TOBy:
THYME COTTAGE

CRAIG PHOENIX

© Copyright held by Craig Phoenix

First published in 2012

Whilst places and buildings in this story may be real, the histories and
facts have been altered to suit the author needs and should not be regarded
as fact. All characters are a work of the author's imagination and any
resemblance to persons living or dead is purely coincidental.

ISBN: 978-0-9557503-6-6
1st edition

Printed and bound by CPI Group (UK) Ltd, Croydon, CR0 4YY
Typeset by Lisa Simmonds at LKSDesigns

www.craigphoenix.co.uk

Cover photographs by Craig Phoenix
Cover artwork by Trudi Couldridge

Acknowledgements

Dad
Trudi
Helen
Lauren
Julie
Tess
Lisa

Thank you for all your comments and feedback it has been invaluable.
Words do not express my gratitude enough.

1

Monday 7th November 2005

Toby turned sharply as the door slammed shut. Thick dust on the windows allowed only a small amount of dusky light from the street lamps outside to penetrate the room. The cottage had been in total darkness when he'd arrived. Despite being asked to call at this untimely hour, Toby had not brought a torch as he had assumed the lights in the deserted cottage would be working

He had queried the late hour and had been reluctant to come, but the housing market was slow and he needed every sale he could get, as he was soon to become a father.

Toby stood nervously in the middle of the twelve-by-twelve upstairs bedroom listening to the silence of the cottage. Tiny pearls of perspiration formed on his brow as he tried to calm his erratic breathing, this fuelled his frightened mind as he churned through memories of the rumours that he'd heard about this place. He was not one to believe in ghost stories, he would always find the logic to any situation. "It's nothing, probably just the wind," he muttered, trying to make himself feel better.

A key turning in the lock broke his rational thought.

Suddenly Toby felt an uneasy presence consume the room. The dread that escape was impossible, filtered into his racing mind. His ears became like radar, picking up every scrape and scuff of someone walking behind him on the bare floorboards. Too terrified to turn around, too frightened to move, he stood motionless, knots tightening in his stomach. He desperately tried to reason with himself that this was all in his imagination, none of it was real. Another sound broke through, making the hairs on his naked arms stand to attention. A breath of wind silently whipped round him, rustling his hair.

His mind raced back to when, as a child of four, he had been locked in his grandparents' garage. It had been late evening and the winter's night had made it feel like a black hole. Frightened and alone, he had waited for his family to find him, too scared to make any sound, his mind creating monsters all around him. It had only been for half an hour but in that time an indelible mark had been made on his impressionable mind. All the haunting sounds permanently etched in his imagination. The wind as it whistled through the rafters, the clanging of metal saws as they hung on hooks and moved in the draught, the scraping of sandpaper as the sheets were blown about on a shelf, and the one noise that had scared him the most, one noise that he couldn't identify, until in his teenage years, when he had discovered a family of mice living in the darkest corner of the garage.

There was even a smell that he associated with times like this, that taunted him, the smell of fear, his fear.

He could feel that familiar feeling rising in him now as he stood rooted to the spot wondering what his next move should be. He had to be brave, wait it out. 'It isn't real, it isn't real', he repeated to himself. He couldn't let fear strike him down. Something brushed past his leg (it felt like a small dog) then was gone, too quickly to tell. Toby's legs almost gave way.

Toby's heart pounded inside his chest as if trying to break out. Tears of fear started to well in the corners of his eyes. Why had he come here at this time? It seemed such a stupid idea now, he could have arranged a more suitable time during the day, said 'it was inconvenient'.

A gunshot rang out from the corner of the room and soon

the smell of the spent cartridge filled the room infiltrating his nasal passages. A warm sensation engulfed Toby's leg and it felt like he was back in that garage again all those years ago, the same smell of fear. His brain told him to scream, told him to go, but normal bodily functions had ceased, fear cutting off any hope that he could move, he now stood like a statue in the middle of the empty room.

Toby heard the sound of a wolf howling outside. Rational thought was making a hasty exit and he couldn't believe what he was hearing. His knee suddenly gave way and for an instant he thought he had received a blow to the back of it, he fell heavily to the ground, putting his hands out to help break the fall. On all fours he heard a low menacing growl which he presumed was from the dog that had brushed past his leg earlier. Now it was sniffing him, it's wet nose at first on his bare arms, then on his back. A cold wetness soaked through the thin material of the sleeveless shirt he wore - it had been incredibly warm for a November night and that too was strange. The dog finished sniffing and emitted a further low menacing growl before scampering into the corner as if commanded by his master. The dog's saliva was still moist on Toby's skin.

As he tried to find his voice his mobile rang. It took nearly a full minute before he answered. A sudden searing pain caused him to drop the phone instantly and the last sound he heard was that of Terri, his wife, calling his name.

2

"Toby. Toby, are you there? Toby?" Terri paused, listening, but there was no reply and panic started to engulf her. Toby had promised her faithfully that he would not go to any more late evening appointments. She hated the fact that this one was even stranger – who wants their house appraised at midnight? It was ridiculous, but Toby had stated that any lead was something as houses were just not selling. She was seven months pregnant with their son or daughter and hated being left in the house by herself. Her hormones were screwing her up, turning her into an emotional wreck. It was understandable, they had already lost one child, which was stillborn the year before, and had two miscarriages – causing no end of trauma for Terri, making her feel like a failure. She was desperate not to lose this one and the slightest peculiarity would set her mind racing over and over, fearing the worst every time. She needed Toby home; she had felt a twinge of pain that didn't seem to be normal. She knew her mother was out and there was no one else she could think of.

"Toby… TOBY!" she screamed harder as the pain intensified, forcing tears to come. She gripped the phone tighter as if this would lessen the pain she was feeling. She fell to her knees, holding her precious bundle, praying that everything would be alright "Please… please… Toby," Terri sobbed into the phone, willing Toby to say something, but there was only silence.

The doorbell suddenly chimed its cheerful ditty, how she hated it, but Toby had insisted that it stay, he liked its cheeriness. Terri struggled to her feet using the arm of the sofa to help her,

4

tears streaming from her eyes. Luckily the door was located in the living room of this two up, two down, house.

Just as she pulled the door open and saw her neighbour standing there, the pain became unbearable and she passed out, falling in a heap in the doorway.

Toby wanted to scream, a searing pain burning every fibre in his body, but no sound emanated from him, his vocal chords paralyzed by the pain. He watched the screen of his phone showing Terri's name. Toby's thoughts ran to her, but all attempts to move were futile. Toby watched in disbelief as Terri's name vanished from the screen. He knew she hated him being out this late, now she was getting close to her term, but he had to work, especially as they now had only one income. The housing market was extremely slow and every opportunity had to be seized.

He had tried to change the time of the appointment but Mr Furrows had insisted that Toby be here at midnight, he had even requested Toby by name. Toby had spent hours racking his brains trying to fathom how Mr Furrows might know of him, but nothing came.

Toby knew this house; rumours of it had abounded. Mysterious disappearances, lights appearing at odd hours of the day and night, yet no one was ever seen. Most of the windows were so thick with dirt and grime they appeared to be blacked out, only a few of the higher ones remained clear enough to make out any details behind. The house always looked deserted, yet never seemed to deteriorate structurally, and it sat uncomfortably at the end of occupied, well kept, terraced railway cottages.

When pushed, Mr Furrows had just said that the house belonged to his father who had passed away recently and so finally he was able to sell the building which had been a millstone around his neck for too many years. As always Toby applied logic and believed that this explained why the house had always looked deserted, 'the old man had probably been off his trolley'.

Toby was blinded by a flash of intense white light followed by the sensation of free falling through space before coming to an abrupt stop. The pain had gone and a strange sense of relief flooded his weightless body. He became aware of someone screaming and soon realised that it was himself.

After what seemed an eternity he landed with a soft thump on the bare floorboards, back in the room he had first entered, almost choking on the dust which flew up in tiny little clouds around him before settling again making him sneeze uncontrollably. He pulled a handkerchief from his pocket and blew his nose but as he continued to sneeze he began to feel hot and clammy.

Suddenly he became aware of a figure standing behind him.

"Good evening, Toby," the flat voice greeted.

From his position on the floor, Toby looked up. In the dim light he saw an immaculately dressed figure in trousers, shirt and jacket. Even in the dusky light his cool burning blue eyes penetrated Toby's soul.

Terri sluggishly opened her eyes, the rocking of the ambulance easing her mind as she found herself comforted by a paramedic, she knew she was in safe hands although she still couldn't escape the anxiety she felt for her unborn child. Gasping, she looked around for Toby but knew he was not there. The female paramedic spoke some indecipherable words of reassurance to her and gently pushed her head back onto the pillow where she slipped back into unconsciousness.

A few minutes passed before the ambulance doors were thrown open and she was wheeled into A & E, with doctors and nurses attending her. She didn't realise the attention that was being lavished on her.

Terri was dreaming, thinking about Toby, she could see

him telling her it was alright. 'Damn you', she was saying, 'why did you have to go out tonight'. Abruptly he vanished. 'Toby', she screamed.

The attending nurse looked at the delirious woman in front of her who was now attracting the attention of all the listening ears in A & E.

3

Groggily, Toby gathered himself together and stood up, brushing the dust from the floor off his clothes. "Mr Furrows?"

Mr Furrows sized up the figure in front of him, soaking up every detail like a portrait artist would covet the image.

Toby quickly tried to gather his thoughts, putting them into some sort of comprehensible order. "Mr Furrows, I'm sorry," he offered his hand to Mr Furrows and scanned the floor for his mobile phone, pad, & tape measure, but there was no trace. Toby spoke nervously at first, not making eye contact. "I hope you don't mind, I let myself in as I was a little early and the door was ajar, I called out, but got no reply." He found his confidence and settled uncomfortably into his usual patter with clients, his eyes still searching the floor for his belongings.

Mr Furrows strolled around the room listening to what was said. Toby guessed he was losing the client since he seemed disinterested and a little distracted, yet he had been requested specifically and this gave him the confidence to carry on.

"I think we can easily get a quick sale, we have various clients on our books and I have a couple in mind that will pay a fai..." Toby stopped mid sentence as he noticed Mr Furrows staring at him.

"You a fair man Toby? Honest?" Mr Furrows enquired.

The questions and the implications threw Toby and he fumbled over his answer. "I... mmm. Yes. What! Yes, I like to think so." He realised he was still holding his handkerchief, he blew his nose one last time and placed it back in his pocket.

Mr Furrows walked in closer to Toby, making him feel a little wary. "Do you know what it is like to know your destiny and not be able to do anything about it?"

Perplexed, Toby was stumped for an answer. "Mmm..."

"This house belonged to my father." Toby felt relief wash over him as the conversation seemed to get back to a more normal subject.

"Yes, you said on the phone."

"I did, you're right." Toby listened, expecting more information, but none was forthcoming for a minute or two. "Well," Mr Furrows paused, "It was actually my best friend's parents, his mother was like the mother I missed." He paced the room again. "My friend died, because of this house." He saw the worried look on Toby's face. "Oh, don't worry, I have all the correct paperwork to sell the house." Mr Furrows was lost in thought for a moment.

"I'll make su..."

"Toby," Mr Furrows interrupted, "I have two choices. I don't like the idea of messing with destiny but I know the outcome if I don't, and believe me when I say it is not pleasant." His stare penetrated Toby, "To watch someone destroy themselves, driven mad by questions they couldn't answer, an impossible conundrum."

"As I, mmm, said, I'll make sure you get a good price for the house. I'll come back tomorrow and measure up," then added apologetically, "as I seem to have misplaced my pad and tape measure. I reckon you can get £125,000 to £135,000. It's got lots of potential, it's a good family house, built around 1910, oodles of charm, especially with the original features that are left. I'll confirm in writing but I can offer our best rate of point seven five percent."

"Mr Grant, how are Terri and Jake?"

Terri slowly came round on the maternity ward, it was the following day, Tuesday, and although she was a little dazed she could remember roughly what had happened. She went to get out of bed but the room spun. She stroked her swollen belly and silently prayed that her baby was okay, remembering the ambulance journey.

The nurse at the end of the ward saw her move and rushed straight to her.

"Now, now Mrs Grant, don't get out of bed, the doctor has said you need to rest, you had a close call last night,"

Panic swept over her, the nurse registered the distress and quickly put her mind at ease. "The baby is fine,"

"Has my husband been in?" she pleaded.

The nurse, knowing the fragile situation Terri was in, thought quickly, and eased Terri back into bed, pressing, the attention button without answering her question. "There, that's better."

"My husband?" Tension made Terri's voice break.

"You just rest. I'll try and find out for you,"

Another nurse quickly appeared at the bedside and before she could speak Terri said weakly, "my husband! Where is he?" Tears pooled in her eyes.

The second nurse spoke. "I'm afraid we haven't been able to contact him, his mobile goes straight to voicemail and, no one is picking up the home phone either."

"Toby!!" Terri started to cry.

4

Clearly Terri was agitated and concerned for her unborn child. The second nurse, Nurse Hayton, fully aware of her medical history, offered, "Is there someone else we can contact?"

"My mother," Terri spoke, struggling to hold in her tears. "Where's my phone? Where's my phone?" panic and every pessimistic thought came forth about what could have happened to Toby.

"Mrs Grant, you need to stay calm, I'm sure there's a perfectly reasonable explanation," the first nurse, Nurse Jones, reassured her.

"His battery is probably flat." added Nurse Hayton. Although they believed it might not make any difference what they said, they still had to try to calm her, for the sake of the unborn child.

"Jake!" Toby almost choked with surprise.

"Your…"

"How the hell did you know?" Toby tried to remain calm but could feel his blood boil. How could this stranger know what Terri and him had discussed as a name for their son, if indeed it was? They had decided not to know what sex the child was because of the instances before, and the heartache they brought. "Who the hell are you?" Toby took a step towards Mr Furrows who coolly retreated.

"Mr Grant. Toby, I'm not your enemy. I'm a friend who wants to help," Mr Furrows paused and strolled to the dirty windows. Toby watched the figure trying to organise his thoughts, "Toby, I want to help. I want to stop what I know I shouldn't. If you knew destiny and could stop it, would you?"

"What sort of a stupid question is that?"

Mr Furrows turned on Toby and the pleasant blue eyes and soft warm features became consumed with rage, "I've watched people I love go insane trying to fathom what was illogical. I watched them drink themselves stupid until eventually it drove them into the brink of madness, destroying not only them, but their family, killing them in one form or another."

"Who are you?" Toby screamed, the words reverberating around the room like an endless echo. The two figures stared at each other and after a long pause Mr Furrows spoke. He had decided.

"I shouldn't have come here tonight. I'm sorry Toby. I shouldn't have interfered," and with that he turned to go.

Stunned Toby stood helpless as Mr Furrows left. He listened as the footsteps faded on the stairs. Shaken, Toby looked around the room one last time, puzzled by everything that had gone on and curious where his phone and tape measure had gone.

Stomping out of the room he slammed the door hard behind him, feeling the vibrations reverberate around the empty house like ripples in a pond. Abruptly he stopped, hearing the loud bark of a dog at the bottom of the stairs, followed by shouted commands.

The scampering of paws racing up the stairs was followed by heavy footfalls sending shockwaves through him, he threw himself against the door of the room when he saw the eyes of a dog in front of him, a torch beam shortly followed. The Alsatian stopped short of him, barking like a crazed animal, saliva like ripped leather hanging from its mouth as his master came into view.

Tuesday 15th November 2005

Terri sat up in her own bed, her mother, Vivien, having brought her home from hospital, against doctor's order, but knowing her daughter wouldn't settle until in her own bed. Toby had not been seen for nearly eight days. Local Radio and TV coverage had been good. The police were doing their best but resources were scarce, only Toby's phone, tape measure, and note pad had been discovered at the scene of his disappearance. No signs of a struggle could be found; the police were genuinely baffled, especially as the company car was parked outside.

Terri was an emotional wreck, devastated that Toby was missing, scared by the thought that she would be having their child alone. Vivien could do little to console her only daughter's emotional turmoil, watching as she tore herself to pieces. Inside Vivien was resigning herself to the fact that her daughter would lose the baby, it had been hard enough to cope with it last time, but now she feared for her daughters' health. Quietly she prayed that the unborn child was going to be okay, it might be the only thing that could save Terri as the police were feeling less and less confident about finding Toby alive, they didn't say it, but she knew it. In her heart she knew it.

The phone rang, Vivien hesitated, so many friends, so many questions, her energy was flagging.

Reluctantly she lifted the handset, "Hello,"

"Mrs Grant? Detective Peters,"

This was the phone call she was dreading, confirmation that all was lost, Toby had been found but was 'gone'. Reluctantly she said. "No, it's her mother, Vivien. Do you want my daughter?" Then, as an afterthought, "Is it something you can tell me?"

"Well..." he paused, Vivien prepared herself for the worst. "We have someone in custody..."

"Oh no..." Shock registered before Detective Peters could finish. How would she tell Terri? Her poor daughter. Toby and Terri had been almost inseparable since they met in the last year of school. They had hated each other at first, but such was the thin line between love and hate, that they had got together one drunken night at a house party and it sealed their fates. But what now? How would she cope?

5

Toby hugged the door as the dog barked on, scared that he might be the dogs next dinner.

"Hold! Max, down!" came the shouted commands. The dog snarled but immediately obeyed his master, "Identify yourself!" The beam of the torch hit Toby's face, blinding him. "Identify yourself!, sir!" The words were spoken with authority.

Toby shook as he stared in the dog's direction trying to find words.

"Sir, identi…" The police officer instantly recognized Toby's face. "To heel, Max." Max suddenly lost his aggression and he returned to sit by his master. "I think you'd better come with me sir."

Toby's voice trembled. "Yeah. Mmm, I was… just doing a valuation, Mr Furrows arranged the appointment. You must have seen him, he only left a second ago." Toby noted the puzzled frown of the officer. "What's wrong?"

"I think we'd better go down to the station, sir,"

"But…"

"Mr Grant, let's go down the station. Control, this is Alpha Romeo, can you let Detective Williams know that I've found Mr Toby Grant, safe and well."

Toby had started down the stairs then balked at the strange terminology, 'safe and well'. What was he on about? The officer followed Toby down the stairs to the waiting police car.

Vivien dropped the phone in shock, when she heard the news, trying to stifle the tears of joys. "Mrs Joyce are you still there?" She could hear muffled sounds coming from the phone.

Picking it up again, Vivien said, "Yes, yes. I have to toll my daughter."

"Mrs Joyce, we just have a few questions for Toby, then he'll be home,"

"Okay," Vivien's voice sounded hollow with disbelief as she replaced the receiver and went to her daughter who was sitting uncomfortably in bed with backache.

"Mum, what is it?" Vivien made no answer as she hovered at the door, wondering how to break the news to her daughter. "Mum?" Terri repeated anxiously. "Oh no, no, they've found Toby's body, haven't they? What will I do?" Terri started to break down.

Vivien rushed to Terri's side knowing her condition was fragile but still amazed by the good news. "Its Toby…"

Terri gasped, bringing her hand up to her face fighting back tears which had been so close to falling over the last few days, expecting confirmation of what she hoped wasn't true.

"No, no, Terri, he's fine." She put her arms around Terri to comfort her as the tears fell, "the police have found him safe and well, he's at the police station now. They have a few questions before they'll let him go. They found him last night."

"Mum… mum…" she cried, tears breaking through the flood gates, words failing her, overwhelming joy.

"It's okay, it's okay." She held her daughter tight.

"MUM!" she screamed breaking her mothers hold and clutching her precious bundle.

"Mr Grant you have caused us great concern and an excessive amount of work over the last few days, so don't tell me you don't know where you have been?" Detective Williams was getting annoyed by Toby's apparent indifference.

"But, I'm telling you, I went to meet Mr Furrows as arranged he…"

"Mr Grant. Do you want me to charge you with wasting police time? Because unless I get some straight answers from you, that is what I will do. Do you understand?"

Toby was about to say something but decided to keep quite, confused and baffled.

"Well?"

Feebly Toby replied, "I don't understand,"

"You don't understand. Frankly, neither do I, nor your belligerence to answering our questions. Now, you arranged to meet this Mr Furrows on Monday 7th November at midnight." Williams shook his head. "and that is the last that is seen of you until today, Tuesday 15th. Where have you been for the last eight days? And, I am warning you, you are treading on very thin ice."

A knock at the door gave Toby, who was now extremely confused, respite. He looked at his watch to confirm the date, it still read 'Mon 7'.

"Sir, there's a message from Mrs Joyce." Toby ears pricked up.
"Terri!"

"Mr Grant's wife has been taken into hospital. She's asking for him."

"Thank you, constable." Detective Williams turned to stare at Toby who eyes pleaded to let him see his wife. The door closed and he sighed sternly before addressing Toby again. "Mr Grant, under the circumstances I am going to let you go. Your wife is obviously in need of you." Pausing to add effect, "but don't think this is over."

Toby left without a word, his mind frantic at the concern for Terri and totally confused. Eight days?

6

"Is she alright?" Toby asked as a nurse showed him to where Terri was.

"She'll be fine, Mr Grant. There she is." The nurse pointed to a bed near the window in a room of only four beds.

Toby hurried across to where Terri was sleeping and grabbed her hand, holding it tightly in his, kissing her fingers. Terri started to stir.

"I'm so sorry."

Groggily she spoke "Mum... mu..." as she opened her eyes, she took in the sight that was Toby, and the tears started again. Anger was mixed with relief. "Toby where've you been? I've been so worried," Terri couldn't control the sobs and Toby hugged her tightly, kissing her hair and trying to re-assure her that everything was alright. "Toby, I thought you were..." she couldn't bring herself to finish the words. "Argh!!" she screamed as another stab of pain took hold of her precious bundle. "Toby!" she cried.

The ward nurse rushed over, pushing Toby aside before he could react.

"Mrs Grant, try to relax." The nurse spoke firmly whilst she examined Terri then pressed the panic button above the bed.

"What's happening? What's wrong with her?" Terror that he was somehow responsible filled Toby's voice.

Two more nurses joined the first. "We need a trolley, we need to get her to the ICU or she'll lose the baby."

'Lose the baby'. Toby hovered, unsure what to do and, as the nurses pushed Terri out of the ward, he followed. Scared for Terri and scared for their unborn child.

After being seen by a doctor it was decided that an emergency C-section was essential and Toby was left spinning, his mind a whirlwind of thoughts and anxieties, in the waiting room. Pacing to and fro endlessly, he sat only occasionally, not being able to settle for any length of time. The last twenty-four hours swam around in his head. Confusion that it was just twenty-four hours for him, but everyone else thought it was eight days. How could that be?

Pacing erratically, he tried to fathom the logic. Was he in another time zone? Had he travelled through time? Was he sleeping and was this just a vivid dream? Yes, that had to be it.

"Please, wake up, I don't like it here," he said out loud.

"Toby, you alright?" Vivien stood looking at her son-in-law.

Toby turned and looked at her. This was no dream. He pinched his forearm, "Ouch."

"Toby?"

"Vivien, Terri's been taken in for a C-section."

Vivien wanted to ask more about Toby's disappearance but it all seemed inconsequential to what really mattered at that moment, that he was here. "Do you want a tea from the machine?"

"Thanks."

Handing Toby his tea, they both waited, without a word being said.

Two hours later they were given the good news that both Terri and son were doing fine, although both would be kept in ICU overnight.

Toby and Vivien viewed the new addition from behind a glass window. Toby was almost in tears at the joy of seeing the small person, his son. And this, for now, pushed aside any thought of the last eight days.

When he was finally dragged away, he spent a restless night in the hospital waiting room trying to sleep, only managing fitful spells whilst Vivien kept her own council and steered clear of talking about his disappearance. The mysterious Mr Furrows continually punctuated his thoughts, disturbing any decent sleep.

What of the strange loss of eight days? How could it be? There was no logical reason. No earthly explanation. How did Mr Furrows know him?

"Mr Grant. Mr Grant." A voice broke through.

"What... who's ther... Oh, where am I? Oh yes." Toby sat up wiping the weariness from his eyes.

"Mr Grant your wife and Jake are doing well. Your wife would like to see you now." The nurse waited whilst Toby tidied himself up the best he could.

"Excuse me, did you say Jake?"

"Yes, Mr Grant, that's what your wife called him," The nurse wondered whether this had been talked about but kept her own counsel. "Is this your first?"

"What? Jake you say? Mmm... yes, yes our first." Toby remembered the endless conversations they had had about names, Jake was their choice for a boy, but it had never seemed real, now he was here, it was very real. Even last night when Mr Furrows had said it and he knew it was real, it still seemed so far off.

"This way."

Toby followed the nurse to the ICU where Terri was sitting up, waiting. Toby hesitated at the door; inside he wanted to run and hug her tightly, but the look in her eyes told him he needed to keep his distance, he had some explaining to do, even though

Terri still looked pale and fragile.

"Terri." Toby hesitated as he searched for the words which escaped him.

"Toby." Terri's voice was croaky. "How is Jake?"

"They say he is fine." Toby took two steps forward. "Look Terri, I... I don't know what to say about the..."

Terri turned her head away and Toby took two more longer steps to her bedside.

"Look, Toby, I don't know what's been going on. I just want to know that everything is alright. Is it?" She stared into Toby's eyes looking for honesty.

"Everything is fine. I don't know what happened."

"Toby, if you can't be truthful to me, then please just go, I'm not in the mood for games. You knew I needed you to be with me." Tears started to well up in her eyes. "Just go. Toby, I can't see you right now. Go."

"But..." words failed him.

"Just make sure you see your son before you go." Toby stood motionless, quivering on the verge of going, but hoping for a reprieve. When none came he turned and solemnly walked away, completely dejected.

7

Toby left the hospital bewildered, hoping that he would wake up from the nightmare. The only consolation was that Jake and Terri were both doing well. His jubilation was tinged with sadness for his parents who would never see their grandson. So, by way of consolation, he headed to Sutton Road Cemetery to visit their graves. The bitter memory of their deaths was always close by, they had longed for a grandchild and now they were not here to witness it. They had died in a car accident in France, the brakes of a lorry had failed and the driver lost control, crushing them into a rock-face at the side of the road. Toby was meant to have been with them, but had broken his leg the week before. How fate worked!

As he kneeled down staring at the headstones, his loving parents' names in gold on the black marble, a tear welled in his eye. He was so happy.

"Mum! Dad! Your grandson is so beautiful. If only you could see him." Toby let the words float through the air. "We've called him Jake. I'm sorry you never got to see him. I miss you both." Toby ran his fingers over the letters of the headstone. Then thoughtfully added. "What's going on?"

Toby heard footsteps behind and turned to see an elderly couple walking hand in hand, he smiled at them, as tears stung his eyes.

After a few more minutes Toby said 'goodbye' and headed home, his heart full of joy and despair. He loved Terri with every part of his being. Her rejection consumed him and, not knowing what to do, he opened a bottle of Rioja that he had been saving from a holiday to Spain, a wine that Terri and he had been saving to celebrate the birth of their child, their son.

As a stupor took hold, his mind wandered to the mysterious Mr Furrows and then something he had said. Like a beacon in the night 'Jake', he asked, 'how was Jake?' How could he have known? Toby sat up on the sofa draining the large glass of wine. How could he have known? It proved too baffling for his already befuddled brain so he switched on the TV, hoping it would help him forget but it only managed to add to his confusion as the news was on and the presenter had just announced the date.

"What happened?" he muttered under his breath. "What the hell happened?" he shouted. His head hurt, ached from the pain and the wine. It was late and raining outside but he couldn't let it rest, he needed answers. Grabbing his keys he slammed the front door closed and walked back to the house that was at the root of his problems.

Thirty-five minutes later he was staring at the front door which stood like a welcome mat. But shrouded in darkness. He contemplated whether he should go in or not.

Terri had finally been allowed to hold her son. Her heart was heavy, she loved Toby so much but couldn't understand his actions, especially as she had been in such a vulnerable condition. As she held Jake's tiny hand in hers she was almost delirious with happiness, if it hadn't been for Toby this would have been the happiest day in her life. She couldn't fight the tears.

"Is everything alright Mrs Grant?"

"Yes I'm just..." She couldn't finish the sentence.

"He's beautiful, isn't he?" The mature nurse smiled at Terri and placed a reassuring hand on her shoulder.

In between sobs she said, "he looks like his father,"

"Come on let's get you back to your bed, you must be tired."

The rain and cold had cleared his head and although the front door beckoned him he felt hungry and decided to walk to the nearest KFC on the London Road.

After eating, Toby found himself back outside the cottage. What was it about this place that called to him? Watching it, he couldn't fend off the temptation any longer, so, making sure the coast was clear he decided to go in again. His common sense told him to go home, but there were too many unanswered questions.

He plucked up the courage and crept through the back gate. The house had old style sash windows and he knew they could be opened with relative ease. First though, he tried the back door, just in case. To his surprise it was unlocked. Being as quiet as possible, Toby twisted the handle and eased it open. Stepping inside, a chill ran down his spine. 'What was he doing?' He knew he was breaking the law. Already he was in trouble with the police and he knew this would not endear him further.

'Damn it,' he muttered, he had forgotten to bring a torch. Tentatively he made his way through the kitchen into the hallway; what little streetlight there was had managed to find its way in, creating shadows that looked ominous. He felt his way along the hall with the stairs running up on his left; he looked up into the black hole, hoping no one was watching him in the darkness, ever conscious of the noise his shoes made on the bare floorboards as he inched along.

Gripping the banister, he placed his foot on the bottom stair. He couldn't recall if there were any loose or creaking boards but then again he hadn't been paying attention the last time. As he eased his weight down, he cringed, expecting a loud creak, and was pleased when all was silent. As he climbed his confidence grew and he hastened his journey upwards, wary for surprises.

Terri lay in her hospital bed wondering whether she had been too hard on Toby, he had always been so loving, they had had their ups and downs, but basically everything was good and she loved him and she knew he loved her. She hoped he would have visited today, Thursday 17th November, but she hadn't seen him and was now getting upset again. She felt so alone without him.

8

"Hi honey. How is my favourite daugh…" Terri burst into tears as her mother walked towards her only child. "Hey, hey what's the matter?" Placing her arms round Terri she hugged her tightly, stroking her hair. The sobs came hard and fast. Terri had been trying to master her emotions for far too long and now she let it all out. "Come on, what's wrong?"

"It's To…by," The words struggled to find any volume through the sobs, "He's left me and…"

"Oh, Baby." Vivien said, immediately feeling hatred at Toby leaving Terri at such a time; as a second thought she knew Toby wouldn't do that. Had there been a misunderstanding? She let her initial anger fall away. "You'll be alright. What do you mean he's left you? He wouldn't."

"But mum!" The words came out more forcibly than Terri had wanted as she pulled her way from her mothers embrace.

"Toby Grant!" The words out came of the darkness, making him freeze at the top of the stairs. Toby knew the voice and a shudder shot down his spine. He turned slowly as he heard the first footsteps on the stairs below him.

"Mr Furrows?"

"Yes, Toby." Toby stepped backwards away from the stairs, as Mr Furrows came closer. "I thought you might return once you found out what had happened. So what does it feel like to lose time?"

The question hit Toby square in the face. "How did you know?" The tension showed in his voice. There was a brief silence as both sized up each other. "How did you know about Jake?"

"This house, Toby," Mr Furrows paused, walking past Toby heading to the back bedroom. "It does strange things."

"Your friend's father, you said before?"

"Yes Toby." It was a loaded reply and wasn't lost on Toby, who followed him into the back bedroom. "I want to break that chain. Do you know anything about this cottage Toby? Have you looked into the history?" Then, before Toby had time to answer. "Do you research the houses you sell?"

"No, no, not normally, I don't need to."

"Argh, ignorance is bliss eh?"

This goaded Toby slightly. "No, not at all. But this is a job and I have a lot of houses to see and I can't..."

"Can't, or won't? Time," Mr Furrows hesitated, "is very important. If only you knew."

Toby was getting annoyed at Mr Furrows' vagueness and apparent rudeness. "Knew what? Now look, you've not really told me anything, yet you seem to expect me to take a lot on face value. And, excuse me, Mr Furrows, if that is indeed your real name, you seem to like playing games. Why don't you just tell me what you've got to tell me and then let me go on my way." The words echoed round the empty room.

There was a stand off.

"Oh, this is ridiculous. If you know what happened to me, can you please tell me? I have a new son..."

"Jake, yes, I know."

"Then you'll also know I need to get back to him."

"Then why did you come back here tonight?"

Again, silence filled the room.

"Toby, I don't want to see your family torn apart. Just stay away from this place, forget it ever existed,"

"Forget it ever existed! Are you stupid? If it hadn't been for you I would never have come here in the first place. You asked for me BY NAME. Remember?" Toby felt his anger getting the better of him.

"Because of what I know,"

"Well, bloody tell me then, because, at the present time, my wife is in hospital with our new son. Jake – which you knew. And, and she doesn't believe me when I tell her I don't know where I have been for the last eight days. Do you understand?"

Mr Furrows stared at Toby, the time had come to tell him the truth. "Toby."

"Yes?"

"You'll inherit this house next year."

9

"He's beautiful Terri. You're right he does look like his father. It's a shame your father couldn't be here to witness it." Vivien reflected, looking at her grandson proudly.

"I know. Do you still miss him?"

"Your father? Yes, of course I do." Vivien looked lovingly at her daughter, who was now a mother and would feel the things she herself used to feel. The love, the uncertainty, the nurturing.

"How did you manage without him?" Terri's question interrupted her reverie.

"Terri, Toby will be back,"

"Will he Mum? He has never stayed away like this, ever. He tells… told me everything."

"He's a man, he's not perfect, your father, bless him, had his quirks."

"Mum, we're talking about disappearing for eight days, not what colour socks he wore, or whether he liked tea or coffee first thing in the morning."

Vivien was taken aback by Terri's vehemence and pictures of Carl flowed through her mind. He did like colourful socks, she smiled, at the time it frustrated her, he would wear a nice suit to go out and yet still wear a pair of garish socks. Now the image was humorous.

"I'm sorry Mum, it's just, just. Oh, I don't know."

"What do you mean I will inherit this house?" Toby asked arrogantly.

Mr Furrows sighed, his voice heavy. "Toby, I knew… know your family,"

"No, you don't," Toby said defensively, hating the feeling of being cornered.

Mr Furrows took a step towards Toby, his eyes losing their warmth and taking on a cold harshness, even in the dark room. "Toby, I was reticent to come here and approach you but I have witnessed how this house has torn apart a family I love. I want to put a stop to it."

Toby's eyes showed his confusion. "You are not making sense."

Mellowing, Mr Furrows stared at Toby for a long time, contemplating his next words. He knew he had to say them, but doubted that Toby would believe them. "Toby you are my best friend's father."

Vivien went to fetch two teas, leaving Terri holding Jake.

"I'll take care of you son."

"Mrs Grant, how is little Jake? Has his father been in yet?" a nurse enquired, as she did her routine visual check that Terri and Jake were okay.

Terri was finding it easier to fight the constant need to cry, although she still felt very emotional. "No, not yet." Her voice was low, almost a whisper. Then she gushed. "Jake is wonderful though. I can't believe I'm a mother."

The nurse waved a few fingers at Jake whose eyes stared innocently forward. "You'll be fine. He won't stay away long, he'll be here. He couldn't stay away from such a beautiful baby. He is probably having a hard time coming to terms with fatherhood. I've seen it many times." She didn't add that she had seen some never come to terms with it.

"Yeah, I hope so," Terri mused, letting Jake grab her finger with his tiny hands.

"What the hell are you on about? Are you crazy? I'm not listening to this." Toby headed towards the door.

"Toby, I ask you again, why did you come here tonight?" The question stopped him in his tracks as he tried to recall why he came back. "How much time did you lose?" the question knocked Toby mentally sideways. "Yes, I know. How else did you think I would know you'd be here tonight?"

Toby walked to the dirt-covered window, quietly answering, looking for solace, "Eight days."

"How are Terri and Jake?"

"They're fine,"

"Have you seen them today?"

"No, I…" the words faded.

"Don't shut them out, they love you."

"I don't know you. How can you be my son's best friend he's only just been born. You're thirty…"

"Twenty-eight, actually. Toby there…"

"No! No! No! No! I have had enough. Who are you?" Toby reached for the door but a hand landed on his shoulder, he turned to face Mr Furrows.

"You have to believe me. Before you walk out of here. Jake destroyed himself trying to fathom what happened to his father. He never got the answers he was looking for." He looked deep into Toby's eyes, "I can't tell you what it is like to watch your best friend piss his life away, then die" His voice was quiet yet forceful.

After a short pause. "Die! Die! I can't listen to this. I don't understand. I've got to go and see my son." Toby pulled open the door and stomped down the hall, his mind in turmoil.

"Toby," Mr Furrows shouted after him, "hold them."

"Just go away. Shut up. I'm not listening to this. You're crazy," he bellowed.

Mr Furrows watched as Toby disappeared down the stairs, his footsteps fading into the night.

"Oh Toby! Please come to your senses before it's too late. Don't come back," he muttered to no one. The empty hallway felt like a death chamber waiting for its next victim. Could the course be changed? Was fate really set in stone? Could he change it? In some way he already had, Toby had experienced a time loss already, yet he knew that it wasn't meant to have happened until next year. Maybe it was enough, he hoped so.

"Terri? Terri? You awake." Toby nudged Terri's shoulder gently. He had tried to sneak past the nurses but the last one had caught him and had been appeased by his pleading eyes and apologetic smile. She also knew that Terri needed to see him, to know he was there for her, even at this late hour, after visiting hours.

"Toby?" she said blearily, wiping the sleep from her eyes.

"Where have you been?" Terri had lost the fight.

"I love you so much Terri." Toby slipped his arms round her, pleased to feel her return his hug.

The embrace was long and heartfelt.

"I love you too. Where have you been for the last two days?"

The words didn't register at first, he looked at his watch. Thursday 17th November, yet a calender just in view at the nurses station had been changed to Saturday 19th November. Another two days had gone by, how?

10

Monday spun round leaving Toby in a whirl. Today he would have to face his work colleagues and boss; he hoped he still had a job. Then would come a visit to the police station. The alarm had been an annoying noise in the wilderness of erratic dreams. Terri and Jake had been kept in for a few more days for observation, so the house was like a stranger without them. Although they were out of any danger zone as far as the doctors were concerned, with her history, they felt safer keeping her in. Toby had spent as much time as possible with Terri and Jake on Sunday; repairing their relationship and trying to explain what had happened for those eight days, and then another two days. Anything Toby had said sounded stupid, but he did manage to convince Terri that he hadn't stayed away by choice.

'8.26' and Toby was standing outside 'Grand Estates' estate agents with nervous energy coursing through his veins. It was exceptionally quiet and he wondered if his watch was actually correct. Phillip, the manager, was usually in by now, opening up. Five minutes went by and still no one turned up. He dived into his pocket for his mobile before remembering that he had lost it at the cottage. He put his face to the window to see if anyone was milling about at the back but all was still.

"Finally, decided to turn up then Toby!" Phillip's voice held a note of quiet sarcasm, making Toby jump.

Toby stepped aside to let Phillip open the door, muttering a greeting and an apology.

"Come on then, let's get this over with shall we," Phillip said resignedly.

Toby followed Phillip inside, shutting the door behind him, and picking up the mail, ever conscious that it may be the last time he did so. The reception had, so far, been cool and in all honesty, what could he expect, he'd not been at work for nearly two weeks, although for the second week, he had a good explanation. Only now he wished he had explained more to his colleague, or called back and spoken to Phillip, but his mind had been at sixes and sevens and rational thought had been too far away. Thinking it through, he doubted he would have a job now.

"Tea, Toby?" Toby nodded, "go on, sit down." Phillip's voice was clinical and cold, "I s'ppose, we should be glad your alive," he said above the noise of the boiling kettle. "How's Terri and son? What's his name?"

"They're good thanks. Jake's wonderful, he so cute." Toby started to gush as if this was a normal day at the office. Then he remembered, two weeks absence without warning or explanation was not acceptable.

There was a couple of awkward minutes. "There you go," Phillip sat down opposite Toby at his desk, "Well?"

Toby sipped his tea, words failing him, his mind racing. He

had rehearsed so many things but now he was here, none of them made sense anymore.

"Come on, Toby, offer me something," Silence. "Do you still want your job? Answer me that,"

"Yes," he answered promptly, almost snatching at the words.

"Well then, give me something," pleaded Phillip.

Toby thought the best thing was honesty, it was the only thing that made any sense. "There is nothing, nothing I can say that, that, will give, will explain, Toby was fumbling over his words. "What happened," he sighed, "look, I went to meet Mr Furrows as arranged. And... and... I don't know what happened. When I left it was eight days later. I know that sounds stupid, but I don't believe in lying, you know that, and that is the truth. As strange as it may be." Phillips face was a picture of disbelief. "See, I know it sounds crazy."

There was silence. Phillip liked Toby, he was a good, hard worker, he got sales with difficult properties, people warmed to him. He would never let Toby go, but he was going to make it a little uncomfortable for a few more minutes. "I don't know Toby."

"Phillip, it won't happen again. I promise. You know Terri and I had it hard with pregnancies in the past. If I could go back and change it, I would. I have never let you down. Never." Genuine heartfelt sincerity was all Phillip needed to hear.

The door opened and in walked Christina. "Morning," she said, yawning, "Toby?"

"Hi, Chris," Toby said, turning to her.

Almost reluctantly Phillip added, "Go on Toby. Get back to work and don't let it happen again."

It took a few seconds for the reality of Phillip's decision to hit home. Then he sprung up and went to his desk to catch up on his emails and messages.

"Toby!" Phillip called.

"Yes," fearing that Phillip might have been joking and had

now changed his mind.

"You'll need these until the police give you yours back."

Phillip placed a new digital measurer and the spare company mobile on the corner of Toby's desk.

Relief flooded through him.

The day was busy and although he had managed to avoid thinking about the cottage over the weekend, it was there, in his head, throughout the day. He was curious about who this Mr Furrows really was; how could he be Jake's best friend? It was impossible. It felt good to be back at work and he almost forgot to go home, Phillip had to usher him out the door telling him to go and see Terri and his new son.

On the drive to the hospital he took a small detour past the cottage, stopping briefly on the other side of the road, curiosity still tearing at his thoughts. Just as he was about to leave he saw movement from inside.

11

Putting the car in gear he told himself, 'No!'. As he started to pull away he felt a dominant urge to stop and, within ten feet, he pulled up, curiosity stinging him like an angry wasp, he couldn't let it go. He hit the steering the wheel with his hands in frustration. Why couldn't he let it go? Staring at the house again, all was still. 'What the hell are you thinking, just go!' But he found himself switching off his engine and getting out, flicking the remote locking as he walked across the street.

He looked at each window in turn, there was no movement and no light anywhere. Standing at the front gate he hesitated, flicking the gate catch up and down, listening to the metallic sound echo in the night air, deliberating what he should do. He had lost eight days already plus another two, he knew he shouldn't go in. But knowing this only drew him on and before he could stop himself he was pushing up an unlocked sash window and climbing through.

The phone in his pocket burst into life, it's annoying catchy ring that once you heard you couldn't forget, breaking the silence of the cottage. Rapidly he searched his pockets to locate it. Finally he whispered "Hello?" 'Number unknown' had shown on the display.

"Toby? Toby."

"Yes," he said, only just audible as he closed the window.

"Toby, you there? You're really faint,"

Scanning the room. "Yes, I'm here. Terri."

"Finally!" She breathed a sigh of relief. "Are you coming in tonight as they've said we can go home tomorrow, Jake is doing well." Terri paused, sensing that she didn't quite have Toby's attention. "Are you alright? Where are you? What happened to you yesterday?" But Toby was busy, looking round the room he found himself in, studying it, not paying attention to what Terri was saying.

"Yeah, yeah I'm fine. I'm just looking over a house."

"Toby, what time are you coming in tonight?"

"I'll be there shortly, just finishing up. Terri how did you get this number?"

"Phillip gave it to me yesterday? I rang whilst you were at lunch. Did you not get my message? I wondered why you never returned my call. What happened to you last night? I thought you would come in." Suddenly Terri felt uneasy. "Toby where are you?"

"I'm checking out a house. Yesterday? What do you mean? I only got this phone today. Phillip gave me the spare until I get my one back from the police."

"Toby. Where are..." the phone went dead.

"Terri... Terri" Toby flipped his phone closed and looked at it for a long moment, shaking his head, confused. Putting the phone back in his pocket he left the room, which he thought was probably the dining room, and made his way into the hallway where he turned right towards the bottom of the stairs. With his hand on the banister he stared up the staircase undecided whether to go up.

Then he realised what it was that had confused him, something Terri said rang alarm bells in his head, 'Phillip gave it to me yesterday', as he churned it around in his head, clarity rang out, 'but I only went in to work today... it's Monday... isn't it?' he checked the date on his phone, it showed Monday 21st November 2005. What is she on about? She must be going mad?'

"No, please don't tell me it has happened again?" he said aloud.

But even that couldn't stop Toby from stealing into the dark gloomy front room where the fireplace had been ripped out and now just bare bricks occupied the space. The grubby wall, the bare floorboards looked unloved. The windows covered by thick layers of dirt were only just letting in some of the street light from outside.

Something in the middle of the floor caught Toby's eye and he stepped keenly towards it, kneeling down to look closer. Whatever it was had gone. He shook his head. 'Probably just a small animal or something' he muttered to himself 'What the hell are you doing Toby?' The question was rhetorical, reprimanding himself.

Leaving the room he strolled purposefully to the dining room.

"I warned you not to come back!" An angry voice made Toby freeze. "What is it that you don't understand, that you'd rather throw your life away trying to solve an unsolvable problem."

Toby sharply replied, "Who the hell are you?"

"I've told you who I am," Mr Furrows said angrily.

"I don't believe you."

"Toby! No good will ever come of you being here. Think of your family?" Mr Furrows was exasperated, the desperation emphasizing his words.

Finally logic seemed to worm its way into Toby's brain. "If you're my son's friend how the hell did you get here?"

12

Mr Furrows stared at Toby, he knew this question would come, he just didn't know when. The pause was long, whilst he tried to think at the best way to answer.

"See, you're so full of rubbish. You can't even answer a simple question like that and yet you expect me to believe you." Toby turned away in disgust.

"Toby, don't come back! Leave it. Leave it where it belongs."

Turning back to Mr Furrows. "Stop speaking in bloody riddles, you're really pissing me off."

Retaliating. "Good, then maybe you'll take notice."

"You've already told me I inherit this house next year, from who though?" The anger burst out of Toby and he struck out in frustration, kicking a piece of rubbish on the floor; it flew into the corner of the room.

He felt the force of a powerful blow hit his chest knocking

the wind out of him. A second later he found himself flat on his back on the floor completely flustered and shocked. Finding his voice, the anger replaced with disbelief. "Who are you?"

Mr Furrows towered over Toby. "I am, your son's best friend, Toby. I let him die. I may as well have held him in my hands and watch his life force ebb away. It was this place that killed him. He never knew his father… you … because this place took you from him. You were consumed by this place."

"I don't understand."

"That's the point. You never do. Neither does your son." Mr Furrows looked tearful but held them back.

"But how did it all start? I don't have any relatives. How can I inherit this house?" Toby sat up, staring at the figure in front of him.

"The house, this house gets left to you by friends."

"A friend?" Toby sat up, rubbing the back of his head and feeling the bump where it had hit the floor.

"No, friends."

"I don't know any friends who own this house."

"Yes, you do."

"Who?" There was silence,

"I don't know. I was never told."

"This is just a big joke, isn't it?" Toby said getting up and brushing himself down. "Everyone's in on it, aren't they? Work? Terri? It's not real. None of this is real. This is just a bad nightmare that I haven't woken up from that's all. You are a figment of my imagination. Terri's probably asleep at home, in bed, this very minute, trying to wake me up."

Mr Furrows grabbed Toby by his jacket picking him up off the floor and forcing him backwards.

Toby stared at the figure whose face was inches from his own.

"My name is Edward, and I am your son's best friend. I'm sorry, but you must believe this is no dream, or nightmare as you know it." Then thinking quickly, Edward asked again. "Tell me, how does it feel to lose eight days, then another two?"

Toby struggled to get his reply out. "Baffling,"

"And how much time have you lost now. A day, two days, three days?"

"What?" Toby stood, free from Edward's hold, "No!"

"Yes, Toby. When you climbed through that window you lost one day. The longer you stay, the longer you are gone. How do you think it made your Terri feel. She doesn't hear from you for a whole day, maybe more. What about work?"

"Oh god, work! NO! Phil will kill me,"

"Yes, now do you see how it begins? One action leads to another and that is what happens. That is what destroys your family."

"So what should I do?"

"I don't know, I am trying to solve that, but don't ever come here again."

"How about if I sell it? We could do with the money. It could give us the start we need, especially now we have Jake." Thoughts ran rapidly through Toby's mind.

"You want someone else's family to go through what your family did."

"What! You just want it to sit empty?"

13

There was silence as Toby weighed up the consequences, struggling to get his head around the implications of what Edward was telling him.

"Go, now Toby, go back to Terri and when you inherit this house, dispose of it, get rid of it, don't let anyone live here again. And... don't come back here. Ever!"

Toby slowly turned round in thought, then turned on Edward but he had vanished, as quickly as he had appeared. "Mr Furrows... Mr Furrows? Edward?" Suddenly Toby felt frightened. What or who was Edward? Toby felt a chill shoot down his spine. What was he dealing with? Was this real? He knew he needed to get out of the house as the perplexing conundrum tumbled over in his mind.

Toby left the same way he had arrived. Outside he stared back at the house. How on earth do I inherit it? What could I do with it? As the questions churned over his thoughts ran to Terri and Jake. Pulling his phone out of his pocket he noticed that the battery was dead.

'By climbing through that window you have just lost one day, maybe two or three'. The words echoed inside. "My God!" he gasped and ran through the back gate to the front garden and then to his car, he could still feel the pull of the house, like a magnet, and for an instant he hesitated holding the door half open.

"No. Just go," he told himself, but still he remained rooted to the spot.

Terri had been trying Toby's phone all night, on the hour every hour, her emotions in turmoil. 'How could he do it again?' 'Why?'

Vivien had done her best to comfort her daughter. She had no sympathy for Toby, not now, not after the first time. Once, even twice, she could forgive – just – maybe put it down to the responsibility of facing fatherhood. But to do it again! His family needed him.

It was Wednesday and they were due to go home. The doctors were concerned over her health, whilst mother and child had been doing well, the extra stress caused by Toby's reluctance to show up could easily affect Terri's already unstable emotional state. They had watched as the first few hours passed and still no word from Toby. Her appetite gone, the doctors almost considered keeping her in.

In the end Vivien had arranged a taxi and, as grandmother, mother and son reached the main entrance to the hospital, they saw Toby running across the car park to meet them.

Terri fainted, Vivien just managing to catch baby Jake.

"Terri!" Toby screamed as he launched into a sprint. "Terri? Terri?"

"Decided to turn up then?" Vivien injected scournfully. "You've got a lot of explaining to do my boy." Vivien's statement was cutting and it wasn't lost on Toby. "Now, go and get some help," she commanded, holding Jake close to her.

Toby ran into the lobby but already an eagle-eyed porter was rushing to her aid. Toby helped the porter lift Terri into a wheelchair a nurse had brought out.

"Toby. I hope you're happy now?" Vivien stated.

Toby couldn't control his frustration any longer and replied meekly.

"I'm sorry, okay. I can't explain what's happening 'cause I don't know. You know I love Terri and would never do anything to hurt her. Now, why don't you give it a rest, eh?"

Chastised Vivien remained silent. She loved Toby like her own son and was surprised by his behaviour and that was what hurt so much. She could only put it down to the fact that she was now a proud grandmother and just wanted everything to be perfect. It had been a long journey to get to this point. Terri had suffered far more than she deserved, two miscarriages and a still born. Finally she had given birth to a beautiful baby boy and it all seemed as though it was going to fall apart. She didn't want that to happen.

Anger in both Toby and Vivien faded. "How is Jake, Vivien'?"

"He's good," she paused as Jake peered up, his big innocent inquisitive eyes like saucers. "I think he needs his father,"

Toby took Jake in his arms and followed the porter and nurse back into the hospital.

14

Terri was rushed through A & E, followed closely by Toby and Vivien, her blood pressure and iron levels were very low despite the supplements she had been given, but they could find nothing else wrong. She had drifted in and out of consciousness throughout and it was deemed best to keep her in for yet another night. Toby was told he could take Jake home, rest was what everyone needed.

Vivien insisted on accompanying Toby home and staying the night, so that he could go into work. Vivien had been curt and polite, and he knew as soon as he was indoors it would go one of two ways; either she would mellow, or blow her top. Thankfully during the drive home she calmed down and as they stood in front of the house, Vivien turned to Toby.

"He is finally home. I am so pleased for you both. If only Carl was here." Vivien started to well up.

Toby placed his arm around her. "I know, Terri misses her father as well, at least we can introduce Jake to his new home." Placing him in his cot with a monitor on the bedside cabinet Toby and Vivien stood and watched him in silence, it was magical. New life, peacefully resting.

Finally Vivien broke the moment. "I'll put some dinner on. You must be hungry."

Toby glanced over to her. "Thank you." He could feel her eyes questioning him, vying for an explanation, but what could he say. How much had Terri told her Mum. "I…"

"You don't have to explain to me Toby," she said lovingly.

"But…"

"Look, Toby." Her motherly tones told Toby he was going to get a 'polite' lecture, "What goes on between you and Terri stays between you two. If she wants to talk to me, then I'll listen, but I won't pass judgement. I'm not stupid, neither of you have had it easy and I know you have both wanted Jake for a long time. Terri is not the strongest healthwise, and little Jake has taken a lot out of her." Vivien put up her hand to stop Toby interrupting her, "… and I know you love her," Vivien let the comment rest on Toby's shoulders the way only mothers can, "make sure she knows it. She needs you Toby, and you need her. Jake needs you both. Don't let anyone else get in the way of that."

Toby sighed, the weight of the world resting on his slim shoulders, then suddenly he realised what Vivien had implied

"There's no one else Vivien, honest to god, I would never, never… not to Terri. Whatever happens I would never. She doesn't believe…" Toby anxiously looked round the room trying to fathom how he could convince Vivien of that. Suddenly Jake started to cry.

"You see to your son." Vivien walked away leaving Toby alone, contemplating his next move, and telling himself how stupid he'd been.

The rest of evening passed without conversation, there was no need. Toby was consumed by regret and this continued to his dreams which were filled with curiosities about the cottage. As much as he tried to think of other things he would always come back to the cottage via some whacky route that didn't fit his dream.

Jake disturbed his dreams once about 3am and wearily he crawled out of bed wondering whether this was what being a father was going to be like. Vivien also got up after hearing Jake. She told Toby to go back to bed but he insisted that he'd get used to it, which made Vivien feel a little put out, although she knew it was for the best. She loved her first grandchild and found it difficult to be parted from him. She watched discreetly from the doorway as father and son bonded properly, son taking a feed from his father's bottle.

"It's alright you can come in," which caught Vivien by surprise.

"Sorry I di…"

"He's beautiful, isn't he?"

Vivien put her arm round her son-in-law and let Jake grip her little finger with his whole hand, his eyes struggling to stay open. Finally with Jake now asleep, Toby yawned and put him back in his cot.

When the alarm sounded its morning chorus Toby hid under the bed covers dreading what faced him at work.

15

"Nice of you to turn up Toby. Do you still work here?" Martin's sarcasm sounded like thunder in Toby's head but he knew he deserved it so took what was coming to him on the chin.

"How is Phillip?" The question was a reluctant one and Toby grimaced, afraid of the answer as he took his seat, not sure if he still had a job.

"I'll tell you, you are so lucky," Martin smiled and continued before Toby could respond, "Phillip has been ill for last couple of days." Martin liked playing games especially at other people's expense.

"And?… What did he say when I didn't turn up?"

Martin walked into the small kitchen, "Tea?" he called over the noise of the water, filling the kettle.

"Martin! What did he say?" Toby walked to the kitchen door. Martin still didn't answer preferring to play this game for all it was worth, "Martin?!"

After a long pause, "You are so lucky you have nice work colleagues,"

"Come on what…"

"We covered for you said you had gone to view a couple of houses with prospective clients,"

Toby sighed, "Thanks, I owe you,"

"Too right, I'm keeping a total,"

"Thought you might be."

"How are Jake, and the new mother? I take it you were looking after them."

Toby hadn't even thought of that as an excuse but, thinking

quickly, he added "Yeah... Yes... mmm, Terri took a turn for the worse and we had to rush her back into the hospital but she's alright now. It all happened so quickly I didn't even think of calling,"

"Yes... we had noticed. Actually that was what we told Phillip."

Toby stood open mouthed. "But, you."

"Two nil! Sorry I couldn't resist it." Toby stared at Martin's back as he made the tea, spitting daggers. "As long as they're alright that's the important thing and they're back at home?" Martin turned and handed Toby a mug of tea, "here."

Toby took the offering. The front door opened distracting them both. It was Christina.

"Oh, Toby, is everything alright? I was so worried when you didn't come in yesterday. Phillip said he hopes that everything is alright and can you give him a ring at home."

"Yes, and thanks, she is. Terri collapsed and had to go back into hospital again. Terri's Mum's at home with Jake now, he is fine."

"So, what's it like being a new father?"

"It's great." The words didn't come across very strongly, after all, it had only been one night for him, although when he had held Jake at 3am he'd felt the first real feelings of fatherhood grip him and the apprehension at the daunting prospect lying ahead of him. "Yeah, it's good thanks," The words sounded like he believed them.

"You couldn't talk to my Matthew could you, he still doesn't want kids, I keep trying to convince him. I think one day I'll just accidentally get pregnant."

Toby didn't know how to respond so let the statement float in the air and proceeded to start up his computer. While it booted he rang the hospital to check on Terri. She was okay, just had to watch her blood pressure and they wanted to keep her in for another couple of days. Toby said he would bring

Jake in to see her later.

The phone didn't stop ringing all day and Toby found he had a full day of viewings on Saturday. Occasionally during the day his mind wondered to the cottage and the mysterious Edward Furrows, supposedly Jake's best friend from the future. His mind still couldn't fathom it, how? It was like a movie.

He did find time to make an enquiry at the land registry website as to who owned the property, the result was a Mr & Mrs Hutchinson who had owned the property for over thirty-five years.

"Who are they?" He puzzled aloud, reading the email document. "How can I inherit a property from people I don't know?" He decided it was all a hoax and felt relief wash over him. There was still no answer to the eight or two days that he had lost, or the previous day.

16

Toby found himself driving a route to the hospital that took him past the cottage again. Stopping outside he watched it with strange affection and curiosity. His mind flitted back to the land registry entry. Who were Ronald Peter and Elizabeth Audrey Hutchinson? He didn't know anyone of that name. Why would they leave this house to him? No one lives there. No one has lived there, from what he could remember, for at least seventeen years. Why would you own a house and do nothing with it? Could it be that they knew about the mysterious happenings? But why would they then pass it onto him? Surely they would know the consequences. With no apparent answers he pulled away.

Arriving at the hospital, Vivien was already there with Jake.

Terri looked pale but delighted to see her son in his father's arms. Toby locked eyes with Terri, there was love, regret and affection there. Toby saw what had drawn him to her. He knew then he had to put the cottage, once and for all out of his mind. He hugged Terri and Jake and smiled at Vivien who understood the only way a mother could, she reciprocated.

Tuesday 11th January 2006

Mother and child were doing great, a routine had settled them all and, although Toby was finding it tiring, he loved his family and let every moment he could, be taken with them. Vivien had said no more about Toby's disappearances and Toby had let the cottage slip from his mind.

"Hi, Pete. How you doing?" Toby yawned his greeting as he closed the front door.

"Little Jake keeping you awake at night" Pete chirped back.

"Too right, the little bugger, just when you think he is gone, he kicks off full throttle."

"The joys of being a father, eh!"

"Yeah. How's Betty?"

"Not bad. The doctor says she needs to get up and walk about, keep the circulation going, that last fall was quite bad."

Toby surreptitiously glanced at his watch, he knew he was going to be late, as Pete was a talker. The joys of retirement. Why did he get up so early? Always out at the crack of dawn, both of them, well that was until Betty tripped and fractured her hip.

"I'm sure she'll be fine. The doctors are doing their best, she has to go back tomorrow for a check up," Pete sighed.

"Look Pete, I don't wish to be rude but I really must dash, things are difficult enough as it is."

"Yes, of course. Anyway, I must be going too - got things to do." Pete smiled.

"Give my best to Betty. Why don't you both pop round for a drink later, it'd be nice to catch up properly."

"Thank you Toby, that would be nice, and I know Betty would love to see little Jake."

"Great. We'll see you about eightish?"

"Thank you. See you later." Pete hot-stepped down the street leaving Toby wondering what on earth Pete had to rush to, and amazed at how sprightly he was for his seventy-six years.

Fifteen minutes later Toby was at the office.

"Sorry I'm late, got collared by Pete, our neighbour." Toby closed the door behind him, shutting out the winter wind.

"Morning Toby." The words were spoken solemnly, which was not lost on Toby.

He glanced around the office, Christina was not her usual chatty self, and Martin was also very subdued. "What's up?"

Phillip walked to the door and turned the lock to stop anyone walking in, not that it had been a problem recently, the onset of a recession was starting to bite. Turning on his employees, sadness was apparent in his eyes.

"I'm not going to draw this out." The words settled in the air as everyone's shoulders sank. "You all know it has been really quiet recently, even more so than normal for this time of year. Well, that's an understatement." Phillip was finding this harder than he'd imagined it to be. He'd rehearsed the lines again and again. "Look, I have considered every option possible but there isn't a viable one. I'm going to have to close. Basically, I've run out of options, the bank won't extend my overdaft," Phillip sat down on the nearest desk as he felt their despair at his own desperate situation. Looking at each of his employees in turn, he found it hard to fight the tears, acceptance that his business was failing and everyone would suffer. He had been putting this off, month after month. The decision had weighed heavily on his shoulders but it couldn't be put off any longer otherwise he would lose his own home. His eyes landed on Toby and he became even more deflated knowing that this would be a terrible start to fatherhood.

17

Toby felt the weight of the world on his shoulders as he cleared the few personal possessions from his desk. The decision was made and Phillip had decided it would be best if it happened with immediate effect. Phillip had managed to scrape together enough money to pay everyone three months salary and a little extra on top, as a thank you. Knowing for some it would at least go some way to easing the financial stress as they searched for new employment. Phillip avoided eye contact with Toby knowing he had a new family to take care of, however, his hands were tied. The office was subdued and eventually they left, one by one. Martin had mooted the idea of meeting up for a drink at lunchtime but no one was in the mood.

Phillip had said the company car still had another month to run therefore Toby might as well make use of it. He slumped into the driver's seat. Toby looked at the road ahead, staring into oblivion for a good ten minutes before turning on the ignition. His thoughts ran to Terri and Jake. Instead of turning right at the traffic lights as usual to go home, he went straight on and headed for the seafront, parking by the Menzies shelter in Chalkwell.

After finding money for the meter, he walked along the sea wall buffeted by the wind that was blowing the grey clouds along at a rate of knots. The day looked bleak, the future looked bleak. What was he to do? He'd always been an estate agent ever since leaving school, the outlook was desolate. In time he knew it would pick up again, yet with a family to support he just couldn't wait. He'd used most of their savings preparing for Jake's arrival. He did not blame Phillip, he had been good to Toby over the years and any decision he had made had been after much soul searching. That didn't help Toby's situation, he'd heard other estate agents were laying people off, cutting back where they could to ride out the storm of recession. What else could he do?

The hours drifted by and no miracles had landed at his feet and wearily he made his way home.

As he turned the corner he could see the narrow street was blocked by an ambulance, red and blue lights reflecting off the windows of the nearby houses. Toby's heart leapt into his mouth, panic rose inside, finding a parking space and leaving his car badly parked, he ran along the street. It was only then he saw paramedics coming out of someone else's house. He stopped in his tracks relieved that it wasn't his house. Instantly realising it was Pete's house he saw the dejected look on the paramedic's brow as they stretchered out Betty who was securely strapped in with an oxygen mask covering her face.

Toby's stomach churned, he knew he ought to go indoors and talk to Terri but he wanted to eek out the inevitable. Marching over to Pete's he called out.

The face that acknowledged him was pale and distraught, a beaten man.

"Pete. What happened? Is Betty alrig...?" Tears started to leak from Pete's eyes. Toby turned to the paramedics, "She's going to be okay isn't she?"

The one at the back tried to sound positive. "We've managed to resuscitate, now we just need to get her to the hospital."

"Pete. Is there anything I can do?"

Pete closed the front door and handed Toby a set of keys, "Can you feed Rex & Judy for me?"

"Of course, of course." With that Pete climbed into the ambulance, a broken man, deep down knowing that Betty wasn't going to make it.

After the Ambulance left, Toby turned and looked up at his own terraced house and thought of the daunting task that now faced him. Reluctantly, he stepped up to the front door, hesitating before inserting the key. What was he going to say? What were they going to do? Three months money and the bonus would not keep them going for long. Deep inside he wanted to run away, hide, but he couldn't, he was a husband, a father. Terri hadn't returned to work and wasn't due to return for another twelve months, making the most of her maternity leave.

Opening the door, he was met by silence. Glancing at his watch he saw it was ten past three. Throwing his jacket on the settee he walked into the kitchen and flicked the kettle on. Pulling a mug off the mug-tree and placing it on the work surface he sighed heavily. He racked his brain for ideas of what profession he should move into, with the housing market as it was, there were no options there.

He was broken from his thoughts by a key turning in the door and Jake's screaming. "Alright Jake, alright, give me a chance." Terri's voice was loud and frantic.

Toby rushed into the hall.

Terri almost stepped back through the open front door, "What are you doing here? Yes Jake, hold on." She knew Jake didn't understand, he just wanted his nappy changed.

Toby stared at his family.

"What is it? Toby?"

18

Terri looked at the bags of shopping she had just bought, small things for Jake that now seemed an unnecessary extravagance. Listening to Toby whilst he changed Jake, despair started to rest uneasily on Terri's shoulders. Making tea for them both she moved to the settee and sat glumly cradling Jake. She tried to remain upbeat as she saw how dejected Toby looked.

As an afterthought Toby had added, "We have got the car until the end of March. Phillip said the lease was covered until then, although he didn't do that for everyone."

"I'll go back to work sooner," Terri added resolutely, "they're desperate for me to go back anyway and it will all help. If we keep ahead of things it will all be alright. I know it's not much but…" Silence rested between them as Jake settled down.

Breaking the silence, Toby offered, "Betty's been taken into hospital. Not sure what happened but when I got home there was an ambulance outside. Pete looked awful, really frail. I've got to go and feed the dogs later. Only this morning I'd invited them round for the evening. Why does everything happen on the same day, eh?"

Terri nodded, but her mind was lost in her own thoughts.

It was Wednesday morning and Terri rang work, reluctant but excited at going back, she loved her job, yet hated the fact that she would be parted from Jake. Necessity was necessity, her decision was met with relief from her boss. Toby had risen as usual but was sitting at the computer compiling his CV, staring at the two thirds of the page on screen that looked pitiful, the cursor blinking at him, as if trying to urge him to write more.

An hour later he was at the first agency. The lady sounded very positive insisting that they had plenty of vacancies to offer, but when she showed him some of them, he knew he wasn't qualified for any of them, however, she brightly carried on. Thirty minutes later he left, dreading the next one. Passing a couple of other estate agents he popped in and left his CV with the managers, although most said there was nothing at the moment, Toby understood.

Saturday trickled round and Toby found it hard to hide his melancholy as he sat and watched TV with Jake asleep on his lap.

At about half past nine he walked across the road to Pete's house to check on the dogs. They barked excitedly as he put the key in the door and stood disappointed when they saw it was Toby. Toby hadn't seen Pete for a few days and was concerned, although even that took second place to his own predicament.

"Yes I know, I know I'm not your master however I'll have to do for now," As he replenished the crunchies and topped up the water bowl he talked to them. "Don't s'ppose you know how Betty is do you?" Turning back round from the sink he saw Rex's head cocked to one side as if to ask, 'What do you think we are? We're dogs', "You never know miracles might happen. I hope she's alright. It's unusual not to have seen Pete. I hope she's doing okay?" Deep down Toby feared the worst.

It was Sunday when Pete came home, Toby was already

feeding the dogs, he had let them out in the garden regularly over the last few days, surprised that Pete hadn't been home at all. He turned as the dogs ran to the door to greet their master. Although Pete bent down to stroke his friends there was something lack lustre about the process.

"Are you...?" Toby didn't get to finish.

"She's gone Toby. She's gone. Passed away this morning. I don't know what to do." Pete hugged his two best friends tightly, tears falling into their fur. Like good friends they licked him excitedly, trying to reassure him that life was okay.

"I'll put the kettle on." As Toby said it he thought it sounded pathetic but he didn't know what else to do.

"I can't take it in. She was doing so well." Pete sat on the stairs in the hallway the dogs licking at his face. "What am I going to do?" He looked at Toby, the sprightly man a million miles away, replaced by a sallow, empty vessel.

"You and me both, you and me both," Toby concurred.

Toby handed Pete a cup of tea and spent the rest of the evening sitting with him. Not sure if Pete wanted him there or not, but he felt he couldn't leave.

Wednesday 22nd February 2006

"Come in, Pete. We've been expecting you. Hello Judy, Rex." Judy and Rex followed Pete into Toby's house. It had been a month since Betty's death. Toby and Terri had made a point of keeping in contact with Pete as he looked lost without Betty. Even the dogs' boundless energy seemed to have waned. Pete brightened when he saw Jake. Judy and Rex were content to wile away the hours curled up on the floor together, Rex resting his head on Judy as if she were a pillow. "We've got Vivien's famous shepherd's pie tonight. Hope that's alright?"

"It's very kind of you, you don't have to you know. How is

the little man?" Pete tried to sound cheerful, but it was hard.

"He is good thank you. Sleeping through the night now, thank goodness."

"Any luck with a job?" Pete always enquired, ever hopeful that Toby would have a different answer.

"No, but got to keep at it." Toby replied buoyantly

"I've bought this, a little thank you to you both for putting up with an old fool," Pete handed Toby a carrier bag full of baby clothes.

"Hello Pete," Terri said, as she walked in the front room.

"Look what Pete's given us." Toby showed Terri the carrier bag.

"Oh, Pete, you shouldn't have." Terri kissed Pete on the cheek.

Pete looked somewhat awkward, he hated a fuss being made. "Yes, I should, you've both been very kind since Betty... I appreciate your kindness."

"You're welcome, and we enjoy having you over. Now come on let's have a glass of wine and sit down while the dinner's still hot."

Tuesday 8th March 2006

Judy had become very ill and had to be put down, a heartbreaking decision for Pete, all Toby could do was watch and offer a consoling word or two. Another cruel blow came when Rex shortly followed, probably from a broken heart. Now Pete was spending more and more time with Terri, Toby and Jake and although it was a godsend they were starting to find it claustrophobic. If he wasn't with them he didn't go out anymore. The occasional meal was now a regular meal just so they knew he ate properly. He loved little Jake and at times, when he held him, you could see a spark ignite in his eyes. It was only then that he explained how Betty and he had lost both their two boys during childbirth.

19

Toby's redundancy money was running out. Everyday he scoured the net for jobs, desperate to find something. As he looked at the reams of jobs, Toby's mind wandered to the cottage which he had managed successfully to put out of his mind. It took him unaware that he should find himself thinking about it, but like a fish hook it had snared him. He found himself looking at the Land Registry document again, studying it for clues, yet nothing shone through, it was just a standard Land Registry entry.

"Leave it," he muttered, "you're meant to be job hunting." Closing down his emails he noticed a trainee management position being advertised for McDonalds – no experience necessary. As much as the thought of working in McDonalds made him shudder, it was a job. The fact that you very rarely saw a branch close, to him it equalled security, at least until the job market changed. Anyway, he did quite like the odd burger. Filling in the on-line application took all of twenty minutes but finally he pressed submit.

Terri had taken Jake to Vivien's so the house sat quiet. Terri was loving being back at work, she missed Jake but liked the fact that Toby got to spend time with him, and it kept money coming in and the bills paid. Glancing at his watch Toby realised he had been at the computer for three hours. He needed to stretch his legs and decided a walk would be good, maybe to the job agencies. The cottage flashed in his consciousness like bright neon.

An hour later he was standing outside it looking up at the dirty cottage windows remembering that first meeting with

Edward, 'you inherit the house'. "What was the crazy man on about?" he said under his breath.

"Excuse me?"

Toby spun round to see an elderly lady staring at him.

"Sorry? Oh, no I was thinking out loud." Suddenly he was hit by a thought. "Have you lived around here long?"

"Sorry," the old lady remarked.

"Have you lived here long?"

"Me, well yes, since 1933, when I was just seven, moved down from…"

"Have you ever seen anyone live here?" Toby interrupted, pointing to the cottage, his mind racing to find answers.

"Where dear?"

"There." He pointed behind him.

The old lady squinted as she looked at the cottage. "Mmm, no dear, I don't think I have. My memory's not as good as it used to be."

"Oh." Toby moved closer to the gate, tentatively putting a hand on it 'Toby, I don't want to see your family torn apart. Just stay away from this place, forget it ever existed'.

He turned back to the old lady but all he saw was a frail figure disappearing down the road.

Looking at the cottage he said, "What's your secret?" Temptation to enter boiled under the surface.

His mobile sprang into life playing 'Life of Riley'.

It was one of the many job agencies Toby had signed up with, they had an interview lined up for him.

The job interview had turned out be a job he wasn't qualified for and both he and the interviewer were bewildered as to why he had been sent there. However, luck changed and after another three weeks Toby got the job on the trainee management program for McDonalds. Pete's visits were having a positive effect on everyone especially as Toby had to work evenings.

Terri would always have company, whether it was Vivien or Pete.

Life was going great guns, both were working, the little bit of debt that had built up whilst Toby was out of work had been cleared and a holiday was being looked at, nothing flash just something simple, Brighton or Yarmouth, a caravan or chalet. Ten months of hard work had paid off.

One day Pete failed to turn up as arranged, it was so out of the ordinary that Terri rang Toby, who came home during his lunch hour. At first Toby had been quite calm until he remembered that it was close to the anniversary of Betty's death. When he got no answer he used his spare set of keys and went in.

"Pete, Pete? Are you alright." The house was eerily quiet. Toby crept upstairs to find Pete in bed, finally at rest, and hopefully, with all his family.

20

Thursday 18th January 2007

Angrily Toby dialed the number he was beginning to know by heart. He had been passed from pillar to post. It was the mortuary, where Pete's body had been taken. It rang five times before being answered.

"Dr Buxton," rang the cheerful voice.

"Hello," Toby stated, trying to control his frustration, "yes, I am trying to find out if a friend's body can be released for burial, I spoke to you yesterday and the day before."

"And you are?"

"Toby Grant. It is my neighbour Pete, who died on…"

"Pete who?"

"I don't know, I've never asked his surname. I told you this yesterday."

"I'm sorry, I don't recall, it's been very busy…" Suddenly he remembered. "Oh, yes, yes, sorry about that. Seems everyone's been dying to get hold of me recently." Dr Buxton chuckled. Toby didn't even crack a smile and the silence was quickly broken by Dr Buxton. "Hold on, I'll just go and check."

"Thank you," Toby was surprised by the lack of compassion he was being greeted with.

A few minutes later. "Sir, yes, the body was sent for cremation yesterday."

"YESTERDAY!" Toby stammered, "you told me to ring back today at this time."

Dr Buxton's tone changed as he realised the genuine error that had been made.

"Please accept my sincere apologies sir, there was a mix up and my colleague who was working the late shift let the body go…"

"But?!"

"I really am sorry sir, unfortunately, with the older generation, when there are no relatives, the state issues protocol, and my colleague followed that. I know it is no consolation and it is with deep regret that I have to advise you of this."

"I was going to arrange his funeral, he was our friend." Toby lost all fight. "Do you know where I can at least get the ashes?"

There was a brief silence. "sir, you have to understand that under the circumstances, the cremations take place with others.

I know that it is no…"

Toby slammed down the phone swearing, angry at the sacrilege, it was a knife in the heart. Toby knew that Betty had been cremated and Pete had expressed his wish to have his ashes scattered with hers. The pain was too much to bear for Toby and he sat heavily in the armchair resting his head in his hands and offering an apology to Pete.

"I'm sorry, Pete, so sorry."

In the three years since Toby and Terri had moved into their house Pete and Betty had become more like friends than neighbours, and since Betty's death Pete was like a granddad that neither had had.

"What is it?" Terri asked, walking in to the lounge.

"They cremated the body. I can't bloody believe it, they tell me to ring up today, I do and they've already done it."

Terri placed a hand on Toby's shoulder, rubbing it affectionately. It was little consolation, and as time came for Toby to head off to work, the regret was biting him leaving a dark cloud hanging overhead. Work could do little to take his mind of how he felt he had let Pete down.

Tuesday 6th February 2007

A letter arrived from Bartlett and Barrington Solicitors addressed to both Toby and Terri. Terri sat it on the mantle until Toby arrived home from his late shift. It was official-looking and she just had 'a feeling that it was best to be left'.

Toby breezed through the front door at eleven-thirty. Terri was cradling Jake who was crying. "Hi ya. Jake not asleep?"

"He won't settle. I don't know what's bothering…" Terri stopped suddenly as Jake fell silent.

Toby stepped toward his family, "I guess he just misses his dad, doesn't he, little Jakey wakey. Yes, you do, don't you. Don't like daddy working late." Terri turned to Toby and poked her tongue out at Toby, frowning at his sarcasm.

"There's better things to do with that." Toby imparted as he took Jake from Terri.

Terri shivered inexplicably. "Something's not right Toby."

"He's fine. Look, he's smiling," Toby replied, rocking his son gently looking at the big brown eyes staring back at him.

"No, Toby, I don't know what it is, but something's not right."

"Your Mum's okay isn't she? You've spoken to her today?"

"She's upstairs changing the bed." They both listened carefully and they could hear her humming away to herself.

"See everything is fine. Look even Jake is feeling tired now." Sure enough Jake's eyes were closing.

Abruptly the room turned colder, and even Toby felt it, the lights dimmed slightly, there was a noise by the door through to the kitchen/diner.

Toby and Terri turned sharply.

21

"Pete!" Toby exclaimed in horror, the colour draining from his face.

Suddenly Betty appeared next to Pete with Rex and Judy looking sprightly and agile by their side. Pete stared at Toby for what could have been minutes, Terri gripped Toby's arm disbelieving her eyes.

"Thank you both, you have been like two of our own children. We want you to have a good future, enjoy what we give you. And give Jake everything. Especially the love you both have."

Toby stood opened mouthed gawping at the spirits in front of him and suddenly a third figure appeared just behind Peter.

"Oh my god," Toby stammered

"What is it Toby?" asked Terri

"It's Mr Furrows."

"Who?" Terri quizzed.

Pete took a step towards Toby and reached out as if to shake his hand. Toby responded instinctively ignoring Terri's question.

"Take heed in his advice Toby." Pete indicated Mr Furrows. "He knows things we didn't."

"But I don't understand. What do you know?"

"Bye Toby. God bless you both."

The spirits left and another chill swept through the room leaving Toby and Terri consumed by silence.

Vivien appeared round the door frame.

"Mum," Terri shouted, "you'll never guess…"

"Yes, I will," she said, quite pale herself.

"You saw?"

"Yes. What did he mean, Toby?"

"I… I, I'm not sure,"

Toby slumped down on the settee still not believing what he saw was real, he looked up at Terri, her eyes confirmed he wasn't dreaming.

Toby replayed what Pete had said 'Take heed in his advice Toby. He knows things we didn't'

But how did Pete know about the cottage? What was Pete's connection with Mr Furrows? Except for his short stop not long ago, Toby hadn't been there in months, he'd left it well alone, as advised to do, he had already lost ten days of his life in total, a fact he still couldn't fathom clearly.

Little more was said between the three of them as Jake was put down in his cot, shock had its hold over everyone. None had experienced anything of the sort before.

In bed Toby's mind could not let go of the cottage. It loomed up larger than life, Edward Furrows' voice booming out his warning to stay away. Confusion racked his mind, if Edward hadn't contacted him in the first place then he wouldn't have known about it, talk about being led into insanity.

The next day Toby found himself outside the cottage, which stood like a mystical structure.

Toby's eye caught something on the wall next to the front door, hidden beneath a now dead plant that had snaked its way up. Opening the gate he immediately felt an intense unease, suppressing any possible regret, he steeled forth and broke away as much of the dead plant as possible. Underneath was a name plaque. On it, in faded lettering was, 'Thyme Cottage'. Toby shuddered as the house appeared to fall in the shadow of a big black cloud, making him look up.

"Toby!"

Toby turned sharply and saw Terri standing at the gate, her face pale.

"Terri what are you doing here? I said I'd be back in an hour." Terri's face contorted in dismay, suddenly he noticed her hair was a different colour and longer than he remembered. "Terri are you okay?"

Terri was struggling with her emotions, seeing Toby standing before her looking exactly as he had done when he left the year before.

22

The Police hadn't taken her seriously when she had reported him missing because he had disappeared for eight days before.

"Terri what's wrong?" She stumbled to her left, grabbing hold of the garden wall. Toby stepped towards her to help.

"Stay away from me." Toby stopped short, surprised by her words. Tears started to well in her eyes, her composure was breaking.

"But Terri."

"How could you?" Anger brewed inside Terri. The hurt for the last twelve months, leaving her to look after Jake on her own. She had known Pete's death had affected Toby hard, but to walk out and leave them. She couldn't forgive that.

"What? I don't understand."

"Neither do I, Toby Grant," It was too much for her and she turned to go. Toby followed. "Don't." She turned on him as she heard his footsteps behind, "I don't know you anymore. I thought you loved me."

"I do Terri, with all my heart. You know I do. And Jake."

"You bastard!" the tears were in full flow, "Jake's been without his father for a whole year. How dare you say..."

"No. NO!" Toby screamed. "Oh God, no. Please don't tell me it's happened again. Terri you've got to believe me I didn't leave you, I would never leave you," Toby pleaded, trying to sound sure of himself but there was a hollowness in his words.

"Just go away Toby, I hate you," Terri stumbled away from

him wiping her eyes with the sleeves of her coat. Toby went to run after her but then thought better of it. He looked back at the cottage, rage coursing through his veins.

"You idiot. You absolute bloody idiot." He kicked the garden wall, which rocked precariously but remained standing. Impulsively he turned to run after Terri, he needed her to understand, understand that he hadn't left her, he would never leave her. She was already out of sight, so he ran all the way home.

Hesitating at the front door he prepared himself for the onslaught that he would probably get, bravely trying to think of how to quell the anger and the hurt she must be feeling. It sickened him to think that he had let it happen again. He had promised himself that he would never, never go back to that cottage. What sort of a father did that make him? He couldn't even keep a promise to himself. Maybe they were better off without him?

In his mind he saw Terri standing at the gate to the cottage. She looked so well. Her clothes new, her hair and make-up immaculate, she'd lost a few pounds making her features look sharper and more defined. She had always looked beautiful to him, but now there was a new guise about her, a fresh look.

"How did she know where I would be if it had been a year?" he muttered.

The door opened and Toby quickly composed himself ready for what would be. Yet staggered backwards when he saw a stranger standing there.

"Hello," came the curt greeting from a small, rotund, woman.

Toby blinked, trying to clear his eyes. Then he checked the property next door to confirm he was at the right house.

"No. Yes. Where's Terri? This is my house."

Another face appeared.

"Can we help you?" The man's gruff tones betrayed his pleasant looking his eyes.

"This is my house," Toby stammered, confused.

"I don't think so." The words were strong and forceful. "We bought this house five months ago. I don't know where Miss Grant went if that's who you're after."

Stepping back onto the street Toby stared at the couple. After a couple of minutes they closed the door shaking their heads.

23

Toby found himself back at Thyme Cottage standing outside the boundary of the property feeling defeated. He couldn't believe a whole year had passed in a blink of an eye. He thought about Jake and how he had missed his first year.

Where had Terri gone?

The walk back to the cottage had been on autopilot, his brain not capable of thinking where else he could go.

Toby still held the key to the house he used to share with Terri and becoming aware of it only gave him a cold reminder that his life was unravelling. Were Edward's words coming true? Why had he gone to the cottage that day? Why couldn't he just leave well alone? He'd been warned enough. He had to find Terri and Jake – the only hope was that Vivien would know, unless she too had moved.

"You idiot!" he shouted as he threw his key at one of the windows trying to release the fury he felt locked inside himself. He watched, as if in slow motion, the key arc towards a large pane in the front bay window. Without warning it vanished in mid flight.

Toby's eyes widened in surprise, his anger instantly quelled. "What the…?" He was about to investigate, "No. What are you doing? Go and find Terri." The words were instructions for himself. Turning to walk away he was stopped by a familiar voice. It was Terri.

"Toby," she spoke calmly, the anger gone.

"Terri. I'm so sorry," The words poured forth almost making them a muddle of sound. Shock registered as he realised she was standing on the garden path that led to the front door, "Terri come out of there quickly." His voice exploded, waving his arms about to urge her towards him. Terri looked at him her face a picture of puzzlement. "Please Terri, we've got to get away from here."

"Why, it was good enough for you. I thought I'd come and see what the attraction was. What it is that has kept you away from your family for so long."

"Please, Terri, that place hasn't done me any favours. Come out of there now. Let's go home. I promise I won't ever go near it again."

"Why Toby? Why?" She edged along the path towards the gate.

"I can't explain, please come out of there. It is too difficult to explain. I don't know what happens. Please come." Toby moved to the gate. his hand outstretched.

"We own this you know?" Toby shivered as the words sunk in. "What?"

"I said we own it, Pete left it to us in his will. That's what he meant when he said he'd look after us. He left us a house. This house." Terri looked at the weathered, impressive two storey cottage. "I was surprised too, he also left us this." Terri pulled an envelope from a pocket and held it out for Toby, there was twenty feet between them. Toby looked at the envelope and then at Terri. "Take it," she demanded.

Hesitantly Toby stepped towards her and took the envelope.

Dear Toby and Terri,

I hope by leaving you 'Thyme Cottage', it helps you with your future. You have been so kind to Betty and myself, especially to me after she passed away. I know you have not had it easy recently and I hope you can make the cottage a nice family home for yourselves and little Jake.

You may wonder why it is in such a bad way and why we never lived there, it held so many memories of a friend I knew once. He disappeared one night and I never saw him again, it tore his family apart. The cottage was left to me after they chose not to live there, or even visit it. By that time we had our own place but I never had the heart to sell it or rent it out.

Now, knowing the end is close by I would like you to have it and turn it back into the home it deserves to be.

I hope you'll be happy there.

Your friend and neighbour,

Pete.
(Ronald Peter Hutchinson)

PS: I have instructed my solicitor to forward to you upon sale of my home the sum of £30,000 to help with renovations.

Toby looked at Terri. "We can't stay here."

"But it's ours Toby. I couldn't bear to live here without you and as much as I hate you for what you've done, I do love you. And now you're back, Jake needs his father. Let's make it a home for ourselves, and start again. Please Toby. Maybe one day you will explain to me why you left me." Terri had been fighting hard with her emotions, the turmoil at seeing Toby after a year and the fact that she still loved him, despite everything. She didn't understand herself, she'd promised faithfully that she would never take him back if he ever showed up again, but seeing him was like a warm blanket that hugs you close and keeps you safe.

"It's this house," Toby lamely stated. "I don't know what but it keeps stealing time from me. We need to..." A dark cloud ran across the sky and Toby had an uncomfortable feeling. Impatiently he grabbed for Terri's hand to pull her towards the gate.

24

"Toby!" Terri screamed, as her arm was almost wrenched from its socket.

As she was pulled through the open front gate the sound of breaking glass reached Toby's ears, he could see no movement, but glancing at the bay window, he saw a broken pane of glass. Terri stumbled into him, knocking him sideways. "OH NO!"

"Toby what's going on?"

"We need to get home." Toby pulled Terri firmly behind him.

"What? What's going on? Toby, my arm."

"I'm sorry but we need to get home. It'll become clear when we get there. I think. You'll understand Terri, you won't like it, but you'll understand." Terri stared at the back of Toby's head as he quickened his pace. When he turned to face her he looked as though he would be sick. Allowing her to catch up he put his arm around her.

"I love you so much Terri."

Terri didn't answer, she was totally confused, her mind racing with emotions and questions.

"Toby I liv..."

"I know, at your Mum's."

Taken aback, again she didn't answer but held onto to him.

Vivien's was only a twenty minute walk from the cottage and after ten minutes of silence, finally, Terri spoke.

"Where did you go?" Her words were soft and barely audible.

"When?"

"Don't play games with me Toby. For the last year." Anger sprang back like a wild cat attacking its prey.

Toby stopped and turned Terri towards him holding both her hands in his. "Terri Grant. I love you with every beat of my heart. I would never knowingly leave you." Terri went to speak but Toby put his finger to her lips whilst still holding her hand. "I have a feeling you will believe me when we get home." He kissed her gently on the lips. The old excitement tingled inside them both and for a few seconds they were lost in the pleasures of a first kiss and how good it felt, washing away the anger, the torment, the frustration.

Terri pulled out her key and opened the door to Vivien's detached bungalow.

"Mum, I'm home." Terri's words were hesitant and wary.

Toby gingerly followed her. The bungalow was quiet.

"That's strange," Terri said, yet Toby knew what to expect.

"What?" Toby asked,

"Well it's Sunday, Mum's friend, Shirley, usually pops round and they play cards."

Toby closed the door behind them and followed Terri along the hallway to the lounge door. Toby checked the dining room which was opposite the lounge. Terri called out for her mum but again got no reply. She walked into the kitchen whilst Toby checked the bedrooms off the hallway, all were quiet. Jake's room was unnervingly tidy.

"Toby," Terri yelled.

He rushed into the kitchen to find Terri staring at the front page of the Evening Echo with a headline which read, 'Mother missing'. Toby scanned the article and saw Terri's name highlighted in bold, followed by two paragraphs and then his own name and a sentence stating that he had disappeared one year ago to the day.

Terri walked to the window putting her hands on the worktop and staring at the garden drenched in the late afternoon sun.

"What's happened Toby?" Terri's voice was weak.

"This is dated Thursday 21st February," Toby walked to the calendar, hanging on the wall. Vivien crossed off the days with regularity, the date showed it was Tuesday 11th March 2008. Terri walked up behind Toby who was staring at the calendar. Her voice trembling as she stated urgently.

"What's going on Toby? Tell me. What is going on?" Anger was breaking through as every rational thought cascaded into a myriad of pictures and doubts.

25

Meekly, Toby turned to face Terri, his face pale. It was still hard for him to believe he had been gone a whole year. And now another three weeks, this time Terri had been party to it, sickening him further to think he had dragged her into it.

"I don't know exactly." It was said barely above a whisper.

Instantly the confusion in Terri's eyes cleared and was replaced again with the anger.

"You don't know, exactly! What have you done?" She pounded her fists against Toby's chest and he let her, knowing she would finally give in. All he could do was wrap his arms around her. "I hate you," she sniffed, the tears coming readily.

"I'm sorry. I…" Toby couldn't find any words that said exactly what he was thinking, so he let the silence surround them, broken only by the sound of Terri quietly sobbing.

Minutes passed before Terri composed herself. "I need to find my Mum and Jake." She withdrew from Toby's arms, looking into his eyes, looking for solace, looking for proof that he loved her. Toby was deep in thought about the cottage and the lost time. Terri turned, disappointed, but not surprised. Pulling out her mobile she pressed speed dial before grabbing a piece of kitchen roll to blow her nose.

It rang four times before going to voicemail. Terri went to speak but suddenly didn't know what to say and after a pause hung up, immediately regretting it and pressing redial. This time she left a message.

"Mum, it's me. Just want to let you know." What could she say? It had been three weeks. "I'm alright mum. I'm at home.

I'll exp…" she stopped mid-word, "just call me when you get this," she hung up still sniffing.

"Now what, Toby?"

He looked at her. "I'm so sorry Terri. I love you so much. I never…" leaving the sentence unfinished Toby walked to her taking her hands in his. Terri surprised him by retracting them instantly. She felt a void had opened up between them.

"I need to see Jake. Make sure he is okay." She walked to the window and stared out into the garden where only earlier that day she had been playing with him in the sun. She mentally corrected herself, it had been a Sunday and a few weeks ago. His laugh rattled through her as she remembered blowing raspberries on his stomach.

"Do you want a tea?" Toby asked hoping to start a conversation.

Terri shook her head 'no', but said "yes."

Vivien was at Carol and Tracy's house, they had been good to her when her daughter had disappeared one year to the day that her son-in-law had gone. She felt her family, her world, falling apart. Just when one thing starts to work for the better there was another blow that shook the foundations under her feet. Had she missed the signs that Terri wasn't coping? She looked as though she was. What would she tell Jake about his parents? That his father walked out on him after a few weeks, then his mother one year later. What would that do to the poor fellow? Not much of a start.

"Here you go Vivien." Carol handed her a cup of coffee. "Black and plenty of sugar."

"Thank you." There was silence, Jake had worn himself out running about and was now asleep on a pile of cushions on the floor, his bum sticking up in the air.

"He's so cute Viv," Tracy said as she knelt down beside him. "Carol and I were thinking of adopting. Well it's either that or find a man." Carol and Tracy glanced at each other then together said,

"But we don't fancy that idea much." They both laughed. Vivien half-smiled as she drank the hot sweet liquid.

"Look do you want something stronger Viv", Tracy added, seeing the despondency resting on her shoulders.

"I'm sorry. I just needed to get out of the house, it seems so strange knowing they are both gone. I just wish Terri would ring. Right now, I'd even settle for Toby. I can't believe he left her like that, he just doesn't… didn't seem the type."

"That's men for you," Carol rebuked.

Instantly a phone started ringing, it's muted tones coming from inside a pocket or a bag.

"Right on cue." Tracy jumped up reaching into her pocket for her mobile. "No, not mine. Must be yours Carol."

"Can you get it for me, Hon'."

"Okay, master." Tracy added sarcastically, returning a minute later. "nope, not yours either."

"There it is again. Viv it must be yours."

"Sorry Carol!"

"I think your phone is ringing." Tracy sat on the arm of the settee and stroked Carol's hair affectionately.

Vivien fished in her handbag for her mobile. As she withdrew the phone the ringing got louder the display showed, 'Terri's mobile'.

26

Vivien fainted, dropping her coffee over the carpet, narrowly missing Jake with the scolding liquid.

"Vivien! Vivien! Tracy, go and get a glass of water." Carol rushed to Vivien's side. Vivien wearily opened her eyes. The phone beeped, signifying there was a message. Vivien looked at Carol, her eyes showing bewilderment, her mind wondering whether she was dreaming, or if this was some kind of a joke at her expense. "You alright Vivien?"

"I… I." Vivien picked up her phone.

"Here you go, Vivien." Tracy walked back into the lounge carrying a glass of water, a towel and a cloth. Jake stirred, burbling away to himself at first before starting to play with the toy car he had been playing with when he fell asleep. It was like someone had hit a pause button and stopped him mid-motion.

"It's Terri," Vivien stammered, "she's called." Carol looked at Tracey and then back to Vivien, who had come over in a cold flush. Dialling 901 Vivien retrieved the message. "She's at home. My god, I can't believe it, she's alright, she's at home. I need to go." Vivien glanced round trying to workout what to do first. "Coat. Where's my coat?"

"It's in the hallway," Carol said, trying to calm her down.

"Oh, yes. Bag? Where's my bag?"

"It's by the side of the chair, Vivien." Tracy added, "Calm down!"

"But she's home, my baby's home. I'm sorry. It's just a shock. A pleasant one, but still a shock."

Twenty minutes later Vivien was standing outside her front door tentatively wondering whether she had imagined the call. Rechecking her phone she saw the missed number listed as Terri's. Jake was kicking the pushchair ferociously, unhappy that he had been stopped from playing. Fumbling with her keys like a nervous child, she slowly opened the door, expecting to hear the deafening silence that had haunted her for three weeks.

Voices, she heard voices, she recognised them. Terri and, and, Toby, and they were talking, as if everything was normal, they hadn't heard the opening of the door.

Vivien found it hard to comprehend that Toby was there and for a split second thought her ears were deceiving her as she listened on. She knew it was him. Anger started to rise up inside, the raw feeling that had taken over when he had first deserted Terri a year ago.

Easing the pushchair over the footplate of the door and releasing Jake she closed the door more firmly than she intended causing the voices to stop abruptly.

"… now you see, I never meant to leave you or Jake. You know I wouldn't."

"When you first went, I kept telling myself 'something must have happened, he would never desert me' but when you never came back, I thought I'd done something wrong."

"Never, you could never do anything wrong." Toby held Terri's hand reassuringly.

"Except that time I washed your white shirts with my red t-shirt," Terri didn't know what made her suddenly think of that, for a moment Toby looked confused before smiling and adding, "That's right. I had to go to work for two days with pale pink shirts. I looked so stupid."

"I don't know, I thought pink actually suited you."

Normal life had returned.

Suddenly they became aware of a noise, then hearing the door slam rushed out into the hall to see Vivien standing behind the pushchair and Jake disappearring into the lounge.

27

Vivien gasped, her anger fading instantly at both her daughter and son-in-law, well and alive; her legs turning to jelly she put out a hand to steady herself.

"Mum," Terri said feebly.

"I was so worried about you," Vivien spoke quietly, overjoyed with happiness.

"Mum, I…" the words were lost as she ran to hug her mum.

Toby walked to Jake, who stared at him as if he was a stranger. He went to pick him up but Jake stepped backwards initially very frightened, his lips pouted as he tried to remember the person in front of him.

"Wow, you've grown so big?" Jake's pout seemed to soften. "It's me Jake, your dad. Come on." Toby stepped forward to hug him.

"It's your father, Jake," Terri confirmed from the doorway but he still stood unsure.

Toby was shell-shocked, his own son didn't recognize him. Toby picked him up and although Jake didn't resist, he didn't reciprocate the gesture. Guilt tore through Toby, guilt at being away and turning to face Terri, tears started to form in his eyes, tears of joy. Terri joined in the group hug and for a few minutes or so, that was all that was needed. Finally, Jake relaxed as the familiar smell of his father registered.

Vivien choked back her happiness. "He missed you," she said, as she sidled up to her daughter and son-in-law.

"I, I…" Toby couldn't find any words that fitted, it was still the same day for him, a matter of hours, but the reality was over a year had passed.

"I'll make tea. I think we need to talk," Terri said.

"No. I'll do it. You two just sit down." The truth was Vivien needed a few more minutes to compose herself.

The evening passed full of awkward conversations, Vivien finding it difficult to take in all that Toby and Terri had to say. It was science fiction to her, a storyline films were made of, not something that her daughter and son-in-law experienced. But she couldn't deny them the sincerity of their words. And when she looked more closely at them she saw that the clothes they wore were still as they had been the days both had disappeared.

Jake spent hours playing, showing his father all his new toys, his new bed, Toby had last seen him sleeping in a cot, now he was grown up, sleeping in a bed. It was a revelation to Toby, an unnerving situation, a year going by in an hour. How? Toby read Jake a story and tried to settle him down, but he was excited at having his father back. It took an hour and two books before he finally gave in.

Back in the lounge the question of what to tell the police reared its ugly head. It was not going to be easy. Toby's history would only open him up to possible prosecution for wasting police time. Terri could find herself dragged into the fray. It had been hard enough for Vivien to convince the police when she had disappeared.

With Toby, the police had at first refused to spend any effort looking for him, too many cries of 'wolf'.

The phone call was put-off until morning. An uneasy night's

sleep beset everyone, except Jake who appeared blissfully un-aware of the repercussions of recent events, settling straight back into normality in a wink. Toby had an uncomfortable night on the settee, Terri believed Toby's excuses for not coming home, how could she not? But she still felt betrayed and despite the aching to have him by her side, she wanted a night to sleep on it.

Breakfast happened in relative quietness, Jake playing joyfully with his food, despite efforts to stop him. Toby decided to help Vivien clear up the plates whilst Terri got Jake dressed. The atmosphere was frosty and Toby knew he had bridges to build but didn't know how to. It was so odd, he hadn't cheated on anyone, he hadn't killed or robbed anyone, the time had gone, that time in his life, vanished, taken like a possession. He could have kicked himself for being such a fool.

As he dried up the last bowl and placed it in the cupboard he spoke

"Vivien. I am..." Words wanted to come but there was still so much confusion – how was all this possible?

Vivien turned to him, only twenty-four hours ago she thought it was just Jake and her, then both her son-in-law and her daughter turn up alive and well. "I won't pretend to understand anything of what you have told me, in fact what both of you have told me, it is impossible to comprehend. You're like the son I never had and I just want you both to be happy."

"I know, I know. If I could turn back..." Toby suddenly stopped hearing the irony in his own words.

"If that house is the key to all this, then don't go back, please."

"I promise you, I am never going back. The cottage is history."

"Good."

"But what do we do with it?" Toby asked. It was an asset, and worthless standing empty.

28

Toby stared off into oblivion, his mind whirring, turning over thoughts of the cottage which they now owned. "S'ppose I'd better go down the station and let the police know we're okay."

"What will you tell them?" Terri said from the kitchen doorway holding Jake who was playing with her hair.

Toby's face looked blank as he stared at her. "I don't know. What can I say?"

"I think it'd be best if we all went together. It will look better if we can show solidarity," Vivien stroked Toby's arm with a mother's affection before leaving the kitchen to get ready. She had got over her initial anger at Toby and was just glad that her whole family were back together.

Terri stared silently at Toby, although the annoyance was now gone her thoughts were still confused. She had mixed feelings for Toby and how the cottage was affecting their lives. Terri had spent the night fighting with herself, turning over and over in her mind every possible scenario from this day forward, and whichever way she looked at it she wanted Toby to be with her, he loved her and Jake, she knew that deep down and she loved him with all her heart.

She strolled over to Toby and surprised him by planting a kiss on his lips which took him a full second to respond to.

"I missed you so much." Terri said as she slipped her free arm around his waist. Toby was surprised but pleased by the show of affection. He responded by kissing her gently on the head. Jake was oblivious to all the proceedings yet he was caught up in it, somewhere along the line, according to Edward Furrows.

At last, Toby spoke. "I'm scared of what the police are going to do Terri."

"So am I." She hesitated, "We don't exactly have a good track record do we, what with you last year."

"I could never leave you Terri."

"I know, I know, I just can't believe what's happened. In some respects it would be easier to know that you left me for someone else, it's far more plausible."

Toby stepped back, breaking their embrace, "No, it's not. I love you and always have. I don't want anyone else." His voice was rough with emotion.

"Good. I'm glad to hear it." Terri added, resolutely.

The police were unimpressed by Terri's sudden re-appearance, even more so when she couldn't offer any believable excuse, everything she had thought of on the way had sounded lame, the idea of going on holiday and her mum forgetting sounded great for at least ten seconds but soon unravelled as quickly as it had come together. Three weeks was a lot of time to account for, the amount of police energy that had been wasted on searching the local area, questioning people about her disappearance, had added up. It was only when Toby spoke up that they forgot about Terri completely. The threat of prosecution for wasting police time was an imminent possibility, and when Toby offered no feasible explanation, the threat turned into reality.

Suddenly a dark cloud gathered overhead. Terri and Vivien tried their best to placate the officers but even they had to concede that it hadn't been just a one off and no explanation could be given.

Toby was duly processed and allowed to leave some two hours later, details of his impending court case would arrive in the post.

The three walked back past the park in silence. It was a pleasant afternoon and there was nothing left to do except to start building some bridges, quality time as a family.

The topic of jobs cropped up, both Terri and Toby had steered clear of this subject; Toby had a whole year to catch up on, including the sale of their home.

Terri explained that after three months she couldn't afford to keep it going so she had applied to the court for special dispensation to sell without Toby's consent and with no formal death apparent. The court had taken some convincing but had finally ruled in her favour and it meant that they would make a small profit. The money and the cottage that Pete had left them had got tied up in red tape initially so she couldn't have used that. It was better if she forgot about the cottage for the time being and move in with her mother, where it would be easier to manage working part-time, and caring for Jake. With Toby now gone, she had received a letter from his employers saying, as much as they understood and sympathized with her predicament, they had to terminate Toby's employment.

Finally the money from Pete's estate had come through but she didn't have the heart to spend any of it. The only saving grace was now they had money to live on for a while until they got themselves sorted out.

"My court case could take most of that though, Terri."

"Oh give me strength, can't I at least enjoy some respite and have some sanctuary, just for a while," Terri said, firmly. Her words had an edge to them that was razor sharp. She didn't mean them and realized that Toby was only making sure they didn't lose track of the reality of the effect the cottage was having.

Abashed, Toby kicked at the ground as they walked. The house was determined to destroy them one way or the other.

Vivien listened without comment, too much had passed, she was glad they were both alive and well and here with her. She suggested lunch in a café as a way to break the mood that was settling uneasily between them.

29

As the days passed, a routine was established although it was far from normal, the playful rapport between Terri and Toby, that had always existed so readily, was gone. A chasm was opening up and it tore at Vivien to watch. It was like each was being consumed by their own guilt and neither would talk about it, a forbidden subject.

After a week of relative uneasy conversation Vivien paid for Terri and Toby to go out for a romantic meal alone, in the hope that they could find their equilibrium again.

She didn't hear them come back but the following morning both were glowing, the spark re-ignited. It was what they had needed.

Relieved, life started to get back to normality and Toby started to look for another job. He knew it would be hard, having just disappeared, he wouldn't be able to get a reference.

Friday 18th April 2008

The weeks started to sail by at a rate of knots, Toby and Terri had got back to where they had been and spent time enjoying each other's company. However, as the money started dwindling cracks began to show, reality was only just around the corner. Toby had applied for jobs but was having a difficult time getting past the application stage due to his year long absence from work, despite spinning yarns about taking a year off to look after his son. Although it didn't bother him as much as before he knew the longer he stayed out of work the harder it would be to get back. He lowered his sights. Anything to get started.

Toby found himself surfing the net more and more, trawling the endless jobs sights and agencies but with no urgency. There had always been a niggling thought in the back of his mind, Thyme Cottage. He had managed to push it to one side up to now, Terri and he had made a pact never to go there again, but that also left them in a quandary - 'What to do with the place that they now owned?"

Nonchalantly he punched the words into Google, curious as to what it might throw up, expecting nothing. There were 1045 references. Taken aback, Toby started to scan through them. Some were for holiday cottages, others picked up on individual words. Page after page he churned, engrossed by some of the obscure connections that Google turned up.

His tired eyes suddenly stopped scanning and locked onto an entry with the date '1908' in the text. Opening it, he read what was an extract from an old newspaper article dated 1958:

'The last of the railway cottages built in 1908 has been sold at auction today. 'Thyme Cottage', which has never been lived in since it was built, was the last lot to be sold after the council failed to find the original owners. A court judge ruled that the local council could seize the property and sell it as it was attracting unwanted attention from vagrants. The police had been called to the place many times over an 18 month period.

Mr and Mrs Smith bought the property in which to raise their son.'

The article rambled on with neighbours' comments, yet nothing more of interest.

With renewed interest, Toby skimmed through more of the entries, time was passing as he found himself engrossed in his search of the history of the cottage and didn't hear Terri arrive back with Jake. He jumped when she tapped him on the shoulder, the music he been playing in the background covering her footsteps.

"Jesus, you frightened the life out of me."

"Sorry what are you doi…" Terri saw the two words in the search box, the two words which had played havoc with their lives for so long "You said you'd stay away. You promised me Toby. We agreed."

"Terri, I just thought I'd find out a bit of history about the place."

"But Toby."

"I wasn't going to go back there. No way. That place has messed us about too much, but we have got to do something with it."

"Sell it. Let's just sell it. It can be someone else's problem."

"In all honesty, can we really let someone go through that?"

Terri looked abashed for a second, she knew it deep down, but that didn't stop her being afraid. If Toby was searching the net for information she knew it would only be a matter of time before he went back there. She knew she could lose him again. "Promise me you'll never go back there, promise me for Jake's sake." Jake turned round when his name was mentioned, but carried on playing on the floor when he wasn't acknowledged. Terri's request was met with hesitancy.

"I promise. Terri, do you really think I am going to put you through all that again. I've already got one court case pending for wasting police time."

Toby switched off the computer. "Look, come here." Toby gave her hug before going over to Jake. "So what's little Jake been up to today then?"

Jake spun round. "We went to park." He caught Toby in the eye with his elbow.

"Nice shot Jake," he said sarcastically.

Terri watched the scene, fearing that she could not believe Toby's promise.

30

Toby found it more and more difficult, as the days drifted by, to forget about the cottage. It was like a screw being tightened every day, the tighter it got the more he had to know. He knew it would be better if he had a job all this sitting around the house was driving him insane. Terri tried to watch him closely, her distrust of his words growing inside her, toying with her own insecurity.

Finally Toby managed to find an excuse to stay behind whilst everyone else went out for a walk. He had been ill during the night, so Terri thought it might be best if he stayed indoors. He rushed to the computer when he knew they were far enough away and continued his search for facts and information about the cottage. In the past few days he had come up with a different angle – missing people – feeling that he can't have been the only person to have… travelled through time. He shuddered at the thought.

Punching in 'missing persons in Southend-on-Sea' Google returned over 25,000 entries. Changing the criteria to 'reported missing' people only increased that figure to 28 million. Flicking back to his original search, after a few attempts to narrow the field failed, he went through some of the more interesting sites.

A lot were about tracing relatives and friends and not actually people vanishing. There was a lot about books and films, comments, reviews. Page after page Toby sifted, every now and then checking his watch for fear that Terri would catch him. As melancholy set in he started to skip pages of results, hoping that maybe an obscure one nearer the end would be more fruitful.

In the bleariness of tiredness he almost missed an entry titled 'railway cottage mystery'. Opening it he read an extract that had been posted on an 'unusual occurrences' website by a Diane Forrester.

'After many hours of research through local papers in Southend library, I came across an intriguing story about the railway cottages in Prittlewell, Railway Terrace, and one in particular. The end terraced cottage was only ever occupied for a brief time in the early 1900's. Rumours at the time pointed at some odd goings on, particularly, before it was occupied when animals, cats and dogs, went missing. Early assumptions were that Witchcraft was responsible with the animals being taken for use in spells by a band of local gypsies camped nearby. However, the interesting thing I found was that after the gypsies had been driven off, the strange occurrences still continued.

I could find no firm dates, as I say, it is all rumour and conjecture. But, to make it to the local papers meant there must have been some substance to it.

Things really took off twelve months later when the keys were given to the new owner 'Ivan Briggs'.

Toby sat bolt upright, stretching his back and reading on.

'Mr Briggs took ownership on 12th February 1909, the house being a gift from GWR as a reward for all his hard work during the construction of new rail links. There was a big ceremony and presentation. Unfortunately, Mr Briggs's family arrived a day late due to a derailment bringing them from their home in Hereford. Nothing untoward happened after this, the disappearances of cats and dogs ceased until the day of Wednesday 11th August 1909. On that day the family, Ivan, his wife –Imelda, and two sons Joseph and Peter were last seen at around tea time. It was the next day when a neighbour, whose name I can't find recorded anywhere, came calling, as agreed with Imelda. The cottage was deserted. Venturing in she found the breakfast things laid out and a pot of hot water boiling over the open fire. Calling out she apparently got no reply and searched the rest of the house. All the Briggs's possessions were there, although few. The strange thing was Mr Briggs's work boots were ready by the front door. No one ever saw them again and from that day the cottage has lain empty, surrounded by myth and rumours.'

Toby scrolled down to the bottom of the post, it was dated 23rd April 1999.

Underneath there was a further entry.

'I have located the actual cottage. I will upload some pictures when I have scanned them in. Have tried to locate if there any owners alive today but have been unsuccessful. Am going round later to have a look for myself'.

In Toby's head he screamed out 'NO' but he knew it was too late, there were no more entries for Diane Forrester.

31

Toby scrolled frantically up and down scouring for further entries, but none came to light. Leaving the website he hurriedly opened other sites looking for signs of Diane Forrester or even Ivan Briggs and his family. Nothing. They had literally disappeared.

He stared at the flickering cursor wondering what to type in next. He tried Diane Forrester, 160,000 entries came back. Some with only her first name, some with only her second name, and after searching through the listings, none on the first thirty pages referred to the Diane Forrester he was looking for.

'Damn', he muttered.

"What is it?" Came a voice behind him, making him jump, before trying to close the site whilst turning in his seat to face Terri.

"Oh, nothing, just a job I thought sounded good was past its application date." He couldn't believe how swift he had come up with that and how plausible it sounded.

"What was it for? You feeling okay now?"

Toby froze momentarily before turning back to the screen as if looking at the job. Whatever he pressed in his haste was making the computer scroll rapidly through pages and pages of search material. "Oh, just a depot manager's job for some wine merchant, it was uptown. And, yes, it must have been that Kebab I had last night."

"Oh," Terri said, scanning the computer screen. "What's it doing? I told you not to have one, but would you listen."

"I don't know, I must have pressed some bloody short cut

key." Toby was punching the escape button furiously trying to make it stop. Trying 'control, alt, delete', still wouldn't stop it. Toby slapped the side of the screen. "Stupid bloody thing."

"Yeah, like that is really going to help Toby." Terri added sarcastically. Part of Toby's frustration was that he had been nearly caught out.

"How's Jake anyway? Enjoy his walk?"

"What he didn't sleep through. Yes."

"As long as he doesn't..." The computer suddenly stopped flicking through pages and Toby caught sight of a few words in bold that chilled him before the screen went black followed by task manager.

Diane Forrester found walking dazed and confused, claims to be a woman who disappeared almost seven years earlier...

"No, you stupid bleeding computer, don't do this to me now." Toby struck the escape key. "Pen, paper?" He scrabbled around the computer desk desperately looking for something to write on. "Oh come on, come on. Don't do this to me."

"You alright Toby?"

"A-ha." Toby said jubilantly uncovering an old envelope and blunt pencil before scribbling frantically. "What was the date it said?" he asked rhetorically, thinking hard to reconstruct the image of the sentences in his mind. "Damn it, it's gone."

"Toby what are you doing?" Terri lifted Jake out of his pushchair and walked over to Toby. "I'm not sure Jake's okay, you know. He's never normally been this quiet and lethargic.

Toby thought quickly. "Just trying to remember some contact details before the computer completely dies on me. Damn thing!" He folded the piece of paper up and placed it in his jeans for safe-keeping. Then switched the machine off. "What did you say about Jake? Oh right. Did Jake have a bad kebab last night?"

Terri eyed Toby quizzically, "Like I am going to allow you to give him that rubbish at his age, he'll have plenty of opportunity for junk food when he's in his teens, I'm sure."

Toby changed tack. "Maybe he's just got a bit of a cold. Does he have a temperature?"

Terri placed a hand on his forehead. "No."

"It's probably nothing then. Do you fancy seeing a film tonight, if your mum doesn't mind watching Jake. Hello little fellow? Come to Daddy" Toby took Jake from Terri. "How's my favourite boy?" Jake barely responded. "That's not like him."

"Exactly." Terri held Jake's hand and tried his forehead again. "Seems normal though."

"Maybe he's just tired. I'm sure he'll be fine. Won't you mate?"

Terri watched Toby carry Jake out of the room before staring at the now blank screen of the computer, her curiosity pricked. Something didn't feel right but she couldn't put her finger on it.

She didn't want to accuse Toby of anything without proof.

Following him out of the room "I suppose. What do you want to see?"

"Don't mind."

He was suddenly being very nice.

Toby appeared distracted as they queued to pay for tickets for the film 'Leatherheads', which Terri had insisted on seeing as she quite fancied George Clooney. She held his hand tightly. He turned and smiled at her even though his thoughts were elsewhere. Toby felt the back pocket of his jeans, the crumpled piece of paper was still there, he was eager to investigate further but knew he would have to be careful. The Library, he thought, that would be the best option to search further, he would make his excuses tomorrow and check it out.

After getting their tickets Toby indulged them with sweets and a massive box of popcorn, just like when they first dated.

Terri laughed as Toby danced around the pick and mix, scooping sweets into the large paper bag like he was a mad professor.

"Toby Grant you're embarrassing." She giggled as he threw a cola bottle into the air and went to catch it in his mouth almost tripping over a blonde eighteen year old nymph-like girl standing behind him.

"Sorry." He apologized blushing red, the girl smiled flirtingly at him, amused by his antics.

"No problem," she smiled demurely.

"Come on, Toby," Terri added, the jocularity gone from her voice.

"Ooops!" He smiled at the girl who smirked at Toby's embarrassment.

32

The following morning Toby made the excuse of visiting the job centre and various agencies but headed to the library instead. With one hour free on the computers to use the internet, he withdrew the piece of paper from his back pocket and typed in what it said.

His typed words had brought up 12,000 entries. "Bloody search engines. I know what I want to see, just take me to the bloody article." And so started the laborious task of sifting through the articles. One minute turned into ten which turned into thirty.

"Come on, come on, you're here somewhere I know you are," he muttered to himself, managing to draw unwanted glances from other net users nearby.

"A-ha. Got ya." Toby scanned the article.

Diane Forrester was found dazed and confused near her supposed former home. Police had been called by the current owners when the woman entered the premises using her door key. An argument ensued and police arrived to sort the matter out.

Accusing the current owners of stealing her home, the police were quick to do an identity check on Miss Forrester, only to be astounded that it was actually her, despite her disappearing five years previously. Her distant cousin, Ruth Johnson, had appealed to the courts to legally take possession of Diane's assets as she couldn't be found. Ruth had subsequently died two years later and her estate, including Miss Forrester's assets, had been sold and divided between relatives.

The most baffling thing for the police was the fact that Miss Forrester looked exactly as she did the day she disappeared. There was no sign of her sleeping rough, her clothes, hair and make up were immaculate as if she had just gone out for a walk for a short time.

Miss Forrester is now under psychiatric evaluation to establish whether she had entered some kind of 'Fugue' state that had lasted five years, despite her insistence that it was 23rd April 1999, although her appearance could not be explained. Police had appealed for witnesses as to her whereabouts for those five years but just like at the time of her disappearance, no information was forthcoming.

Toby drummed his fingers on the table.

"Shush," came the stern reprimand from a man next to him.

"Sorry," Toby whispered.

He scanned to the end of the article to see who it was written by, Matthew Gilbert. Searching the newspapers website he jotted down the phone number.

It took two days for the Matthew Gilbert to call Toby's mobile, and unfortunately Terri was within earshot.

"Toby Grant?" the voice questioned.

"Yes, that's me."

"Matthew Gilbert, returning your call."

Toby stood up, ever conscious that Terri was with him

"Hi, thanks for returning my call. Hold on a sec'." Toby put his hand over the phone and mouthed to Terri that he'd go outside.

"It's alright Toby," but Toby had left the lounge, triggering Terri's suspicion. He had never before left the room answering a call unless the TV was on, but they had been talking. She felt uneasy, something wasn't right and slowly she got up.

"Sorry about that." Toby hoped that Matthew would mention Diane's name, so he didn't have to, in case Terri heard.

"No problem. What can I do for you?" Damn, Toby thought, glancing over his shoulder to check Terri wasn't listening in. "Hello, Mr Grant?"

"Yes. Sorry. It's about the article you wrote about Diane Forrester. I was curious whether you knew her whereabouts, I would like to talk to her."

"Diane who?" Came the short reply.

Toby hated having to say her name once, but twice. "Diane Forrester. You wrote the article about her. She was the one who was found dazed and confused, claims to have lost five years."

"Dazed and conf... Oh her." The memories of the article came flooding back. "Yes I remember now. Strange one that, looked exactly the same as the day she disappeared."

"Yes, yes, I read the article. Do you know what happened to her?"

"Got sent to some care place or other, can't remember off-hand where. Right story she told, baffled the police…"

Toby interrupted Matthew's recollections. "Is there any way I can find out where she went or ended up?" Silence, followed by Matthew blowing out a long breath.

"Not off-hand, you could ask the…" Matthew changed tack. "Why do you want to know? What is it you need to talk to her about? Maybe I can help."

Damn, Toby thought he should have known it could get complicated and suddenly he tried to think of a valid reason for needing to contact her. The pause was longer that he intended. "I'm just looking to find out something about what the cottage…" Toby swore at himself, nothing he was saying was making sense.

"Sorry? What was that?" Matthew spoke, wary that this sounded like a crank call "Look, I've got to go."

"No, no, please. I'm trying to piece together some information about mysterious disappearances in the local area, it's a sort of project."

"Right." Matthew sounded dis-interested.

Toby's brain started to turn over faster and faster, he needed to keep Matthew talking. "Look my father disappeared when I was younger and I was looking into it when I came across other people who had also disappeared. The strange thing is that no one has ever returned in the cases I have come across except this Diane Forrester, I thought it would be good to talk to her, sort of find out what it was like to go for so long and then return."

"I see." There was silence and Toby thought the phone call was over. "I'll check through my notes, I normally keep them safe, see if there is something I can find out. Maybe a contact in the police, that's probably your best bet."

"Thank you, that would be really helpful."

"I can't promise anything, but if I can I'll call you back." Matthew cut the connection.

Toby stood there motionless thinking. The police, that made sense, it hadn't occurred to him to follow that route. He would try them tomorrow.

"Toby what was that about?"

33

Fear shot through Toby like a stake in the heart. How long had Terri been standing there?

"Toby?" Terri's voice shook with fear

Answers tumbled over and over in his mind "Oh, it was just an agent asking if I had found any work yet," he hoped she hadn't heard the whole conversation.

"What agent? Didn't sound like an agent to me." Terri's own insecurity crept back into her like a frost settling on the grass. They had always said that they would never lie to each other.

Toby turned to face Terri. "Oh, a new one 'Matthew's'. It's a guy who worked for one of the many I'm on. He has set up on his own, always got on quite well with him we were just chatting. You know."

Terri tried to hide her doubt of Toby's word. She had only caught the tail end of the conversation and then only the odd word of Toby's hushed tones. Toby stared at her for a long moment.

"Come on let's take Jake down the park."

"It's raining," came the curt reply.

"So, come on, we used to love walking in the rain."

"Toby, Jake will catch his death."

A fraught tension hung in the air like a storm cloud.

"Come on, he'll be fine, the buggie's got a rain cover."

Toby was almost convinced Terri had heard more than she was letting on but he didn't want to come clean, as it would surely cause a row if she knew he was still investigating the cottage. He cursed his own curiosity that kept him so wrapped up in the mystery. He wanted to know more.

"Okay" Terri sighed, finally giving in. They did used to enjoy walking in the rain. There weren't so many people about, and this made it feel that the seafront or park was their private playground.

"What?" Toby responded, suddenly shaken from his thoughts.

"Walk. You know what you suggested not a second ago." Terri couldn't hide the sarcasm in her voice.

"Good! Excellent!" Toby pushed his mobile phone firmly back in his pocket and went to get Jake ready.

An hour later they were walking along the seafront, there was a slight breeze and the rain had turned to a drizzle creating a mist over the flat sea.

"Toby?" Terri said, breaking the relaxed silence between them.

"Yes,"

"You would tell me if something was going on wouldn't you?"

"Tell you what?" Toby felt Terri's curiosity rising and he cursed himself again. He should have taken the call out in the garden or asked to call back.

"Anything! You can talk to me you know. I love you and want to help."

"I know you do. And I do talk to you. What's brought this

on?" Toby played it as innocent as he could.

Terri let the question settle whilst she compiled her thoughts. The phone call had bugged her, hitting a nerve, and she couldn't figure out why it upset her so. She put that together with the computer incident a few days earlier and felt Toby was hiding something. Although she had told him it was over if he ever went back to the cottage, her intuition told her he was toying with the idea. He was certainly covering up something.

Toby had a few seconds to think. "Look, I just don't like this not working. I thought it would be good, you know spend time with you and Jake. But, but, I don't know I'm bored... no, no not bored, restless," he corrected as Terri's face showed her shock. "I know that sounds horrible but I feel in limbo. I need something for me to focus on, focus my mind."

Toby stopped walking and faced Terri.

"Does that make sense?"

Terri glanced down at the ground before looking into Toby's eyes. "Yes," she paused. "and no. I don't know," She was lost for words. Suddenly she felt that Toby was saying he was bored with his family that they didn't interest him, she was enjoying work and in some respects she sort of understood what Toby was getting at.

"I love you, I always will, both of you." Toby kissed Terri on the lips.

Her mind turned over the last time he had said those words just before he disappeared.

34

The next day at home Terri couldn't allay her fears that Toby was going to visit the cottage again, she wanted to confront him yet didn't want to have an argument. She hated arguments. She didn't feel they solved anything. She also believed if she pushed it, she would eventually drive him away and she didn't want to be on her own with Jake, that one year had been enough. She had missed him so much and Jake needed his father.

Terri did start to wonder about the cottage herself, it was sitting there doing nothing for them, accept laying temptation at Toby's feet. She smiled slightly as she pictured herself demolishing it using a wrecking ball. She imagined it as a large pile of debris and her standing on top of it satisfied that it was all finished, over, done and dealt with. Then she saw the world change around her and a dark cloud form above her head, a laughing, smiling cloud.

"You alright?" Toby interrupted her thoughts.

"Yeah. Yes. I was just... doesn't matter." Still Terri held the picture in her head only now there were flames leaping twenty feet into the air as she lit a life size match.

"I'm just popping out okay? Shouldn't be long."

"Where are you going?" The words tumbled out so quickly it sounded like an accusation more than a question.

"To visit the agencies in Leigh." Toby replied, surprised by Terri's reaction.

"Oh, okay." She bit her bottom lip, debating what she should do.

"I'll try not to be too long." Toby kissed Terri on the lips and lingered there awhile but Terri didn't react. "I'll see you later. Shall I get fish and chips for tea?"

Terri's mouth opened as if to say something more but she though better of it. "Yes okay, text me when you're at the chip shop and I'll get some plates in the oven."

Toby grabbed his coat and left.

Terri's distrust kicked in immediately; she stood up and walked quickly to the door to call Toby back. She wanted to question him, get his reassurance that he wasn't going back to the cottage but as she ran to the edge of the garden path Toby was disappearing from view at the end of the street, turning left. She stood shaking, racked with fear, her brain turning everything over in her mind.

He'd turned left! Leigh was right, at the end of the street. She felt a surge of panic like poison. She wanted to run after him but she couldn't leave Jake on his own. Where was her mother when she needed her? Suddenly she was angry with everyone. Toby for being drawn to the cottage like a kid to sweets, and her Mum for going out with her friends.

She went back inside, slamming the door. Finding her mobile and using speed dial she called Toby. She didn't know what she was going to say but was determined to get him back, anything to prevent him from visiting the cottage. The phone started to ring as she paced the lounge, as it rang she became aware of a noise in the house, music. Walking into the hall with her mobile stuck to her ear she listened to the music, following it to its destination. In Jake's bedroom she saw Toby's phone lying on Jake's bed. Horrified she cut the connection and stood staring at it in disbelief.

She speed dialed her mum and let the phone ring and ring.

"Come on, come on, please answer." After the fifth ring it was answered

"Terri?"

"Mum, he's gone!" Vivien's heart leapt.

"What? Where? Who?" Vivien panicked, trying to fathom what her daughter was talking about.

"Back to the cottage. Mum I've lost him again. I don't know what to do."

"I'm sure he hasn't, he promised." Vivien said, reassuringly.

"Then why did he lie to me? Oh Mum." Terri's phone went dead.

"Terri? Terri?" Vivien looked at her phone curiously but the little screen showed the connection had been broken.

She quickly called back but Terri's phone went straight to voicemail.

Terri cursed her phone battery, which had gone flat, she knew she had to ring her mum back. She looked at Toby's phone and pressed the keypad, but it had security code requirement. Toby had never done that before. That only deepened her unease.

Two hours passed and distractedly she played with Jake, although he seemed more interested in watching TV, knowing there was little else she could do. A key turning in the door broke her dark mood and she rushed into the hall.

"Toby?" She sighed at the sight of her Mum.

"Terri, what's going on? I was so worried I had to come home. I couldn't get home sooner as the buses weren't running very well."

Terri looked at her Mum as she turned over in her mind everything she wanted to tell her. Everything that had been kept from her since the cottage had come into their lives. "Terri. You alright, you look as white as a ghost?"

Terri nibbled on her bottom lip just like she had done as a child whenever she was making up a tall story. Should she say, or should she not.

"Terri, you're worrying me." Vivien walked towards her daughter.

"I'm sorry Mum." She paused. "Sorry, we just had a bit of an argument. I think Toby's getting a bit down not being able to find a job."

Vivien eyed her daughter, she recognized the telltale signs of white lies, but she had also learnt that in time the truth always came out. Patience was the best tactic.

"I'm sorry mum, I didn't meant to drag you away from your..."

"It's alright. Come on, let's have a cup of tea. How's my grandson?"

"Watching cartoons."

"He does love his cartoons."

35

Toby marched purposefully on, guilt playing on his mind that he had told Terri so many white lies. He knew he was treading on dangerous ground but compulsion kept him going. He tried to allay his own guilt by telling himself that he would visit the job agencies as well whilst he was out, but first things first.

He spent the rest of his twenty minute walk to Southend Police Station working out what he was going to say. As the station loomed up in front of him he felt himself perspiring. Why would they help him after all the trouble he had caused? It was a long shot but he felt that he had got his story straight. With mock confidence he walked into the reception - it was a throwback to the seventies with its dark hard wood veneered doors and counter tops, posters about crime prevention, security and other spurious matter littering the walls. The counter was un-manned but a notice stated 'press for attention'. Hesitantly he did so. The electronic buzz grated against the silence.

Suddenly the door he had come through opened and he turned to see a respectable large built man in a suit dragging a young girl of about ten by the arm. Her reluctance to be there was evident as she fought to break free of the powerful grip.

"Yes, can I help you sir?" Toby turned sharply to see a young WPC standing behind the counter. Everything Toby wanted to say was forgotten.

"Yes, I been asked to bring this bloody idiot in. Stop struggling or I'll belt you one. You've caused enough trouble already. Bloody be the death of me."

"Dad, I told you I didn't do it," the girl protested, fighting against his fierce grip.

"Yeah, and the Pope's not Catholic." The girl finally managed to break the grip her father had on her.

"Sorry sir, I'll be with you in a second. This gentleman was first."

Toby stared at the WPC for a few moments.

"I haven't got all day, the bleeding idiot has already lost me half a day's wages," the man stated, annoyed.

"Yes, well I am sorry sir, but this gentleman was first."

"No, no, it's okay, please see to him first." Toby only just managed to speak with a level tone.

"Kind of you," the bullish man stated, trying to sound as polite as he could, but his tone was brusque and aggressive.

The WPC acknowledged Toby's acquiescence with a non-committal smile. Toby took a seat whilst the man dealt with his daughter who had been caught shoplifting but was to receive only a caution.

After ten minutes it was Toby's turn.

"Yes can I help you now sir? Thank you for letting... I know you, don't I sir?"

Toby was dreading that sentence but knew that it might occur and wearily he agreed.

"Unfortunately, you probably do."

The woman's pleasant face became severe as she remembered.

"Did the disappearing act. Twice!"

Toby felt so small and it didn't help that the counter and the floor behind were set at a higher level.

Words were slow to form.

"Look sir, if you have come to waste more time then I would think very seriously about it." The implication was not lost on Toby.

"No. No, I haven't, I know I have caused problems but I am trying to do something about it. I am trying to get some answers and I think I know of someone who can help me but I need some information." Toby let those words settle to gauge her reaction. She didn't shift position or change her facial expression and Toby knew this was going to be hard work.

"I know this isn't going to make sense but..."

"Is there a point to any of this anytime soon?" The question was sarcastic. "I do have more deserving things to be doing."

Frantically, Toby searched his mind for something to say that would signify that he wasn't wasting her time.

"Diane Forrester. I am trying to locate Diane Forrester."

"Disappeared as well has she?" It was a question that sounded more like a statement.

Toby sighed inwardly, this was futile.

"Wait a minute. That name rings a bell."

Embarrassed Toby continued, "She disappeared a few years back for five to seven years. Then turned up again, without an explanation."

"Another time waster. Relative? And what of it?"

"I am trying to find her, I understand she went into a home

of some sort. It's just that I think she might have some answers for me."

The WPC stared at Toby for a long time seeing a truth and honesty laying behind his eyes, a sincerity that he was serious about trying to get answers.

"Please." It sounded so feeble "I am trying to get my wife to understand."

"Look, sir, we don't give out information. Afternoon Sarge," she said, as a man appeared from the door where the WPC had appeared.

"Have you got the file on the house burglary from Hainault Road?" The WPC scribbled a note down on a piece of paper as the Sergeant went out of earshot, Toby standing awkwardly wondering what she was going to say next.

"It's on my desk Sarge."

"Thanks."

"As I said we can't give information about people's whereabouts." She paused to make a point.

"Thanks…" Toby said reluctantly turning to leave.

"But…" she continued, regaining his attention, "I seem to remember her being rather fraught and upset and, I don't really know what's going on but, actually you seem quite honest. Try this place, it's where we go to get help for some people of, shall we say an unstable disposition." The statement was loaded. "They might be able to help."

"Thank you." Toby half-smiled, pleasantly surprised that the WPC helped, looking at the piece paper he saw the name of Fennel's Care Home, it sounded familiar.

Leaving the police station he glanced at his watch, 15.07, just time to go the job agencies in Leigh if he caught the number 26 bus, he thought it was an almost hopeless task but at least he would have gone and therefore, strictly speaking he hadn't lied to Terri.

36

Terri and Vivien sat quietly in the kitchen, Terri staring intently at Toby's phone, wondering why it was locked with a security pin.

"Why would he do it Mum? He promised."

Vivien knew her daughter was right but didn't want to believe that Toby would go back on his word. "You don't know for sure." Vivien's words sounded hollow.

"Mum, he walked in the wrong direction." The hurt in her voice was heartbreaking.

"Maybe one of the agency's is…"

"No, it isn't. He said he was going to Leigh, and he hasn't…"

The slamming of the front door broke into Terri's tirade.

Toby beamed as he walked home, he had a job interview lined up for tomorrow. It was up in London for a Lloyd's underwriter, a junior position but the prospects were good. It would mean a fresh start. He couldn't wait to tell Terri, she'd be so pleased.

As he opened the door he heard Terri's raised voice which stopped suddenly. She came racing to the kitchen doorway, furious with him.

"Hi ya, you'll never guess," he said, a smile planted firmly across his face.

"How could you Toby Grant? You promised." She ran towards him, fists clenched.

"Whoa, What? What's going on?" His face a picture of innocence.

"I saw you. You went back to the cottage."

"I didn't," he stated defensively.

"But I saw you," she shouted, her anger bursting out.

"I bloody didn't go back to it. I promised you," Toby raged back.

"Then where did you go?"

"To the agencies."

"You're a liar Toby Grant, a bloody liar."

Toby knew he had told a white lie, but the truth was he hadn't gone to the cottage. "I'm not, how dare you call me a liar," he said furiously.

"Liar, liar, liar," Terri shouted, taunting him.

"I'm not…"

"Yes, you are."

Vivien had heard enough to know that the argument was going to fester and not get anywhere. "Alright you two. Enough, you're like a pair of teenagers. I ought to bang your heads together."

"But he's lying to me Mum and he…"

"Enough Teresa!" Terri stiffened, struck rigid at being called a name she hated.

"Vivien, I have not lied…"

"Just be quiet, the pair of you. It's like being back at playschool. You should be ashamed."

"But…" Terri interrupted.

"I have spoken." Vivien commanded. Terri leaned back against the wall. "We are going to sit down like the adults we are and talk about this sensibly.

Toby couldn't hold it in any longer. "I've got a job interview for tomorrow, that's what the problem is. I got offered the interview whilst at D & A's Job Agency, they rang up the company whilst I was there, we had a quick conversation on the phone and they offered me an interview. It's as simple as that." Toby folded his arms across his chest and looked at Terri whose eyes showed her embarrassment.

"But I saw you turn left at the top of the road."

"So I thought I'd take a long route and get you these." Toby pulled out a plastic carrier bag from inside his jacket.

Terri looked at the Thornton's carrier bag and then down at the floor.

"Take it then," Toby commanded bitterly.

Reluctantly she took it and as Toby removed his jacket she looked in the bag. Inside was a selection box of fudge, her favourites.

She turned to her Mum, who gave her a look of 'think before you speak'.

37

Toby brushed past Vivien to the kitchen to put the kettle on.

"I'm sorry Toby," Terri said mournfully, following him.

"Look, I promised didn't I?" Toby placed three mugs on the counter top. "Tea Vivien?" he called.

"Yes, please," came the reply from Jake's room where Vivien had gone to check on Jake.

Terri stood looking at Toby, feeling guilty for accusing him. "Thank you for the fudge."

"You're welcome." He walked over and wrapped his arms around her and she reciprocated. Toby knew he'd been lucky, thank goodness for the job interview. And the fortuity of buying the fudge. He knew he would have to be careful about the little notes he had. "We'll have to decide what to do with the cottage at some point, we can't just leave it to rot."

"I don't understand how what happened, happened."

"Neither do I, and I guess we never will." He was determined to find out and, hopefully, Diane Forrester would know something.

"But it is not logical. It's not possible to lose time. It's not real."

"It was real. Very real and we both know it."

"Yes, but how?"

"Mmm, I thought I was meant to be to the curious one." Toby thought for a second about telling her what he had found out so far, then decided against it.

"Yeah, you're right. Anyway tell us more about this job."

Toby broke their embrace and made the tea. Filling her in on the details concluding with," damn, I forgot the fish and chips."

The following day Toby was up early, his interview was at eleven-thirty and he wanted to catch the nine-o'seven train to Fenchurch Street, to make sure he was on time. He wanted this job, if only to give his mind something else to fathom. He was dreading questions about why he left the fast food chain training scheme and ran through the answers he could give. The initial phone conversation had gone well, if only taking him by surprise, it seemed an unusual way of doing things yet made him feel positive about the outcome.

Terri finished dressing Jake.

"Here you go." Vivien placed a mug of tea on the chest of drawers next to Jake's bed. "How is Toby this morning?"

"Quite excited. I think he feels positive, the guy sounded really nice apparently. Yes, Jake, that's mummy's nose."

"What time have you got to be at work?"

"Not starting 'til one. I thought I might go in a little earlier if you don't mind looking after Jake. There's a couple of bits I want to do first." Terri hadn't slept well all night, the cottage was an alarm clock going off everytime she closed her eyes. There had to be something they could do, it was a wasted asset, and she knew it would be lovely to buy their own home again, especially now Toby was back. The big question was what. Selling it was the obvious option, but her own sense of morality pulled the plug on that idea. Then her conscience would kick-in and say 'Why shouldn't we sell it? It is not our problem'. She needed to visit the cottage to see if inspiration would strike.

"That's no problem, I don't mind looking after my grandson."

"Thanks Mum."

Standing outside 'Thyme Cottage', Terri studied the decaying monument, amazed that it had remained empty for so long, it looked so inviting, so homely, a lovely place to raise Jake. The potential shone like a beacon, good size front garden and the back appeared to stretch to about one-hundred feet.

"What are we going to do with it?" she muttered to herself. As if on cue a shadow moved across the house. She looked up at the sky but it was a lovely clear day, just a few wisps of white cloud hung decorating the sky's blanket. Looking again at the house something had changed but she couldn't figure out what, something small, something almost indecipherable.

Sudden fear gripped her and she checked to see whether she had accidentally stood in the grounds of the house, afraid that once again she would lose time. But she was outside on the pavement. When she saw movement in an upstairs window her first reaction was to run in, and confront whoever it was. But terror held her back.

"Toby," she cried out.

38

The train journey home from London was blissful, the interview had gone really well and he was almost positive he was going to be offered the job. Every question he answered calmly and succinctly, impressing Harvey Buckworth, the HR manager, of Heath & Smiths Underwriters Agency.

Grabbing a piece of paper from his wallet, he telephoned Fennell's Care Facility, only to be told that Diane Forrester had been discharged a long time ago and that they didn't know where she was.

Feeling pleased with himself he didn't let it worry him. As the train pulled into Prittlewell station his phone rang; number withheld.

"Hello?"

"Mr Grant?"

"Oh, Hello Mr Buckworth."

"Toby, I'll come straight to the point." Toby sat still, thinking the worst. "We'd like to offer you the job." Toby almost dropped the phone, "We like you start a week Monday. You did say you could start fairly promptly?"

"Absolutely. That's great, thank you."

"Good. Well I'll get a letter in the post confirming salary as discussed and everything else and we'll see you Monday week."

"Yes, certainly."

"Oh, and if you can bring in your bank account details and P60 etcetera."

As Toby disconnected the call the train was pulling out of his station, but he didn't care, he had a job. A celebration was called for tonight, a massive Thai take away and a bottle of Champagne.

Toby entered the bungalow cheerfully whistling to himself, two bottles of champagne clinking in a carrier bag. Vivien's bungalow was cloaked with a strange quietness which he immediately found disconcerting.

"Hello." He looked at his watch. "Vivien?" It was four o'clock, suddenly he remembered Terri was working until six tonight, so Vivien had probably just taken Jake out for a walk. He settled in front of the computer to continue his search on Thyme Cottage.

As the cursor blinked away at him, he wondered what he should try next, Diane Forrester was a dead end. Inspiration struck and he looked up ordnance survey maps of the area before the cottages were built, unfortunately the images that came back were blurred and hard to read.

"Hello Toby. How did the interview go? What's that you're looking up?"

Toby spun round.

"Hi Vivien. I didn't hear you come in."

"Obviously too engrossed in the computer. What is that?" Vivien said, unbuckling Jake from the pushchair and moving over to Toby.

"Oh, I was just curious…" Vivien shot a warning glance at Toby "… no, I wasn't checking up on the cottage, but it did get me thinking about what this area looked like before all the houses were built." Toby took Jake from Vivien. "Guess what son? Daddy's got himself a job. What do you think of that, eh?"

"Daddy, job." He repeated, twisting and turning, trying to break free from Toby's grip.

"Really Toby?"

"Yes, start a week Monday. It will be so nice to get some routine back in to my life."

"Terri will be pleased."

"I know. I thought we'd celebrate tonight get a Thai takeaway and I bought a couple of bottles of bubbly, well cheap stuff anyway" Toby looked at his watch. "Where is Terri anyway?"

"So whereabouts is this?" Vivien pointed to the screen. "She said she is working until six tonight."

Letting Jake down, he turned back to the screen, Jake made a grab for the keyboard, which Toby manage to avert. "Go and play with your toys, it's nearly your bath time."

"No," Jake shouted.

"Yes." Toby replied.

"Don't want to."

"You'll do as you're told my boy otherwise you won't get any tea."

"No," Jake replied again, but before Toby could respond Jake ran out of the kitchen. He heard Jake's bedroom door slam and left it, he knew he would play quietly for a little while.

"As far as I can make out that is Prittlewell in about 1840. Six you said? But it is nearly seven.

39

Terri stood at the gate on the verge of stepping over the threshold, convinced that she had seen Toby's shadow dancing about the walls inside the cottage. Her hand rested on the gate latch.

"Toby, you said you wouldn't, you promised. You said you had an interview," Terri muttered.

"Look lads, she's three cans short of a four pack." A scrawny teenager called out to his three friends who laughed.

Terri turned sharply feeling scared by the three loud lads.

"What's wrong love, can't find the loony bin?" called one wearing a faded black t-shirt."

Terri watched nervously as they eyed her from the other side of the road. They seemed to hesitate as if thinking about approaching her. Gulping she tried to fathom her best option, uncomfortably she toyed with entering the cottage convincing herself that it was Toby she saw.

"'Ere Mike, I think she fancies you."

"Yeah, well who wouldn't?" Mike replied

"You attract all the nutters..."

The boys vanished and when Terri looked down at the ground she saw she was standing inside the grounds of the cottage. Panic swept through her, her mind in turmoil, thoughts of Jake racing through her. Turning on the spot she looked up at the cottage, then back out at the street.

"Oh god," she cried, before fainting.

Vivien looked at her watch, "Oh, so it is, my, how times flies. Maybe she had some paperwork to finish and stayed late."

"Yeah, probably. I'll give Jake a bath." Toby left the room.

"Do you want a cup of tea?" Vivien called, sitting down at the computer and staring at the map in front of her.

"Yeah, that'd be nice. Hope Terri won't be too long, I'm starving."

"I'm sure she'll be home by the time Jake's bathed. I'll make tea and then go and pick up the takeaway. I'm so pleased for you Toby."

"Sorry, what was that?" Toby called from the bathroom where he was running a bath.

"Never mind," Vivien said, distracted by the old map on screen.

Bathed and ready for bed, Toby realised that they hadn't given Jake his tea. "Oops, I suppose we ought to give you some tea. Not normally wise after your bath but hey-ho. I wonder where mummy's got to eh?" he asked, watching Jake playing with his hair which was so soft it looked as though it was statically charged. "There you go." Vivien placed a mug of tea on the chest of drawers.

"We haven't given him his tea yet?" Toby said, admonishing himself slightly.

"Oh gawd, no." Vivien agreed. "What awful people we are? Look why don't you do that, I'll get the takeaway."

"Okay. Here." Toby handed Vivien three twenty-pound notes.

"Bet your both starving," Vivien called as she closed the door quietly, aware that Jake would, hopefully, be asleep.

She placed her coat in the cloak cupboard and looked at Toby. "What's wrong?"

"Terri's not back yet."

For a second, confusion played on both their minds. Vivien looked at her watch.

"But it's eight-thirty."

"I know."

"Have you tried her mobile?"

"Yes, goes straight to voice mail" Toby stated, dreading the worst, hoping she hadn't gone back to the cottage, after all the promises she had made him make. Surely she wouldn't have? Vivien rang Terri's mobile whilst Toby carried the Thai meal into the kitchen. Coming back into the hall he saw the mystified look on Vivien face.

"Nothing. It's dead."

40

"Dead? What do you mean dead. Surely it goes to voice mail? It did earlier."

"There's nothing," Vivien said, her words a whisper.

"Let me try," Toby commanded, dread throwing its cloak over him.

Toby dialled the number he knew by heart, fear driving its stake into him.

Nothing!

Toby stared at the phone in disbelief.

"Toby!" Vivien said trying hard to fight the panic that was growing inside her. "Toby!"

"You're right, it's dead." Toby tried to think rationally, but in his mind, thoughts of the cottage rushed around.

"We ought to ring the police, report her to missing persons."

"She did go to work didn't she?"

"Of course she did, where else would she go?" Vivien suddenly realised Toby's implication. "She wouldn't, it has caused enough trouble with you!"

Toby felt the weight of Vivien's accusation and deep down he wanted to believe that Terri wouldn't, but he knew she wanted to find a solution to the property. He was confident she wouldn't have entered, not after last time.

"Then she must have gone to a friends, or out for a drink after work," Toby added.

"But her phone would work."

"Maybe the battery died?"

"Then it would go to voicemail."

Toby knew Vivien was right. A feeling inside nagged him, dread about the cottage.

"I'm going out to look for her."

"Toby?" Vivien stared at Toby, also concerned about the pull the cottage seemed to have on her family, and how implicitly it tore them apart.

"I've got to do something." Toby snatched his jacket from the cupboard.

"Toby, don't go to the cottage. Please."

Toby stood looking at Vivien. "I won't, I promise, but she is never late and she would always tell us if she was going out after work. I've got to look at least."

Vivien watched as the door closed. An aching in her heart. Why did they have to be burdened with the cottage, it had been meant as a gift but was turning into a death knell.

Vivien stood and listened to her bungalow breathing, the loneliness sinking into her bones. She wanted to believe Toby but she doubted his words were honest.

Toby walked along the road, the cold night air making him shiver as he muttered to himself. "Terri, please say you didn't. Please, please. I promised you, don't let it have suckered you in." His walk turned almost into a brisk trot as anxiety took control.

It didn't take long before he was standing outside the cottage, staring up at the fading façade, that looked so intimidating in the night.

"Terri, I hope you didn't go in." After five minutes staring at the cottage in vain, hoping that Terri would re-appear, he turned to leave, only to be distracted by a faint glow of a light in an upstairs bedroom.

"Terri!" He uttered loudly, catching his breath, hope rising inside.

Vivien listened to Jake sleeping, the only comfort she could find. The Thai meal was slowly going cold in the kitchen, but it didn't appeal anymore. Finally a fretful sleep consumed her as she sat in the rocking chair next to Jake's bed.

41

Jake's crying woke Vivien, frantically she tried to recollect her thoughts of how she had come to be sleeping in the rocking chair. As she stood up to tend to Jake she felt the stiffness in her back, the wooden rocking chair not conducive to comfortable sleeping.

Like a jolt she remembered the conversation with Toby, and Terri's disappearance; ignoring Jake's cries she rushed to check on her daughter's room. Turning on the light she saw the bed lay empty, no sign of any occupation, the digital clock radio read, 03.47, she checked her watch, it only confirmed the time. Jake's cries were still ringing in the background as she checked the rest of her bungalow, worried that she had lost both Terri and Toby.

Would Jake be parentless?

Every room was vacant.

"Oh Vivien, what have they done?" she said to herself as she headed back to Jake's room to reassure him.

Hugging him tight she thought back to a time when it was her daughter who had had a nightmare and for a second it was her she was consoling.

"Don't worry grandma's here, you're safe" Jake didn't respond only hugged his Gran tightly, he couldn't remember what his dream had been about. Once his tears had been brushed aside he settled down quickly and Vivien felt uncomfortable as the silence engulfed the bungalow.

In the kitchen she made herself a cup of tea, although she didn't really feel like it. She had to do something. She sat at the kitchen table but couldn't settle so she went into the lounge to let the TV try and take her mind away from her lost ones. But the pictures of her happy family that sat on the mantelpiece haunted her.

"Oh Carl, how could they do this?" She held a picture of her late husband, Terri's father, who had passed away eighteen years previously after an industrial accident. She pulled the picture to her chest, hugging it like a safety blanket. "Please bring them both back to me, for Jake's sake."

The TV did nothing to settle Vivien and she found herself wandering tirelessly around her bungalow, hesitating at Terri and Toby's room, wishing they were there, back in the fold of her family, checking it to make sure she hadn't imagined it.

"Why? Why couldn't you just let it go? You'd been warned about what it does to you." Her words were lost in the silence of the house breathing.

She knew the inevitable call to the police was edging closer and dread filled her, she knew they wouldn't take her seriously, not after the last couple of times. They would file the missing report at the back of the cabinet and only refer to it if they had time available. She could understand it after so much wasted time, but it held little comfort.

Slowly dawn began to break and a deep sadness slipped over Vivien. The question of 'when would her children be returned to her?' consumed her. Did she have to wait a week, a month, a year? How would Jake cope growing up without them? They needed to be here.

Finally she tried Toby's mobile, it went straight to voicemail. Sinking down in the armchair Vivien reflected on the tarnished gleam of family life letting sadness swallow her.

Taking out her handkerchief, she dabbed at her eyes as tears started to fall.

"Toby? Toby?" Terri called out, she followed the noise and the light she had spotted outside. The stairs creaked under her steps. "Toby!" she repeated, less enthusiastically. She reached the door to the middle bedroom and pushed the door open.

A low flickering light lit the shell of a room.

"Who are you?" Terri asked. "What are you doing in my house?"

42

Toby stared up at the cottage, he had hated lying to Vivien about coming here, but it was just the one place he needed to check. In his heart he hoped Terri hadn't come. What was it about the cottage that seemed to be able to destroy everyone who ever knew it?

He stood in the darkness. There was no sign of life. No sign that Terri had ever been there. He hoped he would find a glove, just something, so he knew for definite. Nothing. The house looked deserted and he dared not enter.

"Terri, if you went in, I hope you come back soon. I can't

follow you this time, Jake needs us. I hope I see you soon."

Abruptly Toby's mobile burst into life. Excitedly he pulled it from his pocket hoping that it was Terri, but the screen displayed a 'number withheld'.

"Hello." He said sullenly.

"Is that Toby Grant?"

"Yes, who's this?"

"Matthew Gilbert, you spoke to me about Diane Forrester and that cottage."

"Oh yes, yes. What did you find out?"

"She moved to Scotland not long ago to start a new life."

"Really? Have you got any contact details? It might be good if I could speak to her."

"I don't think that is very likely." Matthew's voice turned cold.

"At least give me a hint or something so I can do my own search for her."

"It's not that Mr Grant, she committed suicide three weeks ago. An associate of mine was doing research on Diane's past and contacted me as she had come from down this way."

"Oh."

"Yes, not good I know, but I thought I would let you know, as you seemed interested."

"Thank you."

There was a moment of silence before Matthew added. "Look, Toby, I was thinking of maybe running another article on this Diane Forrester and you seem to be interested, maybe we could meet up and discuss this further, perhaps at the cottage itself. I think I remember where it is."

"No!" Toby said sharply. "I mean, I don't think it is a good idea, do you? A mad woman disappears for several years, there's not much of a story there, is there?" Toby thought about his own predicament and then wondered how many people had entered this cottage over the years.

"If I remember correctly I think the property has been empty for years now hasn't it.?"

"Yes, no, I mean I don't know."

"Excuse me?"

"I mean I don't think it would be of interest to too many people."

"I don't know, I think I could find the right angle."

"Why not just let it lie? She probably just made the whole story up."

"Disappearing for several years and re-appearing looking exactly as she did the day she disappeared, I don't think you could make that up. Yes, definitely something I overlooked originally. I shall have to check it out."

Toby felt the tension rising inside him, he wanted to protect anyone he could. He didn't want anyone else going through this.

"Please, just stay away from the cottage. It will do you no good."

"You do know something don't you? What is it?"

Toby thought for a few seconds, but could think of nothing to placate the journalist. "Just stay away." Toby hung up and looked up at the cottage.

"Why?" He kicked the gate hard and then walked away, hoping that Matthew Gilbert wouldn't remember where the cottage was. Storming down the road Toby wondered whether he should torch the place. But what about Terri? If he set light to it how would she get back? If indeed she was there.

43

Toby roamed the streets, trying to think where else she could have gone, knowing that the truth was probably the cottage, cursing their misfortune. Cursing the initial contact Edward Furrows had made. If he'd never known about the place all would have been alright. Why had Pete left it to them? Why hadn't he just sold it earlier? 'Damn, damn, damn', he cursed. Distracted, he made his way to Terri's workplace, hoping, wishing for any sign of her. He checked a couple of pubs he knew she might possibly go into, but there was no sign of her. As his heart sank he ordered a pint hoping to drown all the dread he felt growing inside like a ball.

Suddenly he was bumped into by a raucous group of lads, turning sharply.

"Watch it!"

A tall blonde good looking lad with angular chin and smooth skin stared at him in disgust. For a moment Toby was ready for a fight but thought better of it as two more lads joined the blonde one at the bar. He took his pint and went to sit in the corner. After a while he ordered a second pint. Every now and then he looked at his phone in vain hope that there would be a missed call from either Vivien or Terri. No messages.

Necking the rest of his pint he slunk out of the pub into the cold air, lost for somewhere to look next, he knew a few of her friends and walked round to where they lived. At the first two, the lights were off. He glanced at his watch it was eleven, when he reached Sandra's house he noticed the flickering of a TV behind the thick curtains and for brief second felt his heart jump. He tapped on the window to avoid waking the children he knew them to have. The curtains were brushed aside and Toby saw Sandra with a cigarette wedged between her lips. Recognizing Toby she came to the door.

"Toby, what you doing here?"

The question only confirmed what he feared, but he asked anyway.

"Have you seen Terri?"

"Terri? No. Why, did she say she was coming here?"

"No, it's just that…" Toby let the rest of the sentence fall silent, "It doesn't matter."

"Toby, what's wrong?"

Toby turned to go, he was now sure he knew where Terri was and there was nothing he could do or say, it was too late.

"Toby, come in."

"Thank you, but I really ought to get home. Say 'Hi' to James."

Toby walked off into the night leaving Sandra staring quizzically after him. His thoughts were far from going home and he made his way to the seafront, a place where they used to go when they were dating. Staring at the sea he could hear her voice, remember the good times, and the arguments they used to have on a regular basis.

As it turned colder he pulled his coat tighter before resorting to the Menzies shelter that gave him protection from the wind and the rain that had started to fall lightly. As the night slowly drifted on he decided he would do something decisive to end the mystery of the cottage.

Yawning, he noticed the time was 6am, he shivered unaware how cold he had become. He knew it was time to head home, but first he walked back to the cottage. It was time to end it all. Standing at the gate he viewed the property with a heavy heart and willed Terri to appear at the door, but the longer he stared the more hope faded.

After thirty minutes he withdrew a lighter which he had

bought at a newsagents, along with a tin of lighter fuel. It was part insanity.

"Terri, I'm so sorry, I hope you find a way back."

44

Vivien had finally dozed off on the settee, her eyes too weary to stay open, her heart ached from despair as thoughts of her and Jake resounded through her head. Now alone in the world, wondering how long it would be before Terri and Toby turned up again, if ever?

Abruptly she was disturbed from her restless sleep by the sound of the front door closing. For a few seconds she couldn't believe her ears. Was it a dream or real life? Was she awake? As the questions remained unanswered another noise broke into her thoughts.

Hauling herself up as quickly as possible she went into the hallway, hoping beyond hope that Terri would be standing there. Instead a weary Toby bowed his head in greeting. Vivien stared at him for a second before tears started to fall, part in relief, part in sorrow that it had not been Terri, part in guilt for wishing it was Terri instead of Toby.

"I'm sorry, I couldn't find her," Toby said tiredly, embracing Vivien.

"That bloody house. I wish it had never come into our family, it's done nothing but tear us apart. It is determined to ruin everything we ever had. Why? Why us? Why my family?"

"I don't…" Toby couldn't find any words to placate Vivien and just thought of Terri and how he missed her already. His great news of a new job was now tainted. "How is Jake?" he finally asked.

"He's asleep." As if on cue Jake woke up and Toby went to tend to him, and gave him his breakfast.

A while later, Toby and Vivien ate breakfast in silence whilst Jake sat in front of the TV watching cartoons. Vivien still felt sick to her stomach that Terri had gone.

"We'd better report her to the police," Vivien said sorrowfully.

"Why?" Toby stated matter-of-factly. Which ignited Vivien's anger.

"Why?! Why? Don't you bloody care? My daughter is missing. My grandson, Jake has lost his mother!" Toby looked at Vivien, his eyes full of hurt, as her words landed at his feet. "I can't bloody believe you. I thought you loved my Terri." Toby had heard enough.

"You know I do. And do you know what else? I wish we had never set eyes on that bloody cottage. I wish we could go back a year, forget all that has happened, but we can't. What's happened has happened and as much as I hate it, and miss Terri, there is nothing I can do. And do you know what?" Vivien stared at Toby as she understood every sentiment underlying Toby's words. "If we go to the police they will have us locked up so fast, and put Jake in care, life would never be the same again, whether Terri gets back or not."

Vivien and Toby sat in silence as the truth of his words cut like a knife. She knew that with Toby's pending court case he was right. But it hurt to do nothing except sit back hoping she would turn up some time, providing she had visited the cottage. If not, she could be lying somewhere.

Vivien decided to go out for a walk. She grabbed her coat from the coat cupboard, knocking Toby's jacket to the floor.

As she picked it up the lighter fuel and cigarette lighter fell from his pocket. She stared unblinking at them thinking, 'Toby doesn't smoke'.

Instantly the thought was gone and another had entered her mind. She rushed into the kitchen thrusting the objects at Toby.

"Tell me you didn't. Please tell me you didn't. She'll never get back if you did." Toby looked up at Vivien, his eyes betraying his guilt.

"No!" Vivien screamed. "You bastard, how could you." She pictured the cottage a charred ruin, and Terri, stuck wherever she was, never to return.

45

"No, I haven't burnt it down," Toby stated, although he nearly had. He had only been seconds away from starting the fire when the thought that Terri might not be able to get back terrified him.

Vivien could see Toby thinking about his answer. "What are we going to do?"

"I don't know. If Terri were here now, I think I would be tempted to burn it down and hope that would put an end to all the mystery, but she's not. And I don't know why she would have ventured in there anyway, after all we've been through."

The sound of the phone ringing broke the discussion. Toby went and answered.

"Hello."

"Hi, it's Bob, Terri's boss. I am just wondering whether she will be in today? Is she there? We didn't see her yesterday and it is not like her to miss a day without a call. Is she okay?"

"Yes, yes, she's fine, well, no, I mean she is not feeling very well. I do apologize we were meant to ring yesterday and… and I don't have a good reason for not, except to say sorry, I forgot."

"Oh." Bob was clearly not pleased, even though he appreciated the honesty.

Toby decided he needed to buy them some time at least, in the hope that she turned up within a few days.

"I don't really think she'll be in for the rest of the week, she's got a fever and has been vomiting, not a pretty sight."

"Oh, okay, I see," Bob sighed. He was short staffed already and this only added to his problems. "Would it be possible just to chat to her for a couple of minutes, I just have a couple of questions?"

Toby's mind swirled with various answers. "Do you mind if she doesn't, she has been up half the night and only just got to sleep. I'd hate to wake her now."

Reluctantly Bob agreed and hung up, leaving a standing request for her to call, when she woke up.

"Who was that?" Vivien asked.

"Terri's work. She didn't turn up yesterday either."

"At least we know when she disappeared."

"And what good will that do?" Toby snapped. "Sorry! Look, do you want another cup of tea?" Vivien nodded. "I am going to go to the library later to see if I can dig up some more information about the history of the cottage." The look Vivien shot at Toby spoke volumes. "No, I am not going to the cottage, but I have got to do something, I can't just sit here, and next week I won't be able to as I have a new job to go to."

"Yes, yes of course." Silence consumed the kitchen, both thinking about Terri.

"I said who are you and what are you doing in my house?"

The figure looked at Terri, eyeing her curiously. The small sandy-coloured labrador by the figure's side sat up, his tongue hanging out of his mouth, it's gentle eyes pleading to be stroked. Terri eyed the dog cautiously.

"It's alright he won't bite. He is a lovely dog and Norton likes you."

The statement caught Terri off guard.

"Likes me?"

"Yes, always had a soft spot for you."

Goose pimples rose on Terri's arms, setting alarm bells ringing in her head.

"I've never see him before in my life."

The figure rose, his bright features were only outshone by the vivid blue eyes. His long hair gave him a rugged look, enhanced only by his five o'clock shadow. He stretched out a long, spindly arm, the boney hand betrayed his youthful look.

"I'm Edward, Edward Furrows. Your son's best friend."

46

Terri stepped back, surprised, putting her hand to her mouth.

"I was watching you as you stood outside. I hoped you wouldn't come in. But this place has a habit of provoking curiosity in people. I told Toby to stay away and he didn't."

Terri still looked shocked, unable to fathom an understanding.

"Why can't people just listen? It will do no one any good. I wanted to save Jake the pain this will lead to. But you all seem so hell-bent on screwing up anyway."

"I don't understand…"

"No, you don't," Edward responded angrily, "and you never will. Just accept it an' stay away." Norton got up to go to Terri. "Norton stay!" The dog turned to look at his master, pleading to be allowed to continue. "She won't understand boy."

Gathering her thoughts and composing herself she said. "So how come you can come and go as you please?"

"Questions, bloody questions. Alright. Go on boy."

Norton sprang forward excited at being stroked by Terri, she saw the delight in the dogs face and knelt down to greet him. She was scared of dogs normally but somehow he had broken down the barrier to a memory of being attacked by a dog when she was just eight years old. Norton bounded into Terri's arms, licking her face she felt his cold fur. Somehow it created a memory in her that was unfamiliar. She stroked his back as the dog licked at her face, then suddenly its substance was gone.

She fell forward as the weight of the dog disappeared. "What the…?"

"He's not anymore, neither am I. Not here. We were once."

"But he was… there he is…" Norton was sitting in front of her and, as she looked, she saw right through him.

"Who are you?" Terri's voice deepened as she looked around the room to check that it was real, that she was actually there.

"It is real. All very real. Have no fear of that. But have fear of what this place brings, how it tears your family apart. I watched I saw how it affected Jake, my best friend. I always liked you. You treated me like one of your own. Jake couldn't handle it when you told him about his father, but you wanted him to know the truth. I thought by coming here I could change things, but all it seems to have done is speed up the cycle. At this rate Jake will never know either of his parents. What have I done?" Edward turned back to the window, staring at the new street scene beyond the garden wall.

Edward started to fade out.

"Wait. I don't understand, I want to, but it is... I don't know, it's just too... bewildering."

"I know," Edward added.

Terri shook her head. "I can't believe that you talk about my son as a grown up when he is only two-and-a-half."

"I've known him most of my life, right from infant school, twenty-four years."

Feeling her legs go weak she walked over to the window to look at the world outside. "That means..."

"Yes, I know what it means and how it appears to you. It is not an easy thing to comprehend. That's why I hoped my warning would ward Toby off. Jake had done a little research and found out when you inherited this house and then I found a way back and thought I could repay all the favours that Jake ever did for me. I though it would be easy, I didn't realise the cost."

47

"The cost? What cost?" Terri asked, still struggling to take it all in.

"You've hardly changed." Edward spoke, changing the subject, as the hurt of the price he had paid to help his best friend solve a lifelong riddle. The price of failure.

"I'm sorry?"

"You've hardly changed from what I remember growing up.

You age well."

"You said you paid a cost. What was it?"

Edward stared at Terri for a long moment. "My life, I paid with my life."

Staring incredulously at the man before her, she laughed nervously. "This is a joke isn't it? I've been set up. This is some kind of sick joke, a dream… no, a nightmare."

"Terri Grant, this is no joke."

"It has to be, this can't be real." Terri started to get hysterical as she tried to discount everything that had happened since they had inherited the cottage. "I'm going mad, aren't I? I've lost my marbles. Living in some kind of delusional mind…"

"Terri!" Edward shouted, his eyes still calm, breaking Terri's train of thought.

She looked at Edward, her eyes trying to rationalise the situation. "I'm going back to my family."

"Good. And don't ever come back."

Terri took in Edward's rough handsome features one more time before turning to leave.

At the library Toby had been directed to the map section, reams and reams of maps dating back to the thirteenth century. Nothing on the maps showed anything untoward, just fields and farm buildings. He didn't know what he had hoped to find but something unusual, anything that would indicate what was so strange about the cottage.

Walking back to reception he asked to be directed to a section on local history and was politely told that the books resided on the second floor. "You can't miss it," the lady had said and when he arrived he realised why, hundreds upon hundreds of books were stacked on metal shelves covering all manner of things.

"God, this is going to take forever," he said, too loudly, provoking looks of annoyance from people nearby.

Browsing the spines it seemed hopeless, books on picture

houses, books of farming in the local area, books on recent history 1960 onwards, the seafront, the pier, the hotels, manufacturing. Nothing gave him hope of answering the questions that he had and he left dejected after an hour of pointless searching.

Standing outside the enormous stone and glass building he looked to the sky for inspiration and silently said, 'I'm trying Terri, I am, but I don't know where to start'. A cold wind blew up and he shoved his hands deep into his pockets and turned to walk to Southend High Street in search of a hot coffee. After a few steps he reached an Edwardian building, which he had forgotten existed. Outside sat an 'A' frame with a notice confirming the museum was open. He had never been inside but thought maybe it was time that changed.

Entering through the double oak doors, a musty historical smell greeted him and, for a second, he wasn't sure if it was a good idea or not.

"Museum is closing in about half an hour," said a polite, elderly gentleman dressed in casual trousers, shirt and jumper.

"Oh, okay."

"Please feel to look around though, I just wanted to let you know."

Toby looked at his watch, it was just gone four-thirty. "I'll be as quick as I can then."

The gentleman smiled and turned to go.

"Excuse me, actually, maybe you can help me." Toby noticed that the small museum was deserted except for the two of them.

"Of course, if I can."

48

"I'm trying to find out about a cottage, well actually about the history of it and the land it occupies. I've tried the library but the maps didn't seem to help, and there were so many local history books that I didn't know where to begin."

The elderly gentleman brightened, most people who came to the museum barely uttered a 'hello' let alone asked questions.

"Do you mind me asking where the cottage is?"

"No, sure, it is on the corner of Railway Terrace, Prittlewell. It is the corner one."

"I'm not quite sure where you mean. Hold on a minute." The elderly gentleman walked away with a spring in his step. He was on a mission and it felt good, returning five minutes later with a rolled up map in his hand.

"Right, now let me see." He looked around for somewhere to place the map, beckoning Toby to one of the large display cases showing a replica 3-D model of Southend seafront in the 1920's. "Ah yes, here we are."

"Thank you, I'm Toby by the way."

"Alfred Jenkins, but most who know me call me Jenks, and I like it, reminds me of my youth."

"Okay, Jenks it is." Toby smiled, relieved at getting some help.

Jenks eyed the map with some difficulty before reluctantly resorting to using a pair of thick black-framed glasses he pulled from a deep pocket. "That's better. As much as I remember my youth, it has long past." The comment needed no response.

Unrolled, it wasn't one map but thirteen, each approximately four-by-three feet. Jenks sifted through them until he came to one which was clearly labelled 'Prittlewell – 1947'.

"These are as far back as we have here, I expect you have seen older ones in the library."

"Back to the thirteenth century."

"For some reason they won't let us keep them here. Now where did you say your cottage was?"

"Railway Terrace." Toby pointed to the place on the map. It showed that opposite the road was open ground next to the railway sidings. The cottage was clearly shown within walking distance of Prittlewell station. "That's it." Jenks frowned, which caught Toby's eye. "What is it?"

"I'm not sure." He paused for a second or two. "Somewhere in my memory I recall some stories. I'm sure they were in Prittlewell. It's difficult to tell these days, they keep naming roads in different areas with the same names, it gets confusing."

"But you think they relate to this road?" Toby pushed.

"Well, if they do, they were just stories told by children to scare each other."

"Have you lived here all your life?"

"So far, yes," Jenks replied, his mind still distracted by muddled memories.

"So far?" Toby quizzed.

"Eh, oh, yes, well I'm not dead yet young man."

"I see." Toby glanced at his watch, feeling this was going nowhere, the map didn't show him anything new relative to the cottage. "Are there any maps showing what was on the site before the railway was built. I don't know, a church or something religious, a monastery perhaps?"

"Oh no, there was nothing like that there, I remember playing around that area as a child."

"How old are you?" Toby asked, surprised. "I mean, I don't mean to be rude but the railway cottages were built around 1908, if I remember correctly." Suddenly Toby knew he was wasting his time as that would make the fellow over 100 years old, and he only looked seventy at most.

49

Jenks became flustered. "No, that's not right." He balled up his left hand and put it to his mouth, "That would make me, oh fiddle, but I remember it so vividly, the sun was hiding behind the greying cloud, I was eight at the time. I was there with my brothers, William and Albert, they were younger than me. No, no they were older. Why do I remember them as being younger?" Confusion wrapped Jenks in its cold blanket.

Toby looked towards the door and thought about making his excuses, although deep down, he felt sorry for the old man, guessing that he was probably the first person to actually talk to him for ages. Toby noticed a wedding band, so he surmised that Jenks might just be lonely, his wife gone, possibly. But it wasn't helping the cause.

"It was 1905 and the railway was being built, we were playing. I hid. That's it. I remember hiding in an old twisted tree, an old oak tree, it was hollow inside. I must have hid there for ages. They never found me." Jenks stared at Toby, despair in his ageing features, in the space of their short conversation he had aged visibly, his skin appearing greyer and more like dry leather, as if the memory had triggered the ageing process. "I waited and waited. Finally night came. I'd been there so long I had got stuck. I called out frantically but no one came, my brothers had gone. Eventually I clawed my way free."

Toby scanned the room for a chair as Jenks wilted, with the memories becoming more vivid.

"It had started to rain by the time I got free. But I wasn't in the tree, I was in a house. I don't understand." His eyes glazed over. "I ran, and ran, all the way home. I was frightened my father would skin my hide."

Jenks stopped abruptly as tears welled in is eyes. He pulled his glasses off and held them tightly in his shaky hand. Toby pulled a chair over and helped Jenks into it. Glancing at his watch again and feeling callous for doing so, Jenks was clearly disturbed. Toby took the initiative to pull in the 'A' frame board as it was now past five and then closed the doors.

Quickly scouting round the large room, he looked for signs of a kitchenette or staff room so he could make Jenks a tea or get him a glass of water. When he returned, Jenks had become even paler.

"Are you alright?" Toby asked, with growing concern. "Is there someone I can call?"

"I smell burning, yes burning." Jenks paused again, trying to put in order the snippits of information his frail mind was pulling together.

"Your parents' house was on fire?"

"No." He paused. "All around me in the tree, I remember hiding in the tree. But, but…" Confusion racked Jenks features.

"Look is there someone I can call?"

"There's no one anymore. I was in a house, I hid in a tree and came out of a house."

"Jees Toby, what have you started here?" Toby muttered under his breath.

"It was dark and raining, there were explosions all around me. I ran and ran as fast as my legs would carry me." Jenks turned to Toby and grasped his arm. "I ran back to my parents' house, I was scared, so scared. I knew I'd get the belt. I ran to the back door. We always used the back door. Another explosion went off nearby. It frightened me. I ran into the door expecting it to be open but it was locked, I banged and banged, the noises all around me were getting louder. This man in a tin hat found me crying on the step. He tried to take me away but I wouldn't go with him. I kept calling out for my mother or father, he said something but I didn't know what he meant at the time. 'Air raid shelter'.

"As the loud bangs got closer he picked me up, I fought him with as much strength as an eight year old can, but he was too strong and I couldn't get free. I remember the smells all around me." Jenks looked into Toby's eyes and Toby saw fear in them. "They were different from what I remembered. After a couple of minutes I was hauled into a metal shelter with about thirty people in it.

"A dim light shone into my face followed by a scream. Everything went black."

50

"Finally this long, loud noise, a siren I found out later, sounded and we left the shelter. It was daylight by this time. I looked at all the people around me and the houses. It didn't feel right. Something was wrong." Toby felt Jenks' distress and wondered whether he ought to call the Museum owners.

"As people left, I found myself on my own. I didn't know where I was then suddenly I heard a familiar voice 'Alfred'. It was my mum's voice. I turned round in a daze waiting to get a clump but instead. I heard another voice and saw where it came from, it was my father's voice, but the man looked old, so did the woman."

"Sarah, it's not him. Our boy died over thirty-odd year ago."

"But it's him, it is, it's our Alfred, he's come back to us."

"Sarah, don't talk such rubbish. Go on lad go back to your parents, they'll be worried about you."

"I am Alfred, father. What's going on?"

"The man, my father took a swing at me, catching me across the face." Toby stood listening in disbelief and amazed as he started to piece together the importance of Jenks' story.

"That is not funny. I don't know who you are but if you come near my family again I'll... I'll tan your hide until your own parents won't recognize you."

"But father..." The man raised his hand above his shoulder and took another swing, this time catching me square in the side of the head and sending me to the ground where I stayed for fear of another helping.

"As they walked off I saw my brother William, he looked so old, so grown up." Jenks stopped and let go of Toby's arm. The pain in Jenks face cut Toby to the quick and he saw another victim of the cottage in front of him. How cruel was the world? He wanted to ask more questions but Jenks looked exhausted, tired, and as if ready for his own demise.

Guilt ripped through Toby, if he hadn't had come in then Jenks would be alright instead of looking like death was knocking at his door.

"Look, have you got to lock up or something?"

Jenks did his best to compose himself staring at Toby. "I lock up at five, that's when it closes." He said like it was a mantra and would steady his fitful mind. Then, looking at his silver wristwatch, "My, is that the time? I'm sorry young man but it really is time to lock up. You'll have to come back another day."

"Did you ever find out anymore about the tree or cottage?"

"What?" Jenks saw the maps on the display case. "What are these doing out?"

"You were showing them to... are you alright?"

"Don't be so impertinent. That's the trouble with the youth of today. Come on out you go."

"But..." Jenks glared at Toby.

"What?"

"Are you alright?"

"Of course I am. How rude!"

Toby left the museum confused, Jenks clearly looked disturbed, like he was trying to forget something. As the door closed he felt compassion for the man and wondered if he lived alone.

Inside the museum Jenks pushed the last bolt home. The museum was locked safely for the night. He finally let the memories wash over him completely. How could he have forgotten? Pictures of William, Albert and his mother and father flashed up in his mind. The despair he felt when he was taken to an orphanage and regarded as a casualty of the war. Over time he had let their memories fade, almost pretending that he had been given up at birth. Now like sharp knives they were back, his true life, his real family and how he had come to be so completely alone in the world. What had happened in those forty years?

As a tear pinched his eye he felt his chest tighten. Sitting down, the pain eased as he glanced around the main room of the museum, picturing his life. Slowly he faded away not to be discovered until the following morning, when it would be too late.

51

When Toby got home Vivien was doing some finger painting with Jake to keep him distracted and entertained.

"Hi ya. How is he?" Toby's words didn't have the love behind them that he intended.

Jake looked up. "Daddy, I is here."

"I am here," Toby corrected, amazed at how quickly he was growing up.

"Yes," Jake said, simply. Toby smiled as he tousled his hair. Vivien struggled to smile, her tired eyes lacking nothing but dejection at the loss of her daughter.

"He's fine. Did you find anything out?"

Toby threw his coat over the back of the chair. "No."

"You've been gone all this time and you found nothing?"

Switching the kettle on, Toby tried to not let Vivien's mood affect him. He went to fridge and absentmindedly pulled out a can of Pepsi. "I found loads of maps and none of them showed anything. I spent hours going through them. I even looked at history books of the area but there were hundreds. I glanced at a couple but they didn't help." Vivien looked at her son-in-law, "They covered all sorts of things but none of it seemed relevant." He pulled the tab on the can and drank from it, much to Vivien's admonishing stare. When he caught on, he got a glass and poured the remainder into it.

"How do you know until you read them whether they are relevant?"

"Do you want a tea?"

"How do you know?" Vivien repeated, wiping Jake's hands

clean.

"I could spend days, weeks reading them and it doesn't mean I would find anything significant."

"But surely you've got to try. Does my daughter mean so little to you?"

Flabbergasted, Toby turned on Vivien. "Actually, Terri and Jake, mean the world to me. I don't know what to do. I don't know what will help. I just want her back. I don't understand why she even went to the house."

"Cottage," Vivien corrected.

"Cottage, house. What the hell does it matter? She shouldn't have gone. She knew it would only bring bad news. I can't believe she'd be so stupid."

"She probably went looking for you. You seem to be so fascinated by it."

Toby stood frozen in disgust, speechless.

"I'm going out." He slammed his glass down and crushed the can in one swift movement.

"That's it, just walk out." Toby had very rarely been on the receiving end of Vivien's razor sharp tongue and he knew better than to stay. It was far better to go out and let her cool down. It had happened only twice before and one of those was when Terri first fell pregnant, a completely unplanned episode, very early on, when they had been dating. Toby had walked away pretending that it wasn't his, accusing her of sleeping around. They had been only seventeen at the time and Toby was a bit wild and free with his oats, he thought everyone had been like him. Vivien had come round to his house and told him exactly what she had thought of him. In hindsight he knew he'd deserved it but not at the time and he had argued until Vivien slapped him so hard his cheek glowed for hours after. It did the trick and knocked some sense into him.

Two days after he had sent a bouquet of roses to Terri to apologise and bought some chocolates for Vivien to make amends, but she hadn't made it easy. They had lost the baby shortly afterwards but the episode had brought them closer together.

Vivien had been a godsend when his parents had been killed in France. She helped him sort out the financial mess and debt they had left him with.

He slammed the door as he left the house.

Jake looked up at Vivien vying for her attention.

"What's happening Jake?"

"Look nanny." He had painted a mess, but to him it was a picture and she had to smile at his innocence.

"Very nice, Jake. Well done." But her thoughts were elsewhere.

52

Toby stormed along the road. Everything the mysterious Edward Furrows had said was starting to come true, his world was coming apart at the seams. Stopping at the corner of the road he realised that walking away was not going to solve anything. Sighing he watched his breath rise in the cold air, little clouds, ever expanding until they dissipated into the night air. Turning around he headed back.

Sullenly walking back into the kitchen he said, "I'm sorry." Vivien's hard face didn't register anything. "I just want Terri back. But I don't know where to start. How can any of this be normal? It doesn't happen in the real world, it's the stuff of films. What do I do? Who can I speak to about it who won't think I'm mad?" He paused, before flumping down onto a kitchen chair. "I went to the museum after I left the library. I asked the old guy there about the cottage. He had loads of maps, there was nothing there before the cottage, oh, except a tree, a twisted oak tree. Then he went off on one, telling me some story about being around in 1905, with his brothers, playing in the fields before the cottages were built. Before his family disowned him around the war, he said the second world war. I'm not sure if he was getting confused. If he wasn't then he's experienced it as well. He only looked about seventy."

Vivien listened but didn't say anything, her annoyance mixed with bitterness, she only wanted the best for Terri and Toby and the cottage was tearing them apart.

Finally she broke her silence, as Toby started to make himself a tea before he remembered the glass of Pepsi.

"White, two sugars for me, please." She placed a hand on his shoulder, it said more than words could. Toby made the tea for her, sipping his drink whilst the kettle boiled. "I'll do it, you play with your son, I think he wants his dad."

Smiling, Toby went over to Jake. "What we gonna do eh?" Jake just looked at him questioningly.

The weekend pulled round and there was still no sign of Terri, in their hearts they had feared that might be the case. They also knew that they would have to report Terri missing to the police otherwise it might look suspicious, especially as Sandra had already rung saying she couldn't get hold of Terri's mobile, which only led to leading questions about her whereabouts. She couldn't understand Toby's reluctance to go to the police when he had said he hadn't reported her missing, he tried re-iterating the tale about last time she had disappeared, Sandra knew a little of the story but not all and she wouldn't let it go, in the end issuing an ultimatum either

Toby, report her missing or she would.

Reluctantly he made the call on Saturday, knowing he would be going to work in his new job on Monday. Life had to carry on as normal. She would be back, but when.

The call was made with a heavy heart and an expectation of disbelief.

"Hello, Southend police, how may we help?" the polite voice enquired.

"Hi, I'd like to report a missing person, please," Toby stated hesitantly.

"I'll just transfer you." The line went quite, Toby knew what to expect and was not looking forward to it.

"Hello, I understand you wish to report a missing person. Can I ask how long they have been missing?" The kind but firm male voice asked.

"About four days now," Toby sighed.

"Four days!" exclaimed the voice, immediately triggering the next stage of the enquiry. "Have they gone missing before?"

There it was, the question Toby feared. "Yes, I'm afraid she has. Look, I don't want to waste police time but thought it would be best to say something, that's all." How lame did that sound, he thought.

"And exactly how long has she been missing previously?" The person sounded flustered.

"A few weeks. I'm sure she'll be fine," Toby responded, much to the amazement of the controller.

"Right," and then checking that he had heard correctly. "You did say a few weeks?"

"Yes."

"We'd better take some details. Can you tell me your name?" Toby did so and was surprised when he got no reaction. "And this is your... ?"

"Wife, Terri, Theresa Elizabeth Grant."

"Age? Hold on." Toby knew what was coming. "Did you say,

Grant, as in went missing for a year?"

Toby held his breath momentarily, not wanting to confirm or deny.

"I see." The voice changed, a note of cynicism evident.

"Look, I know what you must…"

"No, I don't think you do sir!" The contempt in the voice told Toby exactly what he knew. "I think we have her details on file. We'll keep an eye out of course, but I have to say we are very busy at the moment. I'm sure an officer will be round to see you at some point." Toby could feel the disdain.

"Thank you," he said, replacing the receiver and cutting the connection.

53

Monday crawled round and although Toby was excited about the new job, his joy was tainted with worries about Terri. He was quite sure it was a 'when' and not an 'if'. But it still played on his mind during the train journey to London, this in itself was a welcome distraction, the feeling of working again, or at least travelling to work.

After being introduced to everyone in the office he was shown how the computer system worked and this occupied his thoughts for a few hours as the day became a blur of information, so many new things to take in, the syndicates, what the syndicate numbers represented, the clients, so many overseas investors, it was a welcome minefield. Five o'clock spun round and he felt pleased to have done a full day's work, if a little overwhelmed. The train was crowded and uncomfortable but his mind was once again taken by thoughts of Terri and the cottage – and no answer as to what to do with it clear in his mind.

Absentmindedly he bought the Evening Echo at the station and started the twenty minute walk home. Inside he threw the paper on the kitchen table and went to find Jake and Vivien in the bathroom.

"Still no sign then? Hello son." Jake was splashing the water and playing with the bubbles.

"Hello. No."

"Have you had a good day?" Toby knelt down beside Vivien and started splashing water over Jake who laughed and thrashed his feet harder.

"How was your first day?" Vivien asked.

Toby filled Vivien in, finding it hard to hide his excitement about the job, a step towards normality.

With Jake in bed, Vivien dished up Toby's dinner, whilst he studied the front page.

"Oh my god!" he exclaimed, rousing Vivien's curiosity
"What?"

"Matthew Gilbert's gone missing."

"Who?" Vivien placed a large portion of Shepherd's Pie in front of Toby and sat down with a smaller one for herself.

"He's a reporter, I spoke to him about the cottage. It says here, 'Matthew Gilbert was last seen Wednesday 30th April, when he told a colleague he was going to meet a story at a private residence. He has not been seen since, his mobile registers as dead and police are concerned about his safety'."

Vivien forked a mouthful of food daintily into her mouth without question, but her eyes enquired for more information.

"I rang him about someone else who had disappeared, and re-appeared after five years." Vivien stopped chewing her food as the five years exploded like fireworks in her mind. "He said he wanted to know more about the cottage and why I was so interested, I bet he went there." Vivien placed her cutlery neatly on her plate, her appetite diminished.

"Five years?"

Toby put the paper down and folded it so he could carry on reading, not registering what Vivien had said.

"Sorry?"

"Did you say five years?"

"Oh, I'm sorry Vivien."

"She'll miss Jake growing up." Her eyes showed fear and apprehension.

"I'm sure she won't be gone that long."

"But how can you be so sure? You were gone a whole year."

Staring at her he was lost for what to say to reassure her. A year was a blink of an eye.

"I just… I'm just sure she won't, call it a gut feeling. Five years was probably just a fluke. You know a one-off." Toby's argument didn't have any real force behind it and quite out of the blue his mind thought of Albert Jenkins. Forty years.

"Are you alright Toby?" Vivien enquired wiping her nose. "You've gone quite pale."

"Oh my god. Why didn't I see it? You stupid idiot."

"What is it? Toby." Suddenly he wasn't hungry anymore.

54

Terri thundered down the stairs desperate to get out of the house, everything Edward had said replayed in her erratic thoughts. At the bottom she stopped, turned and looked up at the staircase, knowing she wasn't dreaming this nightmare, it was real.

Questions rallied her mind, goading her to go back upstairs. 'Get the answers now while she could'. One step at a time she climbed the bare staircase. At the top she entered the room she had left just a moment ago. The door inched open.

It was empty.

Edward was no longer there. She took a sharp intake of breath before edging in further. She knew she had spoken to him, he was real. She was sure of that. But where had he gone? He certainly couldn't have rushed past her. She walked around the empty room just as Toby had done when the nightmare had begun.

"Edward? Edward?" She heard a low growl and froze. Something brushed her leg, she gulped, "Edward?" Her voice reverberated around the empty room. A soft breeze ruffled her hair, electrifying her senses. "This isn't funny anymore."

Her empty voice filled the room. As she turned to leave the door slammed shut. Frightened she eased back against wall, again a breeze ruffled her hair.

Reaching into her pocket she pulled out her mobile phone, as the screen illuminated she noticed that it showed no signal.

"Damn."

Suddenly it rang, unknown number, she pressed the green

button. "Hello, help me please."

The phone went dead, but she heard Edward's voice echo round the room. "I told you to go Terri. You said you would go back to your family."

"No. Not until you tell me more about this place. How do we end this? How do we get our lives back?"

The screen on her phone went dark and she replaced it back in her pocket. The door burst open. With trepidation Terri stepped forward, her courage fading like the evening sun. Looking along the hallway, all was quiet, the dark only brightened by the feeble light of the streetlamps beyond the windows.

"Toby where are you when I need you?"

"Hello!" came a call from down the stairs.

Terri shuddered. It didn't sound like Edward. Moving back against the wall she held her breath trying to remain silent.

"Hello?" the voice repeated. It sounded friendly enough. "Is anyone there?"

Terri edged along the hallway towards the front bedroom. Suddenly she heard a step on the stairs and her heart sank.

Timidly she called out, trying to sound brave. "Who are you?"

"There is someone here, thank god for that, I was so worried, thought I was going mad."

She still couldn't force herself towards the stairs.

"Yes. What do you want?"

"I heard a scream and I thought someone was being attacked. I live next door."

'Next door'. Terri felt a morsel of relief and she started for the stairs.

"Just stay where you are, I'm coming down." She didn't want to find herself trapped upstairs, if the voice couldn't be trusted.

"If you say so, but I won't hurt you. I promise. My wife insisted I check the house out. We've lived here since the cottages were built and after the first family, the Coopers, disappeared, ten years ago, no one will come near the place. Think it's haunted like."

Terri took three steps down the stairs and then caught what was said and froze.

"Ten years ago. First family?"

"Who are you?"

55

"The tree, The cottage. No. No it can't possibly be. Surely?"

"Toby? What is it?"

"Something that the old guy at the museum said, you know the one I told you about, a bit loopy. Maybe he wasn't?"

Vivien pushed her plate of food away from her and drank from a glass of wine she had poured earlier. Toby got up.

"Where are you going?" she continued harshly.

"To the cottage. I've got to check something out."

Vivien's face turned to fury at the mere mention of the cottage. "Toby Grant, what the hell do you think you're doing? You know damn well that place is no good."

"But I have got to look, it…"

Vivien slammed her glass down heavily on the table, breaking the stem. "Oh! Damn! See! That place only causes trouble." Her words were like fire.

"But don't you see," Toby started to explain. "Jenks experienced it too. Before the house was even built. So it's not the house is it?" Toby headed into the hallway, leaving Vivien to clear up the broken glass.

"Toby, come back! Do you hear me?" She rushed out after him, leaving the wine dripping slowly onto the floor. "Toby. What about Jake? Everytime you go to that place you go missing."

"Then what should I do?" Toby's words were full of venom, the anxiety of missing Terri flashing in his eyes. He knew she would appear at some point but also that Jenks had disappeared for forty years. He couldn't wait that long. "I need to do something. There must be some way to stop this happening and the answer is not going to present itself whilst I sit around here and carry on as normal."

Vivien grabbed Toby's jacket as he opened the door and, with as much force as she could muster, dragged him back from the open door, surprising Toby with her strength. Standing between him and the door she was like a ferocious animal toying with her prey. He had never seen her quite like this.

"Toby Grant, I have lost too many people in this world to let another go without doing my damndest to stop you." She paused, whilst she calmed down. "Just think what you are doing. Think about your son."

"I am, he needs his mother. I need his mother."

"And you visiting that place is going to accomplish what, exactly?"

Toby stared at Vivien, he knew she was right, but also knew he needed to do something. "But don't you see, if it is a tree, or something, and we can burn or cut it down and end this then everything will be alright." His determination waned and he started to take his jacket off.

"I understand how you feel," Vivien continued, placating him, "and I want my daughter back, but we have to do this sensibly."

"How?" He sounded hollow.

"I don't know. Let's just finish our dinner first."

Wearily, Toby walked back into the kitchen and slumped in

front of his dinner. It looked nice but his appetite had gone, so he pushed it to one side.

Looking at the paper again and the story of Matthew Gilbert he said. "You idiot, I told you not to go there."

"What?"

"Nothing" Toby added, letting silence hang between them as he flicked through the rest of the paper.

After a pause and whilst Vivien mopped up her spilt wine, she said, "why don't you go and speak to this Jenks character again." Vivien placed a beer in front of Toby. "What is it?"
Toby was staring at an article in the paper, dismay obvious on his face. He too, had had the same idea about talking to Jenks, but the headline read 'A Final Goodbye to a trusted and valued worker of Southend Musuem - Albert Jenkins'.

56

Terri stepped cautiously down the stairs towards the gentleman, trying to comprehend what he had just said.

"What did you say?" Her voice incredulous.

"You alright love?"

"No, no I don't think I am."

He took two steps towards her and frowned, taking in the strange clothes she was wearing.

"What?" Terri stammered.

"Sorry, I don't mean to be rude. Just, never seen clothes like that before. But then, I'm not up on fashion."

Studying the gentleman, Terri drank in the details of his leathery skin, his dull collarless shirt, cardigan and plain workman-style thick trousers. The flat cap he was wearing made his eyes look like bottomless pits in the dark of the house.

"Come on love, you look terrified, I'll get my Ida to make you a pot of tea. How does that sound?" He held out a hand to guide her down the rest of the stairs.

Surprising herself, she took it, his firm grip easing any unrest she might have had.

"There you go. Come on."

Terri felt questions burning her mind but shock started to settle and she let them fade from her thoughts. At the front door she hesitated, glancing back into the cottage.

"What is it love?"

Turning back to the gentleman, she withdrew her hand.

"What's your name? How long did you say you lived next door?"

"Joseph's me name, and about eight year now, moved in not long after cottage were built, that be about 1911."

"So you think it is 1919?"

"That be a strange question, but aye, I do. Come on love ya catch your death of cold."

"It can't be." Terri stumbled back down the hallway. "Edward, Edward Furrows what's going on?" she called.

Joseph followed, curious at her reaction. "There's no one here love. Well not downstairs. I checked."

"Edward what is going on?"

"Obviously you don't need my help. Sorry to have troubled you." Joseph shook his head and turned to go out through the open front door.

Terri took the first couple of steps up the stairs then looked at Joseph, trying to analyze what was happening, the dates, Toby had only ever skipped time forwards. Had he ever gone backwards? Was it possible? If it was then could she get back?

"You've got to help me." Terri called, when Joseph had one foot outside. "I need to get back to Toby and Jake."

"I see," was the puzzled response.

Terri walked quickly to him. "1919 you say?"

"Aye. 27th September 1919 to be precise."

"Have you ever seen anyone living here?"

"Not since the Cooper's disappeared, people say it is haunted. Come on love, come next door and we can talk more of it with a brew."

"Thank you." Terri looked past Joseph at the street scene outside and the parked cars, two Ford Mondeo's, a Fiesta, a Peugot, three Renault's.

"What is it love? You look as though you've seen ghost. Come on, Ida will be worrying where I've got to."

"This must be a joke, it's got to be."

Joseph stretched out his hand, Terri automatically took it then felt it tighten in fright as Joseph noticed the unfamiliar street outside. His knees buckled and Terri had to steady him as they made their way to the gate. Terri glanced over her shoulder once more at the mysterious cottage that was determined to ruin people's lives.

57

Toby was at a loss as he re-read the article about Albert Jenkins. Vivien sat down opposite him.

"It's got something to do with the tree that Albert told me about. I don't know what, I at least need to go and look. Maybe it holds the key to all this. May it will free Terri. Allow her to return to us." He paused, expecting rebuke from Vivien but none came. "I can't enter the premises though, that will only…" he left the sentence unfinished.

Vivien took a sip from the new glass of wine she had poured, after deciding she needed something a bit stronger than tea.

"Be careful, Toby." It was a simple and heartfelt instruction and he felt guilt at making her so angry earlier. He took the fork from his discarded plate and picked at the food.

Then surprising Toby, Vivien spoke. "Maybe we should all go, at least we'd all be together."

"No," Toby exclaimed. "I promise I won't enter the premises at all. His words were full of determination. "I just want to look. I need to do something. Come with me by all means. We'll go at the weekend. If we take Jake for a walk maybe we could ask some of the neighbours if they know anything."

"What, a sort of house to house?"

"Well, you never know, there might be someone whose family has lived there long enough."

The rest of week was a combination of workdays rushing by, and evenings dragging, Thursday he decided to visit the library again following a different tangent, something that was more fable than fact. The occurrences which he, Diane Forrester and Albert Jenkins had experienced were the normal source of factual information, so maybe there was hope in fiction, or myth, something in Prittlewell's history.

Once again he found himself amongst the reams of books, sifting fact from fiction; an hour passed and although the library was open until ten o'clock, time was fast running out as he scanned titles and chapter headings. The endless search was proving fruitless. Finally he decided to ask a librarian sorting books nearby.

He was directed to a small reference section, hidden, out of the way and, judging by the neatness of the books, hardly used.

Straightaway he saw a title that grabbed him. 'Unexplained Essex'. Picking it up he flicked through the chapter and sub-headings. There was nothing on Prittlewell. In fact, it was more about reported hauntings – why wasn't it in the other section, it fitted in with it. Shaking his head, bewildered, he posted it back into its slot.

Next he pulled out a book, 'The Hanging Tree by Harry Johnson'. It was a factual history of a horse chestnut tree in what is now Blenheim Park and was used for hanging supposed witches. He pulled out four more books but they didn't elaborate about locations until after a couple of pages. Time was ticking by and Toby didn't feel his search was being any more helpful than the last one over the weekend. It was a shame Albert had died, he felt he could probably have got more information from him.

A small random book caught his eye, 'Lost but not forgotten by James L Tinker'. It had a plain mauve cover with gold embossed lettering. It was a thin book, no larger than a paperback. Pulling it out he noted the old style print and pages, flicking the first few pages he saw the publication date as 1897. There was a preface which read:

After losing faith in our Lord above I search for reason. I search to establish fact where once there was but foolish guise. I have set myself a task to master all that is unholy and unnatural, unmask the deceitful, decloak the vagary of the spoken ill. Banish from this world, ill that should be forgotten.

Toby frowned, but something intrigued him so he turned the pages and caught sight of 'The Prittlewell Passage'. Settling down on a nearby table he started to read more, only to be interrupted by an announcement that the library was closing in five minutes. Looking at his watch he was surprised how quickly the last hour had gone and made his way to the desk to check the book out.

"That's fifty pence please sir."

"Sorry, I thought it was free to take books out."

"It is sir, but the shelf that book came from are the ones we are getting rid of, making way for new books."

"But it's an old book, surely it is worth more that fifty pence?"

"Most of those books, despite how old they may be, are not that rare, and…" She scanned the bar code. "You'll be the first person to have looked at that book since 1968."

"The computer goes back that far?"

"No. But if you look inside the back cover you can see the last stamp." She showed him.

Toby fished around his pocket for the money and left.

58

Toby sat in bed, a cup of tea on the bedside table, ensconced in the book.

James L Tinker, it turned out, had been a monk residing at the newly re-established Cedric Abbey, Somerset before he was defrocked in 1887 after a disagreement. The book was an investigation into myths, legends, and other phenomena that the church had explained as acts of God. It was a strange book, written almost by a would-be modern Ghosthunter. The Prittlewell Passage was a strip of ground that ran between St Mary's Church, Prittlewell and the school next door. A vicar, Father Michael, of St Mary's reported in the seventeenth century that he repeatedly saw the figure of a woman in a white dress float along the strip of ground, which was not owned by the church or the school, to a place down the hill and disappearing by a tree.

Toby's heart raced, his tea was getting cold and it was late, but he kept reading, feeling that finally he was going to get an answer, that is until he realised that St Mary's was half a mile away from the cottage. Fascinated, he finished the story. The woman was meant to be that of Margaret Hinchley, the upper class wife of a local businessman who had an affair with a farm worker. She was later convicted of murdering her husband and her spirit was thought to visit the place where her husband died.

James found out that Father Michael was rather fond of alcohol and other medicine of the era and, as he had been the only witness to such a paranormal phenomenon concluded that it was indeed bunkum.

Toby smiled, it was not what he had expected, but he found James's narrative had a candour that appealed. Looking at his watch, he saw that it was approaching one in the morning. He had work the following day, but felt compelled to continue reading, four chapters later, Toby finally conceded and gave in to tiredness.

The alarm on Toby's phone got louder the longer it rang until finally it gave up, but not before waking Vivien, who listened to what had become the usual fumblings of Toby's early starts, when they weren't apparent she went into his room to wake him.

Forty minutes later he was on the train to work, his mind still immersed in the book.

During my investigations into the vexing matters, I have come across many a rapacious story enough to stir even the most intelligent of noblemen. One such instance was the story of the twisted oak tree, that grew in the field behind a Blacksmiths in West Street, Prittlewell. Prittlewell is thought to be a Saxon Village that dates back to the 6th or 7th century. From the 13th to 16th Century it was a busy market town.

The Blacksmith dates back eight generations and was reportedly once the source of much-rumoured black magic, until a Harry Roberts took over what had become a derelict barn. The original owners had disappeared, thought to have been murdered. It was not until 1834 that Harry Roberts was to be heard talking about a ghostly apparition, whilst partaking of entertainment in The Blue Boar Inn. He stated repeatedly that he often saw a variety of people marching toward the Twisted Oak tree in his field at the back of the stable block.

Many a time, he stated clearly, he had watched folk disappear right before his eyes. One night after tankards of ale had been consumed, he took a party of people back to witness the stories he had recounted countless times. After much cajoling, expectant eyes watched from the stable block as night settled in. More tankards of ale were consumed and, after much merriment, the men fell asleep, only to be awoken by screaming as fire engulfed the blacksmith's workshop and the menfolk watched in horror as Harry Roberts ran screaming from the burning barn toward the Twisted Oak. The men howled with laughter thinking he was just having fun with them. Too late they realised it was not Harry's foolery, by which time the Twisted Oak tree was burning as bright as the Blacksmith's barn.

The men ran after him but no trace was ever found of Harry Roberts and so started the rumour of The Twisted Oak.

59

The train pulled into the station and Toby had to stop reading. As he exited the carriage he was pulled along by the throng of people and the pace carried on throughout the day. His brain took in all the new tasks he faced as he became engulfed in his new job, with not a spare moment for the cottage, it's history, or sadly, Terri, who he missed with all his heart.

As his colleague, Trevor, bade him goodbye he realised he would have to rush to catch the 5.23 from Liverpool Street. He loved the job but even with just a week of travelling, hated the journey on the train. Again he found himself without a seat and standing like a sardine between two overweight sweaty banker-types, one who sniffed every thirty seconds, and the other wheezing as if he was about to have a heart attack.

As the train rattled along the track. He thought about reading his book which he could feel in his jacket pocket but there was not even enough space for that. The wheezing banker sneezed without covering his face and Toby wiped globules of saliva disdainfully from his coat. Wheezy smiled apologetically.

Finally he arrived home tired and weary, Vivien greeted him with a sigh as he closed the door. She had still hoped the next person to walk through was Terri, but it wasn't. Terri was a big part of their lives and they were missing her, even so a routine was quickly being established, if only just to keep them going. Toby didn't even ask about Terri knowing the answer and not wanting it confirmed, if he didn't ask he couldn't be disappointed.

"How's Jake?" Toby enquired.

Vivien answered whilst dishing up dinner, "he's in bed. If you hurry he might still be awake."

Toby went and said goodnight to Jake, who was already half asleep.

After dinner Toby got out the book again and picked up where he had left off.

'The following day folk tended to the ruins of the barn and tree in the hope of finding poor Harry's body, alas none was found, or ever was. From that time on no one dared rebuild the barn.

Another story I have stumbled upon was one of Arthur Digget, in 1875, an apprentice at the local carpentry shop. He was out courting the local landlord's daughter making pleasure in the field when they saw a burning figure stumble from beyond the remains of the Twisted Oak

Tree. Story was that the figure appeared like a ghost. After the initial shock Arthur ran to the burning figure with the blanket upon which they had been sitting, by which time it was too late to save the poor soul. The strange thing about it was that at the time, the identity of the poor fellow could not be established. All the villagers were accounted for and no one had seen any strangers in the area.

Although records for the time are scarce, I have come across other tall tales. Mostly they are about strange people turning up in the village dazed and full of bewilderment at their surroundings. Two such cases were recorded by the vicar at the time, who put the two gentlemen up in the rectory in hope of curing their ailment of the mind. Alas both gentlemen died within a few weeks, their minds broken. The two in question were Robert L Harris and James Williamson.

Robert L Harris, aged 42, appeared in 1732 – the vicar, Father William wrote 'a landed gentleman, full of air and graces but with his mind weak. The places he talks about are gone, vanished. He mentioned 'Landford house', which was a country manor in the village of Canewdon until it burned down in 1689 killing all the Harris family. He is most vexed by his disposition, certain on his lineage and insistent that he sees the family home. Upon arrival he fell to the ground with heavy heart and with some reluctance I took him to the graves, where he literally broke down and died.'

In 1741, a James Williamson, turned up at the Blue Boar in a most agitated way, demanding to know whereabouts of Miss Fanny Holmes and her family. The landlord, known only as Cutter, a kindly fellow, informed him that the Holmes family moved on when their daughter died of a broken heart. Mr Williamson demanded to know where they went and was surprised when the landlord informed him that it was thirty years hence and that he has no further information as it was his father who was landlord then. Mr Williamson, believing he was the victim of a practical joke, became livid at being made to look like a fool in front of the patrons, demanded Cutter tell him the truth. Mr Williamson attacked Cutter when he didn't answer him.

Cutter threw Mr Williamson out of his inn and the local sheriff locked him in the stocks until Father William ended his incarceration and released him. Mr Williamson died a day or so later.

It is a most peculiar matter and the two instances vexed Father William, plaguing him until his death in 1753.

60

Toby stared, perplexed at the pages in front of him and was only disturbed from his thoughts when Vivien entered.

"You alright Toby, you look confused?" Life without Terri was settling into it's own rhythm.

"I have evidence here of more instances."

"Instanc… oh." Vivien physically looked shaken. "When exactly?" she asked reluctantly.

Toby told what he had found out, concluding that it didn't matter if the cottage stood or not.

"Also, there is a sketch of the area at the front of the book with marks showing where every story takes place. From what I can make out, it is exactly where the cottage is today."

Vivien stared at the sketch piecing together the landmarks of pubs, churches and other historic buildings she knew in the area.

"What do we do?" She asked, taking the book from him.

"What can we do? We wait for Terri to come back and hope that it is isn't as long as these stories have depicted."

Vivien's shoulders drooped and she sank into her favourite armchair, despondency enveloping her. Silently she prayed for Terri's return. Toby, in turn ,felt guilt, even though it was not his fault as they sat staring into oblivion without a word shared.

"Lord above, what is… ?" Joseph turned back to Terri. "I… I…" he looked again at the clothes she was wearing before his eyes rolled around in his head. As he started to fall Terri tried to catch Joseph's small frame, but as she struggled she found herself being forced back in to the cottage, before falling to the floor under Joseph's weight. Banging her head she screamed out in pain. The ceiling started to spin in front of her and slowly she closed her eyes.

Saturday 29th June 2008

Nearly two months had passed and Toby received a nice letter from Terri's office. Firstly apologising for the lateness of the letter and then, advising that they had terminated her employment. They thanked her for her dedicated service and forwarded a cheque for the five weeks she had supposedly been ill, wishing her well in her recovery.

Toby took Jake out on the cold but bright sunny day as was the routine on a Saturday, quality time for them both, especially as his new job meant he didn't get in until gone seven, when Jake was in bed. The walks took them past the cottage where momentarily they would stop, Toby staring longingly at it, wondering about the mysteriousness of it. Hoping an answer to the conundrum would present itself.

"What we gonna do Jake?" But Jake didn't answer, he was too busy picking up a pebble on the pavement. Toby had been back to the library to find more books about the Twisted Oak tree, that appeared to be the root of the problem, but the hours he spent sieving through pages and pages of books were fruitless and meant he was spending less and less time with Jake. The internet heralded little further advancement.

Toby began to feel very lonely without Terri. He missed the cosy nights in and the contentment they shared. He thought about the night Jake was conceived. It had been nine months since the last miscarriage and their relationship had been at breaking point. Vivien had told them to go out for a meal and talk things through; she had seen the cracks in their relationship widening. The restaurant of choice was the one they went to on their first real date, Tandi's Thai Noodle bar in Hamlet Court Road. It wasn't the plush place that Toby had imagined, when he had found it in the Yellow Pages. He had been trying to impress Terri after making a complete idiot of himself in front of her friends and embarrassing her by spinning her eagerly round to hug her, but he had forgotten that it was icy and she had slipped over.

The plastic seats and tables made Toby's heart sink when he saw them. The tacky decorations made it look like an attempt to dress up grandma's front room. They were shown to their table, given two sun-faded menus and asked what they would like to drink. Ordering a bottle of red wine which turned out to be 'gnats piss' only added to the awful ambience. The food wasn't much better but the gesture of the evening was enough to prove Toby's sincerity.

The reconciliation that they had been commanded, by Vivien, to have, had been fraught, the arguments, the angry words, the wrongful accusations all betrayed how they really felt and at first the evening look set to kill their relationship completely.

61

Toby arrived first, half expecting Terri not to turn up, the last time they had spoken she had hung up on him. Vivien had booked this place knowing it was where they had really bonded, despite the awfulness of it, she hoped that it was better now. It wasn't. He sat at the table they occupied on their first date. The restaurant had not changed one bit, the owners either believing it was impeccably decorated or didn't care. He drank a glass of Tiger beer. The memories of their first date came flooding back, he couldn't believe he hadn't remembered it when Vivien had mentioned its name. They had hated it the first time they had come here, why bother coming back.

"What the bloody hell am I doing here? My mates were going to the footie and I am bloody here. I don't know what Vivien 'the interfering cow', hopes to achieve," Toby uttered, swigging from his beer, feeling very self conscious.

"Oh, is she now? That's my mother you're talking about." Terri had appeared from nowhere.

Toby went red, his nerves rattled. "You know what I mean?" Then correcting himself, "No, no that's not what I mean."

"No, actually Toby Grant, I think it is." Terri started to admonish him. "My mum has been really good to you. So don't you start talking about her as if…"

"I'm sorry. I only meant that I don't see the point of this, you made it perfectly clear last time we spoke that it was over." Toby's words hid the undercurrent of frustration boiling inside, he thought he had tried everything. The marriage was teetering on the brink and he wondered if it really was worth saving. Once they had thought they were soulmates, invincible, now he wasn't so sure. It was as if Terri didn't understand that Toby was also hurting at the loss of their unborn children. They were both desperate to be parents but fate was working against them.

"Toby, I have just lost a baby, I am entitled to be a bit emotional." Terri sat down heavily. She didn't know whether she wanted to stay with Toby anymore. There was so much they'd gone through that had appeared to drive them apart.

Toby stood up sharply, "Do you think I don't feel anything, they are my sons or daughters too you know."

"Well, why don't you act like it then?" She cut him down. The other four diners were looking at them. The waitress smiled awkwardly, not wanting to getting involved.

"You're unreal."

"Please, you are disturbing other guests." The waitress finally interrupted in her poor broken English. "You like Tiger beer?"

For some unknown reason Toby smirked, it was the opposite of everything that had gone on between them in the last few months and Toby saw the humour that the offer of 'a beer' would make a difference. The waitress, baffled, continued, "Lady like wine, we have house red, house white?"

"A Tiger beer, that's really going to change everything," Toby said aloud, making the waitress and Terri glare at him as though he was mad. He sank back down into his chair leaving Terri poised as if to leave. She was fighting the urge to walk out but the half smile across Toby's face reminded her of the first time they had laughed together and she felt her heart grow warm for his touch.

"Lady like wine?" the waitress chipped in.

"No. Tiger beer too."

"Two Tiger beers?"

"No, just one, but for me too."

"So three Tiger beers?" the waitress said, confused.

"No, just Tiger for me," Terri said, sitting down and placing her coat on the back of the chair.

"Just one Tiger beer?"

"And a Tiger beer for me too," Toby added playfully, adding to the waitress's confusion, all the time trying to conceal his laughter.

"So three Tiger beer?"

Toby was going to add something when Terri touched his hand for him to stop toying with the waitress.

"Yes," he added, instead of his original answer which would have created more confusion. Toby took hold of Terri's hand before she could stop him. Electricity flowed between them, the spark that had been hidden. They both looked into each other's eyes and saw the depth of feeling behind them.

"I love you Teresa Grant." Although Terri hated being called that somehow when Toby said it showed sincerity. She couldn't understand why, but let the words settle between them and simply smiled, letting the anger and arguments slip away unnoticed. Stripped of the facade they knew how they felt about each other, the spark that held them together, Vivien had known, they just needed to see it. But why this restaurant? They had no idea. It wasn't a plush eating house, or even a moderate one, but they enjoyed the meal without actually saying a lot. For once silence seemed to be the appropriate conversation.

62

"You'll always be in my heart, my soulmate."

"Ah." Toby turned and saw an older couple walking past. They smiled and he nodded. Looking back at the cottage with its jaded stonework he noticed thick black dust that settled on every part, years of toxic car fumes, the garden was overgrown but he had never seen it get to the stage where it was like a jungle. The peeling paint on the door was permanently stuck in limbo, never falling off just curling up, allowing the wood underneath to fade to a silvery grey.

For the first time he really studied the cottage, and drank in the details, trying to pry the answers from it, the secrets it held. Turning around on the spot he mentally pictured how the land had once looked, picturing the houses over the rough sketches drawn in the books he'd read, wondering how far in history this mystery went back. Did it go back to the Romans, the Vikings, back to the caveman. What had started the cycle? What or who had been the first to experience the loss of time. It wasn't time travel as you couldn't travel backwards. Or could you? Maybe there was a way to go back? Maybe he just needed to find out what it was? Edward had hadn't he?

Toby knew the risk of stepping into the garden as he looked back at his son who was blissfully unaware of how the cottage teased his parents. What would he ever know about them?
Toby eased along the street looking for a way to view the back garden. It was at least one hundred feet long, finally he found the entrance to an alley that ran along the back of the garden, though it had been blocked by piles of discarded rubbish.

Lifting Jake up, much to Jake's annoyance, he climbed over the rubbish.

The alleyway was overgrown with weeds and tree branches from the gardens on either side. The shrubbery and trees clawed at their clothes, as Toby fought his way along to what looked like a good vantage point to see the back of the cottage. As he made his way to the spot, he noted he could still see the blue hood of Jake's pushchair on the pavement. The first few spots of rain landed on his face which he tried to ignore.

"Raining," Jake stated so matter-of-factly that Toby had to smile.

"I know, we won't be long. Just give me a couple of minutes, I just want to check this place out." Toby tried to sound calm even though he didn't feel it.

"It's wet daddy."

"Yes, I know, but you'll be alright, just give me a couple of minutes. Anyway it's only spitting."

Jake screwed up his face, he was good with words and advanced for his age, which pleased both Toby and Terri, although occasionally he didn't understand and instead of asking he would frown and wait until someone explained.

For reassurance Toby glanced towards the pushchair at the entrance to the alley.

His heart sank, he couldn't see it. Suddenly his mind was in freefall, panic casting its shadow over him. Losing his footing he slipped, swinging Jake around like a cuddly toy.

"Phew!" he muttered as the pushchair came back into view. "Okay, Jake, okay you win. We'll go." Glancing back at the cottage. "You and me have got some unanswered business."

"Daddy, you're funny." Jake said innocently.

"Oh am ..."

Something caught his attention. For a moment he couldn't work out what it was. He stared back into the garden. It was something about the garden. What was it? What was he not seeing?

Jake started to thump Toby's head as the rain turned to stair-rods making them wet very quickly. Toby took Jake's hands in his. "Okay Jake, okay son, we'll go, just give me a…"

Toby was sure he knew what it was that had caught his eye, something inexplicable, yet there. He adjusted his footing and tried to haul himself up on a lump of wood, so he could get a better view over the five foot fence into the garden.

It hit him like a bolt from the blue!

63

Terri dragged herself out from under Joseph and felt for his pulse, which was faint but still there.

"Joseph, Joseph. Are you alright?" He didn't stir.

Terri stared at the street scene outside, the same cars sat waiting to be stirred into life, then she noticed a wire mesh between her and the roadway. Massive eight foot wire mesh fencing panels to stop her from reaching the pavement.

"What the…" Her words fell silent as she heard footsteps behind her. "Don't come out here Joseph. It's not for you." But Terri felt a hand on her shoulder followed by words that were so hollow they sounded childlike.

"I don't understand."

Terri turned and looked at Joseph, whose ashen face showed sadness and confusion beyond her comprehension.

Joseph walked up to the wire mesh security fence, touching it tentatively with the tips of his fingers, instantly retracting them as though he had received an electric shock. He hesitated before turning to her.

"What's going on?" Terri took in his sadness which compounded her own. She hoped it was only a matter of hours, days, that she had missed Toby, Jake and her mother. What must it be like for Joseph, nearly a hundred years has passed, his family would definitely have passed away.

Placing a reassuring hand on his shoulder she desperately searched her mind for words that would make it seem alright, but nothing would come forward because she knew, in part, what he was feeling and it made her uneasy. The feeling grew as panic started to manifest itself. What if it had been years she had been missing? How old would Jake be? Would he know his mother?

She looked along the edge of the property and saw the security fence stretching the full length of the boundary. Walking along, she scoured it for a way out. She was no good at climbing, she never had been. At the corner of the front garden she saw a buckled panel that might just allow them room to crawl under it. Turning she called Joseph, but he had gone, at first she was shocked, but then she believed it might be for the better, he was lost in time, nothing would bring him happiness now. She felt empathy with his plight and knelt down on the ground to try and wriggle under the fence.

"Where are you going? You can't leave me here. I don't know where I am." Joseph's words caught her by surprise.

"We've got to get out of here. I need to get home to see my son." She wriggled some more and finally broke free. Standing up she stared into the sorrowful face of Joseph behind the wire mesh like a prisoner. In the twenty minutes or so she had known him he had aged visibly, even his movement was slower.

"Come on, slide under the fence. You're coming back to my place. We'll sort this out there." His eyes pleaded with Terri that he didn't know what to do. "It'll be alright, I promise." But her words didn't have sincerity behind them.

Joseph turned once more to the cottage that had torn his life apart, his mind questioning what had happened to Ida and his three children. Slowly and methodically Joseph eased under the fence and after a couple of minutes stood outside the security fence, viewing the cottage like a grotesque monument. Terri took his hand and tried to pull him away but he remained firmly anchored. Spinning around he noted the houses, the strange metal boxes with four wheels, the smooth tarmac roads with bright lines painted on them. The metal street lamps that stood like giants, the trees loomed up into the sky. The world started to spin again as he reached out for Terri to steady himself.

"I've got to tell Ida what's happened." He pushed himself away from Terri before she could stop him and trundled to the next cottage along. He was on auto pilot as he knocked on the door, still bewildered, trying to fathom what had happened.

A woman in her forties wearing a black dressing gown opened the door, wiping sleep from her eyes. Joseph stared at her, unable to speak.

"What? Do you know what time it is?" said the annoyed, groggy voice.

"Mmmm, I need to speak with Ida Cole."

"Who?"

"My wife, Ida. I need to know where she is."

"That's all I need, a bloody crank at five-thirty in the morning. Go away. Go back to whatever home you escaped from. Some of us have to get up for work you know." The woman slammed the door shut.

"But you don't understand…" Joseph started to say.

"Come on, let's get you home." Terri pulled at Joseph's shoulders trying gently to pull him away. She was filled with dread. Could that be the reception she'd receive.

64

"The rose bush. That wasn't there a minute ago," Toby said aloud.

"Excuse me, can I help you?" a voice called from behind.

Turning sharply, Toby almost lost his footing again, he saw a middle aged man standing in the gateway to a garden. Seconds passed as he collected his thoughts.

"This is a private alleyway and we try and keep it that way." The man looked at the entrance and saw where Toby had pushed the debris out of the way.

"I'm sorry, I just, I just. I thought I saw something in the garden." He indicated behind him.

"You probably did. But this is private property and I'd be obliged if it stayed that way. There's been enough burglaries recently…"

"I own that house, cottage." The words came out discordantly.

The man frowned. "Really?"

Toby regained composure, changing Jake's position so he rested on his left arm, as Jake was beginning to get heavy.

"Bit strange then to be skulking round the back?"

"I know." Toby glanced at the pushchair. "Have you lived

here long?" Toby had forgotten about the rain that was cascading down.

"Daddy, I'm cold."

"Alright son."

"Look you're wet, and your son will catch his death, why don't you come inside and warm up if it's the house you want to talk about?" The question caught Toby by surprise, *if it's the house you want to talk about.*

"It is. If you're sure? I'll just grab the buggy."

"Come round the front, whilst I block the alley up again."

Excitement raced round Toby's body as he strapped Jake back in the pushchair. The man had introduced himself as Gareth.

What did he know about the cottage?

Once inside the house, Toby got Jake out of his wet clothes and wrapped him in a warm bath sheet supplied by Gareth's wife, Eileen, who then placed the wet clothes on a radiator to dry off. She seemed to be enjoying the fact that there was a small child in the house once again. She asked all the usual questions of a gushing would-be grandmother and Jake was soon settled, talking ten to the dozen with Eileen as she fussed over him.

Gareth brought a tray of tea and biscuits into the dated front room.

"Get this down you, it will soon warm you up." Gareth's tone had become friendly and curious." After a pause he continued. "How long have you owned that place?"

"What? Thyme Cottage? About a year an' a half."

"You looking to move in? It'd be nice to see someone actually live there. We've lived here nearly forty years and never seen anyone go near it." Gareth paused, wondering whether to continue his train of thought. "I blame the rumours," he said, gauging the reaction.

Toby had been watching Eileen playing with Jake, but also studied Gareth intently, noting the creases on his youthful looking skin and the grey cropped hair and trimmed beard which made him appear much older.

"Rumours?" Toby quizzed, playing ignorant.

Gareth looked to Eileen for her permission. She smiled, raising her eyebrows in a gesture that roused Toby's curiosity. Toby wondered what he was going to hear and whether he could divulge any of what he knew.

"What exactly are these rumours?" Toby pushed.

Gareth edged forward on his seat as if to whisper a secret. "The first family to ever have lived there disappeared never to be seen again." Toby relaxed, he already knew about the Coopers and thought this was now just Gareth's way to grab some attention in his retirement.

"And the house has been empty ever since," finished Toby.

Gareth looked flummoxed and taken aback. Toby didn't wish to cause offence so quickly added. "There is also a story about a Diane Forrester who similarly disappeared and re-appeared about five years later."

Gareth looked astonished to hear that and glanced at his wife who was too busy playing with Jake to pay any further attention.

"I didn't know that. When did that happen?"

"About 1999, re-appearing in 2004, looking exactly as she did when she disappeared."

"Most strange." Gareth thought for a second. "That sort of tallies up with what I was going to tell you. The Coopers turned up again about twenty, no, nearly thirty years ago. 1976 or 77, I can't quite remember."

Toby was intrigued "What happened to them?"

"That's just it, they were dead."

65

"Dead. Are you sure it was them?"

"Well, that's what caused the news stories. I'll show you." Gareth got up and left the room returning a few minutes later with five papers carefully folded and stored in a white shoe box. Meanwhile, Toby searched his memory for some snippet of recollection to a story in his search. Why hadn't it come up?

"Massacre of an unknown family." Gareth read the headline, passing the first paper to Toby, who took it keenly.

> A family of five were found brutally murdered in a garden in Prittlewell. The man, wife and three children are thought to be the victims of a vicious burglary that went wrong and now police are hunting the callous criminals.
>
> The bodies were discovered near the front door of the house on the corner of Railway Terrace and East Street at 6am by a passing milkman. The attending coroner has stated the time of death as somewhere between 2 and 4 am, a knife has been recovered at the scene and has been sent away for finger printing.
>
> The police are still baffled as to the identity of the family as the house has been empty for years. The current owners are being located.
>
> It is thought that maybe they had been to a fancy dress party earlier that evening as the clothing dates to around the first world war.
>
> Witnesses are being urged to contact DI Frank Jones of Southend police with any information.

"How did you associate that with... ?" Gareth handed Toby another paper.

> Police are no closer to discovering the identity of the family of five brutally murdered in Prittlewell. The unusual step of authenticating the clothing has only turned up more questions than answers, as it has been determined to be original and from around 1900.
>
> This reporter has done some checking into the history of the house and found that a family of five, The Coopers, Robert, Maud, their sons Harry & William, and only daughter Grace disappeared around 1909, the house was found deserted and no sighting of any of them has been seen. With photography in its infancy it was rare for a family to ever have a portrait taken but I have managed to find just such an archive at a local portrait photographers, Phillips and Sons, a business that has it roots stretched back to 1897. The picture I have has a striking resemblance to the dead family.

Gareth sat waiting for the inevitable statement that he always got when he showed these newspapers to people, 'that's impossible'. But he was disappointed as Toby sat stone-faced, taking it all in.

"There must be more. What did the police make of it?"

Surprised Gareth got out the next paper which had the large headline

'MURDERED FAMILY OF 5 A HOAX'

"A hoax. You're kidding?"

"Read on," Gareth instructed.

> The murdered family of five recently discovered in the

garden of a house in Prittlewell, is now thought to be an elaborate prank by people, or persons unknown.

As forensic tests were carried out on the bodies in the morgue the flesh reportedly crumbled away, instantly turning to ash, leaving nothing but the skeletal remains. Carbon dating has been subsequently carried out on the skeletons and they have been found to be the remains of persons unknown from around the beginning of the twentieth century. Police are now fearing the desecration of graves and are currently urging all clergy to be vigilant for grave robbers.

66

"They can't be serious. They can't really think that someone would play an elaborate joke like that."

Gareth looked curiously at Toby. "What do you know about this cottage then?"

"What?"

"You know something more, don't you? There is more, I've got two more articles here. Toby reached for the box but Gareth grabbed it quickly." Elaine smiled at the pair as they were like excited school children with a project. Gareth had been fascinated by the empty cottage ever since they had moved into their home; curious that it had remained untouched and unloved for so long. He had noticed things, although never daring to enter the premises, that would be breaking the law. "You said something about a rose bush when I first saw you."

Toby looked at Jake who was settled and enjoying Elaine's company. She had some old toys that were left from when there children were at home. Filled with confidence he began to speak.

"What do you want to know?"

"The rose bush."

"It wasn't there when I first looked in and when it did appear it was wild looking as though it hadn't been tended to for a long time." Gareth cocked his head curiously but was apparently not surprised.

After a moment's hesitation he looked at his wife. "I told you Elaine, I knew it. I kept telling Elaine that the garden sometimes looked different but she didn't believe me. Did you?"

Reluctantly she nodded her agreement. Toby filled in Gareth on everything he knew so far, the strange time lapses and the loss of Terri. Gareth listened, excited at the news of a real-life mystery. He then handed Toby another newspaper.

'Two Detectives missing'

DI Frank Jones and Detective Harry Uxbridge have been reported missing. They were last seen a week ago entering the scene of the reported 'Hoax murders'. Their car has been recovered at the scene and police are conducting enquiries into the disappearance, although no signs of abduction have be found police are not ruling out the possibility of the organisers of the 'Hoax murders' being involved.

Toby finished the article which only re-iterated previous ones and drew unwarranted conclusions. Gareth handed Toby the final paper, a broad smile on his face.

'A miracle for detectives'

One week after DI Frank Jones and Detective Harry Uxbridge disappeared, the detectives have been found dazed and confused and unable to make a coherent argument for where they have been. An investigation is now being made into the pair and their connection with the 'Hoax murders'. The pair, renowned for their practical jokes within the force, are on suspension with full pay.

It is thought the two concocted the plan after a drinking session at The Golden Lion in Victoria Avenue, a favourite haunt for them and their colleagues.

Regulars overheard the pair many times inventing practical jokes to play on their department heads. It appears this time the joke went too far.

Toby held the paper in disbelief.
"See." Gareth beamed.

67

"Have you found anything else out about the place other than what I've told you?"

"My wife thinks I'm mad but I keep a diary of anything unusual, and notes from any investigations I carry out." He pulled out of the box an A5 notebook. Toby's eyes widened as it appeared to be full of pieces of paper and carefully crafted notes.

"Wow, you have done a lot. Did you find anything going back further than the fire of the twisted oak tree and the barn?"

"Not exactly."

"Sorry."

"Well there's not exactly anyone I could ask, is there?" Toby looked suitably rebuked. "I started a conversation with some local ghost hunters, and although they didn't have any information, they did put me in contact with a coven of white witches, who had delved back into their roots and found that secret meetings had taken place at Black Crack which was somewhere is Prittlewell. Unfortunately, due to persecution at the time no one kept maps.

"I can see you two are going to be at this for quite some time. Would you like another tea?" Elaine chipped in, gathering the empty cups.

"Yes, please." Suddenly Toby felt guilty leaving Elaine to look after Jake. "Are you okay with Jake?"

"We're fine, don't you worry about us," Elaine said, smiling at Jake, who was playing quietly on the floor with some toy cars.

"Anyway, as I was saying, "Gareth continued, pleased to have someone with whom to discuss, so openly, what had become his infatuation. Toby flicked through the pages of the notebook, reading extracts whilst Gareth carried on speaking. "I went to the museum to see if I could find any maps dating back centuries. There were a few, nothing accurate, however I did manage to photocopy this." Gareth unfolded an A4 size piece of paper. "Just here is St Mary's Church."

"That's the Blue Boar."

"Precisely, that's the crossroads we now know as Victoria Avenue and East and West Streets. I have marked on here where I think the station is nowadays and where I think we are." Toby looked at the square Gareth had carefully drawn.

"What year is this map from?"

"1567."

"I didn't think the Blue Boar was that old?"

"It's not. There has always been an inn on that site but the Blue Boar wasn't built until 1899. The original was demolished to make way for the new road. There was a medieval house 'Reynold's' next door but that…"

"It says here," Toby interrupted, keen to stay on the point "that 'witches burned other witches'. Why would they do that?"

"It's a strange one, I suppose, but sort of makes sense. Even back then there was a code of conduct that witches, spiritual types and wizards adhered to, and if you were caught breaking those rules then punishment was meted out in whatever form was apt for the time." Gareth clicked his fingers. "That's just reminded me, I thought of something relevant at the time, but not knowing any of what you have told me today I didn't put much substance to it." Excitedly Gareth grabbed the notebook from Toby and flicked through the pages, desperately trying to locate the information. "Ah, here we go." He handed it back to Toby.

> 1683– High Priest Michael and High Priestess Isobel have been tried by the coven for using powers to bewitch the landed gentry, Lord Gray, that has brought untold attention to the coven. Burning at the stake or even the ducking stool is likely to be the punishment sought, should they be caught by the authorities. It has been deemed that banishment from the coven and the stripping of their powers be the only answer. The Black Crack Coven shall gather on the eve of all hallows when power will be the highest.

"What's the relevance? Where did you get it from?" Toby felt the stiff paper, the rough texture and almost brittleness.

"It fell out of a book."

"Does this…" he scanned the paper again for the name, "Black Crack Coven still exist to day?"

68

"No, they don't" Gareth replied.

"So we don't know what happened?"

"That's not exactly true." Gareth loved to drip-feed information, almost torturing Toby, who sat expectant. "I spoke with another coven 'The White Hats'"

"Sounds more like an American hockey team."

"They are a fairly new coven, only been in existence about 100 years, but some of the family's histories go back to 'The Black Crack'." Toby wanted to urge Gareth on as he delighted in enjoying every moment of retelling the history he discovered. "Story is that the high priestess and high priest were to be expelled from the coven and their powers stripped."

"Witches, wizards can strip other witches', wizards', powers?"

"Not exactly, but apparently a coven working together can strip any powers."

"Wow, and I thought it was all myth and good TV."

"Here you go boys, I've brought you some biscuits too, but don't spoil your dinner now." Elaine teased them playfully as Toby glanced at his watch, three o'clock.

"According to stories I've heard many people have had powers stripped. One shouldn't disbelieve," Gareth imparted gleefully.

"After coming into contact with that house, I'll believe anything." Toby picked up his tea and sipped.

"As I was saying, the high priest and priestess were stripped of their powers and, according to the story, it didn't go according to plan. The night in question was all-hallows eve 1653." Gareth turned to the relevant page in his notebook. "It was a crescent moon and a meeting had been summoned, thirteen witches and wizards, in total, gathered by the twisted oak tree." Gareth stopped to drip-feed another bit of information, "which was not twisted before that night." Toby's eyes widened as he took a bite of a garibaldi. "Michael and Isobel knew why they had been summoned and hoped to lessen the seriousness of the matter in their favour. They had planted Pineapple Amethyst crystals in the ground where they knew the coven were set to stand. This in turn should have turned the negative energy, they knew would be focused at them, into positive, in effect strengthening their own powers rather than stripping them. However, unbeknownst to them, other magic had been set into play earlier that evening so when they started, in earnest, to defend their actions with the coven, it had dire consequences for Michael and Isobel baffling and scaring the coven so much that they never met again." Gareth stopped abruptly leaving Toby looking on intrigued.

"And?" he asked excitedly, munching another biscuit.

"That's it, I'm afraid."

"What do you mean, that's it, it can't stop there." Toby spat crumbs over himself, then quickly brushed them into his hand and back onto the plate, slightly embarrassed.

"Well, Sophia Knock , she's was the white witch I was talking to, suffered a heart attack and died."

"Did you not speak to anyone else?"

"They refused to talk to me after that, something about," Gareth started to read from his notes again, "the secrets of the coven so shall remain, for unto earth and ash must the spirit unite, the ill be forgotten and remain unspoken and the future heal the rift and remain unbroken."

"What?" Toby exclaimed.

"That was the strange reply I got to my further enquiries."

"They wouldn't tell you anymore?"

"Nope! 'The curse lives on' is all they would say." Gareth sat back in his chair munching on a biscuit and leaving Toby perplexed, his mind racing with thoughts, trying to decipher the cryptic curse.

"So where do we go now?"

"That my dear fellow is a really good question," Gareth stated, doing his best Sherlock Homes impersonation, "and a question I have been asking myself for the last nine years."

"Nine years?"

"That's when I discovered all that information."

Toby continued to flick through Gareth's notebook, amazed at the information it contained, making his own efforts to fade into insignificance. Absentmindedly he looked at his watch. Another half an hour had passed and he should head home, but his excitement was riding high.

69

After a further twenty-minute discussion with Gareth, Toby made his excuses and left. The rain had stopped and he felt a little brighter than he had done now he'd been able to talk to someone openly about everything, other than Vivien.

Outside Thyme Cottage he looked up one last time at it's frozen in time facade.

"What's your secret, house? eh!"

Some giggling behind broke him from his reverie and he saw two girls walking along the street arm in arm.

Embarrassed, he started to walk away, pushing Jake. Then out of the corner of his eye he caught sight of the cottage front door opening, it beckoned him.

Terri and Joseph walked slowly along the streets that wound the way back to Vivien's bungalow. Joseph's eyes were hollow and showed the weariness behind them. His footsteps were automated rather than normal as he turned over thoughts in his head. His family, gone. How? Why? Where was he? Was he sleeping? Yet all appeared very real. He recollected hearing the screams next door and going to investigate - it was incomprehensible.

Terri tried to be reassuring, seeing the strain on Joseph's face and how much it had physically aged him, and how quickly, but her own thoughts were for her family and the question of how much time had passed.

Finally Joseph found the strength to speak, albeit his voice was quiet and he sounded frightened.

"What am I to do?"

Terri gulped. The question was an obvious one yet there was no answer she could give. How could a person fit back into life after nearly 100 years. Society had moved on. His family had gone. The life he knew was in the past, society no longer knew who he was except for the question in history 'what happened to him on that night in 1911?'.

"I..." she started to say, as they walked past a garage, instead she rushed up to the newspaper stand outside and looked at the dates, checking each to be sure she was reading correctly what she saw.

Tuesday 10th May 2011.

She felt herself go weak and staggered backwards into Joseph who had followed her full of curiousity. But when he checked the date the world started to spin again and, in the end both went careering to the ground in a heap.

Two bystanders and one member of staff came to their aid, helping both up.

"I saw what happened, I saw him, he grabbed her." A young slim twenty-something pointed an accusation at Joseph, who was now open-mouthed and flummoxed half getting up.

"No, he didn't," the member of staff retorted. "You alright miss? Would you like a drink of water?"

"He grabbed her. I swear. I saw it," the young man said vehemently, not liking having his witness statement brought into question.

"I think you are mistaken young man," a woman wearing a flowery print dress added.

Suitably rebuked, the young man shifted awkwardly from foot to foot before sloping off quietly.

"No, no, I'm fine, I just want to get home." Terri fidgeted, uncomfortably. Over three years she thought. Her words were filled with dread but she managed to gather enough control and, grabbed hold of Joseph, "come on Joseph." Joseph's stared at Terri as she hauled him with her.

"May 2011!" he stated without conviction, much to the bewilderment of the member of staff who was still standing within earshot.

"Yes, I know," Terri said aggressively, as panic started to rise inside her, she had been gone three and a half years, it still only felt like she had been gone a day at most. "Come on we've got to get you home." The member of staff shook her head and went back inside.

As they stood outside Vivien's bungalow, Terri felt scared, although she tried to put on a brave face for Joseph's sake. She hoped her mum still lived there, especially as it didn't look as well tended as it used to. She hesitantly pulled out her keys from her bag, watched anxiously by Joseph, then gulped and stepped up to the blue door. Tentatively she pushed the key in and turned it, the lock moved easily and she edged the door open.

70

At first glance nothing looked to have changed. But as she stepped in she noted the dust on the top edge of the skirting board. The house appeared to have lost the shine which comes from a good clean.

Unsteadily she inched into the house, questioning whether her mother still lived there. It was unusual for the house not to be meticulously and regularly cleaned. Joseph stood outside studying the street, the strange unfamiliar vehicles, the general ambient noise, people talking seemingly into their hands, others with pieces of wire dangling from their ears and the strange, brightly coloured, clothes. 'What strange world had he turned up in?' he thought to himself, still hoping he was in some sort of vicious nightmare that didn't want to end.

As Terri made her way further in she glanced into the lounge on her right. The furniture looked familiar, easing her mind that her Mum did still live there.

"Mum," she called apprehensively, not sure of the reaction her return would garner. There was no answer and for a moment she felt relief at the delay of their initial meeting, after being missing for almost three-and-half years. Turning, she beckoned Joseph to enter, insisting that she would make him a cup of tea. Joseph's eyes pleaded for the nightmare to end and she sensed his anxiety.

Terri steered Joseph to the kitchen where he sat sullenly, not quite sure what to make of the cupboards, and the gadgets which made strange unfamiliar noises. Terri busied herself making tea. Again the kitchen appeared different to how she remembered, less organised, less looked after. Opening one of the cupboards, she couldn't find her favourite mug, which read, 'I love New York', it wasn't there. She checked the dishwasher but that appeared as though it hadn't been used for months.

'Strange' she thought.

As she placed two cups of steaming tea on the table she heard a key in the front door and rushed into the hall, her heart pumping so hard she thought it would burst.

"Mu…" She didn't finish the word as a woman in her fifties wearing a light blue top and black trousers stood in the doorway.

There was hesitation in both women as they stood facing each other.

"Can I help you?" Terri said at the same time as the woman said

"Who are you?" the woman asked, closing the door.

Indignant Terri replied, "this is my mum's bungalow, do you mind telling me what you are doing here? And what you are doing with a key?"

"Your mum's… that means you're Terri." The woman caught on quickly.

"That's right. Now what are you doing here?" Terri snapped, striding forward.

"I'm from Harris's Homecare. We come in twice a day to

look after Vivien."

"Look after, what do you mean look after? Anyway she's not here."

"Oh," the woman said, momentarily stunned. "She should be, she hasn't left this house for almost a year."

"What are you talking about? My mum is…" Terri let her words fade. She hadn't checked the rooms, only assumed that after she called out and got no answer that she was out. She dashed into her Mum's bedroom, followed shortly by the carer.

In the bedroom Terri stood, stunned, looking at the frail woman who occupied her Mum's bed.

"No!" she stammered, unable to comprehend the change from when she had last seen her. Her vibrant sharp face was just a greying reflection of its former self. Her hands looked bony and as though the skin was now too big for it and her limbs had a spindly look about them.

"I'm afraid she been getting weaker for a while now. My name's Denise by the way."

"What's wrong with her?" Terri stood frozen by the bedroom door as Denise eased herself past.

"Nothing."

"Nothing. What do you mean, nothing? There's obviously something wrong, look at her, that's not my Mum."

"Come on Mrs Joyce, time to get up." She gently nudged her shoulder. "Come on Vivien, I have someone here to see you."

Terri walked gingerly to the bed and looked down at the frail lady before her.

71

"Mum."

Vivien stirred.

"There you go." Denise tried to help Vivien sit up but she fought the help, "Vivien, it's your daughter to see you. Come on, you can't stay in bed all day."

"Who?" Vivien asked, her weak voice had lost the harsh tone it used to have.

"Your daughter, Terri. Teresa Joyce."

"Grant," Terri added, still in shock at how frail and different her mother looked. It was as if she had aged forty years.

"Daughter. I don't have a daughter, do I?" Denise managed to get Vivien sitting up straight, wedging pillows behind her back. "I had one once. I had a husband once. I don't know what happened to them. Do you know?" She directed her question at Terri who sat, feeling disillusioned, on the edge of the bed, distressed at the sight of her mother. She reached out to hold her hand.

"Who are you?" Vivien snapped, retracting her hand at lightning speed, belying how she looked. Her voice suddenly brusque.

Hurt, Terri stared helplessly at her mother. "It's me, Terri, Teresa your daughter. You remember me don't you?" She paused for a few seconds, hoping a memory would snare itself. "Mum, it's me."

"She has good days and bad days now. She used to talk about you all the time when I first started calling... well." Denise was trying to be tactful, "That was about seven months ago. Unfortunately, she has deteriorated a lot in the last two months, I think we are going to have to get her assessed for a home, as she struggles on her..." Denise broke off seeing the hatred in Terri's eyes. "I'm so sorry, it's just that... that I get asked a lot about how people are doing and I switch into autopilot. I am very sorry. If you and your partner are back then that does change the situation, she glanced at Joseph who was watching from the doorway.

"What? No, he is not my partner, and yes, I'm am back, for good."

"I'll just give your mother a wash and get her dressed. Have you been travelling? Anywhere nice?" The questions were innocent enough but Terri felt bitterness in not have a justifiable answer.

Joseph glanced at Terri with soulless eyes and Terri felt every ounce of her hatred for Thyme Cottage rise to the surface.

"Where's Toby and Jake?" She barked, making Denise's hackles rise up.

"I'm sorry who?" she replied, trying to sound friendly.

"My husband and my son." Denise looked baffled and a little taken aback by the sudden change. "She doesn't like that pullover," Terri said, sharply rising and walking round the bed to take over from Denise.

"Well, she's been wearing it for the last few months." Denise tried to moderate her tone.

"Don't take that tone with me, she's my mother and I should know."

"I'll get her breakfast sorted." Denise sighed inwardly.

"No, I'll do it, in a minute. Now please tell me about my son and my husband."

"I don't know about either or them I'm afraid. They certainly haven't been around since I have been coming here."

"But... no." Terri's strength faded instantly and she sank onto the bed. Denise was about ready to turn and go but felt a strange sympathy for the young woman who was almost as confused as Vivien.

"Terri, you've come back. My daughter, she's back." Vivien said to Denise, stretching out a frail hand to touch Terri's shoulder, making her brighten.

All Terri's emotions came flooding out.

72

Terri rolled forward onto Vivien's lap and cried.

"I'm so sorry Mum, I didn't mean to leave you like this."

Denise looked on, then decided maybe it was best to make tea before she left to continue her rounds. She knew she would have to let the authorities know that Terri was back.

It was a touching reunion between mother and daughter and for a few minutes they didn't move, Vivien stroking Terri's hair. Terri felt the years fall away and remembered a time, once after school, when she had been verbally torn to shreds by a teacher for doing the wrong homework. How, when she had come home crying, they had sat on the settee exactly as they were now, hardly a word being said but the tender touch of a mother wiping away the hurt.

"Where's Toby and Jake?" Terri finally asked, feeling relaxed.

"Who?"

Terri sat up, staring strangely at her mother. "Jake, your grandson."

"I'm sorry love, I don't know who you mean. It's a lovely name though."

"Mum, what do you mean you don't…"

"My goodness, I'm not your mother, what would she say if she heard you calling me your mother, she'd be most upset." Vivien got up but her legs were only just able to support her weight, she really had become a frail old lady.

Inside Terri was torn apart. Her mother didn't know her, Toby and Jake were nowhere to be seen and no one knew where they were?

Vivien struggled out of the room using the walls as a support, as Terri sat helpless and lost. Vivien walked without purpose and, at the door, didn't know where she wanted to go, so stopped and turned, looking confused.

"I don't know where the time goes these days." She stepped back towards the bed.

"Come on Vivien, it's not bedtime yet," Denise said pleasantly, tilting her head at Terri sympathetically.

"I have spoken to the office and asked them about your husband and son." Terri perked up.

"And?"

"They're going to look into it. There is mention of them in the file. I am back in tomorrow morning, I'll let you know what they find out."

The rest of the day was a blur, like walking through treacle, looking after her mother and settling Joseph into what was Jake's room which looked like the day she had left. Terri felt she knew what it meant, but why would Toby take Jake with him?

Toby stared at the open door wondering, waiting for what or who was about to step out from inside. Waiting.

Nothing happened.

He took a few steps backwards to get a better look inside, to see who was standing there. There was a figure in the shadows, he stared harder trying to decipher the image but it kept changing, showing him a series of images.

"What are you trying to tell me?" A couple of minutes passed and Jake was starting to get restless.

"Alright, alright Jake, we'll go home."

Toby started to walk away. Suddenly the door slammed shut.

"What is it you want from me?" he called out, stopping impatiently. "You've already taken my wife," Toby snapped at the cottage.

A couple walking along, carrying some shopping, stared at him their eyes piercing his back.

Anger and hatred were boiling up inside, Jake started to kick harder making the buggy judder.

"Alright Jake, alright." He gave the buggy a reluctant push, harder than he meant, tipping it up on its two back wheels.

"Toby!"

He stopped in his tracks, it came from the house, a female voice, he swore it was Terri's.

73

Turning round he couldn't see anyone, especially Terri.

"Toby!"

There it was again, Jake was starting to wail loudly, Toby moved round to the front of the pushchair and crouched down to see what the fuss was about.

"Toby!" He lifted Jake out of the pushchair and turned on

the spot looking for someone calling his name.

I'm hearing things he thought. Looking at the cottage he wondered if Terri was calling him from inside. It sounded like her, or was he imagining things.

He checked each window for signs of life inside, careful not to step over the perimeter.

"Alright, Jake, I'll get you home in a moment." He tried to placate Jake who had been good all day.

A shadow moved across the garden but didn't reach the street, confined within the boundaries.

"Terri, are you in there?" Silence was the reply. "I think your daddy is going mad, don't you?"

"Going mad," Jake repeated, thinking it was amusing.

"Yes, totally," Toby concluded, distracted by the memory of the voice calling his name.

Toby saw the front door was open again.

Glancing in, he heard his name called again. Clearly as if Terri was standing next to him. Turning sharply, he checked the street scene; the cold of the day was starting to bite. Toby found himself caught in the face by Jake's tiny hand as he swung his hands about in temper.

"Alright Jake, calm down. I just thought I heard your Mum." Toby grabbed Jake's hand and felt naked skin. "Where's your glove?" He checked the other hand just in case he had left them at Gareth and Elaine's but that hand was still protected from the cold by a bright red woollen glove. Checking the ground where they had walked he was shocked to see it just inside the boundary of Thyme Cottage.

"Oh Jake!" he scolded, hit by indecision, whether to reclaim it or not.

Terri sat at the kitchen table lost and alone. Vivien was sitting in front of the TV happily entertained by the endless pictures that flashed up in front of her. Joseph was still too stunned to ask questions, despite his curiosity at the various new-fangled gadgets and strange surroundings. His own home, the home that was still as fresh as yesterday in his mind, seem so quiet and ordinary, and yet so appealing. He had sat in front of the TV for a brief period, but the noise and flashing images gave him a headache. Everything was so fast, almost no time for a breath, what had happened to the world?

Terri had her head in her hands when Joseph appeared at the door.

"Are you okay?" Terri asked, thoughtfully.

"I don't know what to do." His voice, the strongest she had heard since they had left the cottage.

"Do whatever you want to."

"But I don't know what that should be. This place is so unfamiliar to me. I want my family back" he pleaded.

"So do I," Terri mumbled under her breath, so Joseph wouldn't hear. "We can go to the records office tomorrow and see if we can trace what happened to your family if you like."

Joseph's smile was thankful but lacked any really hope. "I'll go into the garden if that's alright?"

"Of course. I'll sort some dinner out soon. See what's in the freezer." Joseph cocked an surprised eye at her, the kitchen looked so different from what he was used to, where was the open fire or range? "You'd better put a coat on, it looks cold out there. There's probably one of Toby's in the hall." The mention of Toby's name punctuated her own hurt.

"I'll be fine." He went out through the UPVc double-glazed door, feeling the texture and silently questioning it.

74

In the garden Joseph started to feel at ease. It was a world he was familiar with, plants, grass, trees, he didn't need to question them. Vivien's garden had become an overgrown jungle, left untended for nearly twelve months. For want of something to do Joseph grabbed a fork from the garden shed and started to put order back into the flowerbeds. A rose bush looked half-dead and he found a pair of garden shears and started to dead head the faded flowers, then proceeded to pull out weeds. Within half an hour the garden looked better.

Terri finally got up and checked the freezer and fridge for food and found them to be almost empty except for a microwave lasagne and a tub of Sainsbury's ice cream. In the cupboards there were a few tins and when she checked they were well in excess of their 'use by' dates. She slammed the cupboard doors in disgust.

"I thought they were meant to be caring for you, Mum!" she said to no one. Poking her head outside she told Joseph she was just nipping to Sainsbury's. He gave a puzzled frown. She elaborated saying 'supermarket', but he was none the wiser she clarified by saying 'she was getting some food in', Joseph, being a gentleman, offered to come with her, although he found this new world frightening. Terri turned him down and he visibly relaxed. As she left, Denise's colleagues turned up with 'meals on wheels'. She left them to get on with their job.

At the supermarket Terri collected a few essentials and went to pay for them.

"That's £18.57 please," the cashier commanded pleasantly.

Terri handed over a twenty pound note only to be met with a bemused look.

"I'm sorry, this is not legal tender anymore," promptly handing it back.

"What?" Terri stammered, aware of the queue of people standing behind her.

"They changed last year and we are not allowed to accept them anymore. Maybe you want to use a card instead?" The cashier pointed to a machine positioned near Terri.

"Mmm, yes okay." Terri handed over her bank card.

Much to the annoyance of the queue behind, this was also rejected. Terri started to get flustered, her face flushing with embarrassment. Snatching the card back she searched her purse and managed to cobble together enough, using a couple of fivers she found folded up.

Finally, she walked out of the store with her bank card despite the cashiers best attempts to retain it, as prompted by her till.

After tea Joseph and Terri sat in the lounge, letting the TV flash up pictures of the latest news. To Terri it was surprising, to Joseph it was terrifying. The wars and violence, with its shocking images of tanks, aircraft and roadside bombs. After a while Joseph retired to bed wishing that sleep would wake him from the nightmare. Terri decided to call some of her Mum's friends to try and find out what had happened to Toby and Jake, afraid that she may already know the answer.

Toby reached carefully over the fence to pick up Jake's glove, wary of the possible outcome. It disappeared just as he was about to touch it. Instantly retracting his hand, panic surged through him as he looked around to confirm that it was still Saturday and everything was as it should be. He hugged Jake tighter and studied each car, trying to recollect whether it had been there a few minutes ago. The Buggy! Where was buggy? He spun round almost teetering off balance. There it is. Phew!

He sighed.

"Come on, let's go home."

"Hi Vivien." Toby closed the door and took Jake's coat off before folding away the buggy. "Vivien?" he called, but there was no answer. "Vivien?"

He let Jake run into his bedroom and followed.

"Come on son, let me change your clothes, those ones are still a little damp."

"No."

"Jake," came the warning from Toby.

"Don't want to."

Toby walked over to Jake. "You will change your clothes." Jake stood facing his father his face trying to look as determined as he could, his arms folded across his chest in defiance.

"I take it Jake doesn't want any tea then?" Toby paused. "Well okay, but you can't leave your room."

Jake frowned, thinking hard, then finally gave in and tried to pull his jumper off. When he got himself into a tangle Toby helped.

When he came out of Jake's room he almost collided with Vivien, who stood in the doorway, frightening the life out of him.

"Jeez. You scared me half to death." Vivien's face looked pale. "You alright? You look as though you've seen a ghost." Toby's words hit him like a slab of concrete. "You haven't, have you? She's not, is she? Please tell me she's not."

"She's here, I can feel her."

75

"What? What do you mean? She can't be."

"Call it a mother's sixth sense, but I can feel her here."
Vivien's eyes looked bloodshot and, for a split second, Toby
wondered whether she had been drinking.

"She's not here Vivien…" Toby started to console her.

"She is, my Terri is here, now."

Toby felt churned up inside. "Then she must be d…"

Vivien interrupted him. "She's not, she's alive. I know it."

"I'm going to give Jake his tea." Toby pushed past her as he
wondered what on earth had got into her, she was not normally
sensitive to spiritual things, although they had all seen Peter &
Eileen's ghosts.

What was happening? he thought, as she settled Jake at the
table where he immediately started banging the table with his
hands.

"Cartoons."

"No Jake, it's tea time."

"Cartoons. Not hungry." Toby sighed. The last thing he
wanted was Jake playing up.

Out of the blue Jake burped really loudly, much to his own
astonishment, clamping his hand over his month

"I beg your pardon. You haven't even had your tea yet."

Vivien walked into the kitchen, a slightly dazed look on her
face. Toby tried to ignore her but her vagueness wouldn't let
him settle.

"Vivien, she's not here."

"Nanny, watch cartoons?" Jake started to get down from

the table.

"Jake, stop playing about," snapped Toby.

"She is, right now, in the kitchen."

"Where? In the cupboard?" Toby opened the larder style cupboard and called Terri's name. "Nope, no answer." Bitterness raked him inside and he focussed on Jake instead. "Finish your tea, otherwise you're going straight to bed." Jake pouted at his father.

"She's standing here."

Toby turned to see Vivien standing by the sink.

"Oh yes, I can see her, doing the washing up. This isn't funny anymore," Toby snarled. "Jake come back here now." Jake had slid off the chair and was heading to the lounge to watch TV.

"I know," Vivien suddenly steamed. "She's my daughter. I am not some delusional old hag who has lost her marbles, I've lost my daughter. Do you know what that feels like?"

Toby had made it to the door but stopped and turned on Vivien. "Of course I bloody know what it feels like, she is my wife and the mother of our son. I wish she was here now, but she not, she's gone. She went to that stupid bloody house,"

"Cottage," Vivien interrupted.

"What?!"

"Cottage. It's a cottage."

"Don't talk bloody semantics, she's gone, nothing we can do can bring her back. Do you think I don't wish that she would walk through that door at any second. I love her, I love her to bits."

"So why did you get caught up so much in that house?"

"Cottage," Toby added sarcastically.

The slap across the face came from nowhere, knocking Toby sideways.

"Don't get smart with me Toby Grant, this is my home and you're a guest."

Cut down, Toby held his cheek as it stung from the sharpness of Vivien's hand. They stared at each other in silence, contemplating the heated words.

Finally Toby spoke.

"Fine, I'll pack some things tonight and we'll be gone. I'll come back for everything else later."

Vivien's bottom lip quivered as the summit of their heated exchange settled in her aching mind, but before she could say anything Toby had headed after Jake telling him to get his coat on. Slamming the door to the bedroom, he packed a small bag with some clothes before doing the same for Jake. In the hall Jake was making a fuss but eventually Toby got his coat on him, grabbed his own and stormed out of the bungalow. He had no idea where he was going to go. He had a few friends but none he thought he could stay with; they only had small flats and no kids.

As he slammed the door, the cold night air was freezing on his warm cheek, the slap still fresh in his mind.

Vivien heard the door close and the weight of her worries rested on her weary shoulders.

Thirty minutes later Toby stood outside Thyme Cottage looking for inspiration. Looking for a place to stay for the night.

76

Terri stood by the sink. She had spent five minutes standing in the doorway to Jake's room picturing in her mind the scene that should have greeted her. Finally her stomach had rumbled and hunger bit in, although she didn't want to eat. The day had been spent with Joseph viewing town records, trying to discover what had happened to his family. They had found a missing persons report in the name of Joseph Harrison, dated the night he had investigated the screams in his neighbour's house. Ida Harrison and her three children had eventually been evicted from the house for failure to pay the rent. There were no other records, not for any deaths or children in relation to his family.

Terri had received a phone call from a David Radison, Head of Social Services and responsible for Vivien. He had stated that they were starting the process of taking Vivien into permanent care and this would involve the selling of her property to pay for the care - her mental health had deteriorated somewhat drastically over the last few months. Terri had got very upset and started to argue but David said that the case would be reviewed immediately and, after giving her his number, he requested that she call back in an hour.

"Sorry about that."

"It's alright. I understand. I can be a little clinical when it comes to discussing these matters although I don't wish to be so, but..." He let the sentence go unfinished. He knew she wasn't really interested. "As I was saying, papers have been submitted to the Courts in order to get the relevant go-ahead as we could not locate yourself or your husband..." David flicked through the folder in front of him. "Toby, isn't it?"

"Where's Jake?" Terri spat out. She was finding it hard to take in all the information she was being given, her mind temporarily flicking back to her childhood. How her Mum used to look after her, especially after her Dad had died. Mum always found extra time to spend with her only daughter. During the summer months they would go for walks at the weekends, just like they had done when her father was alive, except now, in her mind, they were more like one day sabbaticals.

They'd head off as the sun rose with a full picnic basket and cool box packed in the car. Terri would have to pack her homework in a bright yellow rucksack, as well as any other bits and pieces - they'd drive to Danbury, Maldon, Hockley, Hadleigh or Colchester. The day would be spent talking, walking, playing, doing homework, reading, anything that took their fancy. It was always just the two of them. It would be that way for a couple of years until Terri started wanting to go out with her friends. Instantly she felt guilty for taking away those precious days and wanting to do something else. A memory from those days reared up in her mind, her Mum writing in a book. She had forgotten that. She had asked her mum what she was doing and she would just say 'oh just making some notes for work'. One day Terri had sneaked a look and immediately felt shame, it was her Mother's diary.

She made a mental note to look for the diary after the call.

"Mrs Grant?"

"Jake, my son." Terri could hear David fingering through the file.

"I'm sorry, there's no mention of a Jake."

"He must be somewhere." She hadn't thought through her questioning, "He can't just disappear." She fell silent and, for a second, David didn't respond.

"There's nothing showing up here. Hold on while I check

the computer. Can you give me your son's full name."

"Jake Samuel Grant," she said, each name carrying her concern.

David repeated it as he punched in the letters on the computer and did a search, not just through Vivien's file, but also a general search.

The seconds were like minutes, and the minutes were like hours as the phone lay silent whilst the search took place.

"Jake Samuel Grant! Here we go. Oh!"

77

"Oh! What do you mean, Oh?" Terri's heart jumped into her mouth, panic seeping into every nerve.

David paused, reading the message flashing up on screen, 'Refer to Section 18'.

"Hello," Terri said, failing to control the dread she felt.

"Sorry." David cleared his throat. "There is a record of a Jake Samuel Grant but…"

"What do you mean there is a record? He is my son," Terri interrupted.

"As I was going to say, a record exists but I do not have access to it, the file, it appears, has been referred to Section 18."

"Section 18! What does that mean?" Again Terri broke in.

"It is nothing to worry about…"

"Nothing to worry about." Terri lost her patience. The one

thing she now wanted more than anything was being kept from her.

"Apologies, I just meant…"

"What? Meant what?"

"If you would let me finish," David interrupted, aggressively. Terri held the phone momentarily away from her ear.

"Section 18 is Child Welfare Services. Now, I don't have access to any of their information, and if I did, I would not be able to tell you anything…"

"But he is MY son."

David sensed his patience slipping away. "I would not be able to tell you anything over the phone without confirming your identity." Terri was about to interrupt and David could sense her anxiety so quickly he ran on. "As cases with children are treated with the utmost security, both to protect the child first and foremost, and then the parents. I can arrange a meeting so you can come in and speak to someone who will be able to help you, and maybe even tell you where your son is." As soon as he finished he knew he had said the wrong thing.

Terri jumped on his words sharply. "May be able to tell me where my son is? What's this maybe? I'm his bloody mother, I have rights." David sighed audibly. He hated one-sided conversations where the parents thought they were always right. If they hadn't been missing in the first place Section 18 would never have got involved. He wanted to scream this down the phone but bit his tongue. "I am going to…" Terri's mind ran to the fact that she had been missing for three-and-a-half years, she didn't know where Toby was and her mum wasn't very well.

The picture became crystal clear in her head.

"I'm sorry," she said wearily, surprising David. It wasn't very often he heard that after the start of a rant. "Can you please make an appointment so I can find my son as quickly as possible?"

A few minutes later Terri was sitting at the kitchen table thinking about her son, wondering what he was up to and where he was. Instantly her thoughts slipped to Joseph. He had slunk off to the lounge and now she had more sympathy for what he must be going through. His family gone, he himself lost in another time with a strange woman who had a mentally ill mother and had also lost her husband to the cottage.

She walked into the lounge. Joseph looked devoid of life, staring out of the window, the clear blue sky offering no respite from the pain he held inside.

Terri looked at him wondering what she was going to do with him. How could she get him integrated back into the world, a world he no longer knew? A world that had taken his life from him. How was she going to get herself back into the world? The visit to the supermarket had proved that her bank accounts no longer existed or at least had been frozen. Had she been declared legally dead? She knew she would have to ask her mother, and hope that in a lucid moment she would recall everything.

One glimmer of hope spread over everything and that was that Jake was okay, even if she didn't know where he was.

78

Looking at the cottage, it bayed at him, daring him to enter, it was like a tormentor, Toby knew he couldn't stay in there, he knew what would happen if he did. But where else could he go?

His thought of going back and apologising.

"No, why should I?" he said aloud.

"Why should you what?" said a familiar voice.

He turned to see Gareth standing next to him.

"I thought I recognized you from our window," Gareth said. "I was hoping I'd catch you again. I had a thought about the cottage." Toby started to feel tears well up in the corner of his eyes, so much regret and all of it connected with the cottage. "Are you alright?" Gareth enquired, concerned.

Toby took a couple of seconds to answer. "No, not really, this cottage is doing its damndest to ruin my life. What have I done to deserve it?" Gareth stared at Toby, knowing it was a rhetorical question but also knowing there were answers that needed to be sought.

"Why don't you come inside?" Gareth indicated his own house.

Toby nodded and followed Gareth inside where Elaine made tea. As they sat down, Toby poured out his heart, letting his emotions come tumbling out. It was only then that he realised how much of a millstone the cottage was. Elaine was quick to offer a place to stay, which Toby politely turned down, appreciating the kind offer to a relative stranger. He knew he had to go back and try to make amends. After about half an hour of general chat, Toby remembered what Gareth had said when he first approached him.

"What was it that you wanted me for?"

"What? Oh yes. I had been thinking about our conversation earlier and I thought I'd try a different tack to find out about the high priest and priestess and what happened. Anyway," he waved his hands about as if wiping an invisible white board. I had a thought about how we could," Toby was momentarily surprised how it had suddenly started to sound like a project or hobby, "gain some more information about the Black Crack Coven. I still have some contact numbers for members of The White Hats. I thought that maybe you could try ringing and persuading them that you were... are an ancestor of this Michael or Isobel. Try and dig for some more information."

"Why don't you just try it? I'm sure they would have forgotten your voice by now after, how long? ten or so..."

"Nine years," Elaine chirped in, "and he did, bless him, earlier today after you left, thinking that very same thing. Their memories are long, I'll give them that." Elaine switched the TV on noting it was time for 'The X Factor. "Now, if you want to carry on talking I suggest you go into the kitchen, this is my one weakness and I like peace and quiet."

Gareth and Toby slumped off to the kitchen, leaving Elaine contentedly watching TV with Jake.

Toby cogitated Gareth's suggestion, "I don't know much about this Michael or Isobel, and they are sure to ask me questions that might, you know, expose that." Suddenly an idea struck Toby, a name he remembered. "What do you know about Lord Gray?"

"A little. I did some research a long time ago. I'll go and get it." Gareth returned five minutes later with one of his notebooks open at a page entitled 'Lord Gray'. Toby quickly scanned through the notes.

Lord Gray and Lady Charlotte owned 100 acres of prime farmland that ran from Prittlewell to Rochford. Descended from a long line of farming generations, he was rumoured to have bullied workers and to have had numerous liaisons with fieldworkers. Before Toby could begin to sympathise with Lady Charlotte he read on and saw that she too had various encounters with farmhands. To high society they were the epitome of wealth, charm and generosity. Regular churchgoers, they were held in high regard by those who did not know the truth. It was understood that they had been trying for a family for years but with little success, despite outside dalliances. That is until one year when a Fanny Williams became pregnant with Lord Gray's child.

79

Lord Gray managed to keep the child a secret from his wife for two years. In those two years he had favoured Fanny with clothes and extra food for the baby, who was called John. Eventually Charlotte found out about John's existence and insisted the child be brought to her with the mother, unbeknownst to Lord Gray, who was away on business. A deal was struck that Fanny and the child would leave Prittlewell and travel up north to Charlotte's cousin's farm in Yorkshire where work and accommodation had been arranged, from then, she would have no further contact with Lord Gray and no forward address would be left. It would be as if she had never existed. When Lord Gray returned from his trip he was devastated to find his son gone. One night after drinking all day Lady Charlotte gloated that she knew about her husband's infidelities and was taken aback when Lord Gray boasted of knowing about her escapades with various farmhands. He tore into her, both physically and verbally, with such ferocity that she was laid up for a week, with only a doctor as visitor. There was no remorse from either party, and no details of the whereabouts of Fanny and son, John, were revealed.

Six years went by and finally Lady Charlotte bared a child by Lord Gray. A son and an heir, James Charles Gray, a healthy child was finally born.

"So what's this got to do with the Black Crack Coven."

"Where are you up to?" Gareth studied the page. "Read on, you'll see."

Toby continued.

Another four years had passed and son James was growing into a strapping young lad, for which Lady Charlotte took all the credit, yet it was the nanny and maid that effectively raised the child.

One day Fanny returned to the manor looking for Lord Gray who was once again away on business. Lady Charlotte saw the woman with the bastard child and demanded to know why she had returned. Fanny explained that Lady Charlotte's cousin's farm had been burned down and she was now unemployed and had nowhere to live.

Lady Charlotte apparently dismissed her out of hand demanding to know why Fanny thought it was her responsibility. Fanny only really cared about her son, John's welfare, and asked for him to be taken in. Lady Charlotte was incensed, yet she also had the foresight to see a plan. So she first conceded to Fanny's request, insisting that if she did this thing then Fanny was never to set foot anywhere near the manor or her son, John, ever again. Wishing only good fortune for John, she agreed and left, pleased for her son, but unhappy about her situation.

The following day Lady Charlotte took John out for a tour of the grounds under the pretence of an introduction to the working lands. It was early on a winter's day that she left the stables on horseback together with the bastard child. Four hours later she returned alone with the two horses, leaving them to the stable boy to put away. No mention was made of John, and from that day forward no one saw him again. Only the housemaid and the stable boy knew of his return to the manor and subsequent disappearance. Subjugation was the order of the day and fearing for their own lives both said nothing. When Lord Gray returned from his London trip he knew nothing of the child and carried on as before.

It was months before rumours started to circulate about a boy that had disappeared, and it was six months before remains were found on the Gray's land. No formal identification was ever made and the boy was buried in a small unmarked grave at the local church. It was paid for by Lady Charlotte and Lord Gray as a generous gift for the unfortunate boy who had come to misfortune on their land.

Fanny had kept to her word until the day when money and position had come her way and promised a better life. She then wanted to be reunited with John. She was horrified when she found out that no one knew anything about him. She pleaded with Lady Charlotte to tell her his whereabouts but was dismissed and in the end the local constable was called to remove her from the Gray's land, claiming she was insane.

80

Fanny wasn't insane but because Lord Gray knew nothing about what had happened when she spoke about their liaison he vehemently denied it making sure she was punished, accusing her of lying. She was thrown in the stocks for a day.

Being well known by society for their generosity and church-going ways it was easy for the Grays to escape any suspicion. When Fanny finally made her own secret enquiries, the stable boy confessed to her that he had seen Lady Charlotte take a boy out with her. Distraught, she confronted Lady Charlotte and Lord Gray saying that the stable boy could back up the story but, when he was called he denied everything. Lord Gray did feel some guilt towards the girl and gave her a sum of money. Although she no longer needed their money she took it, thinking in some way it would avenge her son's death.

Wrapped with guilt, for giving John up, she used the money to get drunk, in a local inn, where she told the story to all who would listen. In that crowd were Michael and Isobel Furrows -.

Toby's eyes widened. "Furrows," he whispered.

"What was that?" Gareth enquired.

"Furrows. Edward must be a distant relation to this Michael and Isobel."

Gareth peered at Toby quizzically.

"That's Edward's surname. He must be a relative." Toby eagerly read on.

- overheard the poor girl's story and invited her to join them. They had a long history with Lord Gray in a dispute about land they had rented from him some years before. They had never before been able to gather confirmation about Lord Gray's abuse of employees and so had not taken matters further. But there were a lot of rumours and they saw fit to believe that there was no smoke without fire. With Fanny's story confirming and backing up their own beliefs, they tried to get the Black Crack Coven to act upon the story, but the concensus was against action.

The coven thought no more of the matter until after the death of Lord Gray's son, James, from a mysterious illness. This happened after a supposed, accidental, meeting between Michael Furrows and James, when Michael handed him a special gift, which he kept secret from his parents. After his death, the gift was discovered, both parents handled it and became ill soon after. Stories started to circulate that the family were cursed. Lord Gray passed away, quickly followed by Lady Charlotte, then the servants started to perish in the same manner. In desperation the manor was burned to the ground by locals, intent on stopping the spread of the mysterious illness.

After the Manor House was razed to the ground, all troubles stopped and life continued as normal. That is until it was discovered that Michael and Isobel had collected special ingredients to bring about divine retribution on Lord Gray and Lady Charlotte. In the eyes of the coven Michael and Isobel had gone beyond the realms of what was considered justifiable retribution and punishment needed to be meted out.

Toby sat upright stretching his back. "Wow, that is some story."

"Yes, I know. It took a lot of research to find it out, as well."

"I'm not sure my idea will work now."

"What was it? Oh yeah…" Gareth asked excitedly.

There was silence for couple of seconds whilst both thought further.

"You could still claim to be a distant relative. He was a cad, and so was she for that matter. No one would be able to deny the possibility of another illegitimate child," Gareth imparted excitedly.

"True." Toby smiled, liking the idea.

Between them they worked out a story that Toby could use, with dates and names, in the hope that it would add authenticity to his claim and build credibility. By the time they had done this it was nearly ten, and probably too late to call.

In Gareth's eagerness to be part of the investigation he tried to convince Toby to stay, to allow the air to settle between Toby and his mother-in-law. Toby decided that maybe it would be best, and as Jake had fallen asleep on the settee it seemed appropriate.

In the morning he would make the phone call with their cover story already worked out.

81

When Toby woke up, guilt pounced on him, guilt for upsetting Vivien. She had helped him more than he would sometimes, readily admit and, without her, he would find it almost impossible as a single father. He picked up his phone and looked at the display wondering whether it was too early to ring and apologise. Whatever they had argued about it was not worth splitting up the family, they needed each other, especially now.

The screen showed it was 8.43. He knew she would be awake because Jake would be awake. Where was Jake? He sat bolt upright in bed, panic coursed through him like a train. He had been nestled on the floor on cushions from the settee. Pulling on his jeans Toby left the room taking the stairs two at a time.

He found Elaine in the kitchen feeding a boisterous Jake who was eating and humming at the same time, swinging his legs wildly on the chair.

"Morning," Elaine said cheerfully. "I hope you don't mind, it was just that he was wandering about the house." Toby couldn't believe he had slept through his son waking up.

"I'm sorry." Toby quickly apologised

"No need to be, it's nice to have a young child in the house. Our children don't visit half enough as I would like and I do miss the grandchildren."

For some reason Toby didn't picture them as having grandchildren despite the photos that were so lavishly displayed around the house. It was an idea that didn't quite sit right as they appeared so young and spritely.

"If you want to take a shower. I have put fresh towels in the bathroom for you." Elaine continued.

Toby left the kitchen to ring Vivien, after kissing Jake on the head, sighing before he pressed speed dial, not quite sure how she would react; hopefully refreshed and, like him, feeling guilty for letting the situation get to her. The phone rang and rang, after ten rings he started to get edgy, it was usual for her phone to go to voicemail if unanswered.

Gareth burst into the lounge, Toby turned sharply. Gareth looked flushed.

Vivien had fretted all night, the heated exchange with Toby tearing at her, he and Jake were all she had left. But, however strange it had sounded, she did feel Terri's presence in the house with her, and it wasn't just memories. Toby didn't understand, but a mother knows, she also knew that Terri was alright. She only wished that she could contact her, talk to her, find out how they could reunite the family and move on in their lives.

Dawn drew slowly on and she watched with bleary eyes from the kitchen window as the daylight brightened the world. She stood mesmerized, drinking yet another cup of tea. Listening to the emptiness of the house, where she had hoped to hear Jake rousing from his sleep. Yet silence reigned supreme. She knew she should eat something but breakfast was a lost cause, she grabbed her coat from the hallway, knowing she had to do something.

It was about ten minutes later that she noticed she'd left her mobile in the house, what if Toby tried to call? 'Damn', she thought. She was heading for a couple of friends of Toby that she knew, hoping he was there.

At the first house there was no answer. Looking at her watch she saw, it was early, barely 7.30 on a Sunday morning. She felt some guilt at disturbing people, but that faded into insignificance against the loss of her family. The next friends hadn't seen Toby, nor the friends after that. The more doors she tried, the more 'no's' she got. Her head started to toy with the idea that they had headed to the cottage. It was theirs, they owned it, and maybe in desperation he had stayed there praying that all would be alright in the morning.

The more she turned the thought over in her mind, the more convinced she was that is what he had done. She hastened her walk to Thyme Cottage.

Standing at the gate she tentatively called out, but with no answer. She was tempted to enter, just to be sure.

82

"Toby, there's a woman standing outside the cottage, she looks as though she is going to enter."

"A woman."

"Medium height, short redish hair, gold loop earrings."

"Vivien!" he stated, shocked. "We've got to stop her."

Gareth tried to keep up with Toby as he rushed out the front door.

Vivien pushed the gate open. She knew this place had taken her family from her but she wanted them back. What was it the cottage wanted?

She looked up at a second storey window, behind the dirty obscured glass she could have sworn she saw a pair of eyes watching her. Staring intently at the window there was definitely someone there. She inched forward focussing on the eyes which, this time, hadn't moved away but remained locked on hers.

"Who are you?" she called out. There was no reply.

Her weight shifted onto her front foot. She was now half-in and half-out of the garden. A shadow instantly distracted her. A rose bush to her left burst into bloom like an explosion, the flowers appeared to shatter sending snowflake-like petals falling to the ground. Glancing back at the window the eyes were still there.

"Who are you?" she screamed, still holding the gate firmly in her left hand afraid to let go in case she couldn't get back, her rationale hoping that it would anchor her firmly back in her time.

"Will you shut up. Do you realise what time it is?" an angry neighbour called out.

Turning to see where the voice had come from and seeing no one she started to lose her balance, falling backwards she let go of the gate. In mid-air she twisted her body and saw the white petals of a daffodil quickly fade to brown before turning to dust. The plant appeared dead and lifeless.

Hitting the ground, she heard a crack and let out an almighty cry of pain, before rolling on to her right side, instantly grabbing her left arm.

As tears started to roll down her cheeks she heard her name being called.

Toby sprinted down the path of Gareth's house, turning left, then left again at the corner of the street and running along the length of the six foot fence that edged Gareth's garden, Thyme cottage's front gate was in view, but he couldn't see Vivien.

He shouted out her name, hoping to catch her before she entered. As he rounded on the gate he thought he saw her. Once again he shouted as loud as he could.

"What is it with everyone today? Will you bloody shut up. Some of us are trying to enjoy our Sunday lie in."

Toby ignored the angry voice and stared into the garden, panic sweeping through him.

"Vivien!" he cried. He stood at the gate, frantically hoping that she had walked away, knowing that she couldn't have got out of his sight in the short time it had taken him to get from Gareth's house.

Gareth drew alongside Toby, panting. He was fit for his age, but it had been a long time since he had run that hard.

"Where is she?" he said, in between deep breaths. Gareth looked up and down the street, no one else was about. "She didn't go in, did she?" Gareth guessed the answer without any further explanation from Toby.

Toby grasped the gate tightly in his hands and screamed "Nooooo." Turning back to face Gareth, tears were streaming down his cheeks.

Gareth helped him back to his house.

83

Vivien tasted bile rising up inside her, small beads of perspiration formed on her brow, she may not have been a nurse but she could tell that her arm was broken. She knew the pain would kick in again after the adrenalin stopped flowing. Her eyes widened, as at first, she saw Toby as clear as the sun in the sky and, the next, he had disappeared from view.

What had she done?

Fighting the urge to throw up, she struggled to sit up but screamed as the pain bit into her, draining what little energy she had. She saw the world around her become a blur as the pain faded and a strange tranquility came over her. Slowly the world faded from view.

She heard a voice calling her, it was distant, some way off but it sounded familiar, she knew it, but she couldn't place it. Her mind tried to fathom where she was and what she was doing. It was dark, or were her eyes closed, she couldn't tell as her head thumped out a rhythm that made her cringe. A shot of pain from her arm rang out in her mind and she reached for it remembering the fall. Still the world wouldn't come into focus.

Wearily she sat up, or was she sitting up, was she dreaming? More pain ricocheted through her head. Her eyelids became like iron curtains and she fought their weight convinced they were closed. She passed out as she saw where she was.

Gareth sat Toby down and brought him a nip of brandy – Toby was as grey as a vein in marble.

"I can't believe she would enter that place, she knows what happens. Why? WHY?!" Toby couldn't hide his emotion.

Gareth looked on sympathetically but didn't know what to say and for a few minutes the new friends sat in silence. Finally Gareth spoke, although he didn't know what reaction his suggestion would garner, but it was obvious the way he saw it.

"Maybe we need to find, and cure the origins of this whole mystery, let us make the phone calls, see if we can't get some answers and bring your family back."

Toby stared in bewilderment at Gareth, tiny daggers in his eyes.

"That bloody house, cottage, has caused nothing but misery for me, every time I try and do something it delivers another blow." Toby paused, the anger he felt inside hiding behind his relatively calm words.

Gareth thought of a piece of advice that had always served him well. "Things always look darkest before the dawn. There is an answer out there somewhere and we just have to find it."

Toby's anger exploded. "Find it, find it? You're crazier than I first thought you were." Immediately Toby wished he could retract the words but he couldn't.

He saw Gareth's hurt.

"I'm sorry you feel that way," Gareth said, starchly. "I thought you understood, I thought…" He left the sentence unfinished and hesitated before leaving the room. Toby stood up slowly trying to decide what he should do. His decision was made for him when Gareth brought Jake into the room with his coat on.

"I'm sorry, I…"

"I think, maybe it would be best if you left. I am sorry for your loss, losses but I will not be spoken to like that in my own home."

"Please, I'm sorry, it's just…"

"Please, go, I think it would be best for everyone."

Toby stood for another minute looking at Gareth holding Jake, wishing there was something he could say to change things. Finally he conceded he ought to go.

At the door Gareth added, "I will keep an eye out for your family."

Toby looked at him, his eyes still pleading forgiveness.

"Goodbye Toby."

"Bye," Toby muttered, hoping for a reprieve that never came.

He pushed Jake out of the front gate and turned left to go back to the cottage, he needed to decide what to do with it, he couldn't leave it as it was, it was only causing more heartache. He came to the conclusion that he would have to pay to get a security fence put around the cottage, to stop anyone going in.

84

Back at the bungalow the desolation of his predicament started to hit home and one problem loomed up like a giant rock, he had no one to look after Jake whilst he went to work and he couldn't afford to lose another job because of that bloody cottage.

Frantically he made some phone calls in search of a babysitter or crèche where he could leave Jake, but it was Sunday and everywhere he rang went straight to answer-phone. Jake was playing up as the night drew in, as if he knew something was wrong, his tea ended up all over the floor and, when Toby tried to give him his bath, he started to scream the place down. Getting frustrated he shouted at him to 'shut up', but it only had the effect of Jake staring astonished at his father and then screaming with renewed vigor. At one point in the evening the phone rang whilst the cooker chimed to signify his own dinner, pizza, was ready - at the same time as the doorbell rang - a great eruption of noise causing the knot of stress in his stomach to tighten.

By the time he had put Jake to bed and finally got him settled, his pizza was dry and brittle and only moderately warm. Taking one bite from it, his appetite disappeared.

Finally the house was in silence and, grabbing a beer from the fridge, he slumped down in front of the TV. It was nearly 10pm when the full extent of the loneliness crept into him. Work was a welcoming friend but the thought of what to do with Jake was puzzling him. He didn't want to let work down and phone in sick, but he had no one that he could leave Jake with. He wished Vivien was here, he missed Terri and wondered when she was going to turn up again. He tried to recollect how long it had been, yet his alcohol-fuddled brain couldn't compute anything. Edward Furrows was right; that place was tearing his life apart and destroying his family, although it was not going the way that he said it would. It was meant to have been Toby who disappeared, not Terri, or Vivien.

Toby thought he felt a vibration in his pocket and pulled out his mobile, the screen remained blank.

Forlornly he threw his head back and stared at the ceiling, the TV burbled in the background. Toby was exhausted, emotionally and physically.

Something caught his attention and he reached for the remote to turn up the volume.

Two detectives who were suspended on full pay after a supposed hoax murder of five people have been sacked from the force. The pair known by other officers for their practical jokes are said to have taken the matter too far this time. Chief Inspector Grade released this statement, 'Whilst our officers are under extreme pressure and occasionally need to let off steam, wasting valuable time and resources cannot be accepted. We are expected to be accountable by the public and these officers have abused the trust which is placed in their hands.

The report made him think about all the people who may have been caught up in the cottage and the ones, he knew, who had lost families, and time. He really did need to get it fenced off to stop anyone else getting involved. Finally he decided that bed was beckoning. Despite feeling tired, his restless mind wouldn't let his active imagination settle.

5am came round too soon. Pleasantly, Jake was still asleep. He knew he should get up but with no one to take care of Jake it was going to be pointless, he would just have to phone in sick. He dreaded that phone call, so soon after starting his new job.

Work had been good after Toby decided honesty was the best policy. His immediate line manager, Mark, understood the predicament that Toby was in, the argument with his mother-in-law and the fact that she would no longer look after Jake. He'd listened and, instead of what Toby had expected, was given the number of someone who would probably be able to help. They couldn't, but they knew someone else who had room and, by the end of Tuesday, a crèche had been sorted out. The expense was something he could have done without but at least things could return to normal.

Saturday crawled round slowly as Toby got to grips with life as a single father, holding down a steady job and co-ordinating care for his son.

He stood outside Thyme Cottage, measuring up in his mind how much security fencing he needed. A thought suddenly struck him.

How come the police who had arrested him that very first time, had not travelled through time?

85

Toby's gaze wandered temporarily to Gareth's house. He knew he should go and apologise, he had been out of order and Gareth was the one person who might be able to help with this mystery.

He turned in the direction of Gareth's house. He had only gone about ten yards when sirens broke through the relative peace of Saturday morning. Suddenly a hubbub of people appeared from nowhere and, turning round sharply, he saw an ambulance draw up to the kerb. There were about five or six people milling around the gate of the cottage.

Toby was about to explode with anger when he caught sight of a figure on the ground. A paramedic jumped out of the ambulance and ran in through the open gate, there was a cry of pain. Toby recognised the voice.

Absentmindedly he dragged the pushchair back to the gate, surprised to see Vivien being attended by a paramedic in the grounds of the cottage.

"Vivien," he half-called.

"Out of the way, sir." Toby felt himself being pushed to one side as a stretcher was wheeled through. In the sea of faces he caught sight of Gareth, who smiled curtly.

For a second a whirlwind of thoughts rushed through him. They were inside the boundary yet he could still see them. How?

Toby stood on the threshold of the gate, one hand on the pushchair.

"How is she?" But his words were lost in a haze of noise. Vivien was hoisted onto the stretcher. She looked pale, her eyes haunted. "Vivien are you alright?" He called louder and two people turned to look at him.

"Do you know this woman?" one of the paramedics asked as they hauled the stretcher to the waiting ambulance.

"Yes. She's my mother-in-law." Relief surged through him. She was back and it had only been a week. That wasn't so bad he thought.

"She's got mild hyperthermia and a broken collarbone."
"She's going to be alright though isn't she?"

Toby inadvertently let go of the pushchair as he followed the paramedic.

"Hopefully she'll be fine when we get her to the hospital, but it depends how long she has been outside on the ground."

Toby caught himself about to say, 'since last week', but it changed to "I don't know, I haven't seen her for a while."

The paramedic eyed Toby strangely but carried on.

"Can I come too?"

"Yeah, sure."

"I'll just grab Jake."

"I'm sorry there's only room for one."

"He's my son I can hardly leave him behind he's only two and a bit." Toby turned to point at the pushchair.

His jaw dropped like stone as he saw that the pushchair was gone.

"Jake? Jake?" he called, frantically, fright rising like a beast.

"Look we need to leave now," the paramedic commanded, but Toby wasn't listening as panic racked every fibre of him. How could he have been so stupid? How could he have taken his eye off Jake? It was only a second.

"Jake." He screamed louder. The dispersing crowd looked at him curiously, as though he was mad.

"Gareth?" Toby looked all around. Gareth had smiled at him. But where was he. Where was Jake?

Panic threw its blanket over Toby. Turning sharply, he saw the ambulance roar off, red and blue lights lighting the morning sky.

"Jake? Jake?" Toby collapsed on the ground, tears rolling down his cheeks. Loneliness wrapping its unwelcome arm about his shoulders.

86

Terri was early for her meeting with Section 18 and as she sat in reception waiting to be seen she could sense everyone staring at her with contempt as if she was guilty of some hideous crime against her own family. The reception area was littered with posters and leaflets about child abuse, broken families, adoption and fostering. Despair bit into her with ferocity – she hadn't done anything wrong and she just wanted to shout it out as loud as possible.

The clock slowly crept round to ten, her frustration growing. She just wanted to know where her son was. Was that really such a difficult question? Why did she feel like she was being sized up, graded, pigeon-holed from behind the plain stud walls? She picked up another magazine, flicked through the pages ignoring the contents before throwing it disgruntled back on the pile.

Terri remembered a time like this in the dentist's surgery when she was waiting to have a filling. She hated dentists at the best of times, but that particular time she was kept waiting for forty minutes. She could hear the drills whirring away on the other side of the door. She had watched as a nurse had rushed out, her face flushed, apologising for the delay before rushing through another door, where she came out with another dentist, both disappearing back into the original room. After another ten minutes an ambulance was called and the patient was eventually stretchered out. The nurse followed ten minutes later explaining that they would have to reschedule Terri's appointment, but she never did return, only giving in when the pain got too much and then finding another surgery.

"Mrs Grant?" A voice broke Terri's nightmare. "I'm sorry to have kept you waiting. Would you like a coffee or tea?"

"No, I'm fine." Terri stood up nervously. "Thank you."

"Right this way. Oh, I'm Giles Thompson. David spoke to you I believe." Terri nodded as Giles guided her through a plain seventies-style brown door into a cold interview room with beech furniture that looked like it had seen better days. "Have a seat."

Terri was lost for words, yet so many thoughts were tumbling around her head she almost became dizzy.

"I'm going to be quite frank with you." Terri gulped fearing the worst, "I have reviewed your case file and there are questions that need to be answered."

"Where is my son?" Terri demanded, concerned, her

thoughts crystal clear.

"First, I need to ask you some questions. You have been…"

"Where is my son? You can't keep him from me, he's mine. I'll go to the courts and demand that you tell me." Her voice became fraught as she fought the panic of answering questions she didn't know the answers to.

Giles' heckles rose, he hated dealing with irate mothers who thought they knew the law, when they were the ones at fault in the first place. His experience had taught him how to deal with that. "The courts put him in our care, so please, if you feel that they will come down on your side, then by all means you go to them. But I can assure you you'll end up back here after a few months of struggling, with me asking the same questions as I am going to ask now." Giles folded his arms smugly, letting the truth of the statement filter through.

Terri went to stand up, her temper almost getting the better of her. But staring into Giles' unemotional face she saw she would lose that fight and then might never get her son back. She needed him back in her life.

Finally, relaxing back in the chair, she stared down at a tiny bit of a doodle that had been drawn on the table in blue ink.

"Good! Now, there are many processes we have to go through for you to get your son back but first I need to know where you have been for the last," he flicked through the file as his eyes widened, "three and a half years?"

Terri gulped. What could she say? What excuse would sound reasonable for why she disappeared leaving her one year old son with her mother? If she told the truth she would never get her son back.

Her mouth moved as if to say something, but no sound came out. Her mind was blank, all rational thought gone.

87

Giles stared at Terri, waiting for an explanation, pen poised to note down what she had to say.

"I…" Words failed her as the truth of what three and a half years away meant.

"Look, Mrs Grant." Giles started to soften as he recognized genuine regret. Something he was not used to seeing with some of his clients. "We are not trying to keep parents and children apart. Our aim is to look after the welfare of both, but according to our files there are issues that need to be dealt with.

"According to the files both you and Mr Grant have been absent for a considerable amount of time, leaving Jake under your mother's care. Which, while she was capable of the task, we were happy to let continue. As I am sure you are aware, that did start to become an issue. We were doing monthly checks and noted that about a year ago your mother's health was deteriorating.

"Now, we had no contact details for yourself or Mr Grant, which left us with no option but," he paused, sensing that the point he was making was clear. "In order to reunite you all, I presume Mr Grant is also back?"

"No," Terri answered quietly.

"Oh. Is he due back soon? Are you now separated? Is divorce likely?" The horror on Terri's face made Giles add, "We have to ask. Stability is the key to family life." It sounded like some mantra written in a self-help manual even though Giles managed to say it with utmost sincerity.

All the while Terri was trying to think of a good excuse for her abandoning her son, yet nothing credible came to mind.

"Well, Mrs Grant?" he paused as if it would clarify what he was asking, but Terri sat there dumfounded.

"I was... I couldn't." Terri couldn't believe how bad everything looked.

Toby ran to the corner of the street. Where was Jake? Who had taken him? But they were questions that didn't appear to have an answer. Neither direction showed sign of him or his pushchair.

Panic grew within him as everyone trailed back to their homes, now the excitement of the morning had died down. He spun around on the spot desperate to catch sight of Jake, or his pushchair, there was nothing! He ran to the other end of the street. There were two people just around the corner, he called out but they ignored him. His heart pounding he ran until he caught them up. Spinning the man round he asked if they had seen a pushchair. Immediately the man's anger, at being manhandled by a stranger, came to the fore, luckily he relented when he saw the concern on Toby's face as he asked if they'd seen his son, realising he didn't mean any harm. A sharp 'no' was given and Toby headed back to the cottage.

Reaching the gate, he stared in at the front door. As his breathing returned to normal he tried to recollect all the images of what had happened. Again, why is it that the paramedics hadn't missed time? They had been in the garden with Vivien and she had disappeared a week earlier. What was going on? Why some, but not others?

"What is it that I've done to you? Why do you do it to me?" he yelled, letting out his pent-up emotions.

A hand on his shoulder brought him, shakily, back to reality.

"Would you like that tea now Mrs Grant?" Giles asked, seeing that it was going to be a long interview.

"Please."

"White? Sugar?" Giles asked, as he got up to leave the room. Terri just nodded.

When Giles left the room, it went eerily quiet and the emptiness that Joseph had left enveloped her. Her family were torn to pieces, separated, and all because of that blasted cottage. Anger boiled up inside her.

"Damn you, Peter, why did you have to leave us that cottage?"

"Excuse me?" Giles placed two plastic cups on the table. Terri sighed. "Thank you. We were travelling." The words popped out before she'd thought it through.

"I see. What about your son? It could be considered a bit selfish to leave your son. Hold on, you said we?"

"Yes," Terri replied tentatively, her mind fashioning together a story as the words escaped.

88

"Toby was having problems getting work so we thought about the possibility of working away, maybe making it a permanent thing." Terri's mind recalled all the times they had watched 'Place in the Sun' and talked about starting again in a warm climate, especially after the third miscarriage. The stumbling block had always been Vivien, she didn't want to leave England, and Terri wouldn't go without her.

"Where did you... ?"

"Australia." It was the first place that came to mind.

"I understand that work is thriving out there, I must admit the wife and I have thought about it."

Terri smiled gingerly, wondering how this lie was going to end.

"Toby. Why don't you come inside?" The soft female voice drew Toby's attention. As he turned he saw Elaine standing there.

Toby hung his head in shame.

"But Jake, I can't find Jake."

Elaine's eyes held sadness in them. "He is with Gareth."

"What? How dare he take him without my knowledge, who does…" Toby stopped mid stream, something about her eyes told him that wasn't the case.

"Come on, I'll make us some tea."

Toby put his hand to his mouth as he acknowledged what had probably happened, in his mind he saw Jake's pushchair just by the gate. Looking down he saw the path was uneven and inclined into the garden. He had let go to speak to the paramedic.

"How could I be so stupid."

Elaine took Toby's arm and led him to her house which now held its own sadness. Gareth was gone. Toby sat down in the lounge. When Elaine reappeared he could see that she had been crying, yet in front of him she had held her own counsel.

After a few minutes silence between the two, Toby made a conciliatory promise to sort the situation out and put an end to the problems the house was causing.

Toby pulled out of his pocket the slip of paper with the phone number that Gareth had given him previously. He needed their help, he also knew that they weren't inclined to give it. Staring at the number and his phone he slowly pressed the numbers, still toying with the story he was going to tell. Elaine watched silently.

The phone rang endlessly but he held on, hoping for a voice to break the monotony of the ringing.

Nothing.

Looking at Elaine he said "we will get them back. We will." He could see the question in her eyes, 'yes, but how long?' He dialed the next number. Again it rang for an eternity and just as he was about to hang up, it was answered.

"Hello," came the bright, young, female voice.

"Er, hello," Toby stammered, as he forgot what he had intended to say.

"Can I help you?" The voice changed tone, a slight hint of annoyance.

"I'm sorry. Mmm… yes… mmm. I'm sorry to disturb you, it's just that I am doing some research and I have been led to believe that you might be able to help me."

"Oh, really," said the voice, surprised, and intrigued.

"My name's Toby Grant." Suddenly Toby wondered if he was speaking to the right person. "That is Frances Anderson isn't it?"

"Yes," said Frances cautiously. "What exactly do you want? Where are you ringing from? If you are trying to sell me…"

"No, no, no. I am not trying to sell anything, honest. I'm after some information about the Black Crack Coven." He paused.

"I see," Frances replied harshly. "Who are you?"

"Toby Grant. I am a distant relative of Lord Gray and I understand that about 200…"

"I'm sorry, but we do not talk about that particular part of history." Frances start to reiterate what had been said to Gareth.

Toby tried to interrupt her, "but I am just trying to establish what happened to my great, great, great, great, great grandfather, I understand he was a bastard child of this Lord Gray and…" The phone went dead.

89

"Actually Australia didn't work out." Terri suddenly rethought her story. "We didn't have the right professions." Giles' look questioned the validity of what he was hearing. "So I, we, went to stay with a cousin in Scotland, who did have some work."

"A-ha." Giles relaxed back into his chair, looking forward to hearing the explanation, his mind turning over the change from Australia to Scotland, it was plausible, it just seemed strange.

The pressure on Terri's shoulders increased. "Toby and I were having a bad time of it, not long after Jake was born, and I wasn't coping very well with motherhood."

"Yes, there's a note to say that Toby disappeared himself for a year." Giles said, leaning forward, mentally counting up his winning points, piling on the pressure. He did love it when he was superior.

"Yes, well, that didn't help. We were close. I was hurt when he left, it shook me badly. I was lucky because I had my Mum to fall back on, but, well, I missed Toby. He was my soulmate." All this 'lovey-dovey' stuff didn't wash with Giles, he had heard it all before, although he had to concede the sincerity with which Terri spoke. "For that year I struggled with Jake and it wasn't fair on him, he hadn't asked for it. My Mum was really good and took most of the responsibility." She paused. She couldn't see if she was making Giles feel empathy or not, his eyes remained focussed and unphased.

"Then, Toby turned up again and it was like my whole world had come back to me."

"So why would you leave Jake with his Grandmother?"

Giles's question gave Terri time to think.

"Toby was having problems getting work…"

"Because of his disappearance?" Terri started to wonder how much research they had done into her family, putting her even more on edge.

"Yes," she said nervously. "Anyway my cousin…"

"Name?" he asked officiously, "We don't have any knowledge of any cousins. We have it that your mother, Vivien, was an only child."

"Well, yeah, she is. Morag, my cousin, her Mum Valerie was my Mum's best friend at school and, well, we've always known each other as cousins."

"I see," he said, chewing the end of his pen.

"Her husband had a job for Toby if he wanted it, it was only a one year contract but, if he wanted it, you know. We knew money was going to be tight if we didn't do anything soon, so we decided that he would take it."

"But why not take Jake?"

Terri paused, why did he have to ask so many obvious questions? "We thought one year might help us rebuild our relationship, help us to start again and then we would come back and take care of Jake," she said lamely, "be a proper family again."

"Surely it would have made more sense to take Jake with you? He would always be there, or were you thinking of putting him up for adoption?" Panic spread across Terri's face, she didn't know what to say.

"We'll come back to that. Anyway, what happened?"

Terri felt herself flush even more that she already thought she had. "It was fine to start off with. We stayed with my cousin, Morag, and enjoyed the life up there, we even discussed relocating up there permanently."

"And where is there?"

"Sorry?"

"Whereabouts in Scotland?" Giles asked, pen poised to make a note along with other odd notes he had jotted down so he could write his full report after the interview.

Inside Terri's mind was a jumble of thoughts trying to conjure up a place name, it had been a long time since she'd been to Scotland and they had stayed with friends. Where was it?

"Invergarry," she exclaimed.

"It's nice up there," Giles answered, knowingly, which made Terri wary that another awkward question was coming.

"Bit cold at times, but picturesque, yes." Terri hesitated, but no further question came. Then she crossed her fingers, hating what she was going to say next, in her mind apologising for being so untruthful. He didn't deserve it.

90

"Then Toby started to drink. We started to argue. I said I wanted to come back as I missed Jake. I even asked if we could find somewhere up there and bring Jake to us. But Toby started going to the pub a lot. We fought and fought."

"But you didn't leave him?"

"He wouldn't let me go." Terri knew she was betraying Toby's good nature but the desperation to get her son back was overwhelming and the more she lied the easier it became.

"He became abusive? Did he hit you?" Again he was poised to write down her answer.

This wasn't going where Terri wanted it to go but she couldn't stop it now. "No, not really." Giles furrowed his brow questioningly. "It was just arguments."

"How about after the twelve months were up?"

"What?"

"You said he had a twelve…"

Terri thought frantically, trying to recollect her lies. "Oh yeah, he got offered an extension, which he took without asking me. I felt compelled to stay."

"Why?"

She didn't know what to say, what would be a valid reason if she had really been in that situation. "I just did, I can't explain it. Then another extension and the drinking got worse. Eventually we had to move out of my cousin's. We got a small flat. Time drifted on and it seemed I was locked in some kind of hell. My every movement was watched, I couldn't speak to my Mum without Toby being present. Then one day I left. I'd had enough. I hadn't been allowed to talk to my Mum for nearly two years by then. I didn't know how Jake was, we had also moved three times by then."

Giles wrote in capital letters, 'ABUSIVE and CONTROLLING FATHER'. Terri saw and offered a silent apology to Toby, wherever he was.

"Thank you Mrs Grant, at least that gives me something to offer the courts."

"The Courts?"

"Yes,"

"But when do I get to see my son?"

"That's not for me to decide. We have his best welfare at heart."

"But I thought…" She let the sentence fade.

"Look, I'll see if I can arrange a supervised visit," Giles finally announced as he stood up. The interview was over. Terri was hurt and upset. "I'll be in touch."

Gareth was horrified as the scene around him changed. One minute there were paramedics and people, including Toby and now the street scene that greeted him was one of a quiet late afternoon spring day. For all the investigations and mysterious goings-on that he had witnessed he couldn't believe what had just happened. He'd only wanted to save Jake's pushchair from rolling into the garden, instead he had tripped and pushed it further in, finding it impossible to stop the momentum of forward motion for himself.

As he bent down to check on Jake his knee smarted, and he knew he must have twisted it as he tripped, sinking to the ground, he rubbed it, trying to soothe the stinging pain.

"What have I done, Jake?" Jake didn't answer, just stared out from beneath his warm coat and scarf, his eyes widening, as if focussing on something. "What is it?" Gareth asked, struggling to get up again.

A firm grip took hold of Gareth's upper arm to help him stand up.

Toby stared at the screen of his phone as the connection was cut.

Elaine saw the defeat resting in Toby's eyes. What could they do? They couldn't force people to talk to them.

"I am not putting up with this crap," Toby spat out, pressing redial. "This is not my fault, but no one wants to help." He caught Elaine's gaze and mouthed an apology for swearing. The phone kept ringing. "I know you're there. Come on answer the bloody phone." Suddenly the ringing stopped.

"Hello, hello," Toby called instantly not giving the recipient time to say anything.

91

"I am afraid the person you are calling…" the answer service cut in, only managing to aggravate Toby's temper further. Finally it was time to leave a message. By now Toby was fed up with stories, he just wanted answers.

"Look, I am very sorry that this maybe painful for you," he said sternly, "and you may not want to discuss this part of your history, but it has now taken my wife, my child, and a friend, as well as numerous other people." Toby ranted. "The only answers I can find, or we can find, is that it is connected to an incident that involves the Black Crack Coven somewhere in the 1700's. The way I see it is that you started this, and it needs to be finished. I want my family back. They are my life and I miss them." Toby felt bitter tears start to push out in the corner of his eyes. "I am fed up with being given the brush-off. I am sorry for lying to you. But now you have the truth."

Toby ended the call before realising he hadn't left his own number.

"Bollocks," he said, throwing his phone at a cushion, where it bounced off and settled on the floor, he caught Elaine's look of disapproval. "Sorry," he muttered, still stewing with frustration.

"I understand," Elaine spoke sympathetically.

Toby stormed to the window to look out at Gareth's carefully crafted, perfect, garden, with its gnomes adorning various flowerbeds.

"This is such a crock of shit. Why won't they talk to us? Why do they keep babbling on about the past must stay in the past?

Are they really that shut off? I thought Gareth said they were white witches, aren't they meant to be the good guys?"

Toby heard Elaine blow her nose.

Finally he calmed down. "I hope Jake is okay."

"So do I, Toby, so do I. We know Gareth is with him, he will take care of him." Elaine said it as though he wasn't coming back, ever. Suddenly she went pale as the full force of events hit her. Although Gareth had talked about mysterious incidents and, when Toby had turned up to discuss the time slips, it had all seemed far-fetched but she had allowed them their fantasy, not really comprehending the full physical implications. Now she was faced with hard fact, and that was just sinking in, making her feel unwell.

"Excuse me, I just…" Toby turned in time to see Elaine falter as she went to stand, he went to grab her but she was too far away. She fell, and Toby watched as if in slow motion. She narrowly missed the corner of the coffee table, landing face down.

"You alright old man?" Gareth turned to see a young man towering above him. He was in his thirties, with short brown hair and a crooked nose.

Recognition flashed across Gareth's mind but he couldn't place the face.

"I think so," he said, his mind still trying to fathom where he had seen the face before, "and less of the old please."

The man helped Gareth up.

"Sorry, I didn't mean to offend."

Brushing himself down, Gareth asked the man what he was doing on the property. The man frowned and turned the question round on Gareth, who was getting agitated by the man's belligerence. "This is private property and you shouldn't be here."

"A reporter is allowed to go where he likes when there is a story involved," the man said, turning away from Gareth.

"Reporter?" Gareth stated.

"Yes, Matthew Gilbert. Can't believe how warm it's suddenly got. It was freezing when I arrived, could have sworn night was drawing in, but now look at it, anyone would think it was Spring again. British weather eh?"

When Gareth did not reply Matthew turned round to face him.

"What is it? You look as though you've seen a ghost."

"Matthew Gilbert."

"Yes. Can I ask your name?"

"Gareth Johnson, I live next… you disappeared a few weeks ago."

Matthew stared at Gareth as if he'd gone mad. "What?"

"You vanished. It was on the news. You went to meet someone, the police thought you'd been murdered. Biggest news story in Southend for quite a while."

92

"Yeah, right, and I'm Sadam Hussein in disguise." Matthew laughed, pleased with his own humour, but stopped when Gareth stared incredulously at him like he was a madman, unable to shake the feeling that the man who stood in front of him was serious.

"Why did you come here?" Gareth questioned.

Reeling from Gareth's seriousness, Matthew thought about

his answer for a time. "I got a strange phone call from an informer. Told me about a story." Matthew didn't sound as sure as he should have.

"What story?"

Matthew felt decidedly uncomfortable. "Reporters never give away that information, not until it's written." Normally it would have been said with some bravado, but Matthew was unnerved, he couldn't help feeling that he had missed something. His search of the cottage had proved fruitless. He had half expected Toby to turn up, in some respects he hoped he would. He had wandered around the cottage for about an hour, inspecting all the nooks and crannies, fascinated by the place, surprised at how structurally sound it was, despite not having been lived in for years. It didn't even look as though squatters or homeless people had spent the night there. Matthew's mind slipped to the crystal he had discovered underneath a loose floorboard in the lounge. It had a bluey-mauvish effervescence about it and he found himself drawn to it, so he had pocketed it. He wasn't going to tell Gareth about it though.

"Look you shouldn't be in here, it is private property, and I don't care what…"

"That's good advice, and I advise both of you to heed it." Matthew and Gareth both turned to look at the man that stood in the doorway.

Toby rushed to Elaine's aid, retrieving her glasses and placing them on the coffee table, before helping her back to the settee. She gripped her wrist as her face contorted in pain.

"We ought to get that looked at."

"I'm sure it's fine," she grimaced, "probably just sprained." For the first time since meeting them Elaine looked frail, a look that normally belied her sixty years. The colour in Elaine's face drained rapidly.

"Come on, I'm taking you to the hospital."

Twenty minutes later, after ordering a taxi, they were sitting in A&E. The colour in Elaine's face had come back and, although her wrist still smarted, she appeared more comfortable.

As they sat quietly, Toby's thoughts raced to Vivien, wondering how she was. After making sure that Elaine was okay he asked at the desk about Vivien. Whilst the nurse was checking, a mobile started to ring, its irritatingly cheery jingle, filling the relatively quiet area. It took Toby a few seconds before, embarrassed, he answered, curious at the strange ring tone, which wasn't a normal one for the assigned numbers he had.

Number unknown flashed up on the tiny screen and, cautiously, he answered.

A faint female voice replied to his greeting. "Hello, is that Toby Grant?" He nodded absently before confirming. "It's Frances here, you rang me earlier."

"Yes." Toby spoke, surprised by the change in her voice.

Sensing Toby's reticence, she responded. "I'm sorry about earlier but as a coven we like to follow strict guidelines," Frances hesitated, "and the things you spoke about, have always led to dreadful consequences."

"What do you mean?" Toby brightened, feeling confident that maybe he had found someone who would talk to him.

Frances muttered something under her breath which Toby couldn't make out and for an instant, he wondered whether she would cut the call.

Finally she said, "would you mind coming round to discuss it. I feel it is important to do this face to face."

Toby, still leaning against the reception desk straightened up with heightened curiosity.

"Of course. Where and when?"

"Here you go, sir Vivien Joyce." The receptionist handed Toby a piece of paper with the ward written on it.

"Thank you."

93

Vivien had been checked into a ward in the tower block of Southend Hospital, it looked dated and lacked any cheeriness – it was not likely to inspire a fast recovery. Despite the place, she looked well, her arm was in a sling and, although uncomfortable, she was resting.

Toby sat by her bed, their eyes barely making contact.

"How are you feeling?"

She coughed. She had been outside for a long time, at least through one night. After that she couldn't remember, it had been like a nightmare, she had called out for help but it took forever. Fearing hypothermia as the cold, wet, night had drawn in she had been surprised to survive. Somehow she had felt watched and looked after, even though no one had been present. She had broken her collar bone.

Quietly she replied, "in pain. They had to reset the bone, which was painful, because it had started to heal."

"Why did you go in?"

Vivien turned to her son-in-law and stared harshly at him, "because I thought that that cottage might have taken my grandson from me." Toby bowed his head in shame and noted the reference to grandson and not son-in-law. "I tried all the friends I could think of, and I thought there was nowhere you had left to go." Vivien fought the urge to apologise. She was still angry with Toby for disbelieving her about Terri's spirit, for want of a better word, being in the house. She knew it had been a stupid argument. "I… I had a feeling that you may have chanced your luck in the cottage." She looked slyly around the ward to make sure no one was listening. "How long was I gone?"

Toby drew in closer. "A week."

Her eyes widened in shock and she shivered. "How is Jake?"

The question hit Toby so hard he almost reeled backwards. It was an obvious question for her to ask, and one that hadn't occurred to him for some unknown reason. Why wouldn't she ask? Fearing he'd put her recovery back, he lied. "He's fine, you know Jake, resilient as ever. I have managed to get him into a nursery so I can go to work."

Vivien looked down at her sheets and Toby sat silent. It was an awkward moment. They both knew an apology should be spoken but neither wanted to show weakness. Stupid under the circumstances.

"Look, I'd better go I've got Elaine downstairs in A&E, she should be ready to go home."

"Who's Elaine?"

Toby tried to recollect everything that he had ever told Vivien about the cottage but his memories were starting to melt into one big mess. "It's a long story, I'll tell you more next time. Okay?"

"Bring Jake with you next time. I miss him."

"So do I," Toby muttered under his breath. He couldn't tell her that he had gone as well. "Can I bring you anything next time?"

"What was that? No, I don't think so," she said, anxiously sensing something ominous.

"I said, yeah, sure. Look I'd better…" He got up and started to walk away, toying with whether to tell her about Frances and the possibility of some good news. In the end he didn't, he would wait until he had something firm to say.

An hour later he found himself looking after Elaine at her house, after firstly going back to Vivien's bungalow and grabbing some clothes for work the following day. He would stay there until the morning when Elaine's friend, Stephanie would arrive to look after her leaving Toby to go to work. He had arranged to call at Frances' house at eight the following night, Monday.

The next morning, on his way to the station, he paused outside the cottage that Edward had predicted would tear his family apart. A strange thought occurred to him. The paramedics, they hadn't been affected by it.

He puzzled about the paramedics for the rest of the journey to work. It was like a conundrum waiting to be solved. Why didn't they suffer? Everyone else had.

94

"Who are you and where did you come from?" Matthew turned to face the man in the doorway. The piercing eyes almost making him quiver as he tried to remain strong. Jake started to cry, so Gareth bent down to pick up the poor mite.

The man stepped forward. "It's been a long time, since I've seen you."

Gareth and Matthew exchanged a querying glance. The man stuck out his hand towards Jake, who fell silent immediately. It was as if they shared an affinity.

"Who are you?" Gareth asked politely, eased by the fact that Jake appeared settled by the strange man.

"I'm Edward, this guy's best friend."

Matthew coughed, choking on his own thoughts. "Yeah right, and I'm his Aunt Fanny," He goaded.

"Just because you don't understand, don't question it. You'll never understand. You never do," Edward said, fiercely.

"Excuse me," Matthew challenged.

"What happens here is way beyond your comprehension. It will turn your brain to mush. Drive you insane trying to figure out the answers."

"You're Edward Furrows," Gareth exclaimed, struggling to get the thought out. "Toby mentioned you."

He nodded his agreement solemnly. "What are you doing here? Why is Jake here? I haven't seen Toby."

"I tripped," he paused, hanging his head with regret, "and followed Jake through the gate." Then, with more gusto, "I was trying to stop him from rolling through, Toby was trying to assist with the woman who was here."

"The woman?" Edward queried, "not Terri?"

"No, no, I think it was her mother."

"I told Toby the outcome was not good. Why doesn't everyone stay away?" Edward turned and walked back to the front door. Jake started to kick off.

"It's alright little fellow." Gareth tried to console him.

Matthew was gathering his thoughts yet was still confused. "What the hell are you two on about? Have you both gone stark raving mad. Am I in some sort of delusional world surrounded by nutters?"

Edward took two long, quick strides towards Matthew, grabbing him by the neck and almost choking him.

"You're Matthew Gilbert, who used to work for the Evening Echo, until you disappeared in 2008. When you re-appeared over six months later, you started talking about a man by the name of Edward Furrows, claiming you'd had a conversation with him. Yet when they researched it no trace could be found of the mysterious man. It was like he never existed. A mere figment of your imagination."

Matthew struggled to break free from Edward's vice-like grip and he started to falter as he fought to take a breath. Edward looked deep into Matthew's eyes, watching them as they started to bulge, as his face became crimson.

"Let him go, please," Gareth asked, still holding onto Jake.

Edward turned his head left. "I will when he gives up what he collected from this cottage."

"What?" Gareth added.

"He heard and he knows what I mean."

Matthew's eyes widened even more. How did he know? Had he been watched?

Edward brought Matthew's face closer to his so he could view the dread in his eyes.

"Well?"

95

"It's in my pocket," he tried to say as his throat was crushed under the powerful grip. Edward let go, allowing Matthew to fall to the ground, rubbing his neck.

"You're real," Gareth stated, astonished.

"What, you thought I was an apparition."

Puzzled, Gareth replied, "well yes, the way Toby explained it you were a, are a ghost."

"There are many things that I can be described as. I sacrificed my life to save Toby's, to in turn, save Jake's. Things are not always what they seem."

Both Gareth and Edward had taken their eyes off Matthew, who sunk to the ground, planning his next move. Surreptitiously he felt the bulge in his coat pocket. The crystal was still safe and he didn't want to relinquish it to anyone, a compulsion he'd kept from childhood, whenever his mother had asked him to hand something over, he did the opposite.

As he stood up, he went to push Edward but to his surprise, went straight through him, like he was never there.

"What the…" he started to say as he went careering to the ground again.

Amazed, Gareth stepped back. "I don't…" but before he could finish the sentence, he tripped over the pushchair which was behind him, losing his balance, he instinctively threw out his hands, letting go of Jake. "No!" he screamed, but he couldn't stop the momentum that had started.

On the train home, Toby returned to thoughts of Jake which had distracted him during the day, causing him to make stupid mistakes in work emails. He knew, he hoped, Jake and Gareth were together, he knew they would be alright then. It was just a matter of time, but how much time? What had happened to Terri? Was she alright? Had they all managed to meet up together?

Over and over again, his troubled mind tumbled. Anxiety rose in him as he anticipated the meeting with Frances. What would she have to say? Would he finally be able to put an end to this stupid cycle that was intent on ripping his life to shreds just as Edward Furrows had said it would? Had he not been the one to throw the dice? Would Terri forgive him, if she ever came back?

That solemn thought hit him as the train pulled into Prittlewell station. The walk back to Vivien's was a lonely one, and the cold wind that blew was like an exclamation mark on his life emphasizing the way Terri and his happy life had be shaken up so rapidly.

Vivien's bungalow was lacklustre in its current state. It was missing the very reason for its existence, to be a home. A microwave meal and a change of clothes later Toby left for his appointment with Frances.

The house was a thirty-minute walk and every step made him more hopeful. As the green door of the house loomed into view his step lightened. Yet, as he approached, he heard raised voices talking wildly behind it. An argument was in full swing and for a second he eavesdropped.

"… it stays in the past. It is not open for discussion. Do you know what would happen if we were to interfere?" came the harsh male voice.

"Look, Peter, I have never questioned your authority. None of us have." Toby wondered how many more people were there. "But you've read the newspapers over the years, for Christ sakes…" Toby recognised the slightly nasal tone and delicate crispness of Frances voice.

"Don't take the Lord's name in vain."

"And don't lecture me in what I can and cannot say." There was a pause and an outpouring of breath followed by, "Peter, this has to end, more and more people are getting mixed up in it. We know about it. It is part of our history."

"Yes, but look what happened to Sophia Knock. She died immediately after speaking about it. It is a curse. Something that only Priest Michael and Priestess Isobel would ever think up. We have to let it remain in the past."

"No."

"What?"

"I said no. My family have lived with the knowledge for far too long. It has to end."

There was silence and, for a moment, Toby questioned whether to ring the doorbell or walk away.

96

As he hesitantly reached for the doorbell the door was thrown open and a short slight man with very little hair and an angular nose stood there wearing a heavy raincoat.

"Excuse me," he stated angrily, and barged past Toby, almost knocking him flying.

Regaining his balance he saw a dark haired, olive skinned, woman wearing blue jeans and a thick heavy jumper.

"I guess you must be Toby." She held out a hand awash with gold rings. "Come in." Toby took it and followed her inside.

Directed into the lounge, he sat down on the plush shiny yellow settee.

"I'm sorry about that, but Peter is our High Priest." She saw Toby's bewilderment so she tried to clarify. "Every coven has one, it orders things." Toby still looked bemused and she didn't bother to explain further, another non-believer she thought. "He doesn't always like the way that witchcraft has come into everyday life so much. He preferred it when it all was myth and hocus-pocus." She paused, sizing up Toby. Something about the message he had left on her answer-phone had endeared him to her. It was a love for his family which she could hear in the 'stresses' of his words.

Toby became uncomfortable as she paused for what was almost a minute. He used the time to take in the room, he had expected tomes of old books to litter the shelves, candles everywhere and incense burning. Instead he was sitting in a very luxurious lounge, a little gaudy for his taste, but very refined. A cat was sleeping on a footstool, its long ginger tail flicking from side to side.

"Hold this please." It was this command that caught Toby off guard. Frances handed him a blue Larimar crystal. As he took it he felt a cool breeze scuttle through the room, followed by an energy settling oppressively around him.

"The weight of the world weighs heavy on your shoulders." She held out her hand and indicated for him to pass the crystal back to her. "Please." As he handed it back, the air lifted and a warm buzz trickled though him like a tiny electric charge. Every hair on his arms stood on end. "Thank you."

Toby went to speak, but she held up her hand and beckoned for him to follow. Mystified and uncertain, he slowly got up, the cat flicked open one eyelid briefly, giving his approval.

By the time he reached the hall Frances was disappearing through a door underneath the stairs.

"You want…"

"Come, don't be afraid. There are things you want to learn and there are things that need to be said. The time has come and the journey will be tough."

Toby glanced at the front door, which looked so inviting, however, a nagging curiosity stopped him heading straight out and, slowly, he took the wooden steps down into the basement.

Gareth watched helplessly as Jake started to fall. Before he knew it Edward had Jake safely held in his arms, Gareth didn't even see him move.

"What are you?" Gareth spluttered, landing heavily on the overgrown flowerbed.

There was a sharp movement to his left and he saw Matthew dart through the open gate. Matthew said something but as he faded from view his words took to the wind like tiny bees, becoming just a buzz of white noise.

Gareth trembled with fright as Matthew disappeared from view, haunted by how things change quickly when connected to this cottage.

"I have to get back," he added, urgently fearful for his own existence. "This isn't right. Any of it."

"Go, and tell Toby to put an end to it. I want to know that my sacrifice saves Jake's life. He deserves better."

97

As he stood up, Edward stepped towards him.

"Look after Jake. Now, go before time loses you too."

Gareth hurried through the gate carrying Jake and dragging the pushchair behind him, a few steps away he stopped and looked back. Edward Furrows was gone. Who was he?

Not wanting to waste anymore time he scurried home to find Elaine, cleaning the house, the frail woman a shadow of her former self, but her eyes lit up at the sight of him.

"How long?" he asked, knowing he didn't have to explain the question.

Elaine hugged him and Jake tightly. "Nearly three weeks.

Terri sat at the kitchen table drinking a strong black coffee, something she didn't normally drink, but the interview with Giles Thompson had rattled her and, not wanting to drink alcohol so early in the day, she'd decided coffee would be more sensible. Its bitterness was like paying a penance. She felt ashamed at painting Toby in such a bad light but it was her only

"Thank you Terri. I don't know what I'd do without you." Terri sat on the bed, shocked by the sudden recognition. Vivien took her hand and gripped it tightly and, for an instant there was a connection between mother and daughter. Terri felt the love pouring out of her until her mother spoke again. Joseph left them to it.

"What's happened to Toby, he looks so old?"

Terri pulled back slightly, glaring at her mother in bewilderment.

"Toby's not here mum, he's gone."

"Don't be silly. He was just here."

"That's Joseph, not Toby, I don't know…"

"You think I don't know Toby when I see him." Terri stood up, knowing the moment of brilliance had gone.

"I'll get dinner ready." Terri's voice faltered.

98

As Toby reached the bottom step he found himself amongst five other people as well as Frances. There were rugs and throws as well as scatter cushions all over the floor. Scented candles wafted their rose and lavender fragrance, filling the windowless room.

"Please sit down." Toby was directed to a cushion furthest away from the stairs, it made him feel quite vulnerable. "You are quite safe. Unfortunately, there are a few precautions we need to take," Frances instructed warily.

Gulping, Toby wondered what she meant by 'precautions'. Nervously he sat down eyeing the three women and two men. All looked so normal, most wore jeans and either shirts or blouses, their feet bare.

As if reading his mind Frances spoke. "We take off our shoes and socks in order to ground ourselves, which is also why we are in the basement. All magic needs to be grounded otherwise complications can arise. I will introduce everyone to you in a moment, but first can I ask you to remove your shoes and socks as well."

"Hold on a minute. What's going on here?"

"Toby, you contacted me, and, as much as I was reluctant to help at first, I can see that there is a great wrong that has been going on for too long and needs to be corrected." Frances said, placatingly.

"We hold secret much of our past, never divulging it to strangers," one of the men, who wore a full bushy beard yet had relatively little hair on his head, explained. "It is part of our coven and the particular incident to which you refer has held much in the way of a curse, therefore, we need to protect ourselves and," he stared deep into Toby's eyes, "you," he finished gravely, frightening Toby, who glanced from person to person, his mind conjuring up a whole menagerie of images about how his demise might be met.

Removing his shoes and socks Toby watched Frances take her place in what was obviously a circle and of which he was now a part. She placed the Larimar crystal which he had handled in the centre and then introduced everyone, going clockwise from Toby's left.

Phillip was first. He had deep-set eagle-like eyes, his hair spiked and the tips bleached, he looked about forty going on twenty-five. Annabel was a plump woman in her fifties with short cropped hair giving her face a hard appearance. John was next and was the guy who had spoken to Toby. Harriet, next to John, had a plain pleasant face. Diane, the last one, spoke quietly, her long brown hair tied neatly at the back, exposing diamond studded earrings.

After the introductions were made each showed a Merlinite Crystal, it's two distinctive colours – black and white - interlocked like day and night, which they had been holding in their hands. Placing them out in front they created a circle around the Larimar Crystal Toby had held.

Frances began "Please link hands." Toby did as instructed. "Now, you may think us foolish but please join in with the chant we are about to say. It is very important. It is for protection from a dark magic that is all around us." Toby felt the urge to run. "Stay. To break the circle now will invoke trouble. In turn, you will say the words 'Inostadia fragata intolberate'. This is your part that you have to play as a guest of the White Hat Coven.

Toby felt the words, 'You're all bloody mad', rising inside like a cat ready to pounce.

Harriet chipped in, "Toby, this is the only way to set things right."

"So why wasn't it done before?" Toby asked forthrightly, immediately wishing he could take back the words.

There was silence, yet Toby felt a presence grow within the basement, a dark energy that circled, sniffing out its prey, hungry for a feed.

"Please, Toby, just go along with us, there are forces here that you will not understand," Diane added, this time, her soft and well spoken voice was full of persuasion.

Toby nodded.

Frances started, "Ecoudriata hargola"

"Jigla katadian gorad fremanata" Harriet called out next, followed by Diane who sat to Toby's right.

"Wesferatam hitration luminata."

All eyes turned to Toby, who sat pondering, trying to
remember what he was supposed to say.

99

Like a dream the words came back to him and he added,
"Inostadia fragata intolberate." Saying them made him feel
pretty stupid but he knew he now had little choice.

Phillip appended "Hugtas Jimbus Yamabia," followed by
Annabel.

"Heart Hagaeta Jipostia."

Concluding with John, "dopium controdai gosai moscai."

The basement dripped with a vibrant energy that teased
them all, hanging like a cloud. The crystals rattled, as if they
wanted to dance. Toby watched as his Larimar Crystal glowed a
bright aqualine blue that projected a hue onto the surroundings,
temporarily colouring the candle's flames mauve. Toby noticed
the bare brick walls of the basement had coloured crystals
buried within the cement like tiny jewels.

"We are ready," Frances announced, and suddenly Toby
noticed all outside sounds, that had been penetrating the
basement walls, ceased and they were left as if they were in
some kind of vacuum. Even the echo of their voices was muted.

"What just happened?" Toby enquired, letting go of the
hands of Phillip and Diane

"It was necessary to create a safe zone. A place where the

curse that High Priest Michael and Priestess Isobel concocted cannot get to us, as we have yet to find a way to break it."

Phillip butted in. "Toby don't look so worried, now you are safe, which is more than can be said for the friend that your friend spoke to."

"Why the curse? What is the curse?"

"Death to anyone who divulges information about the night of Michael and Isobel's expulsion," Annabel advised.

"Expulsion! Is that what it was? Gareth said that he had been advised that it was a stripping of power... meant to be a stripping of power," he corrected, "but it went wrong."

All eyes turned to Frances, giving Toby the impression that she was the leader.

"You have to remember, Toby," Frances started. "That night was a long time ago, generations of our families, and yes, those gathered here tonight are all descended directly from the members of the Black Crack Coven. Only direct descendents can discuss what occurred. But as you might surmise, as much as we try to convey an accurate account on what occurs from generation to generation, it does not mean it always happens."

Annabel continued, "the night in question saw the end of that coven, what actually happened should never have occurred. Stripping of powers is just that, it would not make them disappear. But Michael and Isobel were very strong and whatever they invoked that night countered the magic of the others."

"After your friend, Gareth," John emphasized, taking up the story, "spoke to Sophia she was immediately taken by a suffocating pain," he paused for effect. "I know because I was there, she was my wife."

Toby reeled backwards, aghast. "I'm sorry. I just want..."

"We know what you want, and what you ask. Our families have watched reports appear more and more often in the papers over the decades about disappearances of people, people who wouldn't have gone. How did we know?" John let the question sink in. "You, we," John corrected, "read energies. There are many energies around us."

"You felt them tonight when I placed the Larimar crystal in your hand," Frances explained. "When you rang, or rather left a message, the energies lined up and then I knew you were true. Well, let me explain, the Larimar is a heart crystal, it can heal the heart and it can help you find your soulmate." Toby stared on incredulously. "If we are going to take risks, and we believe it is time to set things right, then we need to know you are the right person and that you are true for the one you seek."

"And?" Toby asked, almost afraid of the answer.

"You are a true soulmate. Look" Phillip pointed to the centre of the circle where all the crystals sat.

100

The six Merlinite Crystals were spinning slowly on their axes, a ring of white and black light connected all of them and, slowly, Toby watched as blue tentacles of light reached out from the Larimar Crystal and bonded with the circle of light.

"Woah," Toby cried, pushing himself backwards out of the circle. The blue tentacles of light hesitated.

"Don't get up," Phillip placed a firm hand on Toby's shoulder and held him in place. "Your energy is joining ours, tuning in with all chakra's in this room."

"What was the argument about when I arrived?" Toby boldly asked. "Chakra's? What are you on about?"

"Jeremy doesn't feel that we should mess with the past or the future, we should let the world cruise on," Harriet said, "but what he doesn't realise is that, in some way, it was all started by us and we have let it ride out time, ignoring the consequences. Just because our ancestors didn't act doesn't mean we have to do the same. Chakra is your subtle energy."

"What? Why didn't they stop?"

"Toby, Toby," John stated in a friendly manner, "why does anything happen? We don't know. We cannot know what they were thinking at the time."

"Maybe they didn't know," Frances chimed. "But we do, and as much as we have tried to ignore it, we can't." Frances produced a folder full of newspaper clippings." As she opened it, Toby recognised some of the more recent ones.

"So what do we have to do? How can I get my family back?" Toby urged.

There was silence whilst they all looked at each other.

"Well?" he demanded, more firmly. "When, and how do I get my family back?" he stated again, more determined. "You can get them back can't you?" Again they all sat silent.

Terri's frustration was breaking her. Two people to look after and no news of her son. Two days had gone by since her interview. She had rang Giles' number five times and left five messages on his voicemail. She drained her glass of wine. Alcohol she hoped would numb the pain as the bungalow sat in silence. Her mum lurched from moments of recognition to hours of forgetfulness. Joseph was sinking deeper into despair, the garden no longer occupying his broken heart. He didn't belong where he was and, as much as he had been a healthy thirty-six year old, he looked like a seventy-year old, his hair fading to grey.

"Damn you, Toby!" she hollered, launching the glass at the wall of the lounge, "Damn you, Peter, for ever leaving us that bloody house!" The glass smashed into a thousand tiny shards, which then sprinkled like moon-dust over the carpet. "I just want you back. I just want my life back," she sobbed. Her nose began to run almalgamating with her tears. She threw her head back on the settee. "Why me? Why me? I don't deserve this, I've done nothing wrong."

"I hope you are going to clear up that mess young lady. If your father gets home and sees that he won't be very happy, will he?" Vivien said from the doorway. In her mind Terri was eight years old again and doing her homework, making a mess.

Terri stared at her mother through salty tears, before collapsing onto the pile of cushions, hugging one tight to her chest, wishing it was all over. Willing it to be as it was. Wishing she would wake up from this world.

Suddenly she heard the front door close, shaking her from her delirium. She got up and saw that her Mum was missing. She quickly checked her bedroom, it was empty.

"No, no," she shouted, in a controlled rage, grabbing her coat and keys and rushing out. It was cold and raining. At the end of the footpath she glanced left then right, but there was no sign of her. "Mum, where are you?" Panic started to throw its cold blanket over her as she toyed with which direction to go. Throwing her hands up in despair she turned right, her steps becoming more of a slow run.

101

"You have to understand…" Phillip started, but Frances put her hand up to stop him.

"Toby, what we have to do is something that hasn't been tried before, to our knowledge, and we do not know the outcome of it. What we do know is that we have to put a stop to something that was not directly our doing. Putting right past wrongs."

Thinking for a minute, Toby tried to take it all in, the true implications of what they were saying. "You mean there's a chance I will never see my family again?" The thought sent chills cascading down his spine.

Frances looked suitably solemn. They all understood the crushing possibility of the outcome.

"What happened to this Michael and Isobella?" Toby begged.

"Isobel," Phillip corrected.

"Whatever, what happened to them?" Toby raised his voice unable to stop his annoyance at being corrected over something so minute when there was more at stake.

Furtive glances were exchanged between the coven until Annabel spoke. "It was presumed that they had been killed, hence the breaking up of the coven. It had been told and that is how it stayed, until mysterious happenings - we now know off – were first noted by the members of the coven who had stayed local, our distant ancestors."

"Then what?"

"Excuse me," Harriet queried.

"Then what did they do? They caused this, surely they didn't just leave it?" Toby's frustration was making him angry.

"No Toby, they didn't," Frances countered his anger in her delicate soothing tones. "But they also did not know, exactly, what had happened. It is not like today where reporters are everywhere and almost every little incident becomes front page news," her voice edged with sarcasm. "I'm sorry, but you must understand News did not travel as quickly, people lived shorter lives, it was easier for time to march on." Seeing the annoyance on Toby's face she tried a different tack, "We are going to try our best to put right everything that has happened, but we are dealing with time. A very powerful force that it is not easy to alter. It would seem that all we can do is close the portal that has been opened."

As the words settled, Frances said she would make tea and coffee for everyone. It was so mundane, bearing in mind what they were talking about. She stood up and immediately her crystal stopped spinning and the ring of light faded - all normal outside noises returned, things like the rumble of a car speeding past on the road outside.

"So what do we have to do?" Toby asked.

"We will resume in a minute," Harriet said, softly placing a hand on Toby's knee making him feel uneasy again. "It's alright, it's just that we need to create a hidden void where we can discuss in private, without fear of the curse. How do you think coven's remained so well hidden through the centuries. We created a cloak of silence."

At the end of the street Terri stood in the rain, her Mum was not in sight. Her clothes were soaking wet as the rain got instantly heavier. Her world was falling apart around her, despair like a razor sharp knife cut at her mentally, tearing her to shreds. She turned around in a big circle looking into the dark night, looking for the figure of her mum. As she faced the way she had come she saw Vivien standing looking at the houses.

"Mum," she called, running down the street, trying to

ignore the coldness that was seeping in. "Mum what are you doing out here?"

Vivien turned to her daughter, her brow furrowed. "I think I am old enough to go to the toilet when I need to, don't you."

Terri was dumfounded, she hadn't seen where her mother had gone, she was surprised at how naturally she had sounded. "Let's get inside." Terri grabbed her Mother's arm.

"I think I can find the bathroom door, thank you very much, I am not an invalid."

Perplexed Terri watched as Vivien strolled confidently up the garden path to the front door. Terri followed, saddened.

"I'll have to get your father to fix the roof, it is a bit damp in here."

"Mum, your…" Terri gave up, opening the front door.

102

After a break, everyone rejoined the circle on the floor. The crystals immediately started spinning, creating the circle of light. The break had been so normal, everyone talking about work, gardening, their houses, their families, they were ordinary people with everyday lives. It was so surreal to Toby who just wanted to get to the bottom of Thyme Cottage.

"Now Toby there are certain things that need to be done, and you will play a key part in the process. What we know is that our ancestors used Amethyst Pineapple Crystals to help neutralise the powers of Michael and Isobel, and we know the ritual they should have performed to do this. What we don't know is what Michael and Isobel did to turn things around and we have to make a stab at that. They disappeared, our ancestors thought they had killed them but, from recent events, it would appear that some kind of fourth dimensional hole was opened."

"Fourth dimensional?" Toby quizzed.

"Time, a wormhole of sorts," Frances continued, "however, if it was a wormhole, one would expect it to take all entrants to the same time - this doesn't seem to be the case here and this is where our problems start. We have enough power to be able to close a normal wormhole and bring back into their correct time zone the people that were dispersed." Frances slyly looked at Phillip.

Toby brightened. Life would be as though nothing had ever happened. Suddenly Edward Furrows entered his thoughts, he was the only one he knew who had travelled backwards in time. He had said he was his son's best friend.

"However, I do not feel that will be the case this time," Frances concluded, snapping Toby from his thoughts.

"What do you mean?" Toby said, not masking his concern.

"There is no set key," John added.

"What about Edward?" Toby asked.

"Who's Edward?" Annabel asked. All looked curiously at Toby.

"Didn't I te... no I didn't. He was the man who first contacted me about the cottage and told me that I would inherit it. He said he is, or was, my son's best friend."

Glances shot from one to another.

"Frances, I don't think we can deal with this." John's gravelly tones resounded off the basement walls. The morbid dread was not lost on anyone except Toby.

After a moments reflection, Frances spoke with a serious fervour. "We don't have a choice, we must proceed as planned."

"But Frances, this is something far different than we discussed, we…"

"I know," Frances interrupted Harriet, whose face had gone pale.

"What's the problem? He's only a ghost… I think," Toby added, remembering how he had physically touched Edward.

"A ghost from the future Toby? I think you'll find not," Frances concluded. Toby didn't know what to believe.

"Of course he's a ghost, he's not real, I know I tried to hit him and my hand passed right through like he wasn't there, but then there was…" Toby became baffled as his answers and memories contradicted themselves.

"What is in front of you is not always what it seems." Annabel voiced to no one in particular.

"Look," Toby's annoyance at the riddles was tearing at him, "he told me he had sacrificed his life to save my son's, therefore he must be a ghost." John whispered something to Frances. "Please, don't treat me like an idiot, if you have something to say, say it."

"Excuse John's apparent rudeness, it's just that this casts a different picture on things and we must tread carefully. There has only ever been talk, speculation about a two way wormhole in our history, and only since the event, with Michael and Isobel, did we find out about a one way wormhole that worked. John has advised me of something that I think we need to check out before we make any rash judgements and find ourselves damned into hell. We are going to have to ask you to leave us for tonight so we can consult with our elders and the high priest, who you saw leaving earlier." Toby went to speak. "Please allow us this time. What we are dealing with could have serious repercussions for all involved." Frances stood up and the crystals stopped spinning. She picked up the Blue Larimar and handed it to Toby, who stood up and took it. "Keep it with you, it will ground you to your family, keep the bond strong within."

103

Toby trudged slowly home, confused and baffled by the evening's events, wondering if the situation was ever going to be sorted out. At home he sat on the settee holding the crystal and staring into the blueness as if it was an ocean waiting to be swum in. He had phoned Elaine and made sure that she was alright and to check whether Gareth had reappeared – he hadn't.

In anguish, he toyed with the crystal in his hands, turning it over and over. As his anguish settled he felt a bond tugging at him, craving for his attention. He turned to look at the alcove where it seemed to originate, it was trying to tell him something, yet the secret remained out of reach. Getting up he approached the alcove, the up-lighter was off, and he saw the picture of Terri's father and mother on their wedding day that hung underneath. He touched the light green and white vertical striped wallpaper wistfully almost feeling a connection with the anguish with which Terri had thrown the glass at the wall. A tremor shot down his spine.

After putting her mother to bed again in dry clothes Terri set about clearing up the wine glass that she had thrown. Dragging the Henry Hoover out from the storage cupboard she vacuumed up the glass from the thick carpet. The crunch as it disappeared up the hose soothed her thoughts. After ten minutes she believed she had picked up all the bits. She saw the picture in the alcove, her Mum's wedding photo and tentatively lifted it off the wall and stroked the glass tenderly. "Oh Dad, I wish you were here. We miss you. I know Mum misses you."

Replacing it on the wall, she took her time to straighten it, tenderly letting her fingers run over the figure of her father

She stood there for a further ten minutes, pretending she had been there on their wedding day.

"They look so happy." Joseph said softly, standing behind her, placing a reassuring hand on her shoulder.

She turned to see the aged face contorted with pain at the loss of his family. "Looks a lot grander than my own wedding day." He paused thoughtfully, "I didn't even get to say goodbye. What do they know about me? What would Ida think when I didn't come back that night? I worry that she might think I ran off with another woman, I would love one more chance to explain, to say goodbye." His sad eyes closed as he pictured his family the way he remembered them, a matter of only days before for him but nearly a century ago in reality. "Did you get to say goodbye to your father?"

"Only at the funeral. I will help you find your wife's grave so you can at least try and make peace."

"Yes, that would be nice." Joseph's voice had no strength.

Toby stumbled backwards as he could have sworn he saw the picture move slightly on its hook. He turned round sharply to see if anyone had entered the room, he felt a presence around him, but there was no one. 'Of course, I'm on me own' he said to himself. Yawning, he guessed he must be tired, so he went to bed still holding the crystal, it reassured him that somewhere, somehow, Terri was close by and that Jake was safe.

Frances sat in her lounge, turning events over in her mind. Wishing she could go back and find out what had happened over two centuries ago, at least that way they would know what they could do. Her white witchcraft powers were strong, inherited from her father's side of the family. When Michael and Isobel had been spoken about it had always been briefly, they were strong, some of the strongest witches and wizards that the Black Crack Coven had ever known, hence them rising to High Priest and Priestess. But with power came corruption and in effect it had destroyed the coven, splintering it. Michael and Isobel had not cared about the punishments that had befallen many a witch before them, they thought they could outsmart anyone, including the coven. And it looked as though they had.

104

Frances had arranged for a meeting of all members of the White Hat Coven on Friday night. It was essential that everyone was on board, especially Jeremy who was the High Priest with whom she had argued earlier. She rang him after the meeting and explained the change of circumstances. He had calmed down a lot and even he conceded that the situation needed to be sorted, his only objection was to use an outsider like Toby; he loved secrecy and the less people that knew about their coven the better. Frances explained that Toby was caught in the middle and the risks involved were better to be taken by him than a member of the coven, reminding Jeremy that there was still the chance that he would not survive. In theory Toby was a pawn to them and this appealed to Jeremy.

Toby checked in with Elaine on a daily basis after work, her wrist was recovering well but there was still no sign of Gareth or Jake. Toby tried to sound confident that everything would be alright and it was just a matter of time. He could understand her doubts. The hardest part for her was when friends asked where he was, the first few days had been fine, she could just say 'oh he is just pottering around the garden' or 'he's gone to the shops'. When he didn't ring back she would say 'you know what he's like - would forget his head if it weren't screwed on'. As the days dragged on she hated the lies and just wished for his return, she knew their children were due to visit in a couple of weeks and it terrified her to think that he wouldn't be back in time. What would she say?

Terri lay in bed, it was past ten in the morning but she didn't care, all life had drained from her. The nightmare she was in didn't have an end, and it was heartbreaking to see her mother falling apart. She didn't know what to do with Joseph, he was a spare part in a world that he didn't know. He was lost without his family and she believed that he was now just waiting for death to come and take him away, to carry him to Ida.

It was Thursday before Giles Thompson rang with some news of Jake and as soon as she heard his voice her heart leapt into her mouth, however it wasn't good news.

"As I was saying we know what happened to Jake but at this present time we are unable to make contact with the foster family, they have probably just gone on holiday."

"But surely they would tell you."

"They are supposed to, it's part of the protocol, but they have been looking after him for over a year; he has probably fitted in with the family like one of their own, and they simply didn't give it a second thought." Giles thought the news would be good for Terri to hear, such was the sanitized view of his work.

"He is my son," Terri said ferociously, "don't you do regular checks and remind them that he is not theirs."

"Mrs Grant, you are being totally unreasonable."

"How dare you call me unreasonable. Do you know what it's like to miss your son and want to have him back," Terri protested, hating the fact that she was being treated like a bad parent and in her mind, it had only been a few days when the reality was three-and-half-years,

"You left him, Mrs Grant. We only stepped in when your mother could no longer cope. We take every precaution possible when vetting our foster families, some of whom, have to deal with very difficult circumstances…"

"I don't give a shit," the anger burst out before she could stop it. "I want my son back and I want some answers."

'Mrs Grant, if you persist in using language like that then I will do everything in my power to make sure you never get him back' is what Giles wanted to say, instead he played the congenial card. "Please don't swear Mrs Grant. I am doing everything possible to help, but it is not just me who is dealing with aspects of this case. There are various other departments involved, and each has to consider the child's best interests." Giles said, through gritted teeth. "Look, I am just keeping you updated. I realise how hard this is for you, but please bear in mind we take care of hundreds of children from all sorts of backgrounds, no case is ever the same…"

Terri let Giles' voice fade into oblivion as she tried to conjure up a picture of what Jake would look like now.

105

Friday's meeting of the White Hat Coven was held in Frances' basement. It was cosy with everyone there, but it was the best place for all the thirteen members to meet. Instead of being in a circle they stood facing the High Priest and Priestess, Jeremy and Frances. A general hubbub of conversation filled the basement, rendering the meeting almost a social occasion, until finally Jeremy called the meeting to order.

"Ladies and gentlemen." The basement fell silent. "We all know why we have gathered tonight. Frances and I have already performed a protection ritual so we can all speak freely without fear of 'the curse'. I must admit I was against getting involved as magic should only be corrected, by more magic, under very extreme circumstance. This happens to be just one of those. Not all present here tonight will be familiar with certain family histories as you are not direct descendants, which is why you were not invited to an earlier meeting that was held here. However, something has come to light that spreads despair, in me especially. I speak of Michael and Isobel, of the Black Crack Coven."

Sandra, a tall thin lady, with bleached hair, couldn't contain her curiosity, "Who?"

"An old, coven whose families some of us have descended from," Jeremy repeated, in a serious manner, not wanting to say more than necessary. Finally he concluded. "And that brings us to the reason we are here. We would be foolish to ignore the situation any longer, in fact if our," Jeremy looked at Frances, who dipped her head in agreement, "theory is correct Michael and Isobel are not dead, as was thought, but merely living in a different time."

"I'm sorry, I do not follow." Mark, a fifty year old short guy with bright blue eyes and a thick head of grey wiry hair, started. "We have no proof that they live on. As you said, they disappeared. So there is a time rift, the odd person gets sucked into, so to speak. Surely we'd be better off just enchanting the place to make people stay away? Is it really our concern?"

"Mark…" Jeremy interrupted, "I had that very argument with Frances, but," he paused, grabbing a file from the floor, "these are just some of the disappearances, that can't be accounted for, over the last 200 years." Opening it, he showed the various newspaper clippings, and other notes. "Now you have to remember that as society moved on it became easier to follow, in the news, strange…" he thought for a second, "… events shall we say, such as people disappearing, or re-appearing, in time. As you say Mark, magic to keep people away would have been quite apt, but what has come to light is that someone has come back the other way in time. This could have very serious repercussions, if, we don't close the rift."

Mark was about to speak when Harriet piped in, "I still think it is very risky. I know we spoke with Toby on Monday but since then I have done some research and there are many other spells we could do to contain this."

"I have to agree with Harriet," said Stewart, an Afro-Carribean man, with long dreadlocks and a small goatee, who spoke with a Welsh accent, "we are taking unnecessary risks. My family comes from a long line of medicine men who have practised many of the dark arts and there are always those who operate outside of their limitations, they will reap what they sow. Karma, my friends."

There was a general murmur of approval and Jeremy was struggling to keep his faith in what he and Frances had discussed.

"Please, listen to me." Frances silenced the gathering. "As the White Hat Coven we have been in existence for 170 years, and the major part of our heritage was to do only good." There were nods of agreement from all. "We are not accountable for what has gone before us, that is a given. But, should we refrain in putting right actions of our ancestors when it is in our power? We are mocked in stories and films but we have strived to help those that have come to us and asked. Have we not?"

Not one person disagreed.

"I placed a Larimar Crystal in Toby's hand and it told me that he is true and the one he seeks is his soulmate, and of his lineage."

"But doesn't fate have it written that this is how his life should open up?" Mark added quietly. "Didn't you tell us that this mysterious man tells him of his future and his demise. Is he not himself trying to change fate?"

"But did our ancestors not start this? Do we not have the power to put an end to something that maybe should never have been started? The spell that our ancestors used was only trying to put an end to bad magic used by a priest and priestess. Stripping of powers is not unheard of. They should have accepted their punishment."

106

The discussion raged on for another two hours, dividing the coven. Eventually a decision needed to be made.

"Quiet, please. I think a vote is in order. All in favour raise your hands."

Frances counted all the hands.

"All those against," there was a pause, "then it is decided."

Toby sat in the lounge eating his breakfast. It had just gone eleven on Sunday, he stared vacantly at the picture that played on the TV screen in front of him. He knew the White Hat Coven had met on Friday night and he thought he would have an offer of their help by now. He surmised, by the lack of a phone call, that it was not forthcoming.

In his mind he weighed up the options of what to do with the cottage. There was still no sign of Terri, Gareth, or Jake. He had visited the hospital and finally conceded to Vivien that Jake had become the latest victim of the house. Her fury was like a red hot poker in the heart and after being asked to leave the hospital, he had not been back. Two days later the hospital had called to say that Vivien had taken a turn for the worse and pneumonia had set in. His first inclination was to wait until she got better, before he visited again, but guilt had got the better of him. Although she had been awake and talkative, it was polite chat.

Monday kicked into life and he found his journey to work was jaded with sadness. The day past slowly, every job becoming a chore. Tuesday through Thursday played out much the same, his mind constantly distracted by Terri, Jake, Gareth, and the cottage.

Friday, about midmorning, he was making a tea for himself and his colleagues when his mobile sprang to life. Fishing around in his pocket, he finally pulled it out. It was Elaine.

"They're back. Toby they're back."

Too stunned to talk, he accidentally let the tea he had been holding fall to the floor scalding his ankle and making him dance around the floor much to the amusement of his colleagues.

"I think Toby's trying to demonstrate what he's doing for his turn at the pub tonight." His colleague, Charlie, called out.

"Can he moonwalk?" Tracy shouted.

The phone slipped from Toby's hand as he tried to rip off his shoe and sock, juggling it with both hands before it crashed to the floor.

"This is better than going to the circus. What else can you do?" Charlie added sarcastically.

"Shush," Toby called. Excited and embarrassed at the same time.

"Are you alright?" Elaine asked.

Toby picked up the phone, "Yes, yes. When did they get back?"

"About half an hour ago. They are both fine." Elaine couldn't contain her pleasure.

"I'll be there as soon as I can." Toby hung up the phone, placing it in his pocket before recovering his shoe and sock and rushing in to see his boss.

Twenty minutes later he was on the train home which, despite being the fast train, didn't move quickly enough for him.

At Gareth and Elaine's he gave Jake a firm hug. He was so pleased to have him safely back in his arms. Gareth filled him in on Matthew and Edward and what had occurred. Toby could not believe his ears. "You actually, physically, touched Edward. I thought he was a ghost from the future."

"Yes, I did."

"I need to find out more about this Edward, this isn't right, something isn't right."

Gareth could see the determination in his eyes. "Don't go back in there Toby. Just leave it be. You have already lost your wife, don't lose yourself."

"What should I do then? The White Hat Coven won't help."

"You spoke to them?" Gareth asked, surprised.

Toby filled Gareth in on everything that he now knew.

107

An hour later Toby and Jake were visiting Vivien. Seeing her grandson was a tonic to her and she immediately felt a hundred times better, her emotional frown turning to a jubilant smile that didn't stretch to include Toby. The usual close relationship they had shared appeared to be a fading memory. She still looked ashen, her hair lacked the lustre it once had and her skin had aged ten years. She played with Jake, but there was an awkwardness between her and Toby. He tried to sound positive and upbeat but, by the time he left, he knew it was time for him and Jake to look for a new permanent home.

He was told that Vivien would be allowed home in a couple of days but she would need looking after. Unbeknown to Toby, Carol and Tracy had visited and agreed to come and look after her.

Walking home, Toby felt the urge to ring Frances. It had been over a week with no word, if they weren't going to help he at least preferred to be told outright so he could make his own plans. 'His own plans', he thought, that was a laugh, he had not the slightest clue what he could do, except erect a security fence and wait for the property to fall down, which would probably not be in his lifetime as it didn't seem to deteriorate past its present state.

Frances' phone rang and rang until Toby hung up, disappointed, he had felt sure they would help since she had called a meeting to discuss it. Okay, the information about Edward had changed things but, how? The thought of going back to Vivien's filled him with despair, it wasn't home anymore.

Where could they go? Rented accommodation temporarily, until he could sort out a mortgage and find them a home?

Thoughts about the time since he had met Edward Furrows cascaded through his mind, painting a dark ominous cloud which hovered above his head; everything that had happened was working against them. They had only ever wanted to be the best parents they could when Jake was born and somehow they found themselves torn apart. It was out of their control, albeit started by Toby's own curiosity. In some ways, if Edward had never called him to the cottage in the first place, none of this would have happened. That first week had set all this in motion and now things were spiraling out of control.

Back at work he spent his lunch-hour searching for companies who could supply and erect a security fence around Thyme Cottage. They gave him a two week lead-time once the deposit was paid, which he did by credit card. Sitting back in his chair, he felt a sense of calm envelope him, a sense that finally he had put an end to this chapter in his life. He hoped that Terri would reappear sooner rather than later and that maybe they could rebuild their lives. Maybe he would try and sell the cottage to an unwitting developer, maybe one who deserved it, but he couldn't do anything until Terri was back.

On the train home two thoughts struck him, one was that Edward had said that it was him who disappeared from Jake's life. However, the fact remained that it was Terri who was missing. Two, was Edward really Jake's best friend, or had it been some dreadful practical joke? Toby knew it couldn't be, but something just didn't fit although he couldn't put his finger on it. As the train pulled into Prittlewell Station, there were police officers on the platform; apparently looking for someone, according to a conversation Toby overheard, who had threatened another passenger with a knife.

The event gave rise to the question - twice the emergency services had been onto the property and not suffered any loss of time. What made them so unaffected by the cottage?

As his mind turned this thought over, a car horn squealed its irate blast, breaking Toby's train of thought, he had stepped into the road and had only just missed being hit. He raised his hand in apology only to get a two-fingered salute.

108

After picking up a screaming Jake from the child minder he set off for home, or rather Vivien's home, as he had started to think of it. A place where he was no longer comfortable.

No matter what Toby tried, Jake didn't want to stop crying and screaming. He was worse than a car alarm going off, neighbours twitched their curtains to see where the awful noise originated from.

Finally at Vivien's front door, he lifted Jake out of the pushchair.

"What is it?" Toby said, through gritted teeth, this gave Toby's features an angry look, only aggravating Jake more. "I s'ppose you miss your Mum." Struggling with the key, he opened the door. "Well, I think you'd better get used to not seeing he…" Toby stopped, bewildered that Jake had instantly stopped crying and screaming once inside the bungalow; he welcomed the silence.

Dragging the pushchair in, he slammed the door closed, shutting out the night. Throwing his keys on the small table he let Jake run to the kitchen. There was an odd feeling about the place, a presence that wasn't sinister in any way but was there none the less. It was so strong that at one point, as he fixed Jake some tea, he called, 'Who's there?' expecting an answer, but not receiving one. Jake was quieter, he looked happy, content, his round face like that of a cherub, his brown eyes shone with delight. It made Toby uneasy, the hairs on the back of his neck prickled. He remembered the argument with Vivien, she had said Terri was there. Then he remembered the picture in the lounge, the feeling too that someone was there. Was Vivien right? Had Toby been so closed off that he just hadn't realised?

Terri poured another glass of wine, her fifth that day. Joseph declined. He struggled to understand why he shouldn't. He had witnessed many men getting drunk when life became hard, but he'd had a good wife and family and whilst enjoying the odd night out, family always came first. There wasn't much spare money to waste on drinking.

Joseph had practically remained a voluntary prisoner in the bungalow fearing the strange outside world. He was not a curious man, he was happy with his lot, yet the world had got so much noisier that he couldn't believe how times had changed.

"You're so lucky," Terri slurred, filling her glass from a fresh bottle of wine as they sat at the kitchen table.

Joseph's grey face turned slowly to face her, questioning her words.

"At least you know your family have gone. Mine, I just…" she lost her thought.

Joseph rose, his brow furrowed, "It seems to me that you don't know how lucky you are."

"Ha, lucky, me?"

"Back in my day you wouldn't have had time to sit there and become self-pitying."

He walked from the room. Terri stood up swaying as the

room started to spin around her. "Self pitying. I have lost my family, my mother doesn't even know who I am, no one will tell me where my son is and, my husband…" she emphasized with disdain, "… is more interested in a bloody house than his own family, so much so that he drags us all into it and who has to live with the results?" She paused as if expecting an answer, but none was forthcoming. "Muggins here, I never asked for this." She stumbled through the kitchen doorway into the hall looking for Joseph.

Suddenly he was in front of her, stepping out of Jake's bedroom which he had been using. His face was flushed red with anger, he hated self indulgent people, you got what you deserved by working hard for it, and dealt with life as it came at you.

"Mrs Grant if you were a fellow worker I would knock you from here to kingdom come but you're a woman, and not a particularly good one at that from what I've seen. My Ida is worth ten of you." Terri stood in stunned silence, her mouth open. "I will say this though, you have proved one thing to me, and that is, I cannot stay here and wait for you try and sort this out, as you seem very unlikely to do so. I appreciate your hospitality but good bye." Joseph about turned. His frame had lost its hunched frail look and he looked like the man that he had appeared the first night Terri had met him.

Terri stared at the door as it slammed shut.

"No, no you can't leave. Everyone leaves. Please stay."

"Excuse me my dear this is a hotel not some doss house. Now some of our guests are trying to sleep."

"Oh, shut up mother and go back to bed," Terri snapped.

"How dare you talk to me like that young lady. If you were my daughter I would put you across my knee and teach you some manners." Vivien spun round and slammed the door shut as she returned to bed.

"I wish you would, I wish you would," Terri choked, dropping to the floor, in a pool of emotional turmoil.

109

Joseph left the bungalow with a destination in mind. He felt so out of place where he was. Even if they found any descendents of his family they wouldn't know him and they certainly wouldn't believe him. The cold soon bit into him as he hadn't borrowed a coat, knowing he wouldn't be returning to see Terri again and did not believe in stealing. When he had walked out he was confident that he could locate Thyme Cottage, the cottage next door to his own, but as he trudged through the streets he became lost amongst the concrete jungle that had replaced the small village he knew.

Loneliness seeped into him. The strange noises of machines that he wasn't used to, the pounding of car stereo's thumping as they sped past only adding to his dis-orientation. Silently he prayed for the open spaces where his children had run around. He even missed his work on the railways, a job he had worked hard at and had made good progress. He turned another corner and was met with another picture, houses that he didn't recognise. Frustration ran through him. He saw a couple of people walking on the other side of the street and asked them for directions to places he knew, but which now no longer existed. He was met with blank faces. Despondent, he walked on, growing colder and colder.

Round the next corner he concluded he had walked in a big circle. Still he refused to give up and pushed on further.

Toby tried twice more to contact Frances over the next week, but each time the phone rang and rang, it was as if she had vanished. He now had a date for the security fence going up and looked forward to that with relief.

Another date that loomed, larger than life, was his court hearing for wasting police time. It was three weeks away and he knew he ought to seek a solicitor to defend him, however, he thought it was futile and preferred to try and sort out the matter on his own, a part of him hoped that it would all go away. What could his defence be? He hoped his penalty would not be a prison sentence, not now he had a job and a future as a single parent. What would happen to Jake if it was?

Vivien had arrived home and sleeping arrangements were awkward, as Carol and Tracy were staying to look after her which was driving a wedge further between Toby and herself. The atmosphere was strained. Toby had said he would move out as soon as he could, the bitterness in his voice was evident. Vivien felt the urge to try and stop him but, at the same time, she hated the sight of him, he had brought the family to this. She knew she would miss Jake but would make an effort to see him, even if it was only for a few hours. Maybe she would offer to take care of him for the odd day, giving her the quality time she craved, alone, without Toby.

There was still a strange air about the bungalow, a glow of Terri's presence which both felt but neither openly admitted.

Thursday night came and Toby visited Gareth and Elaine to see how they were and to explain about the security fence. For want of someone to talk to he had told them about the chasm that had grown between him and Vivien, mentioning in passing that he was now looking for a place to move to. Elaine's maternal instinct kicked in and she offered Toby the spare room, much to Gareth's surprise, judging by the sly shocked glance he gave her. Toby thanked them for their hospitality but insisted he couldn't impose but, after much cajoling, the decision to move in temporarily had been made. It wasn't until he left that he felt awkward about the move, he didn't really know them that well.

He stood outside the cottage. It was like a beast grinning at him, an ambivalence rested on his shoulders. Peter had meant well when he had left them the cottage, yet to leave it empty for so many years seemed a preposterous idea. He wondered whether Peter had ever entered the property – he must have done, surely? If he had, did he know about its strange possession over people's lives? Or, was he immune to its powers like the police officers and paramedics.

Questions and more questions burned inside him. The White Hat Coven appeared to know the answers but were not forthcoming. As if on cue, Toby's mobile rang, he looked at the screen, it was Frances.

110

When Joseph finally found the cottage, the cold evaporated from him and the warmth of his family enveloped him, almost burning. Taking off his cardigan he stood awestruck, outside what was once his home next to Thyme Cottage.

"Ida, I am so sorry. I don't know that I'll ever see you again but I have got to try. I don't like it here."

He walked round the corner to the front door of Thyme Cottage, not even hesitating at the front gate.

"No don't go in," he heard a voice scream, breaking the silence that had become midnight by the time he had found his destination. Reluctantly he turned to see where the shout had come from.

Toby sat at the kitchen table twisting the mug of tea around in his hands. Vivien faced the counter and carefully made some cheese on toast, her arm still smarting. Jake had been put to bed and Toby had broken the news about moving to Gareth and Elaine's temporarily, until they found somewhere more permanent. Although it had been expected, even wanted, Vivien was crushed by the actuality of it. She daren't face Toby in case he saw her breaking as the sadness welled like a fountain about to cascade its waters. Finally she could stand it no more.

"I'm sorry, Toby." She still didn't turn round, it was hard enough as it was. "I don't want you both to go."

There was a brief pause, "But you said…"

"I know what I said, but I've changed my mind." Her arm was still in a sling and she rubbed it as if trying to loosen a tight muscle. With the words out she was overcome with a sense of relief, the sadness disappeared. "Women can be fickle." She stated light-heartedly, trying to signify to Toby how sorry she really was, and how hard this was for her. There was silence for a few seconds then she turned and walked to the table hoping to hear the words that would mean everything was okay.

"My God!" Toby exclaimed. Vivien's heart sank, until she saw that he was looking at the paper, and it was not her that he was referring to.

"What?"

"Matthew Gilbert's turned up and has been sectioned after threatening his editor, who believed him to be dead." Toby looked up at Vivien, his own face full of relief, the tension had been broken. "Thank you, by the way. I know how hard that must have been for you. I'm sorry too. It has all got a little out of hand. I wish Peter had never left that place to us. I'm sorry I didn't believe you." Toby hesitated, there was something he wanted to tell her but it sounded alien to him. In the end he could hold it in no longer. "I too can feel her presence, I can't justify it but it's here, in some way."

Vivien smiled, relief flooding through her. "Who's Matthew Gilbert?" Wiping her nose with a handkerchief, pulled from her sling.

"He was, is, a reporter I contacted a while back. He reported on Diane Forrester who also disappeared in the cottage, although no one knew that at the time, despite her blog. She re-appeared five years later." Vivien stared in bewilderment at Toby. "Well, Matthew had done a story on her and I contacted him to get some more information on what had happened to her. He got all excited that there might be more of a story than there actually was and wanted to meet me at the cottage." Vivien's face was a picture of horror. Toby lifted a hand to reassure her. "Anyway, unbeknown to me, he went, Gareth saw him there, and now it seems he is back. Edward said 'he goes mad in the future trying to understand the cottage'." A thought occurred to Toby, "Gareth mentioned that Matthew had hidden something from the cottage in his pocket, a crystal of some sort, Edward said... but Matthew scarpered before Edward could get it back." Toby scanned through the article to see if there was any mention of a crystal, there wasn't. It rang alarm bells with him, but why?

"You alright Toby?" Vivien enquired.

"Yeah, it's just." He didn't finish the sentence, just stared curiously, past Vivien at the kitchen wall.

"What is it?"

Toby sat upright, draining the remainder of his tea. "It's the crystal, it rings a bell with me and I can't think why," after a short pause, "also, something is not quite right. When the paramedics dealt with you they didn't experience any loss of time did they? Nor did the police when I was first arrested? And, how is it that everyone involved loses time yet Edward claims to be Jake's best friend from the future." Vivien stared at Toby as he became quite animated about all the pieces of the puzzle.

"Leave it Toby, please?" She placed her right hand on his shoulder, her eyes pleading for him to leave the mystery that had caused them so much misery.

"But, I've got to go and see Frances, they have a plan to help end this." Belligerence registered on his face. "I need to tell her everything.

Vivien knew he had to go.

111

Toby pulled out his mobile and rang Frances. His excitement was that of a school boy. Vivien wondered if he would ever be able to let the cottage go.

This time Frances answered straightaway. "Hello." Toby rushed to fill her in on all the pieces of information that made up the puzzle, all the pieces that he had not mentioned. "... there was mention of a crystal, that rings a bell but I can't remember why."

"Amethyst Crystals," she said, resignedly.

"Yes?" It was a question not an agreement.

"They were used to start this whole thing. We are aware of them. I have discussed it with the coven and this Friday we will meet you at the cottage at eleven pm, you must remember to bring the Larimar Crystal with you. It ties you and Terri together." As an afterthought she added, "I was going to call you tomorrow. I am sorry it has been so long but there have been things that we had to do, first." Toby nodded, before thanking her, and hanging up. He was thrilled, this was all going to end on Friday a couple of days away.

Joseph looked into the darkness but couldn't see anyone. Staring at the security fence he tried to remember how to get in. A hand suddenly grabbed his arm.

"Don't go in there. It's not right. I don't know how but it's…"

Joseph stared straight into the wild eyes of Matthew Gilbert, gone was the assuredness of a calm exterior, he looked wired.

"… you were there, you must have experienced it," Matthew continued.

"I know what you speak of and that is why I must go in." Joseph's dull eyes pleaded for Matthew to let him go. But Matthew's grip tightened.

"No don't. I lost three months of my life. Three months. How does that happen? It's not right." Matthew sounded insane as he desperately tried to put all the facts into focus.

"Let go of me," Joseph demanded fiercely, trying to wrench his arm free.

"You do know. You have to tell them, tell them I'm not mad."

"Let go of me. I want to go back to my family," and after a pause for reflection, added, "if I can."

"Your family?" Matthew loosened his grip.

"My family lost me in 1911. I don't belong here, I have to try and get back to them." Matthew stepped back in astonishment, letting go of Joseph. "Thank you." Joseph turned back to the security fence but was dragged bodily back from the brink by Matthew. As Joseph fought to break free he was wrestled to the ground shouting, "Let go of me."

Blue lights suddenly lit up the night sky and before they

knew what was going on they found themselves in handcuffs in the back of a police car. Joseph had become quite agitated as the police pulled Matthew off of him. He had tried to run to the gap underneath the security fence but was stopped by a goliath of a police officer and after a brief struggle found himself overpowered.

As they pulled away, Joseph's hope died inside him, trapped in a future that held nothing for him, surrounded by strange things that he didn't understand.

Terri sat alone in the hallway on the floor, life was losing its appeal. It seemed tempting for her just to go to the cottage and disappear again. Maybe Jake would be better off without her. He was probably happily ensconced with his foster family. She wondered whether he even remembered her, he had been just over one year old when she last saw him, now he would be, she had to think, coming up for five. The thought pierced her heart and she dragged herself up to pour herself another glass of wine. The pain was too much and she needed to dull it. After four more glasses she passed out in the lounge.

Her dreams were filled with images of what Jake might look like, both at the age he was and when he was sixteen and twenty-one. Each image was a younger version of Toby. She pictured them all standing together as a family outside a church, someone getting married. Who was it? A bride appeared at Jake's side. As quickly as it had appeared the image faded. Then she was banging on the church doors. There was confetti on the ground, she could hear organ music inside. She banged harder and the sound reverberated around the stone entrance lobby.

Wearily she woke up, her mind groggy, every movement punctuated by a thumping in her head. Lifting her body proved difficult as her muscles groaned with stiffness. Was she still dreaming? She pushed her body up from the settee, her mind curious as to what she was doing there. The room was bathed in a half light, disguising the brightness of the day outside, hidden by the closed curtains.

Finally, sitting up, she heard the pounding on the door again. She couldn't fathom whether she was still dreaming, her mind and body were working as different parts, then nausea swept over her and she stumbled from the room to the bathroom as quickly as she could, banging into each door frame on the way as her legs struggled to co-ordinate properly.

112

Overwhelming joy rallied Toby's thoughts as the prospect of finally ending the mysterious happenings of Thyme Cottage came into view. He searched his room for the Larimar Crystal. It was small but he couldn't remember where he had put it. Searching Terri's jewellery box he looked at each piece with affection, remembering where she had got each bit and what it meant to her. Wandering into the lounge he saw the Crystal on one of the alcove shelves next to a pair of Edinburgh Cyrstal Champagne Flutes that had been given to them by Vivien, each engraved with their names and their wedding date. They had drunk champagne from the flutes on the first day of their married life and both said it was the happiest they'd ever been and these glasses were their pride and joy. The flutes were of such fine glass that they were kept on display at all times ready for any celebration that warranted their use. They were unique to Toby and Terri because of the inscription and what it signified.

Breaking the news to Elaine and Gareth about him and Jake not moving in had been received kindly, they were pleased the situation had been resolved, although Elaine would have loved to have a little one in the house again. Toby told Gareth about Friday and that the end was in sight. Gareth was pleased and said he would watch from the window upstairs and maybe document what occurred. Toby smiled.

Friday trickled round, as Toby waited for the end. It was a cold night but, thankfully, dry. The stars twinkled high above and a light frost was already starting to show on the cars. Anticipation of what was actually going to happen coursed through him. What could they do? He'd had his doubts about witchcraft. It had always been just a mechanism for a story. but now, now his future rested on the powers of these people.

He held the Larimar Crystal tightly enjoyed the warmth it brought, Terri's warmth. He looked forward to celebrating the end of the nightmare and being reunited with Terri. He pictured the champagne flutes filled with their bubbling liquid.

"Hello, Mr Grant," Matthew Gilbert said, startling Toby.

"What? Who are you?"

"Matthew Gilbert, you rang me about this place remember." Toby tried to think quickly, he could do without the press being here.

"I thought I told you to stay away. You went missing."

"Yes, I did, thank you for that."

"I didn't do anything, I told you to stay away, you didn't take my warning."

"I'm a reporter. If someone tells me to stay away, it normally means that they are hiding something, so I thought I'd check it out. I mean that Diane Forrester was a nutcase, well the story she told was…" He didn't finish. "But after experiencing it myself."

"You were sectioned, how did you get out?"

"Yeah, funny how people can react. They don't really believe you when you tell them that you only went out for the day, yet three months pass in a blink of the eye."

"Now you know why Diane went funny in the head after five years of being missing. Anyway that doesn't answer my question. 'What are you doing here?'"

"I got a phone call from a Frances and was told to be here. She spoke to my doctors first, who surprisingly agreed to let me out. Don't know who she is but whatever she said worked, I thought I was going to be locked up for good."

"Well, I want you to go."

"Can't do that. Said I'd keep my word. Plus I'm looking for a good story to get me back into my job." There was a stand-off as both eyed each other cautiously. "Oh, and I was asked, actually told, to bring this," Matthew held out the Amethyst Pineapple Crystal, "I was told it was vital."

113

The White Hat Coven had convened in Frances' basement, preparing to put right what was started over two hundred years before. Thirteen witches and wizards, each with their own task, to unite their powers for one night.

Frances spoke. "We are gathered here tonight to conclude what was started by our ancestors."

Jeremy continued, "we all have our tasks and they need to be completed in the order which I have deemed. It is important that Toby knows nothing of what we are doing as he needs to believe that this will put right all that has gone before."

"So he doesn't know that he is the sacrifice?" John asked.

"No, and we cannot tell him," Jeremy answered.

"We are many things, High Priest, and Priestess, but we are not killers and that is what we are basically consenting to," John stated angrily. "I continued my family tradition for the good, not for the bad."

"Unfortunately, in the pursuit of good, some bad is inevitable, this situation is not of our choosing, however," Jeremy went on, "it has been deemed that we should put it right."

"But we can't be sure what actually happened, and by acting on impulse, we could aggravate the situation."

"John," Frances broke in, "this has all been discussed. As the White Hats we were meant to watch for the re-emergence of Michael and Isobel. Remember, when they first disappeared it was thought they were dead, not something that was meant but, with the powerful magic they used, reacting with the stripping spell, 'Karmation', they opened up some sort of gate, which only became known about, years later, most prolifically when the blacksmith set himself on fire."

"In the great scheme of things these are isolated incidents, the house should be boarded up and left to rot." There was a murmur of consensus with John's idea.

Jeremy decided to change tack. "And what if Michael and Isobel have found a way to use this gate to travel to, where and when, they like, causing all sorts of mayhem." John was about to interrupt but Jeremy signaled for him to keep quiet, "and remember, John, that if they change something in the past, we will not know about it now because it would be set in our history, in our minds and memories." The room fell silent.

They knew the implications, but faced with the fact that they would cause the death of another human being, did not rest easy on their shoulders.

Frances could see the strain on the faces of the eleven people in her basement. "Your families swore to watch time and act if needed, it was one the darkest parts of our history, and one of which we are not proud of, but let us unite our power and turn bad into good." Frances hesitated whilst she thought, "or at least stop more bad from happening. Hasn't this gone on for too long as it is?"

There was a muted murmur but it was neither opposing or agreeing with the course that had been suggested, and set in motion.

"Now, we know the Amethyst Crystals are still on site, with exception of the one taken by the reporter Matthew Gilbert. I have made contact and requested that he be there later tonight along with Toby. I have also made it imperative, for his own sanity, that he bring the Crystal if he wants to know exactly what happened to the three months he has lost."

"More lies," cried Susan, clearly agitated at being involved, knowing that it was essential for her compliance if they were to end what had started so long ago, even though it was not one of her ancestors involved. By being part of the White Hats her involvement was necessary.

"We understand Susan, and it is not something we condone, but it does not matter what we want, or believe, fact is fact." Frances concluded, her tone shaded with heavy notes indicating that she was fed up discussing the morals of the situation, as if she was personally to blame. Families, she thought. Jeremy turned and smiled at her as if in agreement with her thoughts.

"Now have we all got the Groggledyte Stones?" Jeremy observed the bobbing heads concurring. "And have they all been buried for seven days. This is important to ground the energy, remember we are trying to align time and locate Michael and Isobel to neutralise their force." Frances then directed them all to sit in a circle with their Groggledyte Stones in front of them. In the centre of the circle Jeremy had set a small black pot, barely six inches high. In part it looked like a toy cauldron but the purpose of it was soon to become apparent.

114

Jeremy poured a glittering powder into the pot, silently, while everyone watched. The magic they were using was the darkest they had ever had to use. It was almost forgotten magic, doomed, and hoped to lie somewhere in the midst's of centuries past. However, tonight it would rekindle the heretic nature of their families.

The glittering powder hit the sides of the metal cauldron and sounded like a thousand tiny shards of glass popping.

"Dom Que, Dom Quew, Dom Quetin. Let will and time unite and locate Michael and Isobel from times past. I offer up the essence of the lives we seek." Every witch, when they joined the coven, had given a token of some kind for safe keeping. The token needed to have been in contact with the witches' blood, this was their essence. Essences were kept by the families for all time. It was like being a keeper of the gift, ensuring that it would pass from generation to generation. The priest and priestess's essence would be held by a keeper, another of the coven, for use in circumstances, such as the stripping of powers, should they break the sacred heart and oath of the coven.

When Michael and Isobel had disappeared their Essences, in the form of two pieces of metal, had been locked away until the time when they might be required.

Jeremy now held the two pieces which appeared to be no more that old coins that could be kept discretely, ensuring that no normal passer-by would know their true significance.

"Sancranata, Sancranetia, Hold over the power with which we beseech you." He dropped the coins into the pot and they clanged as they landed. The glittery dust puffed up in a cloud above the pot and started to crackle and spit, filling the room with a vaporous mysterious warmth that was caught somewhere between the stench of burning coal and decaying flesh.

All in the circle winced as the pungent smell filtered up their nasal passages. Harriet and Phillip had to fight the urge to vomit, so hideous was the smell.

"And now I must ask you all to 'Judiscata'."

Harriet baulked, but knew she had to acquiesce or face a stripping of her power, ultimately ending her family's tradition.

Jeremy spat into the pot. It hissed. Frances followed suit, and then one by one the others.

"Dark magic is so disgusting I can't think why anyone would want to practice it." Harriet stated obliquely, before doing her bit.

A luminescent glow emanated from the pot, followed by a cry that resided somewhere between a banshee's screech and a crow. The basement was filled with putrid fear.

"Now, take your Groggledyte Stones and hold them in your hands, we will charge them with 'Nookta', the medicine of life." Jeremy took each of the stones and dipped them into the pot. The blue and yellow marbled stones appeared to morph, from an irregular coalition of shards and points, to smooth oval discs, as if they were a malleable substance, before each was handed back to their owners. Each stone had its own chakra that was united with its owner, one could not be passed to another and this would safeguard them through the process that they would follow later that evening.

After Jeremy had dipped the last stone, he announced, "we are ready. Let's meet at the required time and remember to bring your watchers. Tonight they are important as only they will be able to determine what is real and what is not."

"Accussamium, Desanata," All called in unison.

115

Toby felt anger rising inside like bile. "What have they told you?"

Matthew felt a subtle game of secrets coming on. "Why, what's it to you?"

Fighting the urge to lunge at Matthew, Toby turned away, trying to ignore him, preferring to walk along the road towards Gareth's house. Looking up at a back bedroom window he saw Gareth's face. He smiled then looked at his watch. Frances was ten minutes late and Toby doubted they, the coven, would turn up, believing it to be a hopeless case.

"Toby, where are you going? We were told to meet here," Matthew called.

"Why don't you just…"

"Toby, sorry we are late, there were a few preparations we needed to make."

Toby turned sharply to see Frances with twelve other people walking towards him like a group out on a late night ramble, behind them straggled various pets, a few cats, a couple of dogs and even what looked like a rat. Staring at the group Toby became strangely uneasy. Frances held out her gloved hand and shook Toby's in a firm, yet friendly, greeting. "And you must be Matthew." Frances turned to him and seemed to scowl. "You brought the Amethyst crystal with you."

Matthew hesitated before answering. "What's this all about? I mean what do you need the crystal for anyway?"

"To put things right, Mr Gilbert, to put things right." Frances stepped in closer, "You should never take what isn't yours, the consequences could be…" she paused for effect, "beyond your comprehension."

Matthew looked at Toby, his eyes expressing his thoughts that this woman in front of him was mad. "Who are all this lot?" Matthew sidled up to Toby.

Jeremy stepped forward, "How much do you know about this house Mr Gilbert?"

Toby corrected, "cottage," much to Jeremy's consternation. Toby looked suitably rebuked. "They are here to help me get my family back. They are the White Hat Coven."

Matthew's eyes widened in surprise, before answering Jeremy's question. "I know enough. Sounds like a hockey team." Matthew smirked.

Jeremy's eyes pierced Matthew and his face grew very serious. "Do you really Mr Gilbert?" Jeremy asked, menacingly. With no answer, he continued. "You have experienced the power this cottage has," he said pointedly, "yet you still don't believe. And, by taking something that is not yours you may have changed the gate that is in operation and needs to be closed."

"The gate?" Toby exclaimed, shocked, although he couldn't believe he would be so shocked after all he had gone through.

"Toby, it is a generic term we use. But each gate will have its own signature. This is something that was set up by Michael and Isobel."

"Who?" asked Matthew, thrilled at hearing new information, hoping in some way that he could write a story on the cottage and get his job back.

"Never mind." said John, who had now made his way to the front of the group. "Shouldn't we get on? The full moon's energy is at its highest." He snapped shut a small compass-like box. Toby and Matthew exchange a puzzled glance.

"It's a moon crystal. Just another part of what forms very powerful magic," Frances started, "and just like a small part of an intricate maze of things that have to be right, including the moon's energy. Now, we have about ten minutes to get ready."

There was a silent pause. Toby was happy to go ahead with whatever they wanted, he just wanted his family back. Matthew, however, was calculating what game plan to use.

"Who is this Michael and Isobel, and what do they have to do with this?"

"Mr Gilbert, Matthew, do you have the crystal?" Jeremy asked more forcibly, sensing a hesitance to participate, or even hand over the crystal.

"First, I want to know more about what is going on? I know that entering this house kept me missing for three months. How? And who is this Michael and…"

Harriet stepped forward, her six-foot frame cutting quite a powerful figure with her long blue overcoat and matching hat, she held out her large boney hand.

"The crystal, Mr Gilbert!"

Matthew stared at her and saw the moonlight dance with menace in her eyes.

"Matthew, we can do this the easy way or the hard way, but time is of the essence and we will not ask you again," Jeremy affirmed.

116

Slowly Matthew pulled the crystal from his pocket. Harriet's eyes softened when she saw the Pineapple Amethyst Crystal.

"Interesting."

"Yes, Harriet, as we suspected, and it answers a few questions," Frances replied, her face twisted in a half-smile. "Now, Mr Gilbert, do you remember exactly where you found it?"

"Maybe."

Phillip stepped up so he was standing just behind Jeremy. "Mr Gilbert, you think your games are clever but, be warned, there is many a way for you to come unstuck." The menace behind Phillip's words was not lost on Matthew.

"Alright Phillip, I think Matthew knows that he is in grave danger, don't you?"

If Matthew didn't feel scared, Toby did. There was a sinister side he was seeing to the White Hats, who proclaimed to use magic only for good. Yet the threats were there, and he saw that they meant business. For the first time he wondered whether he would survive whatever they had planned. Was this just a trap? Were they really going to help him, or was it to silence him.

Toby was about to speak when Jane, a petite thirty year-old woman with naturally blonde hair, whose make up was immaculate, wandered over to him. "Shush." She placed a woollen gloved hand to his lips. "You have many questions that we do not have time for. We need to act and we need your participation. Toby simply nodded his acquiescence. "We are ready High Priest," she uttered, taking Toby's arm and linking it with hers.

The term, 'High Priest', for some inexplicable reason chilled Matthew to the core and he glared at the group in front of him.

"Please, everyone take up your positions as instructed. The group dispersed so that they were standing at various points around the outside of the perimeter of the property, with the exception of the boundary attached to the neighbour, which they couldn't do much about. Jeremy had instructed John and Harriet to take up positions as close to the neighbouring fence line of the property, at the front and rear gardens to create a 'mirror line'. This would give the illusion that they were surrounding the property in its entirety. The straggle of animals followed their respective masters, sitting or standing directly behind, waiting for their instructions.

All the Groggledyte Stones were placed on the ground in front of the representative person.

Toby, Matthew, Jeremy and Frances stood by the gate.

"You have brought the Larimar Crystal with you?" Jeremy asked.

Matthew looked on curiously, but Toby was the one to speak. "Why…"

"By possessing this for any amount of time it builds up the residue essence of the love you have for a person, and we need that to bond you with your family."

"Yes." Toby pulled the crystal from his pocket.

Jeremy put up his hand to stop Toby from handing it over. "You need to enter the property and take this with you." Jeremy handed Toby a Groggledyte Stone like the ones each member of the coven possessed. Its blue and yellow marble surface felt rough and sharp despite have the appearance of polished stone. It emanated a warmth that was comforting.

"But won't I…"

"Just do it Toby," Frances commanded. "Time is short and we need to complete stage one using the energy the moon exerts on time." She could see Toby's disbelief. "Toby, the reason the original ceremony was conducted on all hallows eve was because the vibrations and strength of energy enhance our powers. We don't have the luxury of waiting until next all hallows, but the strength of the moon is good on this night. It is full, the sky is clear and ideal for what we need. But, you have to trust us.

Now, please go inside, take the stone and the Larimar Crystal that understands your love for Terri."

"Do I need to stand anywhere in particular?"

Jeremy showed relief at a sensible question. "You need to find the…"

"What about the Amethyst thingy," Matthew asked.

"… the spot where it first started," Jeremy concluded.

Frances turned to Matthew. "You need to place it where once it was."

"I'm not going in there, not again."

"But you must, otherwise it will not work."

117

Terri gulped cold water from the tap, trying to lose the taste of bile in her mouth. The pounding on the front door became more insistent. Her head was still thumping, making every movement painful. Staggering towards the door, it slowly came into focus. Disoriented she turned the catch and pulled the door open. Standing in front of her were two police officers.

"Mrs Grant?" the shorter of the two asked as his radio crackled into life. "Mrs Grant? Are you alright?"

Terri teetered to the left, as another wave of nausea swept over her.

The second officer reached out to steady her. "Come on, you'd better sit down." The officer firmly but gently led her into the lounge.

"No, I need the bathr…" The urge to vomit came quickly. Putting her hand over her mouth she stumbled back into the bathroom, swiftly followed by the officer.

"I'll get you a glass of water."

"Pete," the first officer, PC Ferris, who was standing by the lounge door, called. Walking over, he saw the mess, the broken bottle, the wine stain on the carpet, and the general mess of the room. He mimicked someone drinking. Pete smiled at the mockery and fetched some water. The kitchen was littered with dirty plates and half-eaten food.

Hearing the toilet flush, he found a clean glass in the third cupboard he searched and took it to Terri, who was leaning against the bathroom doorframe. Taking it, she gulped down the refreshing liquid.

"Thank you."

"Heavy night?" Pete tried to make light of the situation, but was met with an intense stare from Terri.

"Mrs Grant, I'm PC Smith and this is my colleague, PC Ferris."

"Do you mind if I sit down?" she asked rhetorically, stepping toward the lounge, not waiting for an answer.

"Certainly," Pete took her arm to steady her. "Look, Mrs Grant, we're sorry to disturb you this morning but we have someone in custody who claims to know you, but he cannot give us a credible story…"

"Joseph?"

Both officers looked at each other. "Yes," PC Smith stated

matter-of-factly.

"What's he done?"

"He hasn't done anything as such, but we caught him trying to break into a house, Thyme Cottage. Do you know it?"

Terri was still reeling from her unsettled stomach. Taking another swig of water, she answered, "I, we… no, I own the house, cottage."

Exchanging a curious look, PC Ferris continued. "Mrs Grant can you please clarify what you mean?"

"I don't think I can. Is Joseph alright?" Her mind started to clear. She saw their curiosity. "Look, he is not feeling himself right now, he lost his family quite recently and…"

"He is fine, he just seemed very confused, but that explains everything. Maybe you could come to the station with us."

"Who are you? What are you doing in my home?" Vivien called from the doorway, standing in her underwear."

"Mum, what are you doing?" Terri got up quickly to cover her mother up. "I'm sorry, she is not very well."

"Who's not very well? I am quite well thank you very much young lady. Now please explain what you are doing in my house before I call the police."

PC Ferris stood up. "Mrs Grant, is everything okay?" this was directed at Terri, but Vivien answered.

"I'm not Mrs Grant, young man. How did you get here so quick? Did I call you already? I don't remember calling the police."

"You didn't Mum."

"Do I look like your mother? Where's your father?"

Terri felt her heart sink. Life was getting too much, the bile and tears started to rise."

118

Joseph stared at the cell walls. He couldn't believe he had been put into a cell, he hadn't done anything wrong, he had only tried to help a neighbour. Now he was in a place he didn't know, with people he didn't know, his family gone.

The noise from a drunk in another cell was like an alarm call. He'd been questioned for an hour, the questions causing confusion in his mind. The fast pace at which they came was like gunfire. Every answer he gave seemed to contradict the previous one and the officers just got more and more agitated. He tried to explain where he had come from, but it sounded like gobbledy-gook. In his mind it all made sense, it was the truth after all, but he came across like a crazy person. At one point they had said they were going to call a doctor and get him locked up.

Pleading with them he told them to ask Terri, Terri Grant, she lived with her mother. After much hesitation they had conceded to think about it but in the meantime they would lock him up, to keep him safe.

It was the worst nightmare he could have imagined. He was a hard worker, a gang leader on the railway. He had gained the respect and trust of his employer, that's how he had come to be renting their house. He pictured Ida as the cold cell walls faded from view, his minds picture of Ida drawing his attention. What had happened to her? What had she thought when he didn't return that night?

Matthew stared at Jeremy and Frances, whose faces showed

their frustration. An alternative, if Matthew didn't acquiesce was planned, but they hoped they wouldn't have to resort to those sort of measures, it was always better if people participated willingly.

"Right, you leave us with little choice."

Matthew crumbled. "Alright, alright I'll do it." He had weighed up the consequences of not going along with these people, they scared him, there was a darkness that belied their polite exterior. The house had already proved there was something strange going on. "What do I need to do?"

Frances' face lightened. "You need to return the crystal back to its original position."

"Go now," Jeremy commanded. Toby watched, intimidated. Matthew hesitated briefly at the gate before reluctantly pushing it open. As he stepped over the threshold, his physical presence started to fade.

"How will I get back?" Matthew stammered, but the words got lost in the ethos.

Matthew was gone. Toby shot a glance at Frances and Jeremy tentatively asking.   "What do I have to do?"

"Toby," Frances started, "you have to enter the property, follow your heart and find the strongest point of your love for Terri. The crystal will help focus the Groggledyte Stone. You will feel that love manifest itself in heat. If your love is true then the place will be obvious. Usually it is where all this problem started."

Gulping, Toby turned to look at the cottage. It was a formidable barrier. Was his love true? Before he would never have doubted it, but now he wasn't so sure. Stepping onto the path he turned slowly to look at Frances for confirmation that what he was doing was right.

"What happens if I can't find the spot?" But already Frances and Jeremy had disappeared from view, loneliness was his companion.

With no other option apparent he made his way to the front door twisting the metal loop catch and pushing, as usual it opened easily. With a shudder he stepped in.

The cottage was cold, and sent shivers like icicles through him, he held the Larimar Crystal tightly in his right hand and the stone in his left, expecting guidance. The stone immediately started to warm.

119

Terri found herself at the police station in an interview room, waiting for Joseph to be brought in. She had taken two aspirin but still didn't feel any better. The door opened and a sad looking Joseph was marched in.

"Joseph, are you alright?" Terri stood up, her stomach still queasy and her head pounding under movement. How much did I drink? she thought.

He lifted his face to greet her. He didn't answer. The officer looked at the two people, conceding that he didn't have a case for Joseph to answer and that he had little option but to let him go with Terri.

Outside the police station Terri took Joseph's arm. It was a gesture of comfort but it did little to help ease Joseph's worries. He didn't want to be here, it wasn't his time. Terri felt his despair.

"Come on, I'll take you back to Thyme Cottage."

Without answering he walked with Terri, not knowing

what his destiny was going to be. Where would he end up? Terri stopped off at a 'Seven-eleven' and bought some basic provisions. Not knowing what lay ahead for Joseph she wanted to help him as best she could.

Standing at the cottage security fence, she handed the two carrier bags of provisions to him.

"I'm so sorry." Joseph looked at her. "I don't know what you'll find, but I hope it's better than here."

"Thank you, thank you for your help Terri. You made me feel welcome and I feel I am throwing it back at you."

"In some way, Joseph, I know what you are going through, but at least I have a hope that they may turn up. I know, Jake will at least, somehow I do, I've got to believe that. I wonder what he will look like though."

"Goodbye." Joseph took the carrier bags from Terri, after climbing underneath the fence, his sad eyes filling with salty tears. He said no more but walked solemnly to the front door. Terri watched on, feeling her own grief welling up inside.

"Toby Grant, please come back to me."

"Terri, I wish you were here with me. I miss you so much." The blue and yellow stone grew warmer in his hand as if she was close. "Terri? Terri?" he called hopefully but only silence responded. Toby walked along the hallway to the kitchen. Someone had tried to make something of the basic room, a small tiled area above the butler sink looked as though it had been used not long ago. The single tap protruding from the wall was stark against the bare walls. The stone grew colder and it surprised Toby, who didn't have a lot of faith in its abilities. Turning around he walked to the small dining room. This was an exceptional railway cottage, spacious compared to railway cottages he had sold before, which normally consists of two downstairs rooms and an add-on bathroom at the back, plus two rooms upstairs – this had three.

The stone remained cold in the dining room, only growing warmer at the bottom of the stairs. Taking one step at a time, it grew remarkably warmer as he climbed the stairs gingerly.

"What do I need to do once I find the spot?"

"Toby, I told you to stay away."

Startled, Toby stared straight up into the angry face of Edward.

Frances and Jeremy saw Toby disappear from view, then nodded to each other.

"Stage one completed," Jeremy said satisfied, then signalled to the gathered ones to start, each nodding in turn. "Frances?" Frances took Jeremy's hand.

A luminescence rolled out from the Groggledyte Stones, winding its way from stone to stone until a complete single floating tube of dark blue-yellow smoke effervesced like a wild dream.

Where Harriet and John had created the mirror - a thin line of the smoke flowed along the boundary of property, dissecting the cottages and visually making it look as though the second one wasn't there. It was like opening a blotch paint picture, it showed black hot spots in the same places as the ones on the pavement. Instead of thirteen there were now twenty-six.

120

It was perfect symmetry, as if the property were surrounded on all four sides. Slowly and assiduously a thin veil of smoke rose up, cloaking the property, it reached up twenty feet after about three minutes. Where the stones were placed there was a thick column of black smoke creating what looked like fence posts.

"Ascenua inomdia comcarderata," Jeremy and Frances chanted in unison.

The moon appeared to shine brighter, illuminating the gathering, its bright effervescent light glinting off the slate tiles as if putting the cottage in its own spotlight.

Glancing to their respective sides, Jeremy and Frances signalled that it was time. A second later all thirteen people clasped their hands in front of them, then slowly brought them up to chest height. Finally, in a swift quick motion, they brought their clasped hands into their chests and then pushed them out again.

The vertical black smoke columns phased out temporarily before becoming sharper, like rods of granite. Without warning, the rods imploded back into the Groggledyte Stones. The stones suddenly jumped up five feet to hover ominously in the air in front of their masters.

Exploding they formed dust clouds that held their cohesion. A bold bolt of black light leapt from each dust cloud in another explosion, heading towards the cottage, piercing the walls and appearing to converge at some indeterminate point inside.

The thirteen members of the White Hat Coven began to chant along with their mirrored points.

"Time recant, time repent, time repair, time deny, time realign, time recompose, time reorder." The chant continued, unabated, a quiet hum in the night air.

Gareth watch as the coven set about their business, amazed at the animals following, untethered. Surprised that they all ignored each other, unsure of what they were doing there. As Toby and Matthew had disappeared inside the cottage, he'd wanted to scream out to stop them but his words were soundless. Amazed, he watched the vaporous curtain surround the cottage and rise to where the roof met the walls. The sky suddenly grew brighter as though the moon were being commanded, but it was only over the cottage, the other properties remained in shadow.

Thirteen tiny explosions made him almost fall off his chair as he was drawn in by it all.

A man appeared on the footpath, he had rough features, a sad distant look on his face and was holding two carrier bags. He vanished as quickly as he had appeared. Thyme Cottage started to change before his eyes, becoming newer, gradually the garden burst into life, the flowers in full bloom, the grass a lush green, even the darkness couldn't disguise its brilliance. The window frames became clean and fresh, the dusty, dirty panes of glass like vibrant crystals. Inexplicably he saw a roof slate vanish, followed by another, then another. The house was dismantling following the exact reverse route of its build.

"I have tried every possible thing that I can to save my best friend's family, yet you all still persist in getting drawn into this place." Edward seemingly glided down the stairs towards Toby, making him flinch in response.

"You don't understand, I am trying to put it right..." but before he could finish Edward pushed him hard away from the stairs. Toby flung his arms out to steady himself. The stone and the crystal flew across the hallway in opposite directions, hitting different walls before finally coming to rest ten feet away. Toby's heart leapt into his mouth fearing the worst.

"Get out," Edward exploded, "and don't ever come back here. I sacrificed everything for Jake and this is how you repay it. I wanted to end it. Instead you continue the cycle."

The house resonated with a low growl.

Composing himself, Toby checked the Larimar Crystal and Groggledyte Stone, both were okay. Edward looked around warily. "You don't understand I have found some people who can help me. They are witches and wizards, they know about the origins of this place and why it does what it does. They are going to help me get my family back, but they said I had to come in here and find the spot where mine and Terri's love is strongest, this crystal pinpoints that spot" He quickly picked up the crystal and stones and thrust the crystal at Edward. Toby felt it grow warmer as it neared the stairs. "It's leading me upstairs."

121

Edward stared incredulously at Toby.

"So what about him?" Edward pointed to the lounge door. Inside a shadow was dancing on the wall. Edging towards the door, Toby saw the shape of Matthew with his hand below a floorboard.

Terri walked back to the bungalow, depression sinking its claws into her. A familiar tune broke her from her melancholy. It took a few rings before she recognized it as her mobile.

'Number withheld' flashed up on the tiny screen. She answered cautiously.

"Hello."

"Mrs Grant? Giles Thompson." Terri brightened, hoping to hear good news, which had been absent from her life for a while now.

"Yes," she fumbled.

"I've got some good news for you," He knew it wouldn't be what she wanted to hear, but it was better than nothing as far as he was concerned.

Warmth rose through Terri, happy at the thought of seeing her son, a connection with her memories. She held her breath, waiting for the words she wanted to hear.

"I've managed to arrange a visitation at our offices for tomorrow afternoon."

"Visitation!" she exclaimed.

"Yes, about three-thirty." Giles listened for Terri's reaction, but all that followed was silence. "Mrs Grant? You can make it can't you? If you can't then I don't know when we will be able to fit another time in. We don't like to upset the routine our children get into with the foster parents, it's very important."

"He is my son." Terri struggled to keep her voice level, the emotion tearing at her.

"Mrs Grant, unfortunately you did leave your son." Giles sounded condescending, he knew it and didn't care.

Words started to fail Terri, so reluctantly she conceded that there was no option and agreed that the time was suitable and hung up.

Despite Giles' insinuations about her failings as a mother, she was pleased at the thought of seeing Jake. Suddenly she felt nervous, it had been three years. Would he recognise her?

Would he know she was his mother? Would she recognise him?

At home, looking after her mother became a welcome, hurtful, distraction, but as night drew in, her mind was awash with everything she wanted to say to Jake. All the apologies, all the hopes for the future. She hoped that things were on the up.

Toby startled Matthew, who looked up from what he was doing. "How did you ever find the crystal buried there?" Matthew stared through Toby. "Matthew?" he called again.

"Edward." Matthew walked up to him.

"So you're returning what you took?" Edward asked.

"Why did you take it, and how did you find it?" Toby enquired. Matthew ignored him.

"He can't hear you Toby, you are in two different times," Edward answered, exposing two silver coins in his hands.

"Hey, where did you go?" Matthew asked. He then shook his head in disbelief, and returned to placing the crystal back in its place. "Now what do I do?" But a second's hesitation turned a thought over in his mind. Should he keep it? However he let it go, placing the loose floorboard back before Edward would notice.

"What's he on about Toby?" Edward asked, curious.

"They said he had to return the Pineapple Amethyst Crystal back to where he found it."

"Who is they?" Edward asked.

"The people I was trying to tell you about, the White Hat Coven. They are trying to end this once and for all." Toby filled Edward in on some of the research he'd found out, and on Michael and Isobel.

"Michael and Isobel." Edward smiled. "I have seen them."

"You've seen them?" Toby was astounded.

122

"What do you mean you've seen them? Wait, I need to find the love spot. I want my wife and family back." Toby walked from the room and immediately the Larimar Crystal became warmer in his hand. Turning back to the lounge it chilled, Edward appeared at the lounge door.

"One thing that's puzzled me from the beginning, is that you're the only one I know to travel back in time, everyone else has lost time." He paused, cogitating the thought. "How?"

Edward walked past Toby, and Toby felt the draught. He went to grab him but his hand went through his arm. "What are you?"

"Don't you have to find the love spot?"

"Who are you?" Edward brushed off the question.

"I've told you who I am and what I sacrificed for Jake. Yet that seems to have been thrown back in my face. Doesn't it?"

"But you won't answer my question."

Edward started to walk up the stairs. "I think you'll find the love spot is this way."

"Answer my question," Toby insisted, following Edward thumping his feet in anger on the treads of each step, making plumes of dust. "How come you can go both ways?" Edward vanished and the stone grew hotter. In anger he shoved his front foot down hard on the top stair."Why won't you give me a straight answer?" As he lifted his back foot up, the tread gave way under his full weight. His leg disappeared throwing him off balance, forcing him against the wall yet he still managed to keep hold of the two stones.

"Shit." His hope plunged even though the stone remained warm. Managing to prevent himself from toppling down the stairs, he hauled himself onto the top landing, twisting his ankle awkwardly, unaware it was trapped in a broken board. "Ouch, shit, shit, shit. Give me a break!"

He pulled his foot out from the board and rubbed his ankle placing the stone and crystal on the floor beside him. They sat still briefly before rolling towards the bedroom, where Toby had first encountered Edward, stealing Toby's attention from his ankle. He got up and stumbled after them. Through the open door they rolled until coming to rest on the very spot where Toby had first felt Edward's presence, the stone ahead of the crystal. Auspiciously the stone rose off the floor about six inches emanating great warmth that filled the room. The Larimar Cyrstal rolled directly underneath creating a miniature looking obelisk. Toby stared at the stone and crystal, curious at the way they sat perfectly still, one above the other. After a minute or so he walked to the window to see what the White Hats were doing.

Shocked, he only saw Gareth, in daylight, staring forlornly up at the cottage. Turning back into the room it was still night, sharply he turned back to the window, it was clearly daylight outside.

The room suddenly filled with an eerie humming, an almost droning noise that grew louder the more he listened. The stones still hovered above the floor but appeared to be silent. The constant noise was coming from, everywhere.

"Toby, what have you done?" It was Edward's voice but he couldn't see him.

"Edward," he called, glancing back out of the window. It was night again and this time he could see the White Hats, a veil of black smoke marked the perimeter of the property, with shards of black smoke standing vertically and a horizontal line of black smoke wafting toward the cottage. He caught the eye of Frances as she stared up at the window, she mouthed the word 'Sorry', and, in that moment he realised the truth, it hit him like a landslide - he was not due to get out of this,.

123

Terri waited in the room that had been set aside for the meeting with Jake and his foster parents. Apprehension made her anxious. Why was she so nervous? Jake was her son, but in this time and place it had been over three and half years since he had seen her. She wondered how he would have changed. Would his face be anything like she imagined?

She'd arrived early and Giles had shown her into a plain uninspiring room leaving her as if it was a punishment. She had tried to sit down and settle, but walking around eased her anxious mind. A quick glance at her watch revealed that only two minutes had passed and she still had ten minutes to wait.

Giles' greeting had been cordial but cool. He hadn't even offered her a tea or a coffee. Another glance at her watch, the hands had barely moved, tormenting her. A thousand thoughts tumbled through her racing mind. Words she wanted to say, to try and explain why she had been absent, but every thought sounded lame. How do you explain, to a four year old, his mother's desertion? What was causing her the most difficulty was that it had been unplanned, caught up in some strange mysterious cottage. She put her watch to her ear to check. It was working, the tick sounded as though it was at half speed.

"Oh come on," she said, shaking her wrist trying to speed it up but to no avail.

The door handle creaked as it was drawn down and slowly the door opened.

Frances smiled up at Toby, sudden guilt bit into her about the outcome of the night, she knew he was lost now and mouthing the word "Sorry" was the best she could offer. She knew it was a hollow apology but somehow it justified everything.

Jeremy turned to face Frances. "Ready?" Frances nodded approval and then looked to John, signaling that it was time for the final part. John pulled an ancestral time-line quartz crystal from his pocket. It acted like a lighthouse beam sending an intense bright white flame towards the cottage diagonally upwards, but following the line of the black smoke trail.

John then spoke aloud. "Rectify the time line. Close the window that remains open. Correct the dimensions of time."

Next to him, Phillip did the same, producing another ancestral time-line quartz crystal which reacted the same way, producing a brilliant white flame of light that pierced the cottage somewhere upstairs. In turn, all members of the White Hats repeated the procedure until half of a twenty-two sided pyramid was formed by the bright white flames. The points of which converged directly above the black smoke streams.

Their noise grew as each added their voice to the recital.

Toby watched as day turned to night then back to day outside in quick succession whilst inside in remained night-time. He caught glimpses of the coven as they performed the ritual. These were interspersed with other people staring up at the cottage, Gareth and other unfamiliar faces. One looked like a young Edward but the image faded too quickly for Toby to be sure. At one point he thought he saw Terri with a young boy aged about six or seven but, again, he couldn't be sure.

"Toby," an angry voice called, and he turned to see three people standing in the doorway to the room. Edward flanked by two older looking people.

Gareth watched amazed as the fabulous light and smoke show played out in front of him.

"I brought you some tea love. You've been up here for hours."

"Shush, something's happening. Toby's gone into the cottage."

Elaine walked to the window to view what Gareth was seeing. "What are you looking at?"

"The cottage. Thyme Cottage. They've just produced these stones and you can see the trail of bright white light. From here it looks almost like a many-sided pyramid."

Elaine inched to the window, nudging Gareth over slightly. "Where?"

Astonished, Gareth turned to Elaine and, despite the light being off, looked at her in disbelief. "What do you mean where? It's in front of you."

"I can't see anything."

"Do those glasses work? Look." He stood up sharply and pointed to where he was looking. "See?"

"See what? There's nothing to see."

"Don't be stupid, of course there is. See the thirteen people standing around the property, well they are the White Hat coven…"

"I can't see anyone."

"Are you mad? They're there." He grabbed her shoulder firmly but gently and pushed her closer to the window.

"I can't see anyone."

124

Perplexed, Gareth sat down again.

"Now there is no need to be rude. You can stay up here as long as you like for all I care but don't insult me," Elaine reprimanded.

"But..."

"Goodnight," she said coldly, and left the room.

Gareth looked out of the window trying to fathom who was mad, him or his wife. Still the light show blazed on and within a few seconds he had forgotten the exchange with Elaine, remaining transfixed with the cottage.

Jeremy smiled up at Gareth and for a minute a shiver ran down his spine.

The door opened wider and Terri rocked backwards as a small blondee- haired boy walked into the room holding an adult's hand, his brown eyes shone like beacons. As he saw Terri he buried his face behind the arm of the adult, a tall, slender woman with soft pale features, wearing the minimum of make-up. To Terri she looked kindly and gentle, motherly, which immediately got her back up.

To add insult to injury when she offered words of support to Jake they were full of love and affection. Terri felt every bit of guilt tear into her, from being absent from his life, to returning and taking him away from someone who projected absolute trust.

The woman's voice was confident and friendly. "Come on

Jake, don't be shy." Then turning to face Terri she asked, "Terri?"

Terri's voice caught and barely an acknowledgement came out.

"He's a bit shy I'm afraid. I told him he was going to meet his Mum."

Terri bit her bottom lip as a wave of emotion ran through her. She couldn't believe how much he had grown, she barely saw the baby in the boy before her, but there was no doubt that the eyes were Jake's.

She stepped towards him, causing Jake to squeeze even tighter into the woman's side.

"Come on Jake," the woman offered. "You said you were looking forward to meeting your Mum. We told you she would be back, didn't we?" Jake hid his face from Terri. "I'm sorry Terri, he was looking forward to it." The woman tried to placate.

"That's alright," Terri choked. "I must be like a stranger to him now..." She realised she didn't even know the woman's name.

Almost with ESP ability the woman introduced herself. "Rebecca. Some people call me Becky, Becca, whatever, I'll answer to most things," she joked.

Terri hated this woman, she was so nice and personable, and probably a good mother.

"I hope you don't mind but I brought some of his drawings with us, I thought you might like to see them." Rebecca held out a carrier bag stuffed full of paper.

"No," Jake shouted, reaching for the bag. "Mine."

Rebecca knelt down. "Now, now, Jake. Your mother would like to look at your drawings. Don't you want her to see what a talented young man you are?"

"No!" Jake snatched at the bag, Rebecca looked awkward.

"I'm so sorry Terri." Her face showing the sort of embarrassment, that could only endear sympathy.

"No, it's alright." Terri, managed to sound more confident. "He doesn't know me anymore." Then looked directly at Jake, who tried his best to hide his face again in Rebecca's side. "Don't you remember me Jake? Look, this is you." She pulled a wad of photographs from her bag, which she placed on the floor. "You were only six months old. There's your father, Toby." She pointed to another photo, "and Granny Vivien."

Jake tried to hide his curiosity but one eye peeped at the photos.

"He's normally such a chatty boy, you can't keep him quiet," Rebecca added.

"Look, there's you with your favourite cuddly toy." The picture showed Jake holding a hand-knitted rough looking teddy-bear. Jake moved from Rebecca's side, still holding her hand, and reached into the carrier bag, drawing out the original Teddy. Finally he let go of Rebecca's hand and stepped tentatively toward Terri, who tried to control the flood of tears that were close, joyous that there appeared to be some recognition there.

Holding the Teddy out he said boldly, "Olly."

125

"Toby, these are my parents." Toby stared at Edward incredulously as twenty-six bright light flames pierced the room converging on the Larimar Crystal.

"Your parents?"

"Michael and Isobel," Michael said, offering his hand, "It's so nice to meet you at last, we've known Jake a long time and he talked about you but it was a shame that we never got to meet you." Toby took the hand, which was cold and almost had no substance to it.

Toby felt himself falling backwards, it was all too weird to comprehend, his mind reeling with information overload as the pieces started to slip into place. "Michael and Isobel."

As Jake took another step towards Terri his assuredness grew, briefly glancing back at Rebecca who had been his stand-in mother for the last year and with whom a bond of trust had grown.

"It's alright Jake, Terri's your mother." Then to Terri, "He's a lovely boy, I'll be sad to see him go. I know you shouldn't have favourites, but life's not always that easy."

Terri's ears pricked up. "See him go. Why? Where's he going?" The panic like bile in her throat.

"Oh, didn't they tell you? Maybe I shouldn't have said anything. Well I believe it is just a formality, but there is a court hearing in two weeks to hear the facts and then the decision to return him from care to you will be made. It doesn't happen very often with some of the kids I have homed but you get to recognise the good ones." Terri cocked her head with curiousity. "Sorry, good mothers. Giles said, well maybe it would be best if I let him tell you himself." Rebecca stepped in closer as if to pass on a secret. "It will all be fine."

Terri hadn't noticed that Jake had slipped his hand into hers. "You smell," he said matter-of-factly.

"Sorry."

"Jake, that's rude to talk to people like that." Rebecca admonished forgetting that his real mother was there and should be dishing out any reprimand. But Terri eyed Rebecca thankfully.

The look on Jake's face gave way to what he actually meant.

"I think he recognises your scent," Rebecca added.

Both women smiled and Terri gripped Jake's hand tighter, feeling a well of motherly love brimming over.

"How do you fancy coming home and seeing Granny."

Jake shrugged.

"Thank you. Thank you for taking care of my boy." All hatred for Rebecca vanished, replaced with respect. Terri's realization that her initial resentment was misplaced.

"You're welcome. As I said I wish all the kids were like him, it would be so much easier."

The two women sat down and chatted like old friends, whilst Jake's original reluctance turned into an enthusiastic showing-off, pulling all his drawings out of the carrier bag he spread them out on the floor, before thrusting each one into Terri's hands for her approval and telling her all about it.

"Edward. Edward Furrows." Matthew called. "Toby." There was no answer as he wandered around the cottage. He thought back to the Amethyst Crystal that he had just replaced where he had found it. Temptation to take it again was high on his agenda, his natural curiosity made him hate just following instructions. "Damn it, why should I do as I'm told. It's probably all…" He stopped mid sentence. How could he forget that he had lost time, been missing for weeks, lost his job."

He was in the kitchen and, from below the floor, he saw a bright glow of yellowy-white light, illuminating the cracks that looked like a stave.

"What the…"

126

Inexplicably Matthew felt a glowing presence behind him and, turning, saw another glowing light, then another. Wandering around the ground floor he found thirteen in all creating a circle of light. Black streams of smoke met at a single point in the middle of the circle. A tree started to grow, yet it didn't break the floor boards. Like speeded-up film it rose two, three, four feet, it reached the ceiling and continued through the floor, then there was a flash of lightning and the tree buckled and twisted. A massive split opened up and the top of the tree fell. As it hit the ground it continued to grow. Not once did it affect the building, it had no physical presence.

The tree burst into flames and smoke filled the room, choking Matthew, even though he couldn't feel the heat from the flames or the firmness of the tree. As screams filtered through the room he attempted to run, but the smoke became acrid, making him cough and splutter, the smell of burning flesh irritating his nostrils. Fighting his way to the door he almost collapsed, pure will power keeping him going.

Finally, he reached the front door, yanking it so hard, it almost came off its hinges. The fresh air was like welcome nectar cooling his burning throat. Stepping outside, he noticed it was daylight, the street was empty, the White Hat coven were gone. At the gate his first thought was that he had lost time again but there was an unfamiliar air about the street, an unfamiliar air that was not of the future but more a step back into the past. The houses looked fresh and new. Was he dreaming? He pinched himself to see whether the nightmare had stopped.

It was real.

At the gate he turned back to look at the cottage, petals from roses flew up from the ground of the tended garden and rejoined onto the heads, all the time growing brighter and more vivid in colour. The heads closed up and shrunk, the circle of life spiraling backwards. The grass sprang from the neat lawn to unwieldy, and back again, in quick succession. Voices swirled around in the air, yet he saw no one.

Slate tiles appeared in piles at his feet as the neat gardens turned into a quagmire of debris from building materials. The piles grew higher and quicker. Looking up he saw the roof stripped bare. The pine sarking glistened under a morning dew, this also disappeared, forming a neat pile near the base of the walls, exposing the skeletal roof structure. Turning to the street, the house across the road had vanished, the road had become a dirt track, the trees that lined the road were mere saplings. Spinning around, the house had been reduced to foundations. These gradually faded from view and the ground beneath his feet just a field. The whole row of railway cottages had gone. A barn suddenly appeared and the world started to spin faster and faster in front of Matthew. A voice caught him unaware and he almost tripped over as he steadied himself.

"Can I help you sir?" The figure standing in front of him was dressed in black with a white collar. "Sir are you alright, you look as though the illness has taken you."

"The illness?" Matthew questioned, convinced that it was all a dream. "What illness? Where am I? What's going on?"

The kindly vicar held Matthew's arm and guided him out of the field to a dirt road that led to the church.

"I am afraid sir the whole village is with sickness. People fear it is the plague. You really shouldn't be out. The sheriff has…"

"I don't understand, I… I…" Matthew's breath came quickly as a mist formed in front of his eyes, finally he collapsed at the vicar's feet.

"That's impossible," Toby stammered, stunned at the realisation of his thoughts. "No?" It was a question rather than a statement.

"Why do you find it so hard to believe?" Isobel asked, her voice a rasp.

"You have started what we hoped you wouldn't," Michael added, looking at the light flames converging on the stone and crystal.

"I want my family back. I am doing what needs to be done. Putting an end to all of this, getting back to the beginning. That way Edward won't sacrifice anything for Jake and I will see my family grow up," Toby said, growing more assured with every word.

Edward stepped forward and placed a hand on Toby's shoulder. Toby felt the strength that rested there. Edward's eyes pierced Toby's soul. "Toby, this is exactly what took you away from your family."

127

"No," Toby cried, stepping backwards cutting one of the light flames and scorching his flesh through his jeans, causing him step toward the wall away from Edward and his family. "This will set time straight. They said it would. They said this would close the gate."

"What else did they tell you, Toby?" Michael asked firmly.

Toby's mind ran wildly from clear thought to a vivid imagery of the information he had found out about the cottage, the Black Crack Coven and the history of Prittlewell. A well of information surged around his frantic brain, trying to form some kind of coherent understanding.

Isobel stepped toward Toby, her hand outstretched. "We were wronged Toby, and we have paid a heavy price for that. We could have accepted our new lives but we found out about the repercussions it had on your family and that's when Edward made his sacrifice," She turned, looking affectionately at her son. "He wanted to save Jake and his family, they were friends from Playschool but slowly, in his early teens, Jake became obsessed with this place." She threw her hands out to encompass the cottage. "Slowly but surely it took him as he tried to find out what happened to you." She rested a hand on his shoulder.

"But I've tried to stop that from happening, I've tried…" Toby lamented lamely.

"No, Toby, you've allowed it to bend you to its will and you have followed the path we had so hoped you would avoid." Michael moved in closer.

Toby's legs started buckle, it was all too much for him to take in, everything he thought he had done to prevent this had led him directly to it. As he slumped to his knees, the house filled with an acrid burning smell.

"I don't know what to say. What do I do?" Toby implored, as all hope diminished. Isobel turned to Michael and both turned to Edward, who shrugged.

As Toby stared at the family in front of him. They faded from view like vaporous apparitions. "Don't go. What do I do?"

Edward stared at him as Michael and Isobel dissolved completely. Had he heard Toby? He couldn't tell but the vacant dark eyes remained fixed on him.

"I'm sorry." Suddenly he felt a renewed vigour at the betrayal, they could have just told him in the first place. "Why didn't you just tell me?" he shouted at the figure of Edward, who seemed lost to him now.

The plaster started to vanish from the walls, the lath and plaster ceiling deconstructing itself. Toby heard Terri calling his name.

"Toby, talk to me please, Toby." A mobile phone and a clipboard appeared on the floor. The tiny screen was glowing in the darkened room, his clipboard and tape measure sat beside it. Then he saw himself on all fours before everything vanished from sight.

The air around him turned cold. An impulse made him look up. The roof was gone, the last timber joists faded from view, the internal doors phased out of sight, slowly the walls came down, the windows were now just holes. Looking down he saw the floor had gone, yet he didn't fall. He was suspended in mid air.

He could see the area around the dismantling cottage reverting back to its original state of fields and unobstructed views of farmland.

A tree started to grow, a small sapling turning into a mighty tree that was crooked and bent. It burst into flames and Toby shielded his eyes from the ferocity but felt no pain from the tentacles of fire licking at his body.

A deep cry of pain in the distance caught his attention and he looked over the field towards a burning barn, in time to see a man running from it.

All went quiet as a bright ring of light connecting thirteen pineapple amethyst crystals appeared on the ground. The light source came from below the soil.

Chanting filled the air, and clearly in view were thirteen people wearing full length monk-type cloaks. In the middle of the ring of light, he saw the faces of two people he now knew.

128

Terri's walk home was difficult, she had finally connected with her son, the bonds confirmed as still being there, and she felt the positivity, she would be reunited with him, her son, and soon. Giles had even conceded as much at the end of the session which he had observed from behind a mirrored partition. Even he couldn't deny the love they shared. He had witnessed many a fake attempt when a mother had the time to spend with a daughter or son and he'd seen fear in the child's eyes, the reluctance of the child to enjoy the situation. But Jake's reunion with his mother had been a joy to watch, the love was reciprocated and he'd have no trouble recommending that full ward be granted back to Terri with a stipulation for regular checks.

As Terri neared home, Vivien came into view, she was sitting on the front wall in her nighty. Her joy lapsed as she wondered what she should do with her Mum, whom she loved so much, but who now was just a shell. Vivien was now just an occasional presence, a flash in the darkness. How long would she go on like this? As hurtful as the thought was, she hoped that death would take Vivien. In her heart she knew her Mum would want it, she would hate the confusion, she would hate that she had become a burden on her daughter, and most of all she had always wished for a diginified death.

"What are you doing out here Mum, you'll freeze to death?"

"I've been waiting for the ten-twenty-two bus to Colchester. It seems to be running late. I've never known it to be so late. The driver, George, is a stickler for timing. You ask your father? If it gets much later I'll be late for work."

"Mum you don't work anymore," Terri replied wearily, seeing her usually so 'bright as a new penny' mother falling foul of the disease that was addling her brain.

"Of course I work. Who do you think pays for your new school clothes." Terri lent forward to grab Vivien's arm but she vehemently shook it loose. "Excuse me young woman, what on earth do you think you're doing?"

"Please come inside," Terri pleaded as Vivien's eyes glazed over.

"Where am I?" Vivien asked, confused.

Terri took her arm and silently led her indoors.

"Michael, Isobel," Toby called. They looked up at him as though he was a guardian angel. They both smiled. Looking around the circle of thirteen, he tried to focus on the one voice that cut through the chanting, its gravelly tones like a rumble of thunder.

"High Priest Michael and High Priestess Isobel, you are charged with using black magic for retribution, this is against our charter and you are to be stripped of your powers…"

Michael and Isobel stood silently, not protesting against the charges that were being detailed.

Michael spoke as a cartwheel of bright yellow-white light, emanated from the pineapple crystals buried in the ground. Shock became clearly visible in the body language of the gathered ones.

Michael shouted as a crack thundered through the night sky. "The truth will be with us. The mighty rise tonight, the weak fall. To ourselves we offer protection and to you all we condemn you to eternal damnation."

The cartwheel of light died down and the black night appeared to grow even darker, making it difficult to see anything.

"Michael and Isobel Furrows, we condemn you to a life of normality." But as the moon brightened, the figures stood dismayed, all that remained of Michael and Isobel were two effervescent blue circles on the ground. On closer inspection they were piles of blue powder.

Blank looks passed from one to another, agitation clearly visible, fear casting its blanket.

"What have we done Jacob?" cried Mary.

Sobs came from a member who had fallen to the ground. "I didn't mean it. I only meant to avenge their sadness. I didn't mean for this to happen," a young woman with straggly straw-like hair explained.

"What did you do Betsy?" the man asked, walking over to her, along with the rest of the coven, who had formed a circle around her.

"I put a spell on Lord Gray."

129

Suddenly the image around him became a swirl of smoke. Toby found himself back in the room with Michael and Isobel, their faces solemn, their clothes old-fashioned. His mind clicked the pieces together, this was the Michael and Isobel he had just witnessed, their faces were locked in shock, neither one of them speaking, just staring at the room in which they found themselves.

A minute of silence passed before Isobel found the courage to speak.

"Michael, what just happened?"

"I don't know my sweet. Do you have any idea of where we are?" Michael stood rooted to the spot.

Wandering to the dirty window Isobel looked out but the scene outside made her feel faint and she wobbled backwards, the room spinning deliriously around her.

"Isobel, what is it?" Michael rushed to her aid, catching her as she started to topple. She didn't reply.

Michael helped her gently to the floor where she sat, before he too walked to the window. His eyes widened in alarm. "What happened?" The row of terraced houses stood proudly opposite, curtains still pulled tight to leave the slumbering occupants sheltered from the early morning sunrise. Watching the sunrise reflecting off the coloured metal boxes Michael found himself in shock. Four black wheels, glass reflecting the dazzling sunlight as it broke the sky. He wanted to turn away but found himself questioning reality, blinking, he wanted the outside world to disappear.

Turning back to Isobel, he wanted to reassure her but words failed him. As thoughts turned into realisations, he asked Isobel to get out her Moldavite Crystal which he had gifted to her on their wedding day. It was a rare crystal which he had acquired through his travels to the Continent before they had met. It had been broken in two and they shared halves.

They sat crossed-legged in the middle of the room and placed the Moldavite crystals on their third eyes.

Toby watched as they entered a trance, facing each other. Michael spoke slowly and clearly.

"Father time, Mother nature, assist two souls who have lost their way. Place us at your will and guide us into this new life." Toby stood amazed as the room once again started to fade and the open field reappeared, the twisted oak tree stood proud. A bright circle of white lights glowed in the ground. A figure wearing a shawl was burying Pineapple Amethyst Crystals in the ground, thirteen in total. The actions were hurried with quick glances over the shoulder, wary of onlookers.

Finally the job was done and the figure stood up. Instantly the face became recognisable as Mary Harper, a strange young girl from the village who had weaved her way into the coven so cleverly.

As Toby continued to watch he was amazed at the clarity of the images. Isobel took a sharp intake of breath.

"Be steady my sweet, I think we are close now." Michael eased, stroking Isobel's hand. Michael had seen what Isobel had seen, Mary's disguise, the façade she had used to cover her real identity, it was Fanny. This only managed to open the way for more questions, but at least it answered the question of what had occurred when the coven had met up to strip Michael and Isobel of their powers. Now they just needed to know where they were.

"Are you ready my dear," Michael asked affectionately then together they recited a proclamation.

"Father Time and Mother Nature unite, hide not what time we inhabit, guide us into salvation and let knowledge flow like wine from our minds."

They pulled two Chrysanthemum Stones from a pocket and placed them on the floor in between them. The stones immediately glowed hot and a column of smoke engulfed Michael and Isobel, who were now holding hands, making it difficult for Toby to see what was going on. There was a flash of light so bright that it temporarily blinded Toby. But he could hear voices everywhere, all around him in the room, whispering voices, shouting voices, angry voices, jovial voices.

Everything went black and silence consumed him.

130

The silence was broken by a familiar voice. It was Terri's, yet it had more sophistication to it than he remembered.

"Come on Toby we're going to be late for Jake's twenty-first." The words rocked him gently in a warm fuzzy feeling. Was there still hope that everything would be alright?

"I'm coming," he called absently, carried along by the swell of emotion building up inside. Hope.

"Toby. Toby." another voice called. This time it was a man's and it was unfamiliar.

"Edward, what are you doing here?" Toby asked, but yet another voice filled the room.

"Jake, I've come to try and get you to end this."

"But I want to know why my father found this place more fascinating than me? Why he let it consume him?" Jake cried out, his drunken anger filling the room.

"Come on Jake we've been best friends all our lives, let it go, you can't correct the past. It's gone."

Toby staggered backwards, unsure of what was real. None of it made sense, it was like different time zones being jumbled up together. "Jake, I'm sorry," he pleaded, hoping his future son would hear him somehow.

"NO," Jake shouted. "I want to know what it is about this place that my father sacrificed his life for." Toby heard a bottle smashing on the floor and an ensuing struggle.

Instantly the blackness faded and he was back in the room with Michael, Isobel and Edward.

"What's going on?" Toby exploded.

Solemnly Edward walked up to Toby. "You have started the

course that I so wished to correct."

"Please, there must be a way. I heard him."

"I did all I could do. I gave my life for his, that's how much I cared for him. Terri became like a mother to me after my parents died."

Astonished. Toby faltered, "but, but they are there," he said, pointing to the two figures standing behind Edward.

"We are mere Soulshadows conjured up by our son," Michael explained, "to reunite us as a family."

"So you are all dead." Toby couldn't believe he was saying it so calmly. He didn't believe in ghosts or witchcraft but all that was changing.

"I told you my parents had died," Edward started.

"But that was before I knew it was them," Toby cut in. How do you manage to travel backwards through time, no one else has managed it. Arrrgggghhh," Toby screamed as he felt a searing pain deep within him.

"I am so sorry Toby," Frances said under her breath as she heard Toby's piercing scream. "You had to be our anchor." She felt sympathy and Jeremy picked up on it.

"It was necessary otherwise it would've been one of us. Now it is nearing completion, all the crystals are working with each other."

"Now to finish," Frances said reluctantly. "Fire, earth and sea, bring back unto me, the link that binds thee to thee. Grattadium…" Frances didn't get to finish, a massive explosion of smoke erupted from the room sending tiles and timber everywhere, breaking the concentrations of the white hats. Frances' eyes widened as she saw people escape through the front door.

"Jeremy," she called.

"I know, I see them." He glared at John and then Harriet.

131

John and Harriet looked bemused. All eyes turned towards Frances and Jeremy for guidance, this shouldn't have happened. It was like the house was expelling all the ghosts of its visitors over the centuries. Jeremy gulped, feeling the pressure of the guidance being silently sought, spells had their own power and, through knowledge and experience he, as well as the others, had learnt how to harness that power and control it. But now something was going wrong and he didn't know how to stop it, the spell was too far into its cycle.

Panic swept through him and Frances could sense his unease. What had their ancestors really done, centuries before? He thought that he, and they, all understood. Were the notes, and stories that were passed down from generation to generation incorrect? No, when they had studied the old notes he had used the spell 'Corrartum Interentium' which confirms fact from fiction. Frances had used it on the first telephone conversation she had with Toby. How then could it all be going wrong?

Jeremy watched as ghosts left the house heading towards the gate, where they disappeared, an endless procession of people. All the newspaper clippings and stories about disappearances that Frances and he had collected seemed to account for only half of the people that had actually been pulled into this cottage.

"What are we going to do?" Frances's voice didn't hide her fear. Jeremy didn't answer. He didn't know what to say.

Light started to flash from one room to another inside the cottage, then thirteen beams, like searchlights broke through the roof. The white light flames that were being emitted from the Groggledyte Stones held by the coven wavered and became unsteady as if the energy they emitted was being tuned out.

Gareth blinked wearily, struggling to keep his tired eyes open. He jolted as the line between sleep and awake blurred. Glancing at his watch he noted the time, 1:47. He had seen the White Hats appear, he had observed the dialogue with Toby and Matthew, even watched them walk into the cottage, but after Elaine had left the room they were gone. Had it been over?

He had waited. Maybe he should go and check? He wondered whether he had drifted off at one point. He shook his head and looked at his notebook, the time was noted neatly in the margin but very little else.

The stillness of the night dampened his fading excitement further and, finally, he declared that it was time to give in. There was obviously nothing more to see and he hoped everything had worked out.

He stretched his arms, arching his back, amazed at how stiff it had become sitting still for so long. On cue the sky brightened. At first Gareth thought he had imagined it, but looking out of the window he saw that the sky above the cottage had a bright haze to it, daylight trying to break the stranglehold of night. Scanning the horizon, he looked for a reason, but nothing was visible, in fact, the rest of the town was bathed in slumbering darkness.

The brightness lacked a source yet Gareth instinctively knew it was the cottage. 'What is going on?' he muttered, a little annoyed that he couldn't see anything. An idea struck him and he left the sanctity of the spare bedroom and made his way into the garden as quietly as he could.

It was pitch black as he walked unsteadily across the lawn. He thought he knew his garden like the back of his hand, but when he couldn't see it, he managed to be guided to every flower pot and flowerbed that had been so cleverly woven into his small garden haven. Finally at the fence he peered into the alley beyond. He could see nothing. After a few seconds he felt he was being watched, a strange sense of awareness.

Harriet was staring at Jeremy when she felt the presence of someone close by. She knew their attempt to correct the rift in time was not going well and she was now wary that the cloak they were working under was failing. She turned, trying not to break her concentration, only to see the whites of a pair of eyes staring at her, watching her inquisitively.

132

The pain intensified as Toby doubled over. Thirteen searchlight beams broke through the roof and Toby felt his insides burning. The Larimar Crystal exploded, shards flying everywhere. Toby's instinct was to shield himself but the pain was too great and he succumbed to whatever was to follow.

He smelt Terri's perfume, Eternity, heard the many times she had told him she loved him, felt her tender touch, the closeness of her naked body as they writhed around making love.

"What's happening?" he finally managed to squeeze out.

"You are being anchored to this place. You will never be able to leave." Edward's sad voice echoed round the room as every sound, except his voice, faded from Toby's ears.

"Help me, you must help me," Toby pleaded, as the pain twisted his insides, something finally snapped. Shock registered in his eyes.

In his mind he saw Frances mouth the words, 'I'm sorry Toby', and at last he knew why, they had double-crossed him, the people he thought could help. He went to shout out his profanities but the pain subsided and he became lightheaded, released from any earthly chains.

Terri sat in the lounge with a smile plastered over her face. She had received a letter from the courts confirming that she would be awarded custody of her son. It lay crumpled and tear stained in her hands, it was a torch lighting the way forward. Her only wish was for Toby to be there to share this moment.

"Toby, wherever you are, I hope one day we can be together again."

"What was that Terri?" Vivien said, standing at the door, a vision of her former self, the vagueness of the Alzheimer's that had consumed her was gone, it was as if a reboot had taken place.

"Mum?" Terri quizzed emotionally, curious by the sudden change in her demeanor.

"Don't act so surprised, I do live here. This is my bungalow, if you remember? Now do you want a cup of tea? What's that in your hand?"

"Yes, no, sorry, yes, it's a letter from Section 18, they say I can have custody of Jake."

"Custody of Jake?" Vivien sounded shocked. "Have I missed something?"

"Mum, please, this is no time to..." Terri stopped as she heard the cry of her son.

As the sound hit her ears she raced past Vivien, almost knocking her over, out of the lounge and into Jake's bedroom where he was standing up against the guard rail of the cot, bawling his eyes out. Almost passing out, she turned to see Vivien standing behind her.

"What's wrong Terri?" But when she didn't answer, "Terri?"

"Mum, I... I... I don't know..." Terri turned back to Jake,

convinced she was seeing things, having a bad dream, a cruel twisted nightmare where everything was as it should be, even though she knew it wasn't. Her legs started to go weak and she held onto the door frame to support her weary self.

"I think you had better sit down, you must be coming down with that flu bug that's going round. Tracy and Carol were saying that it has got quite a few at their place. Come on, I'll see to Jake."

"No," Terri snapped. "Sorry, I just need to hold my son."

"Are you sure you're okay?" Vivien peered questioningly at her daughter.

"I'm fine. Fine, couldn't be better." She staggered heavily over to the cot, still shaken, as though she was drunk, and for all intents and purposes she felt it, drunk with happiness.

A niggling curiosity pulled at her and she looked again at the letter in her hand.

133

Harriet felt a burning sensation scorching her heart. She looked at Jeremy and Frances, they looked to be suffering too, all the White Hats felt the same searing pain.

"Frances," Jeremy called, hoping for inspiration.

"I… I… aargh." She let out an ear-splitting scream. Whatever was happening was inexplicably working against them.

Phillip cried out, "Astaaid Fornata Monariar." Phillip's Groggledyte stone started to fizzle like a blue firework, letting off sparks that were alive, cracking and spitting, the white flame of light became pale blue, before changing completely to a vivid mauve. The black horizontal smoke trail that ran below, vaporised.

A shock of fear appeared in Phillip's eyes just as grey mist enveloped him, concealing him from the rest of the coven

There was an ear-piercing 'pop'.

"Phillip," John shouted, fighting the searing pain as best he could, but it was too late. Phillip's now pale blue flame of light disappeared, the black horizontal column of smoke from the Groggledyte Stone had all but gone, to the amazement of the others all that was left of Phillip was a powdery blue luminescent substance on the ground.

"Expeldriata," Jeremy called, knowing that whatever they were battling was too much for them. Their ancestors had manifested something that was far from controllable and now it had taken one of them.

All Jeremy hoped to do was stop everything.

"EXPELDRIATA!" he called again, to no avail.

Gareth watched Harriet gradually come into view, along with the grandeur of the display of magic.

"Oh my gawd!" he exclaimed.

Harriet turned, shouting, "Go, you are in danger.", her voice fighting the pain she felt.

Gareth stumbled backwards, tripping over a pile of plastic flowerpots and falling into his vegetable plot.

An eruption of sound broke the tranquillity of night air as the invisibility cloak the White Hats were using gave up. Lights flicked on in the houses surrounding the cottage as a thunderous explosion illuminated the sky like a battlefield.

Glancing back at the bedroom window he had been using as a lookout post Gareth saw Elaine watching in bewilderment; he tried to wave to her but found his arm caught up in something.

Suddenly there were thirteen high-pitched 'pops', running consecutively at about fifteen second intervals before the night sky started to dim and the noise fade.

All the remaining twelve White Hats chanted 'Expeldriata'. It was meant to cease any magic that was being performed and return an equilibrium to proceedings, but it failed. They watched in horror as John's white flame of light turned a pale blue and his Groggledyte Stone also started to fizz, spouting blue sparks. He tried desperately to drop the crystal he was holding and run; however, much as he tried, he found himself rooted to the spot and completely taken by the magic they had started. A grey vaporous cloud engulfed him just as it had done Phillip, and the remaining White Hats watched in disbelief as he to soon disappeared amidst the same ear piercing 'pop'. Jeremy and Frances glanced at each other in horror and then at the remaining nine. Within seconds Harriet was surrounded by the same mist followed by a 'pop'. One by one each White Hat disappeared to be replaced by a powdery blue substance on the ground.

"Dragodian Mir..." Jeremy didn't get to finish as he too found himself too engulfed in the grey mist.

An uneasy silence rested over the cottage. People came out in their dressing gowns and night clothes to watch the weird display of light and sound, amazed that a place that had remained empty for so long could be the centre of something so unusual.

Toby felt the pain stop suddenly, the light and the noise all gone. Standing up he looked around the room. He felt different but he couldn't think why. Edward walked towards him. He looked different too, and Toby felt a meaty hand grab his shoulder, now it was clear why he looked different, he was real, solid, like a living breathing person.

Hope rose within Toby, jubilation ringing its successful chorus.

134

Terri pulled the letter into focus, still unsure what was happening. The events she remembered were still so vivid in her mind, they were as real as memories of her father. The ink on the paper appeared to grow clearer as she stared at it, her mind still in turmoil. It wasn't headed from Section 18 but from Council offices regarding a proposed extension into the roof of the bungalow.

Terri turned to Vivien. "I don't understand."

"What's that love?" Terri handed the letter to Vivien who looked perplexed at her daughter's vagueness. Vivien took the letter whilst Terri wandered over to pick Jake up and cradle him in her arms.

"Oh, it feels nice to hug you, my boy. If only your daddy were here." She turned to face her mother, who was still looking at the letter.

Looking up she said, "It's the good news I told you about, we don't need planning permission, only building regulations need to be satisfied."

Toby felt his arms and legs, they all felt real. He ran to the window. The scene that greeted him was as he remembered.

"Yes," he let out a jubilant cry, receiving a strange look, in response, from Edward.

"Toby," Michael called softly, "why are you so happy?"

"It worked, it worked. Look." He pointed to the outside world. "Everything is right." He clapped his hands together, "See." Then he patted a wall before dancing jubilantly around the room. "Ye of little faith," he mocked.

"Toby." Edward stepped forward.

"Why the frown, it worked, everything is good."

Edward sighed, bowing his head, "Toby, the truth is…"

"The truth is it worked, don't look so glum."

"Toby," Isobel said sharply. "If it worked why do you think we are here?"

The words cut Toby like a knife, stopping his jubilation in its tracks. "What? But."

"But what?" Michael offered. "If it had worked we would not be here, we would certainly not be clearer to you now than we were. To prove the point Michael grasped Toby's hand and squeezed tightly until Toby squirmed at the discomfort.

"But you're ghosts, how can you…?"

"You have become what we are. You have sacrificed yourself as much as Edward sacrificed himself to save Jake.

"No!" he cried, an empty feeling rising like acid in his stomach. "I feel sick," then immediately his mind caught up, "but I can't feel sick if I am a ghost."

"You are not a ghost as such Toby, neither is Edward. You still feel what you normally feel. You are in an altered state of being," Isobel said soothingly.

"I have to get home, I have to make sure Jake is alright." He started to run from the room.

"You can't leave this place Toby," Edward called, following him out of the room and down the stairs.

"It's lies, it has to be. I've helped to stop all of this." He ran for the front door, almost yanking it off its hinges. "See," he said turning on Edward who was following close behind. Edward stopped a few feet away.

"Then go through Toby. See what happens."

Toby furrowed his brow, a million thoughts rushing like busy bees inside his head, the sweet scent of success turning sour as each second slowly ticked by.

Toby stepped toward the doorstep, digesting all that had happened, questioning whether what he was being told was true. Had Edward ever lied to him?

"No, this can't be true." Toby turned and launched himself through the door.

"Toby." Edward watched, knowing the awful truth, knowing how he had felt at the moment of realisation.

135

Toby was running for the gate, feeling the full freedom of the outside world beckoning to him. At the gate he stopped and looked back at Edward, whose face was fixed in a stare of pleading.

"See, I'm free. Look." Toby spun round. Although his voice sounded confident there was edge of doubt to it. A part of him believed Edward.

Toby pulled the gate open and stepped through.

"Why are you looking at me like that Mum?"

"It's just I haven't heard you mention Toby like that for a while," Vivien answered cautiously.

"Why wouldn't I?" Terri's mind trying to decipher which memories were real and which weren't. It was like a nightmare, twisted recollections of time passing, her Mum's with Alzheimers, losing her son, yet here she was with Jake just over a year old. How?

Vivien shrugged her shoulders. She knew her daughter could be fickle when it came to Toby ever since his disappearance. "Look, why don't you two go and sit in the lounge and I'll make you a cup of tea, then maybe we can go out for a walk. It's a lovely day."

"Okay," Terri agreed, still distracted by her memories. Sitting in the lounge she enjoyed holding Jake, pleased that she wouldn't have to handle a court hearing and trying, once again, to explain the missing years, which no longer existed.

Gareth sat on the ground where he'd fallen, the cloudless night sky like a dark silk sheet, his memory was fuzzy. His reason for being out in the garden at such an untimely hour was unclear. Looking at his watch, 3:15, only made him more curious, his eyes widening in surprise. Had he sleepwalked? He looked at his clothes - he couldn't have.

Slowly he got up, still bemused and turned towards the house, when something tugged at his mind; a curiousity. A tiny thought that wouldn't let go but wouldn't make itself clear either. Tentatively, he turned back to the fence and Thyme Cottage, which stood as a dark silhouette. Peering over his back fence, across the alleyway and into the cottage's garden he almost missed a soft blue effervescent glow coming from the ground that separated the two boundaries. It triggered a recollection that wouldn't hold firm in his mind, it was playing a game of hide and seek.

As he took in the length of the dark alley he noticed another area that glowed the same effervescent blue. Unlocking the back gate he investigated further. Both areas were about fourteen inches in diameter and kneeling down he could feel an eerie coldness that inexplicably clung to the area like a disease. He held his hand above the ground curious at its coldness, the circle of blue remained bright, as though lit from beneath.

Leaving the alley and wandering around the perimeter of Thyme Cottage he found eleven more soft blue effervescent circles on the ground.

Studying the cottage, he wondered what it was that wouldn't come into focus, he knew something, he remembered something, but no matter how hard he thought about it, it remained fuzzy.

Toby stepped backwards through the gate and was amazed when the front of Thyme cottage and Edward disappeared from view and immediately he found himself back in the room upstairs.

"What the?" he pleaded.

Edward entered the room a few seconds later.

"I told you, you can now never leave this place. It is your sacrifice."

"But my family."

136

Edward placed a consoling hand on Toby's shoulder. It made little difference but, in some way helped to calm Toby's racing mind. He also felt a wet nose nuzzle his hand. Norton, Edward's dog, had appeared and Michael and Isobel had gone.

"So I did all this for nothing then? Whose dog is this? Where's your parents?"

"Toby let it go, there is nothing you can do to change what has happened, except..." Edward left the sentence unfinished, knowing the thought he had would probably only upset Toby more. "Norton is mine, I found him as a puppy in the grounds of this place, he appears from time to time. He keeps me company." As if on cue, Norton went and sat next to his master.

"Except what?" Edward looked at Toby. "You said nothing can change what has happened except... Except what?" Toby turned on Edward, rage starting to build.

"Forget it, nothing?" Edward turned and walked away with Norton.

"No, wait, what is it?" Toby half-shouted.

Forlornly, Edward eyed Toby, one hand resting on Norton's back, knowing in some way that it was pointless not to tell him. "Except, when Jake turns up, you can try and do what I did, before it's too late."

"When Jake turns up?" Edward could see confusion manifesting itself in Toby's eyes.

"Toby, this cottage starts to eat at Jake when he is just ten years old. His mother," Edward paused, "Terri, tells him." After another short pause he continued. "It's a school project we get asked to do. What our mums and dads do? He asks Terri. It happens to be on the anniversary of your disappearance and she tells him. She even walks him to the cottage, this place.

"He, or rather we, first visit it about a year later, it was after our fourth day at senior school when he confides in me."

"NO!" Toby stated, Edward nodded, "Then he must experience the time..."

"No," Edward interrupted Toby, knowing where the thought was going, "he doesn't, neither do I."

Toby's face paled as he remembered the question that was haunting him about how some people didn't get affected by it.

"You know," Edward started and, as if bored, Norton faded from view much to Toby's amazement. "I had the same thought, once I understood what we were dealing with. It is something Jake and myself discussed many times and it was, in some ways, the hardest for him to understand and would drive him to drink and drugs. He almost wanted it to happen, to find out why his father would leave him." Seeing Toby search for Norton, he added. "He is his own master and…" Edward didn't finish that thought. "… I don't know where he came from."

"I didn't leave him, I would never leave Jake…"

"I know that, and you will be able to tell him that in about ten years from now."

Toby stared down at the floor, flummoxed. "How do people travel back in time?"

Edward looked at Toby, he knew this would come. "To understand you must know this, and it is something that took me a long time to find out. Every second of time has its own frequency, like a signature and if you can tap into that signature you can go anywhere."

Toby's intense concentration was furrowed on his face as he tried to understand.

"If you treat every second as if it has a different frequency that can be duplicated then you can go anywhere. The problem is you need a key, something that will enable it." Edward lifted a shiny coin from his pocket. An image flashed up in Toby's mind, his first meeting with Edward, he was flicking a coin up in the air and catching it. "Pure silver, look." He flicked it to Toby who caught it in both hands.

"I don't understand," Toby said.

"I will teach you, but, for now, know this, if you can tune this to a certain frequency you can tap into any time you want."

"But how does that explain why you and my son never experienced the time…" Toby searched for the right word which was elusive. "whatevers?"

"Terri gave us both a silver St Christopher for our tenth birthdays. She wanted to make sure we were both looked after.

Silver is the most conductive precious metal there is and so it tunes itself into the frequency of our time and, in some way, roots itself firmly where it starts and the person with it, it makes sure the right combination remains to keep them safe."

137

Toby looked around the room as though a clearer explanation would present itself.

"But how would Terri know that?"

"She doesn't. It was a fluke that she gave us those St Christophers. Unfortunately I lost mine…" Edward paused reflectively, looking through Toby to a point in time on the wall, "when I had a fight with Jake, when the drugs were taking a hold."

"But how did you discover its properties?"

"I found my father's diary. It told me of my parent's origins. Their expulsion from the coven and how they came to be where they were nearly three hundred years from their time." Edward stepped towards Toby, his voice softening. "This time. Imagine their shock at finding themselves here. They knew sorcery and they tried to get back, spending years experimenting, gradually fitting into society. Then they had me and although they kept trying, it wasn't a necessity anymore, they had got used to their new life and as they had me it seemed natural to stay for my sake?"

"But why silver? How?"

"Please, let me finish," Edward asked kindly.

"But they would have experienced the time shifts continually, this house…"

"They didn't stay here Toby." Edward's patience was wearing thin, "You asked and I am trying to explain." Edward turned and started to pace the room. "As far as they were concerned, at first, this was someone else's house, it didn't matter that it was empty, they couldn't guarantee it would stay that way and for a few days it was fine. They were powerful sorcerers who knew how to utilise their power to help them fit in, to establish themselves without causing suspicion.

They would come back every now and then and try different things but nothing seemed to work." Edward turned on Toby his expression dark and intense. "Except once. My mother vanished halfway through their experiment. That would turn out to be their first clue. You have to understand that my parents never altered their rituals, right down to the clothes they wore. Magic can be about finding your own source, your own key if you like, then once you find it you can build on it. There are many guidelines, but magic is an essence, and everyone's essence is slightly different. That said, it confused my father, he came back day after day hoping to find my mother. It was a month and a half before she showed up again. After that, they stopped experimenting, feeling that it was getting nowhere. It baffled and confused them. They had power. But the only thing they couldn't control was this place.

Then they discovered my mother was pregnant with me and they stopped altogether. It wasn't until I got hold of the diaries my father kept that I discovered a difference, something that had not been quite the same on that one occasion."

Toby looked at Edward, waiting for an answer.

In the lounge Terri sat enjoying every moment of Jake, held so tightly in her arms.

"There you go." Vivien placed a tray on the coffee table, two mugs of tea, half a pack of biscuits and a bottle for Jake. Terri juggled with Jake whilst trying to pick up the bottle, but she had sunk so far into the soft settee that she couldn't reach the coffee table. "Here, let me take him."

"NO!" Terri answered sharply, instantly regretting the harshness, she hadn't meant to sound so aggressive. "Sorry Mum."

"Are you alright Terri, you seem a bit…" she thought, searching for the right word, "… lost. I know it must be hard without Toby here, but you can talk to me, you know you can. Although it's not quite the same."

"I know Mum." Terri finally managed to get herself upright with Jake still cradled in her arms. "I…" She wanted to say more, but somehow the words wouldn't formulate in her head, "I don't know."

Vivien smiled and let the matter rest.

138

Two days later Terri inexplicably found herself outside Thyme Cottage, wishing Toby would come back to her. The dilemma of what to do with the cottage hung over her like a dark thunderous cloud. What was the point of owning an asset that they couldn't use? And what had happened to bring her back to a time she knew.

"There was a necklace my mother used to wear. "Edward continued. "A present from their first wedding anniversary, it was a simple silver pendant, pure silver. It had broken and was being repaired. It didn't occur to them that something so small could make such a change, but it was enough to get me thinking. School was good and my stepfather was a genius at chemistry and all the sciences. Unfortunately he had a knack of making science sound boring, but once I had grasped this fact I started to pester him with questions about properties and their make-ups, benefits, uses, anything and everything." Edward looked into Toby's eyes. "What really confirmed it was after that fight with Jake.

I had watched him drink more and more. At first I went along with him, but when he started to divert his attention to drugs, that's when I stopped, sobered up, saw what it was doing to him."

"Do you wanna swig" Jake asked, pulling a bottle of Jack Daniels from his coat pocket and crushing the empty cider can he'd finished.

"Yeah," Edward replied, placing his half-drunk can of cider on the wall. "Why do we always end up here?"

"Cos'," was Jake's gruff reply.

"It won't bring your old man back you know." Jake shrugged his fifteen year old shoulders, staring at the jaded front door of Thyme cottage from the garden wall they were sitting on, legs dangling in the cottages overgrown garden.

"You think I'm stupid?" Jake pushed himself off the wall fronting up to Edward his eyes glazed over in a fog-like daze. Jake had been acting wired all day, as though he was fixing for a fight.

"Woah," Edward replied, spilling Jack Daniels down himself, "calm down, it was just a question. I just thought you'd hate being here knowing it took him."

"Yeah, well, I don't know." Jake paused taking the bottle back and gulping a long lustful draw.

"You ought to move in when you're sixteen. I mean it's yours anyway. Ciggy?" Edward pulled a packet from his jacket pocket. "I'm sure your Mum will be pleased to see it occupied. I still don't understand why she doesn't just move in herself."

"'Cos she won't, stupid mare."

Edward looked sideways at Jake. He liked Terri, she had always treated him like her own, she wasn't a replacement for his own family but he was closer to her than his foster parents, who were nice enough, just boring intellectual types.

"Go easy on her, it must 'ave been hard after your father disappeared."

"What is it with you tonight?" The question struck Edward as strange.

"Nothing, it's just she's nice, your Mum, always been good to me."

"Well, bully for you." Jake's demeanour had an edge to it.

"Come on, Jake, she's been fair to you, never heard you complain before. What's eating you tonight?"

"What is this, twenty fucking questions?" Jake stomped towards the front door, swigging Jack Daniels carelessly.

Edward stood up and followed, amazed by the reaction. "No. Come on, I was just saying, that's all."

"Well don't, I don't want to hear it, I'm fucked off hearing it, you're like a broken record. 'How wonderful my Mum is' and 'oh, how she does this and that'." Jake started mincing around, taking the mickey out of Edward, still swigging from the nearly empty bottle.

"Yeah, well I'd be happy just to have my parents back…"

"Oh, give it a rest."

"What?"

"You heard." Jake kicked the front door, which sprung open

easily.

"God you're an arsehole sometimes. You don't know when you're well off. If I had one of my parents here now, I'd be pleased." Edward's voice became more aggressive antagonizing Jake. "You're so bloody lucky, yet you've let the fact that your father walked out on you, eat at you like a bloody disease. Your Mum has done everything for you, so why don't you tell me what's really eating at you."

139

"Oh, fuck off, you sanctimonious dickhead. You're like a bird, once a month." Jake turned on Edward pushing his shoulder firmly, "Is that it? Your time of month" Jake downed the last of the whisky and threw the empty bottle over Edward's head and into the deep weeds and grass of the front garden, expecting to hear it smash, amazed that only silence followed.

"I'm going, don't you worry." He turned to leave, but stopped after two steps. "I don't know what has got into you recently, and I don't know what it is about this bloody place that you can't let it go. I know it hurts, but letting it eat at you is not going to solve anything."

"Oh give it a rest will you," Jake answered, pulling a tin that Edward didn't recognise from an inside pocket.

"What's that?" Edward asked curiously, his anger fading instantly.

"Something to calm me down after listening to you rage on."

"What, drugs?" Edward exclaimed.

"No, it's not drugs, just a little weed." Jake started to roll a joint with expert precision, shocking Edward.

"Of course it's bloody drugs. Are you stupid? What next, eh?" Jake turned, licking the cigarette paper and skillfully finishing the task. Edward grabbed his shoulder turning him sharply causing Jake to drop the tin and the joint.

Jake's fist struck Edward's right cheek with the force of a hammer blow, sending him reeling sideways into the small fence that separated the front garden from the back, near the front door which was on the side of the house. Edward didn't baulk, the alcohol in his system only fuelling the anger like touch paper.

Within seconds both were on the ground wrestling each other, their faces red and flushed. Jake tried to push Edward away after managing to manoeuvre himself so they were face to face, Edward on top of Jake, pinning him to the ground. Jake's hands grasped at Edward's throat.

"What's wrong with you?" Edward gasped. Jake tore open Edward's shirt sending buttons cascading into the grass.

From nowhere Jake found some extra strength. He was smaller than Edward and had always been the weaker of the two, but now he was overpowering Edward. Edward shot over Jake's head, head first into the wall of the cottage, more buttons tore off, and the rip could be heard as his t-shirt underneath ripped open.

Edward looked down at his chest in disbelief, great red marks showed where Jake's fingernails had scratched him.

Both friends rose to their feet, seething at each other like wild animals ready to pounce, but the fight had gone out of Edward. His best friend stood before him like a crazed animal, a stranger.

"I'm going, you can do what you fucking like," he said, sullenly, straightening his clothes up as best he could.

"Good," Jake growled.

The two boys stared at each other for a few more seconds, before Edward pushed past Jake to the gate.

"Oh, before you go, I believe that is mine," Jake snarled with venom, reaching for Edward's neck and tearing the silver St Christopher free.

Stunned, Edward took a second or two to react. "That's mine," he called, as Jake headed to the front door.

"Fuck off it is." Jake turned to take another swing at Edward but found himself lunging at thin air, Edward gone from view.

Edward blinked as he saw Jake disappearing into the cottage, kicking the door closed behind him. Something was different about him, yet he couldn't place it.

Desolation crept into Edward and he hastily left, wishing he could take it all back. Their friendship seemed finished.

140

Edward walked solemnly back home, playing over the events again and again in his mind. The alcohol's effects had vanished, despite polishing off four cans of cider and a few swigs of Jack Daniels.

"You see, Toby, I knew something was wrong that night, but I couldn't work out what it was. That was my first experience of the time slips which have occurred. My real parents had never had the chance to fill me in on their lives so I never knew. I didn't even know that the silver St Christopher would prove to be part of the key. All I knew was, on that night, I had lost my best friend. I was angry, he was angry." Edward looked at Toby, who stood listening attentively and, as the words filtered through, his thoughts turned to Terri and how he wanted to be part of the tale he was hearing. "I kept calling Jake after that night but he wouldn't answer. When I finally went round he slammed the door in my face. His eyes became more and more vacant, like he had lost his soul.

I even resorted to following him and that was when I discovered the real reason for the change." Edward paused as he was reminded of the loss of his friend again, and how he felt. "It was a Thursday and the school bell had rung signalling the end of the day. School hadn't been the same since our fight. Although we didn't share a lot of the same tutorial groups we used to meet up at break-times, now we didn't and I missed him. I was determined to repair our friendship." Edward smirked. "Even my foster parents had noted that I was staying in a lot more on my own and I hated it. We should have been out partying, having fun.

I waited at the school gate after legging it out of the last lesson like a rabbit on heat but, somehow, I must have missed him, he always left by the west gate on a Thursday. After fifteen minutes I knew he wasn't coming and I left.

I found him though."

Gareth collected some of the blue powder up in a plastic bag, his mind still struggling to reach a memory he knew was there, yet just out of reach. What was it? He remembered doing something? No, it was gone. Still confused he took the collected sample indoors.

"What on earth is that?" Elaine said, startled by the effervescent blue powder.

Gareth furrowed his brow. "It has something to do with the cottage." Elaine rolled her eyes. "There were thirteen circles of this at various places around the perimeter of the property."

"Gareth, I love you dearly but even I wonder sometimes. I can't believe how obsessed you are with that cottage."

"Don't you think it strange? I mean look at it." Gareth wafted the bag in front of Elaine as if she would be interested, instead she batted it out of the way. "Your tea's there. I'm going to sit down and put my feet up." She started to walk from the kitchen, leaving Gareth feeling dismayed.

As she reached the kitchen door the stench hit her nose, almost making her drop her tea. "Oh my... errgh, what on earth is that smell? Smells like burnt flesh." As she finished her words she felt the bile rising up inside and rushed back to the kitchen sink to take a gulp of water. She thrust her tea tray onto the draining board, sending gravy and sausages flying off the plate. Out of the corner of her eye she saw the bag on the floor and Gareth by the open back door choking on the stench.

"Great, just leave it in her..." But she didn't finish her words as vomit rose up and she could no longer hold it in.

Gareth turned to face his wife, who was retching into the sink, the colour slowly came back into his own face. He marched to his shed and found a garden rake and then proceeded to collect the plastic bag of blue powder, carefully catching it in the prongs of the rake and removing it from the kitchen.

Half an hour later all trace of the blue powder was gone from the floor but the smell didn't leave. Elaine opened all the windows and, although it was cold, it let the air flow through.

Two days later the smell was just as strong where the bag had spilled some of its content onto the lino, forcing Gareth to temporarily cut out a section until he could seek replacement for the whole floor.

In all that time he still couldn't fathom what it was, he was sure he should remember.

141

"I walked," Edward continued thoughtfully, remembering the time as if it was yesterday, "my usual route home until I got to the sweet shop near the Cricketers pub about half-way home. There, something made me take a diversion, I don't know what, just an inkling. So I headed down Milton Road towards the Cliffs Pavilion. As I neared the vacant car showroom I noticed another kid from school. I hadn't seen him for a while, I was going to ask him if he had seen Jake when he spewed up. He stood there stunned, not comprehending what had happened. Suddenly I thought I knew where Jake might be, there was a house just off of St Helens Road, it was rumoured to be where you could get drugs, although no police raids had ever found any trace.

Ten minutes later I was standing outside. It was a big house that had been converted into bedsits. It was rundown with piles of black bags left rotting outside in amongst the remnants of an ornate garden wall that had been kicked down. I must have stared up at it for a few minutes when I noticed movement at the side of the house. A rotting back gate that led to an alley was being pulled open. I remember panicking, looking for a place to hide, there was a pillar box nearby so I darted behind it.

Within seconds Jake appeared, carelessly holding something in his right hand. I moved to get a better view. He stopped at the edge of the property and pulled something out of an envelope and threw it into his mouth, throwing his head back as if swigging a beer. I was about to shout to him when I saw someone else appear at the gate, they had a knife in their hand, a three inch blade that glinted in the dim daylight. Words got stuck in my throat as I watched in horror rooted to the spot.

Terri looked up at the building, Thyme Cottage.

"Well you've managed to destroy my family. What I ever did to deserve that I don't know." She let the words dance in the breeze that blew softly from the east.

"Terri!" The voice came from nowhere, taking her by surprise. Startled Terri glanced around her but the streets were empty. "Terri."

Again Terri searched for the voice she recognized. It was so familiar to her that she didn't want to believe. It couldn't be. She desperately wanted it to be, but fear kept her from accepting it.

"Terri, please wait there."

She hadn't even been aware that she had been moving, so natural was her reaction after so many experiences with the cottage. Jake's pushchair snagged on a twig on the ground and she found herself tripping into it.

The voice called again. This time she answered cautiously, "Toby," wondering if she was hallucinating, "No, you're not real. Are you?" She looked into the garden which was empty, she glanced from window to window hoping to catch a glimpse of Toby but she saw nothing. "Toby, is that you?"

The only reply she got was the gate slamming as a sudden gust of wind caught it.

Feeling a cold chill she knelt down in front of Jake and zipped up his jacket to protect him.

"Your Mother's going mad son." She stared longingly at him, seeing Toby's eyes staring back at her. "What am I going to tell you about your father, eh?" Jake stared blankly back. "Come on let's get you home." She stood up, staring at the cottage, hoping to hear her name one last time, but only the wind answered.

"Goodbye Toby. I loved... love you with all my heart. I wish you we here now, you could tell me what to do." Terri pushed Jake home, an aching in her heart that gave her stride a lethargic gait.

"Ter…" The voice stopped abruptly. Terri turned. "Stop it, whoever you are, it's not funny," she shouted.

142

Edward carried on, the emotion of that day showing on his face, tormenting him. "The man approached Jake, grabbing him round the neck and whispering something menacing into his ear, he then pressed the blade of the knife to Jake's neck. I could have sworn I was going to see Jake killed. There appeared to be a stand-off before Jake was pushed away, crashing to the ground and spilling the contents of the envelope into the gutter. I watched, torn up inside as my best friend frantically retrieved the contents, eleven tiny white tablets. The man angrily kicked the gate open and disappeared behind it.

Jake got up, placing the tablets in his coat pocket. He didn't see me as he slunk off in the direction of this cottage, his grey skin aged him, his features were starting to look emaciated. I couldn't believe the transformation in him in such a short time." Edward looked away from Toby, who was still struggling to comprehend that he was listening to stories about his new born son, and his eventual demise.

Edward turned and scuffed the floor with his shoe, like a bored child.

"After a minute or so I followed I wanted to do something, but what? In some way, by following him, I was helping, or so I thought. Yet as I watched another part of him went."

"Why didn't you speak to your foster parents? They could have helped," Toby butted in harshly, airing the guilt he felt.

"They were clever people, but they didn't know about drugs and I didn't feel I could talk to them about it. I thought it might get Jake in trouble with the police." Edward walked to the dirty window and looked forlornly at the garden gate. "Many times I walked right up to the gate, determined to confront him about the drugs, but each time I chickened out of it, scared of another fight, scared I would push him further away from me. I missed him, but a strange thing occurred, just like the night of our fight." Edward turned to face Toby, whose face had gone pale. "It had been a month and a half and we had hardly spoken, he was turning up less and less to school. Break times weren't the same. I had other friends but he was…" Edward paused and Toby looked on expectantly, "It sounds strange maybe, but he was kind of my soulmate. We'd known each other since infant school. Anyway, I didn't even follow him this one night, I just waited outside by that tree." Edward pointed to a tree just beyond the front garden wall which Toby couldn't see from where he was standing. "Didn't have to wait long, he saw me but he turned his face away, hoping I wouldn't see him"

"Is that it Jake? Is that all you can do now, turn away from me? I thought we were mates?" Edward's face was full of hurt.

Jake shrugged his shoulder non-committedly and carried on sauntering past. Edward grabbed his arm and turned him round.

"Piss off, I don't wanna talk to you," Jake grunted.

"Why not? Look, why are you doing this?" Jake stood at the front gate poised to enter. "Well? We used to be mates, what happened?" Edward was struggling to hide his feelings.

Jake's eyes were hollow, the bags under them only emphasized their sunkenness. Edward thought for a second he might get an answer, but Jake pushed open the front gate and headed to the front door,

"Don't bloody answer me then!" Edward shouted, running for the gate. Jake about turned but looked ambivalent as he started to collapse. Edward rushed forward but as he did, Jake vanished from view.

Recoiling, Edward stepped back through the gate. "What the f...?" as he bumped into a man, who stared at him for a long minute. "Sorry," Edward stammered, looking up at the figure.

"What are you doing, going in there?" the man said.

"My mate, he has just, he has, well, he." Edward tried to explain, pointing to the spot where he had seen Jake fall in their fight a few days previously.

"I've seen you around here before haven't I," the man said, Edward shook his head, thinking - deny everything, that's what Jake and he had said as kids 'always deny everything'. "Yes, I have, I only live next door, it was few days ago." Edward looked both surprised and curious. "You followed your mate in here, then left him when he collapsed, is that what it is like to have friends these days. I don't know what the world is coming to." Gareth said.

"No, no, I never. I would..." Edward started to defend himself.

"Yeah, right. If you're that concerned, I called an ambulance." Edward gawped at the man. "Something you should have done. Nearly died by all accounts." Edward started to run off. "Oi, oi, I only live over the back and if I see you..." Gareth shouted but he let the words fade away as Edward rounded the corner. "... I'll call the police. Youth of today. No respect."

143

"Hi Mum." Terri pushed Jake's pushchair into the hall. The day had brightened and the sun shining had finally helped her come to a decision about the cottage. She had got control of her emotions and felt stronger than she had in a long while. Toby had gone and there was nothing she could do about it, and, although she hoped he would turn up one day, she had remembered Edward's words. She had to think about Jake and try and stop him from heading down that path. As hard as it was she knew what she needed to do.

"Hi ya." Vivien wandered from the lounge, "And how's my little Jake then, did he enjoy his walk?"

"I think he did, we went round Priory Park," Terri said, taking off her coat, and releasing Jake from his restraints. "It certainly helped me get my head straight." Vivien cocked her head curiously at Terri. "About the cottage," Terri added, "I'm going to sell it." Terri could see Vivien was about to say something. "Before you start, yes, I have thought about Toby and the... well, experiences, and, to be frank, I don't see why it shouldn't be someone else's problem. Why should we be lumbered with it. Peter obviously didn't care about us, to..." She stopped, realising she was speaking ill of the dead, and it sounded ungrateful. "Sorry, I know he meant well, but it hasn't done us any favours so we might as well get rid of it. If... when Toby comes back to us, it will still be there, he'll still have a way to get back to us."

There was a moment's silence as Vivien pulled Jake from the pushchair.

"How's my favourite grandson?"

"He's your only grandson Mum," Terri stated matter-of-factly.

"Still my favourite," Vivien replied sarcastically. "Anyway, what I was about to say is, I think you are quite right, it does seem silly for it to sit there, an empty asset. Her smile faded. "I hope he does come back soon."

"So do I Mum. Glad you agree though, as I have already asked an estate agent to value it."

"Don't want to waste any time then?" Terri smiled half-heartedly. It had been a hard decision and one she hoped she wouldn't regret.

Edward sat down on the floor, leaning up against a wall. "By the time I got to the hospital Jake had been moved to a specialist ward. He was suffering withdrawal symptons. Before they let me in to see him I had to empty my pockets, to prove I wasn't carrying drugs to feed his habit. I wanted to swear at them.

I had never seen someone suffering like he was. He was sweating profusely, his skin almost icy white, his eyes red and sore, his voice raspy. I looked at him and it was as though he didn't recognise me, but he didn't hide the venom in his words.

'You bastard, why d'you grass me up?'

Shocked, I couldn't answer him, I hadn't grassed him up, I didn't know what he meant.

Then a nurse came in. 'Scary isn't it. It's what drugs can do to you'. Her tone was condescending, as though I had been the one to put him there.

'I tried to stop him,' I said lamely, but she just rolled her eyes and checked Jake's vital signs. 'Can't you give him something to help?'

She looked at me, 'You his friend?'

'Yes. Well used to be.' I looked at Jake for his agreement but it wasn't forthcoming.

'He needs to get out of his system whatever it is he has taken, his body can't cope with it. We're monitoring his progress but I, we don't think there is any more we can do at this point.'

'I hate you, you useless piece of shit. I hate you. Now fuck off,' Jake spat out.

I stared at him and he held my gaze before a violent stomach cramp gripped him making him squeal in pain.

The nurse saw how upset I was, although I was not crying.

'Look, drugs screwed him up, he doesn't mean what he says.'

'Yes, I fucking do, you lame poof. Argh'. The cramps twisting him into an ugly mess.

The nurse led me outside. 'He'll be alright you know'

The truth was I didn't, but she had done her best to console me and, as she left me in the corridor, a coldness seeped into me; the sterile conditions only emphasizing it.

144

"Jake came out five days later to be treated as an outpatient. I had tried to see him everyday, but he still wouldn't speak to me. I kept turning over in my mind what had happened, how had I let it happen, could I have stopped it?"

"You can't change someone's destiny," Toby spoke instinctively, and then noted the implications of what he had said. Edward stared at him. It was like a hammer shattering the glass between reality and a dream.

"Maybe you're right, but I had to try." Toby looked admonished. "It's a shame I couldn't do it sooner, it's a shame I had to watch him die."

"Did you not speak after he came out?" Toby asked after a pause in which he walked to the window to look out on the street scene below.

"Yes, we spoke but it would be for the last time."

Terri and Jake were walking out of the hospital, after Jake's release when they heard Edward calling "Jake, Jake? Mrs Grant?" Edward ran after Jake and Terri. Terri turned.

"Hello Edward. Nice to see you again, it has been a long time." Her tone was friendly, if a little tense. "How is school?" Her voice to Edward was like early morning birdsong, but her eyes showed the strain that Jake's addiction was having.

"Okay, thank you. Mrs Grant."

"Why don't you come back with us, I'm sure you've both got loads to catch up on? I'll do your favourite dinner, egg and chips."

Edward smiled. "Thank you, would it be okay if I ring my foster parents and let them know?"

"Of course, you can."

Jake didn't say a word and walked in front kicking his feet along the ground.

"Jake don't be so rude, come and talk your friend. He came to see you."

"He's not my friend," Jake uttered under his breath so neither could hear.

Terri found her spirits lifted as Edward gushed about things that were happening at school.

"You asked that girl out yet? What was her name?" Edward became shy and blushed crimson. In truth he had a crush on Terri and that is what had made it doubly hard when Jake and he had gone their separate ways. It was just a stupid schoolboy crush, but it felt monumental.

"Jennifer, her name's Jennifer. And no I haven't. I want to, but…" It sounded silly even to him as he said it, so he stopped.

"You should, she'd be mad to miss a catch like you."

Edward grew hot with embarrassment and let the conversation die away.

Fifteen minutes later they were indoors at Vivien's bungalow. "You two go in the lounge and I'll do you egg, sausage, chips and beans." Terri tried to remain cheerful, her son had nearly died, and he refused to speak to Edward whom she regarded as a grounding influence on him. She only hoped that he could help where she felt she had failed. She was worried about Jake, she hadn't noticed the drugs until the phone call from the hospital, it had scared her. Then, watching her only son suffer whilst he was drawn off of the drugs was even harder. Every night she had cried herself to sleep. It brought memories of Toby back to her, how a part of her had missed him, it had been so long, nearly fourteen years. On a selfish level she had missed his touch, his scent, him holding her hand; on a more encompassing level the family unit they could have been, the holidays they could have had.

"Thank you Mrs Grant." Terri watched disconsolately as the two boys went into the lounge.

Jake was the first to speak when Terri was out of earshot. "Why don't you fuck off," he whispered menacingly.

"We're mates. We said we'd always be mates, don't you rememb…" Edward wasn't allowed to finish.

"You only hang around me 'cause you fancy my Mum."

Edward could feel himself blush, but he still denied it. "No. No I don't." Then trying to sound hard, added, "I thought we could go out later and get some ciders, you know go along the seafront."

"You are so boring. Go on, bog off and leave me in peace."

Astonished, Edward stood rooted with indecision, to go or

stay, he thought, naively, that once the drugs were out of his system everything would be back to normal.

145

Finding strength from an unknown place, he stood up to Jake, "What is your fucking problem?"

"You, you interfering twat, you're such a do-gooder. Yes, Mrs Grant, two bags full Mrs Grant."

"You're an arsehole."

"Mummy's boy." Jake saw the hurt in Edward's eyes and in some way regretted saying it as soon as the words came out.

"At least I'd appreciate my mother if she was still here."

"What, instead of fancying mine you mean." Jake was caught out by the speed at which Edward's fist flew at him, sending him reeling backwards towards the settee, but he landed on the floor in front of it. Edward stood shocked by his own actions, Jake looked up at him, his cheek tender but there was no blood. "Truth hurts." Then, cockily getting up, "Well, at least your father didn't leave you, at least he had a good reason for not being there."

Exacerbated Edward raised his voice and shouted, "What, you mean being dead? Like that's so much better. Your Mum told you about your Dad. All I have ever known is that they died when I was six, I remember their faces, I think I remember their smell. You don't know when you've got it so good. I would gladly swap shoes with you, you ungrateful bastard."

"Oooh, get you…"

"What the hell is going on with you two?" Terri stormed into the room, her face explosive with anger, at the gulf opening between her and Jake. They used to be so close.

Jake plonked down on the settee, grabbing the remote and switching on the TV. "He started it."

"Quite frankly I don't care who started it, I won't hear that sort of language in this house." Terri was going to add more but Edward interrupted.

"Sorry Mrs Grant." Edward hung his head respectfully, whilst Terri looked to Jake expecting an apology. Jake said nothing just watched the pictures flash up on screen.

"I don't know what has got into you Jake but it stops now." She could feel every part of her motherly love fighting the urge not to get angry. Jake ignored his mother. "Do you think I have had it easy without your father? Why do you insist on wasting your life? You need to change, it won't do you any good." Jake was still staring intently at the TV and was unaware of the approaching slap round the head. "Bloody look at me when I'm talking to you. Are you so pig ignorant that you don't care." Terri grabbed the remote from Jake's hand and switched off the TV.

Edward stood uneasily watching the scene unfold, he had never seen Terri lose it with Jake, but it was needed.

"Hey, I was watching that," Jake said.

"You'll never watch another thing in this house if you don't get your act together my boy. Your father may not be here but he would be ashamed if he saw you now, what you've become. I've done everything to avoid this, the drugs. We knew this was what was in your destiny, I thought I…" Terri lost all fight as fourteen years of knowing hit home, destiny was ringing its alarm bell. The thought of losing her son, a painful memory of what was to come, even though it was as if she had already lost him.

Jake's eyes widened, Terri had explained about his father, and some of the information about the cottage but she couldn't tell him about the missing time, only saying that it had something to do with Thyme Cottage. It was why Jake kept returning to the cottage, in some way he wanted to be close to his father, find out about him. But somewhere in the hormones as he changed from boy to man, his emotions made him push away the people that cared most.

"I'm outta of here." Jake pushed past Terri, who stood stunned, as he reached Edward he said, "Tosser."

"If you leave this house now then you are not coming back, I have had enough, I can't tak..." It was too late.

Jake slammed the front door shut behind him.

146

Toby looked at Edward, thinking that Terri went through so much trouble with Jake as he grew up and him not being there to help making him feel even more guilty.

"Is that really the last time you spoke to him?" Toby asked tentatively.

"Yes," Edward replied solemnly. "He didn't show up at school after that, at least, I never saw him. The teachers asked about him, they knew we were friends, but I couldn't tell them anything."

There was silence between the two as both reflected on what was to come. It was deflating for Toby knowing he had tried but, by trying, he had only assured the future. He kicked the floor with his feet. Glancing out of the window he looked for solace, everything looked so normal until he suddenly noticed something different about the garden.

"Mrs Grant?" the young enthusiastic man, dressed in grey pin-striped suit, with a Mickey Mouse tie, asked.

"Yes," Terri replied, "thank you for coming today."

"You're welcome. I understand you want to sell this property. Oh, by the way I'm Nigel Davis." He held out his hand, which Terri dutifully took. His handshake was limp.

"Yes. It needs work as you can see, but I think it will make someone a nice home some day," she lied.

"I don't think we will have a problem selling it. Shall we go in and have a look around." Nigel went to open the gate.

"No!" Terri cried.

"Sorry?" Nigel looked at Terri, bewildered.

"Can you not just do what you've got to do from out here?"

Nigel's mind swirled with thoughts, wondering what sort of a 'nutter' he was talking to, and then a thought occurred. "Is it unsafe?"

Like an olive branch Terri grabbed hold of it. "Yes, yes, as you can see, it has been empty for a long time and there does seem to be some uncertainty about its stability."

"Oh, I see," Nigel's face showed his disappointment as, in his head, he saw the commission dwindle unless they arrange a fixed fee – he would discuss that later. "Well, it might make it harder to sell. However if that's the case, do you mind if I look in through the windows so I can get a feel for the place, you know, advise my clients what they can expect." This time he didn't wait for a reply and, within seconds he had a camera out and was wandering into the overgrown jungle. Terri stood perplexed at the gate, watching the young man nervously.

"There's a 'for sale' sign in the garden." Toby noted.

"Where? It's amazing what people throw…" Edward got up and walked to the window. He too saw the sign, standing upright, nailed to the gate post. He turned to look at Toby who returned his concern.

"No, she can't sell it. Or does she?" The question was for Edward, but he didn't answer. "Well, does she?"

"I don't know. I don't know everything."

"I have to let her know I'm here." Toby headed from the room, momentarily forgetting what happened last time he reached the gate and went through. At the front door he stared out at the sign. Upstairs it had appeared shiny and new, now it had green moss growing on its shaft. He sensed Edward sidling up to him.

"Tell me how you control time. Tell me how you managed to go back. I have got to try and talk to her, tell her I'm here."

"What do you hope to accomplish? It didn't work with you. I tried." Edward stepped through the open door.

"I have to try. I can't just stay here and forget about her." Edward glanced back. "Please tell me what you did?" There was a pause whilst Edward thought. Toby changed tack. "How did you discover the secret?"

147

After a pause, Edward continued.

"It was my eighteenth birthday. I hadn't seen Jake for over two years, not to speak to anyway, only in passing, I missed him as a friend. I can't explain it clearly. It was like a part of me was missing. I'd occasionally find myself standing outside the cottage hoping to see him, I did once or twice, but he didn't acknowledge me. In his sallow eyes I saw contempt, the drugs had taken their toll on him.

I'd seen Terri fairly regularly, I could confide in her about my life and what was going on and she seemed to enjoy our chats. I felt a connection with Terri, like I would have been hers if things had turned out differently.

Anyway, my foster parents were taking me out to celebrate, a special dinner, and they had invited Terri, and Jake. They knew he wouldn't go but I think they hoped it might be an olive branch."

Toby turned to face Edward, hating to hear how his family had been torn apart. "Did Jake still live at home?"

"Yes, well, occasionally. He would disappear for days or weeks at a time but, Terri didn't have the heart to follow through on her threat. I don't think her Mum was too pleased, but." Edward left the sentiment unfinished - he could see Toby understood. "As I was saying, it was my eighteenth birthday and as we were about to leave a parcel, well more like a small trunk, arrived by courier.

It was from a firm of solicitors, Harper & Catcham and was a bit out of the blue, and although I was curious, we were running late so it had to wait until we got back."

Toby looked on expectantly, hoping the explanation would come soon; when they had first met, Edward couldn't have been more cryptic, now he just wanted to talk.

"And?"

"It was a box full of my parents' things, notebooks, diaries and a whole load of other paraphernalia, along with a notice of the inheritance due to me on my eighteenth birthday. Eighty-five thousand pounds in total, I couldn't believe it, that was a lot of money. I forgot about the diaries etc. Life started to move on, faster and faster, I bought a car and went to University to study chemistry, biology and physics. I liked the sciences and in the end found my stepfather a lot more interesting because of it." Toby felt his patience running out, he wanted to know how to control time. "Then one day I got a letter from Terri. I remember sitting at the kitchen table in the flat I shared with my girlfriend, Grace, reading that Jake had died of a heart attack at twenty-one. It was a shock for me, I can tell you." Edward stared at the wall behind Toby, who looked shattered by the news.

"Edward you should've have been there today, you missed a corker, Roger got completely taken out by Simon, I never thought I'd see it, it was incredible. Haven't laughed so much in ages." Grace wrapped her arms around Edward and kissed the back of his head. "You alright?"

"Jake's dead." The words came out like a vicious slurry.

"Who? I've never heard you talk about a Jake. Do you want a coffee?" Grace checked, before filling the kettle. "Jackie and Chris have asked whether we want to go down to the pub later. Do you fancy it?"

Edward didn't answer, his thoughts firmly attached to childhood memories, and the final bitter argument that had torn them apart. Guilt ripped into him and he wished he had tried harder. Inexplicably the emptiness of a missing part of him, bit back; a long forgotten feeling that he hated.

"Edward?" Grace turned, realising she had been slightly insensitive. "Who is Jake? Why don't you tell me about him? Why haven't you mentioned him before?" Her voice expressed her warm caring side as she sat down next to Edward, resting a reassuring hand on his knee.

"He was a friend, my best friend." Tears pooled in his eyes and he didn't try stop them, the regret and guilt twisting like a knife. Edward didn't say anything further.

Grace pulled Edward into a hug, which he didn't reciprocate or pull away from. The tears kept flowing for five minutes as more pictures and memories played their final show in his mind. Edward knew she was there for him and he loved her for not pushing the issue. But the guilt he felt wasn't giving up so easily, it started to eat away at him. Edward barely spoke to Grace about Jake, but instead let it fester away inside, and within two months they had split up, after being together for two and a half years.

"It wasn't until then that I went home to visit my foster parents and rediscovered the box with my parents' things. Although I had looked at it years before, I had never given any of it more than a cursory glance. I don't know why, maybe a tinge of betrayal towards my foster parents? I started to sieve through the items, reading their diaries."

148

"That's when I found out about my true past, my parents' true past, and who they were. I spent two days reading the diaries. It was a welcome distraction from the guilt that raked, guilt that I wanted to bury again. There was a letter, from my father, trying to explain their origins and why I had no living relatives."

Edward,

I hoped that you would never have to read this letter and that one day your mother and I would be having this conversation with you. There is no easy way to comprehend where we have come from and where you find yourself. We thought it prudent to leave you something in the way of knowledge should we not survive. The diaries that should be with this chest will help you understand how we coped with the upheaval and the change in our circumstances. Excuse some of the early anomalies, we didn't start making notes until a few months had passed.

There is no easy way for you to understand this, but we came from 1757, then via magic after being wrongly accused of using dark powers against another, find ourselves here. We have investigated many ways to get back alas have had little luck thus far, and now we have you, and as much as we do not feel part of this place, we feel it offers you a better future, so we have ceased *experimenting.*

The location of our arrival is detailed in journal one. If we have not survived and you receive this, it may be nice for you to visit. You will have inherited our powers, even though you would not have been guided in their use, and until such a time as we find a coven who can take you under their wing, we will write down as much information as we can in order that you may learn to use your powers.

We have searched in our hearts for parting words of wisdom to pass on to you. Composing a letter like this is not easy, we don't know what you need to know. However, there is a spell should you need us - it will enhance our essence that is all around you and allow some communication, albeit a limited version.

If you have received this, we are sorry to have left you in this world on your own. Be goode, be true, be wise.

Your loving parents

Isobel and Michael.

"I read the letter again and again. It seemed so alien to me. They were saying I had power, magic power. The journals appeared like hieroglyphics. Some of the early experiments made no sense to me, and I couldn't talk to my foster parents.

Amazed at what I had read, I digested it gradually. I started to understand and began to experiment." Edward could see Toby getting anxious to get to the point of the story and the key, which was important. "At first I did little spells as they had detailed, but I started to get bored and skipped ahead, to my detriment. They were close to pinpointing what it was that sent them through time, although they knew they were missing one crucial element." Edward looked at Toby, who stared back expectantly. "Silver."

"You said it, but how do you tune it in?"

"Science of all things. But you need to know what you are tuning into and that is the difficulty. Thankfully, my education helped to provide an answer, with just a little more information provided by my father, or rather, my foster father."

"Hold on a minute, if you can do that, why did you say you sacrificed your life for Jake's."

"It was a one way deal and one that locked me here in this place. Magic, science, the combination can be fickle things, there are no set rules as such and I am by no means an expert, and because of my limited knowledge, my foster parents now do not know where I am."

149

"You mean you just disappeared one night?"

"Yes, I didn't realise I would, and I hope one day that I can correct that. For the moment that is the way it is. The guilt I felt for Jake made me feel that I had let him down and I hoped I could change that. What would you have done?"

The question vexed Toby as he stared at the jaded 'For Sale' sign. Would he have gone back to save his own son? He guessed, hoped the answer was yes. Somehow it was still hard to comprehend Jake's life story, he only knew him as a child, a child he would never see grow up and who would grow up not knowing his foolish father.

As he stood watching the sign, churning over the hypothetical question, it faded from view temporarily, re-appearing moments later on the ground and the day outside of Thyme Cottage changed with it, to the full bloom of summer. A figure appeared and it took a couple of minutes to recognise the face, it was Terri, her hair neatly cropped short but left longer at the sides, accentuating her soft features. Her face had been opened up, enhancing her beautiful eyes, making her pale complexion radiate warmth; she positively glowed. The figure-hugging black jeans, which were out of the ordinary for her, made her look stunning, shaping her figure nicely. The white crisp top was tucked in neatly, revealing her buxom chest.

"Beautiful isn't she?" Edward asked rhetorically. "I always did fancy her, she had a way about her. A sexine…" Edward stopped, aware of Toby looking at him, regret painted plainly in his eyes before returning to look at her. Toby's heart wrenched at the thought of never seeing her again, never touching her. He remembered the perfume she like so much, 'Opium', a sweet mandarin note that danced around tingling the senses. "Why don't you go to her?"

Toby sprinted through the front door like a giddy schoolchild.

Nigel returned to Terri.

"It certainly looks well proportioned for a railway cottage, it needs a lot of work but the right person, I think, will see its charm. I'm surprised so many original features remain, always a bonus…" He stopped suddenly as Terri stared at him opened-mouthed. "Mrs Grant, are you alright?"

Gulping, Terri took a second to answer. "A-ha, yes, fine, just. Yes, what were you saying?"

Nigel shook his head briefly and carried on. "I was saying that the original features will help, even though it needs a lot of work. I take it the upstairs is in a similar state."

"Yes."

"Right." Nigel made some notes on a pad. "Now, I reckon if we put it into auction with a guide price of £80-90,000 you might achieve £120,000. These places have been selling for around the one-sixty, but that is refurbished. It also depends on what the survey says. How bad is the structural stability of the building?"

"Not sure." Terri shook her head. The thought of deceiving people was hard, but it was pointless for them to keep the cottage, and she knew it would be nice to move out of her Mum's bungalow.

"Right then. Well, I'll firm all that up in a letter and get it sent out to you on Monday. Is that alright?"

"Okay," Terri said, agreeing it was the sensible thing to do now and maybe one way to save her family, however, she made a silent vow to bring Jake here and tell him the truth about his father. "Do I need to sign anything?"

Nigel was surprised, he hadn't expected to get confirmation so quickly and eagerly added, "Oh, yes, back at the office, there are a few formalities if you definitely want to go ahead?"

"Yes." Was her short hesitant reply.

Terri accepted a lift from Nigel to the office to sign the paperwork. As she placed a signature at the bottom of the form, a feeling of giving away a part of her life came to the fore and she went pale, her hand shaking.

"Are you alright Mrs Grant?"

"Fine," she replied, through gritted teeth.

150

Terri was just about to turn away. Toby couldn't believe she hadn't seen him.

"Terri," He screamed louder than he expected. Toby reached the gate just as Terri turned to face him,

"Toby." She reeled backwards as anger, denial, and finally acceptance pulsed through her like a tornado.

After a momentary pause, he reached out to grab her hand, but as his hand became level with the gate a static electric shock forced him to retract it. He hadn't noticed it before when he had ran full pelt through and ended up back in the room upstairs. Dismayed, he looked at his hand and then at Terri for reassurance – it didn't come. Her eyes begged for answers, she stepped to the gate as Toby stumbled backwards, hit once again by the reality that he couldn't leave Thyme cottage.

"I'm sorry Terri." But her eyes were fixed on something behind and he glanced round to see Edward standing in the doorway. He half-smiled a silent greeting, not sure what to say, knowing he just wanted to see her again.

Toby turned back to Terri in time to see her start to open the gate.

"No, don't come in," then more forcefully, adding, "You can't come in."

Terri's anxious eyes were full of more questions, he stared into them, desperately trying to express all the thoughts that rushed around his head. He stepped back to the gate and pushed it firmly closed. "I'm sorry, you can't come in, you mustn't, otherwise I'll lose you again."

Suddenly Terri started to phase out, a shimmering shadow. Desperately Toby called to her. "Terri, Terri," before feeling a hand on his right shoulder. Turning he saw Edward holding out his hand.

"Take this." Edward passed a silver coin to him, the silver coin he had seen him with the first night. Puzzled, Toby frowned. "Take it before you lose her again." Edward pushed it into his open hand, immediately Edward phased out of sight, Toby frantically turned back to where Terri had been standing.

"There you go, Mrs Grant, these are your copies, and, as I said, we'll get it into next month's auction. I know there'll be quite a bit of interest. It's a nice property, well, certainly could be." Nigel handed Terri the copies of the paperwork. She was trying hard not to let her sadness show through, and was choking back the heartache, knowing that it would not be hers, or theirs, any longer. Hoping that somehow it would save her family, although she still found it strange and unbelievable to comprehend that what Edward had said was true and that Toby was gone. Her experience with Joseph only added to her woes as she left the estate agents, eighty or ninety years Joseph had been gone. Generations missed. Would Toby be gone that long? She hoped not.

Ten minutes later she was still standing on the pavement outside the estate agents, lost. Nigel came out.

"Mrs Grant? Would you like to come back in and sit down, you've been out here for a while." His young fresh face showed an honesty to it.

"Thank you, no, I'm just…" She bit back the words, held onto the emotional turmoil inside and walked off, sighing. "A new start, that's what I need, I can't go on like this." It was a decisive moment and one that clearly defined where her life was going from now on.

She left Nigel standing perplexed, but content that a commission was in the bag.

A few hundred metres along the road Terri stopped outside a hairdressers, Fare Hair. It had one customer sitting down being attended to by a middle-aged woman who's long straight blonde hair looked as though it had never been styled other than the length kept in check. A young girl sat in one of the free chairs flicking through the pages of a magazine, looking bored, a Saturday girl swept the floor meticulously, even though it didn't need it.

Terri eyed her reflection in the plate-glass window, her long dark hair was looking a little tired and was making her look older than she was. 'A fresh start' she thought, and, within seconds, was inside.

The bored girl sprang to attention and soon Terri was seated, with the girl fussing over her, talking ten to the dozen, about the many fashionable styles that were around.

"Bobs are in you know, but somehow I think something more striking would suit your face."

Terri started to feel it was bad idea, she liked the way she looked, had never questioned it, Toby liked the way she looked – Toby's not here - she thought.

"Okay," Terri said. "Go for it, in for a penny, in for a pound." Her words were strong but her voice expressed her lack of real courage.

The young girl faltered as delight shot through her, this was her chance to show off her skills, create without objection. Terri became aware that she wasn't sure if she had heard the young girl correctly, but it was too late.

151

Terri watched mortified as lumps of hair were being, what looked like, carelessly chopped off, falling ungracefully to the floor in an untidy pile. Dread filled her. What had she done? The house? Her hair?

It had been shocking enough when she saw her hair bleached. Now, before her very eyes, her face was changing shape, her cheeks looked more prominent, her ears protruded further than she had thought, her gold loop earrings appearing massive now they were clearly on view, her nose looked more pointed and her make up paled against the blonde hair. The hairdresser, Vanessa, chatted away, not paying attention to the worried looked that was slowly growing into a frown, ever confident that what she had suggested would suit. She was pleased that, for once, she had had free reign to try something new and loved the challenge it presented.

Two-and-half hours later Terri stared at the finished article, speechless, it was so different, she didn't know whether to laugh or cry.

For the first time Vanessa noticed that her client was not overly enamoured with her new look and, rather sheepishly, tried to make Terri feel better.

"If I may say so, I think it really shows off your cheek bones, you have got a lovely line down here," Vanessa pointed to Terri's cheek so she could see it in the mirror. "And if you use a slightly different tone of blusher it will bring out the colour of your eyes. I use this one." Vanessa stepped across to her bag, on the floor behind the pay kiosk and pulled out her make up bag full of different eyeliners, lipsticks, lip glosses. "See." Vanessa demonstrated, without waiting to be given permission. The middle-aged blonde woman had not interfered throughout but had carried on attending to her customers with little conversation. She was amused at Vanessa's incessant chat and brash confidence, hoping one day it would backfire on her, but generally, somehow, she won through in the end.

Forty minutes later Terri had a full makeover and approved of her new face, Vanessa had been right, the short crop and change of make up had given her a sexy, sassy look which invoked confidence but left her clothes looking drab and outdated. She left a large tip for Vanessa and booked a follow-up appointment for six weeks, she wanted to keep this look tip-top.

With a spring back in her step she felt the world was not so against her. The thought of a clothes shopping trip excited her. It had been a long time since she had splashed out extravagantly on clothes, it was time to throw out some of the drab comfortable bits she'd been wearing for years and engage her new-found confidence.

Terri looked forlornly at Toby, she reached across the gate and touched his hand. The tenderness showed on their faces, the longing, the love.

"I've missed you," Terri said, pulling Toby into a hug over the gate, as they did so a static charge coursed through making the hairs on their arms stand on end.

"I've missed you too. How long have I been gone?" Toby asked, still feeling the static crackling between them, the sound inexplicable and a little distracting.

"Too long." Terri buried her head in Toby's neck inhaling his essence that was like a sweet nectar, fuelling the emotions she had hidden for nearly two years.

"You look amazing," Toby whispered, not wanting to let go.

Toby felt his shoulder growing wet as tears rolled gently down Terri's cheek. "Hey, what's wrong?" He pushed Terri to arms length so he could take in her splendour.

"I put it on the market, Toby." Terri confessed, expecting a backlash. Toby could only look at his wife with understanding - silently he agreed they should have done that in the first instance now they knew the pain and hurt that Thyme Cottage had caused. After a couple of minutes Terri dried her eyes with a paper tissue from her shoulder bag.

"Come home. Jake's growing up so fast."

Toby choked back the words he knew he had to say. It was the only answer he could give, and he knew it would break her heart again. If only they could stay here, at Thyme Cottage, forever – it was an unobtainable dream, and he knew it. Finally, slowly he said the words that would be thunder. "I can't."

Terri withdrew from him, reeling from the shock, questions buzzing round – why not? What have I done? Don't you love me? His worst dreams were fulfilled. "I can't leave this place. Terri please, no, it's not what you think." But already Terri's face was growing angry, rage re-building the wall around her heart that she had put up to protect herself and which only Toby had the power to knock down instantly. "Terri, please, listen," But she was almost running down the street, trying to stop the hurt, hoping it wouldn't catch up with her.

In a moment of madness, Toby forced open the gate and bounded through, only to find himself back in the room upstairs.

152

"Noooo," Toby sobbed, pounding the wall, determined to lose the aggression that was rising within him. "Why me?" he screamed back at the empty room, loneliness throwing its cloak over him. "Why did you ever tell me about this place?" he yelled at Edward, hoping that wherever he was he would hear it. "Why were you so guarded about its secret, why didn't you just tell me the truth?" Toby sank to his knees, the picture of Terri walking away so fresh, so painful.

Terri burst through the door catching Vivien unexpectedly as she walked from the bathroom.

"You frightened the life out of... my god Terri is that you?" There was a nanosecond before she continued. "You look amazing. What have you had done?"

"Do you like it?"

"Like it, I love it, it really suits you. Not something I imagined would but yes, it looks fabulous." Terri placed her coat on a hook, beaming at the compliment, closing the door with her foot.

"This hairdresser, Vanessa, did it. She said it brought out my eyes and she gave me a list of make-up I should try and loads of tips," she gushed. "I thought it was time for a change."

"I can tell. You look ten years younger, you look brighter. Can I guess why you did it?" Vivien didn't wait for an answer, "Do you want a drink?"

Terri's mood sank momentarily. "Yes, please, and yes I have." A hint of melancholy in her voice emphasized how hard the decision had been. She walked into the lounge and looked at

Jake playing cheerfully on the floor.

"I'm going to look after you, make sure that place doesn't destroy you." Jake ignored Terri and carried on playing with the brightly coloured plastic building bricks.

"Tea or coffee?" Vivien called from the kitchen.

"Coffee please." Terri wandered to the kitchen. "I know you disagree with the sale but I feel it is right. We need to make a fresh start. We don't know how long Toby will be gone and I can't rely on you all the time. I need to be strong for Jake, especially if what Edward said is true."

Vivien turned to face her daughter. "I know, it's just that I actually like you both being here. It reminds me of when your father was alive and you were just a baby, they were happy times. Yes, we had arguments but there weren't many."

"We won't go far away, probably only a couple of roads. I just feel that I need to do it. I know you were planning the loft extension and that would have been great." Terri's positivity about her plans faded a little and she found herself wondering whether it was such a good idea to move out once the cottage was sold. The proposed loft extension was to give her a bedroom and dressing room as well as an en-suite, and she did like living with her Mum now Toby was gone.

Finally Vivien conceded. "I know, I am just being selfish." She stood and rubbed her daughter's upper arm reassuringly. "You need to live your life. I only wish Toby were with you."

"So do I. What is it they say about looking a gift horse in the mouth? We should never have accepted the cottage in the first place."

"Yes, and hindsight is such a wonderful thing. I'd be rich if I had a pound for everytime I'd wished that. Here you go?" Vivien handed Terri a mug of coffee and they walked back into the lounge.

"I wonder what Toby is doing right now? What he knows."

"One day, one day you'll find out."

"Let's hope I'm not too old for him then."

Silence descended on the two as they reflected separately how life was turning out, not as either had expected.

Breaking the quiet Terri's mobile sang out its cheerful ditty.

"Is that Terri?" the voice enquired.

"Yes, speaking."

"It's Jill from Graydon's Employment agency." Terri's face lit up. She had forgotten she had signed up with them. "We've got a job interview available for tomorrow if you're free and still looking." Before Terri could answer, Jill continued. "It's with a local firm of financial advisors, they are looking for a general office manager. They are offering a salary of about twenty-three thousand. I know you said you were only looking for part-time work but they offer a subsidy for childcare if needed." Terri couldn't help but brighten, today indeed seemed to be the first day of a fresh start.

153

Full of anger, Toby got up and sprinted down the stairs and out through front door hurtling as fast as he could to the open gate. A static shock clipped his senses as once again he found himself back in the room. Rage boiled inside him and he set off again as if it would make a difference. After four failed attempts to break free, he lay on the floor breathless, hot and sweaty with bloodshot eyes as the tears wouldn't stop coming.

"Edward, Edward," he shouted, spittle dribbling from the corner of his mouth.

"Toby." Edward appeared from nowhere. Toby sat bolt upright.

"You've got to show me how to go back, how to talk to Terri again." Toby spoke in short bursts as he got his breath back. Suddenly he noticed a small device Edward was holding, it looked like what Toby knew as a voltmeter, but more primitive with two displays.

Edward answered his question before he asked. "Yes, this is what I have used. I carry it with me at all times." Toby looked at him, aghast, fathoming the logic of the sentence. "I made it to help me, Toby. I put it together using information from my education and some of the early theories from my father." Edward set the device on the floor and Toby scooted across to the get a closer look. Edward knelt down and pulled two wires, red and black, from another pocket and plugged them into jack-points.

"What is it? It looks like a voltmeter."

"It doesn't have a name and yes, it is, or rather was, I adapted it and made a few changes but the principles are similar. After my fight with Jake when he tore off my St Christopher, reading my parents notes, along with my experience after that fight, I started to form an idea. It's a shame it took so long to find a common thread. Amongst the stuff I inherited from my parents were the pendants they wore. They were silver and, with my knowledge," Edward paused in thought as Toby looked on attentively, eager for Edward to continue. "Silver is the most conductive of precious metals."

"Yes, you told me."

"So I did. The rationale I followed is that everything has a frequency and if silver is the common key then maybe time does as well. It was the only hypothesis I had that explained how some people were never affected. Now, if that hypothesis, is, was true, then if I could tune a piece of silver to a certain frequency, I should be able to pinpoint a particular time segment in history." Looking at Toby, he could see the questions burgeoning him. "Obviously there isn't a manual so I had to experiment. This device was the culmination of eighteen months work, but using these dials I can tune into an approximate time." Toby stared in disbelief that something so small could help him.

"It wasn't exact, which is why I ended up here, a year before you inherited this place."

A thought exploded in Toby's head. "But surely if you can tune to a time in the past you can go forward again to…" Edward looked solemnly at Toby.

"That's what I thought, but for some reason it only works one way, maybe something to do with the magic as well. For whatever reason, the cottage, or the time fracture that is present, controls future travel, and for only those who do not wear a silver object. If you do wear a silver object it somehow tunes itself to the current time, anchoring them, making it safe to enter this place." Edward pulled another silver coin from his pocket.

"These were in my parent's things. I use these, or rather one of these, as that is all you need."

Toby brightened as another idea blossomed in his fervent mind. "How about if I give one of these to Terri, then she could come in, she could stay, she could live here, we could be together. We could, couldn't we?"

Edward had never given it a thought. Why not? It was a logical suggestion. Maybe because he had only ever wanted to save Jake and not occupy the cottage, but the theory was good. If a silver token was all it took to hold time steady then Toby's idea might be feasible. Objects had certainly not been affected by the time fracture.

"You could be right Toby." Edward's face showed surprise as a slight smile started to appear. There was an end to all of this. There was a way.

154

"Toby you must still remember that you cannot leave this place, neither can I; and that riddle I have not been able to solve. For some unknown reason, travelling backwards in time locks you to this place. Yet, if the house, or the time fracture, projects you forwards in time – like my parents who were transported to 1998 - you can." Edward sensed the question that had been one of his own. "They used magic to establish identities and gain employment. A little incantation that creates a kind of cloak allowing a certain manoeuvreability, shall we say, giving them the chance to fit it normally."

"Hold on." Toby's mind was in turmoil as facts and thoughts raced about. "If we think this through logically, your parents were wearing the silver pendants at the time of their... whatever you want to call it, transportation to 1998. You have established that silver is what holds time steady when in this property, then surely you must be able to tune into the future, you can go home."

"It doesn't work." Edward wasn't a patient person when it came to explaining complicated theories to people who couldn't grasp them and frustration started to boil at repeating himself. Whilst time travel wasn't exactly science, it's roots were in science. His experiments had been extensive and he hated that Toby thought he knew better, despite being open to new ideas. "You think I haven't tried, once I came back and did what I wanted to do, I tried to go back."

"Did the time fracture not take you back?" Toby quick-fired.

"No, not exactly," Edward stood up and walked around the

room, frustrated, "Toby, it is like a game of chance, you can control backward movement, yet forward movement is at the time fracture's will."

"How far forward have you been?"

"Fifty, sixty years. It is difficult to gauge as I can't leave this cottage."

"What about the Pineapple Amethyst Crystals? What relevance do they have in all this?"

For a moment Edward stared at Toby, confused, "Pineapple Amethyst Crystals?"

"Yes, like the one Matthew stole and had to put back, the night I got myself stuck here as well."

Recognition flashed across his face. "They were used to protect my mother and father from having their powers stripped, they were meant to turn the power of the coven on the perpetrator of the deception, but it didn't work and they ended up here." A thought started to crystalise in his mind, a connection that was just out of reach, hidden in the shadows.

"What is it?" Toby enquired.

"I…" Edward hesitated, then ran from the room, his footfalls echoing on the bareboards of the stairs. Toby ran after him, stopping at the door to look at the device on the floor. Not knowing whether it was safe to leave it there or not. Grabbing it, he ran downstairs.

"Edward! Edward!" Toby went from room to room but Edward had vanished and the cottage sat in relative quiet. Suddenly a shadowy figure brushed past him. "Edward?" There was a faint reply which he couldn't make out. Then, without warning, Edward was standing in front him. "Where have you been?"

"Sorry, you got me thinking. All this time I had forgotten about the Pineapple Amethyst Cystals and the role they played."

"You mean we might be able to end this?" Toby asked excitedly.

"I need to make sure that all the original crystals are in

place," Edward said, looking at the floor as if he was sizing up the space.

"How do we do that?"

Edward thought for a second before answering, I can use a locator spell. We know that one of them is already in the lounge, Matthew put it back there."

"Yes, the White Hats said he needed to replace it for their spell to work, I don't know why bec…"

Edward interrupted, "because they are what started this time fracture and without them," he paused, as a thought whirled around his brain. "Of course! That's why it never worked."

"What? What are you talking about 'never worked'?" But before Edward answered he had gone into the lounge, Toby followed. "Edward what are you…?"

Edward had lifted the floorboard that Matthew had discovered as being loose. Toby walked over and stared at the ground below.

155

"Where is it?" Toby asked, perplexed. "They said he had to put it back for the magic to work."

"And he didn't," Edward said, enlightened. A full understanding of what had occurred rallied his thoughts. "That's why your friends, the White Hats, disappeared."

"What?" Toby exclaimed.

"That night they evaporated, the only trace of them is a blue powder. I found the newspaper article of the night in question, although there was no mention of what they were doing. The article only said that a blue powder had been found in thirteen points around this property, a property they were last reported visiting."

"So what happened to them? And what happens now."

"Well if the thirteen crystals are not in place then there is very little we can do."

"So we need to get the thirteenth crystal back from Matthew." Toby paused. "How the hell we are we going to do that?"

The room sank into silence.

"Terri could get it bac..." but Toby had forgotten he couldn't leave the cottage. He was a prisoner stuck in time.

"Mum, are you coming?" Terri called, putting her coat on.

"Sorry." Vivien poked her head out through the kitchen doorway.

"Are you coming to the auction?" she repeated, zipping her coat up before double checking that Jake was wrapped up warm in his pushchair. "I thought you said you wanted to."

Vivien sighed wearily. She felt sorry for Toby, Terri's loss, and she'd had second thoughts that selling the house was the best idea now. What would Toby say if he was here?

"No, I think I'll stay here. I'll take care of Jake if you want?"

"Thank you, but I want him to be with me. I don't know Mum, I just think he needs to be there, it's like I am saying goodbye and I want him too, as well. Does that make sense?"

Vivien stared lovingly at her daughter, "Of course it does. Let me know how it goes."

"Should go well," Terri said cheerfully. "Nigel said there has been quite a bit of interest." Terri paused, he had also told her that some clients had not come back to him and their mobiles were off. Terri feared what had happened and desperately tried to fight the concern that rose inside like an angry beast. She hadn't told Vivien. It was bad enough trying to deal with the guilt on her own, without her Mum knowing that she had let other people get caught up in the cottages mysterious happenings. "See you later."

As the door closed, Vivien moved into the hallway. "I wish you would come back Toby, wherever you are." The plea resounded off the walls, a hollow wish.

After a long pause, Toby started to cogitate on all the events and, more importantly, the first contact Edward had made with him, at the estate agents.

"Wait a minute," Toby started, startling Edward, who was studying the empty lounge, picturing how it could look with love and care. "How did you manage to contact me, or my estate agents? Can't we do that again, whatever you did?"

"Guess work and luck, guess work and luck."

"Eh?" Toby enquired.

"Although I can, as explained, tune to certain frequencies, times, with the silver coins, it is not an exact science, there is no sure measure. I set the frequency, take it out of the machine and, with the help of a little magic, let it guide me back. I then rely on people walking along the street to find out what day, year, etcetera and so forth. The house has its own volatility but as long as I have my machine I can go back."

"But if that's the case how come you haven't found yourself back in your own time? Surely if it sends you far enough into the future you can just go back to the correct time."

Exasperated, Edward looked at Toby. He realised it was a difficult concept to understand. "I did just that…" Toby was about say something when Edward continued, "but I still couldn't leave the house, whatever I had initiated locked me to this place just like you."

156

Dismayed, Toby's eyes showed his confusion.

"I know, I can't explain it very well, but magic has it's own properties as well, mix that with time and science and you have cauldron of steaming reality that does not always follow logic."

Finally Toby spoke. "Can you get me back to a time when Terri was here, or at the gate, like the other day, today, or whenever it actually was?" He finished, his voice rising in excitement at the thought of seeing Terri, talking to her.

"Do we know when that was?"

"What do you mean?"

"When in actual reality it was, to the time we are in now, standing here?" Toby's face glazed over, the truth was more than he could handle.

Edward rummaged in his pocket and pulled out three coins. "See these." Toby nodded. "Well, this one," Edward showed him a coin with an 'E' scratched on the back, "this is set at the time from when I came, my life, a future which I know and want to be part of again, hopefully with Jake in it. This coin." He showed another coin with a black scorch mark on it. "I take as being from my parents' time, again the notes depict a charge running through their bodies and is similar to a mark I saw on the pendants. The third one I use to go between times." Sensing Toby's incredulity, "It will be easier if I show you."

Toby handed the contraption that he had brought downstairs to Edward. "I place the coin with my initial in here as a reference point." He placed the coin into a slot at the side of the device and one of the meter needles sprang to life, registering a reading. "Then I connect the other to the leads and turn this dial," Toby watched, intrigued. "I have roughly calculated that each of these intervals," he pointed at the display, "represents about five years, registering a charge of 1 milliamp, so, using the reading from my initial coin, I work backwards." Edward twisted the knob underneath and together they watched the second needle twitch into life starting at the position of the first and falling to the left.

As the needle reached a certain point Edward stopped.

"And now what?"

"I take the coin with my initial out, turn off the machine and hold the other coin." Toby hadn't seen that Edward had initialised two coins, one was passed to him.

"And that's it?"

"Pretty much, except for a little magic."

Toby almost smirked. It still sounded so alien, despite what had happened,"

"Endecha, Hun chata, Timeline compose, Timeline align. Detruta Karma nathia."

Toby heard what sounded like a gunshot, which made him jump. He looked at Edward disbelievingly as the smell of spent bullet filtered through the room.

"What was…?" But Toby knew. He had smelt and heard the very same on the first night he had entered the cottage and met Edward. He didn't question whether it had worked, it must have done, Edward had done it before, hadn't he?

"Why don't the other coins interfere? You said that each silver object tunes itself to a certain time, surely they would corrupt one another."

"Toby." Edward started angrily, making Toby flinch. "Sorry, yes, it sometimes does, that's why I fade out occasionally. Some frequencies seem to be stronger, have a stronger pull to them. All I know is it generally works. I also have the power to let them fade." Toby looked baffled. "The power of magic, Toby."

"Oh. So what do we do now?"

"Nothing, it is done." Toby looked around the room. "But it still looks the same."

"What did you expect?" Toby shrugged his shoulders. Outside the window the sky was growing brighter. "Come on, we need to go outside and see if anyone is around. Maybe we can borrow a mobile phone."

"Sorry."

"That's what I did. I knew your old office number from some papers that Terri found. I remembered it and so I called it, that's how I contacted you after persuading a nice member of public to let me use their phone."

Toby followed Edward outside, holding the coin securely in his hand, as if his life depended on it.

The street looked empty.

"What now?"

"We wait Toby, we wait."

157

Terri stood at the back of the auction room, which was the ballroom of a local hotel. Nerves tingled as the details of each property were called out and a frantic display of bidding took place. Hands appearing at different places in the room, signals that caught the auctioneer's eyes but were lost to her.

Doubt started to creep into her. Even her new image and the

confidence it gave, couldn't stave it off. Was she doing the right thing? What if someone knocked it down and it broke whatever was going on with the cottage and Toby could never find his way back?

Another lot number was called, breaking her from her painful memories of all that the cottage now represented. The bidding grew even more frantic as hands, bits of paper, and paddles rose into the air, the starting price had been sixty-thousand and within a minute rose to above a hundred thousand, four or five people wanted the house, a four-bedroomed residence in need of modernisation, a small courtyard garden and no off-street parking. The hammer went down, the price had soared to one-hundred-and-fifty-three thousand. The figure flashed like neon in her head and suddenly the prospect of cold, hard, cash beckoned. Terri scanned the list and saw there were only three more properties after this one, before Thyme Cottage. Silently she offered an apology to Toby still wishing he was there, but knowing she had to move on.

"Lots forty-six and forty-seven have been withdrawn, which bring us to lot forty-eight, a fire damaged bungalow in Leigh, two bedrooms, separate lounge, kitchen, garden, garage. I have bids on the books and start the bidding at seventy-five thousand." The auctioneer glanced about the room, slowly a hand rose into the air and the bidding was off.

"Eighty... Eighty-five... Ninety... Ninety-five... One hundred... One-ten." The auctioneer was reading some figures from a page in front of him before throwing it back out to the room, declaring no more registered bids. There was a sudden surge and then the hammer's fall reverberated around the room. It had happened so quick, she wasn't ready, she needed more time, but it was too late.

'This was it', Lot 49, Thyme Cottage. Terri had been pleased by the way the previous bidding had been going and hoped that it was a good sign. Yet, inside she was scared. She pulled a sleeping Jake from his pushchair, the implications not even on his radar. Cuddling her son she felt Toby's essence close to her, and she crossed her fingers as the auctioneer declared the opening gambit.

Silence settled on the room.

"Sixty-five then, come on who will open the bidding at sixty-five for this delightful end terraced three up, three down larger than usual railway cottage with its many original features." Again silence was the response. Terri's heart sank as her dream of a new start crumbled before her very eyes.

"How long is this going to take?" Toby asked, bored, kicking the ground. They had been waiting for over two hours and not one person had passed by the cottage.

"Patience," was Edward's simple reply. Toby was going to object but instead walked back inside the lounge, studying the pulled up floorboard where the crystal should have been.

"Bloody reporter..." but his thoughts were interrupted by Edward's call.

"Toby!"

He dashed from the lounge in time to see Edward rushing down the path towards two ladies walking dogs. He followed.

"Excuse me ladies," Edward politely called, but they initially ignored him as they were too busy chatting. "Excuse me," he called, a little louder, trying to keep his voice polite. "I've got an emergency and my mobile phone has died, could I be cheeky and borrow one of yours if you have one?"

Edward was met with a strange curious look from the taller of the two women who haughtily replied, "I don't have a mobile phone."

"Thank you anyway," Edward responded with a smile.

158

"Come on, Ladies and Gentleman, this is a delightful little cottage with great potential, either as an investment or as a project." His eyes scanned the room meeting Terri's. She quickly diverted her gaze as hope faded.

"I think it's time to go home Jake," Terri whispered.

"Please someone start me at fifty-five."

Terri felt betrayed, it was worth more than that; the truth about the mystery of Thyme Cottage vanishing from her memory like a sweet elixir.

"If there are no takers then I will have…"

A hand in the third row slowly climbed up above the hands.

"Fifty-five thousand sir, thank you. Anymore offers?"

"Fifty-six," a lone voice called.

"Thank you, gentleman at the back of the room." Then the auctioneer peered at the first gentleman. "Sir, do I hear fifty-seven?" There was a pause for consideration but the man shook his head. "Any other offers in the room?" He waited with bated breath and when there was no reply, he called, "No sale. Reserve not met." The gentleman shrugged, non-plussed.

As the auctioneer continued with the next lot Terri slunk away, pushing Jake solemnly from the hotel, deciding to take a walk along the seafront to calm her raging mind, as emotion after emotion ravaged her. The new start a million miles away. All her new found confidence ebbing away too. She didn't want to go home just yet. The sun was trying to break through the low cloud cover.

"Yes, but I do, Jane." The shorter of the two women, Regina, fished in her bag and pulled out a large grey phone, by which time Toby had joined Edward at the garden wall.

"Thank you, you are very kind. We will keep it very short, it's just so my friend can ring his wife, she's meant to be meeting us here, but we think she has got lost."

"There you go. You're welcome. I never use it much myself but my daughter likes me to carry it around."

Edward took the proffered phone and handed it to Toby. "Give her a ring."

Toby dialled Vivien's number.

"It's a lovely day isn't it?" Edward said, smiling at Regina. "Reminds me of the start of that blistering hot summer we had in ninety-seven, wasn't it?" He left it open hoping that one of the ladies would confirm or deny.

Jane, the taller lady, looked away from Edward, annoyed that their early morning saunter had been interrupted, it was always so peaceful at eight o clock on a Sunday, a pleasant time to walk the dogs, who sniffed unperturbed at anything and everything. "I hate the hot weather, perspiring, trying to keep cool," Jane concluded.

Toby was waiting for the phone to be answered, which rang and rang, he couldn't understand what was taking so long.

"Well, I like the summer, although the garden does need careful tendering. That was a dreadful summer for looking after my flowers, they kept wilting. My husband used to water them in the morning and late in the evening, that was always best. That summer was the year after he died." Regina look reflectively at the garden where Edward was standing. "Looks like that could do with some work."

"Yes, I was thinking that myself. We are trying to buy this place, but it needs work. By the time it's finished it will probably be another ten years before we have a summer like…?" Edward added casually trying to keep polite conversation.

"It was only six years ago. Regina," Jane said, more to correct Edward.

"Two-thousand-and-three," Edward muttered to Toby.

"Eh! There's no answ…" Toby caught on. "Wrong number. Sorry do you mind if I…" But Toby didn't wait for confirmation and pressed the digits quickly, it was answered within two rings.

159

"Toby, your tea's getting cold." Terri called out to the garden where Toby was planting a small apple tree.

"I just want to get this planted before we go out, otherwise it will never get done. What time did we say we'd meet Stacey and Mike?"

"About half an hour. Eight-thirty."

"Why did they want to meet at such a stupid hour? It's Sunday morning, do they not believe in sleeping in. They should take it while they can, once they're married with kids, there won't be much sleeping in. There, all done," he said pleased.

"They wanted to meet for breakfast at the Arches…"

Abruptly the phone burst into life.

"I'll get it." Toby said, running through the back door kicking his shoes off.

"You just finish your tea so we can…" Terri started.

Toby had already picked up the phone in the hallway. "Hello, he said, cheerfully. There was silence.

Edward stared at Toby, as his eyes widened in surprise, he hadn't thought of himself, from another time, answering the call. 'It is another three before I disappear' he thought. Lost for words he passed the phone quickly to Edward, who looked baffled.

"Careful, young man, that's not your…" Jane started, but then just sighed heavily as Edward spoke.

"Hello, is Terri there please?"

"Hello, hello," Toby continued, his voice gaining more sarcastic tones as each hello was repeated. "Another one of those cra…"

"Hello, is Terri there please?"

"It's for you Terri," Toby called covering the mouthpiece with his hand. Then added. "Who's calling?"

"It's Edward."

"Edward who?" Toby started, but Terri grabbed the phone off him.

"Finish your tea and get ready, or we'll be late." Terri playfully slapped him.

"It's Edward. " Then he mouthed, 'Who's Edward?'

"Never you mind, now go. Hello Edward." Terri did know an Edward from work and although they had spoken a few times outside of work on the phone, his phone calls were normally prearranged, never unexpected.

"What's up? You don't normally ring me."

"I've got someone who needs to speak with you." The comment caught Terri off-guard and she reeled slightly from the strangeness.

"It's Terri. Now get her here today, It must be today," Edward whispered through gritted teeth, hoping that Regina and Jane wouldn't hear him.

Toby sent a querying look at Edward but didn't have time to say anything as the ladies watched him closely.

"Terri?"

Terri physically baulked at the phone in her hands, she could have sworn she heard Toby's voice. "Did you call, Toby?" she called down the hall.

There was no reply inside the house.

"Terri, please I know this is going to sound strange, but I need you to do me a favour." Toby walked away from the garden wall, the phone planted firmly to his ear.

He heard Terri calling out to Toby

"Toby, are you messing with me? Can't believe I fell for that one. What am I doing, talking to a phone." She slammed the receiver down.

Toby appeared, his shirt unbuttoned displaying his bare hairless chest.

"Very funny." Terri said, walking towards him to thump his chest with her hands, a playful frown on her face, when the phone rang again, she looked at it in disbelief and then back at Toby. "Are you messing with me?"

Toby looked suitably innocent.

Toby looked at the mobile in his hands. "No!" he cried, above a whisper, then pressed redial without thinking.

"Excuse me young man can we have our phone back," Jane asked, her eyes narrowing, giving the impression of a stern school mistress.

160

As Terri picked up the phone Toby started. "Terri, please don't hang up, it really is me. I can't explain how, but just listen." Terri stood perplexed, mystified at the voice she recognised, yet the physical person was standing less than ten feet from her. She glanced sideways, Toby stuck out his tongue, normally she would have responded but she was having problems fathoming what was going on. "You still there? Terri?"

"A-ha," she barely muttered trying to conceal her fright.

"Terri, it is important that I see you, today…"

Terri interjected, her mind on autopilot. "But we've got Stacey and Mike's Wedding Fayre day."

Toby looked at his wife talking on the phone, she had gone slightly pale, her eyes glazing over.

"Are you alright?" he mimed. She stared at him, and then waved him away as confusion left her mind in turmoil.

"Excuse me, young man but I must insist you give us our phone back, this is very rude." Jane aired her disgust at what was turning into a distraction from their morning jaunt.

"It's alright Jane, it's probably important."

"It's not alright, he asked for one phone call and this is two, actually three now."

"This isn't Hill Street Blues," Regina chastised.

Edward butted in, "I am, really sorry ladies, but it is very important, and I do appreciate your patience and generosity.

"Yes, well," Jane scoffed.

Toby was reflecting on the Wedding Fayre, knowing what

a fiasco it had turned out to be. It was what killed Stacey and Mike's relationship, as Mike tried to watch the purse strings, Stacey got carried away with all the delightful add-ons she could get for the big day.

"Terri, please, come to Railway Terrace this afternoon, you'll be finished at the Fayre by three. This is really difficult to explain but it is about our future, I have limited time and need to see you, I have something to give to you that will save our son's life."

Toby shook his head and walked back into the bedroom to get ready, he indicated his watch to Terri who still held the phone, flabbergasted.

Quietly she spoke, "Look, I don't know who you are but this isn't funny. I don't even have a son. And you'd know that."

Terri was about to slam the phone down again when Toby offered some information.

Kicking a nearby tuft of grass Toby tried to let out his frustration. He understood how she was thinking, and there was a time when he would have agreed with it

"Terri, Stacey doesn't get married. They have a big row, with Mike trying to curb Stacey's spending, the Wedding Fayre is what sets it off." Suddenly a clearer vision of the day came to him. "Look, about two o'clock, we are all standing looking at the wedding cars, Stacey wants to go for a Silver Phantom Rolls Royce, Mike wants a white limo. It is so stupid, up to that point, Mike wasn't fussed, but they will pay out over eight hundred pounds in deposits at the fayre. Mike realises that it is all getting out of hand but doesn't know how to stop it. They have a big row in the middle of the Fayre and we head home with Stacey about three.

Terri, Terri..." Toby pulled the phone away from his ear. "Think, think," he said to himself. It was as if he was talking to a complete stranger, yet he had known Terri since school, they were soulmates, they had an understanding of each other that was so deep, they would believe each other, always. Putting the phone back to his ear there was just silence. "Just meet me at the Corner of East Street and Railway Terrace, after the Fayre. You'll see I'm right." He paused, waiting for her confirmation, but it didn't come, and after a half a minute the phone went dead.

161

Terri looked at the phone as if it was a stranger, she'd heard everything Toby had said but she didn't believe it, even though something inside tugged at her heart strings making her want to believe, to believe that it really was Toby she was talking to, yet it couldn't be.

Slowly she replaced the receiver, leaving her hand resting on it as she tried to work out what was going on, her natural curiosity wanting her to go to the Cottage.

Suddenly Toby's arms were around her waist and he was kissing the nape of her neck, shaking her from her thoughts, making her jump...

"Bloody hell Toby, you frightened the life out of me." She tried to turn but Toby held her tightly, gently caressing the right cheek of her bum with one hand, and slipping the other under her top stroking her stomach tenderly. She tingled with the first yearnings of excitement. "Toby, we're going to be late.

We haven't got time," she said, her mind still curious about the conversation. She tried to fight the lust as Toby's hand rounded her breast and he started to nibble her ear. "Toby, no, we've got to get going." But her words were losing their forcefulness. He kissed her cheek, Terri's head moved back in submission. Toby's other hand fumbled with her other breast and he felt her nipples go hard. He knew, with a little tender kissing on the back of her neck, she would not be able to resist the messages her body was sending, to let Toby take her, the urgency of her desire. She thought her chest was her best asset and loved Toby playing with it, it excited her and he knew it was one of her many weak spots. Turning her, Toby pulled her top up and over her head. Her buxom chest supported by a red lacy bra was a welcome sight and as he easily unclipped the catch with one hand Terri let herself succumb to the lust, the physicality that she loved about them.

Distractedly Toby handed the phone back to Regina. A quiet 'thank you' was all he managed, ignoring the sarcastic remark from Jane, who grabbed Regina's arm and almost frog-marched her along the road, the dogs struggling to keep up.

"Is she coming?" Edward asked, afraid that the answer would be 'no'.

"I don't know. I don't know if she believed me." Toby turned to look at the cottage.

"Well I guess we wait then," Edward muttered, but Toby was lost in his thoughts.

"Hi Stace, sorry we're late. Toby wanted to plant that apple tree we bought about six weeks ago. Why he picked today I'll never know." Terri eyed Toby knowingly, still feeling the excitement of their 'quickie' before hugging Stacey.

"You sure that's all you planted mate, looking a bit flushed, shall we say," Mike insinuated, making Terri go red. Toby just raised his eyebrows in acknowledgement.

"Well mate, a man's got to do what a man's got to do."

Terri swung her arm backwards catching Toby in the stomach. "Easy, mind the merchandise." Terri shot an embarrassed look at Toby, to which he replied sarcastically. "Love you."

"Yeah, well I don't love you," Terri joked, linking arms with Stacey, the telephone conversation still on her mind albeit in the background of the excited wedding talk from Stacey.

"I want a nice fluffy meringue with a fifty-foot train, twenty bridesmaids and a pageboy. Six cars, horse and carriage. I thought I might book St Paul's. What do you think?"

"Sounds lovely, I'm sure they'd be honoured to have you there." Terri went along with Stacey's joke.

"You alright mate? You look as though the third and fourth mortgage won't cover it," Toby enquired. Mike smiled falsely. He was worried that they couldn't afford what Stacey wanted. Her parents had given them five thousand pounds and they had saved up another five, but deep down he knew it would fall short of her expectations for the day she had planned for as long as she could remember. Even though he overheard Stacey's joke list with Terri, he knew that, in truth, it wasn't far off what she really wanted.

"What's the time?" Toby enquired, bored of waiting.

"About ten minutes since you last asked," replied Edward.

"Hold on a minute," Toby said, as a thought occurred to him that was so sublime he couldn't believe he hadn't thought of it before.

"What?" Edward played along dully.

"Food. I don't feel hungry and it must be hours, days since we've eaten."

"One of the side effects, and no, I don't know why. You don't age, you don't need to eat, it is strange, I grant you. But, it is what it is."

Toby got up from where they had been sitting on the doorstep. "So is there anything else we can do, or is this some kind of hellish limbo?"

162

The time passed slowly, and the sun started to fade from the sky.

"I guess she didn't believe me." Toby sighed, before adding. "What do we do now?"

We neutralise the coins and see where the cottage takes us next, we need her to get that crystal back. As I said..."

"It's not an exact science," Toby concluded.

"Yes, and we just have to find a time when Terri does believe. I was hoping we'd have ended up back nearer the time after you inherit this house, it would have been easier as she would already..." Edward stopped mid flow.

Terri appeared at the corner of the property hesitantly peering at the two figures standing in the falling shadow of the afternoon sun. Immediately she recognised Toby's more mature face and her step faltered, feeling for the wall she steadied herself. Toby ran down the edge of the garden to reassure her but as he got close she stepped back.

"I don't believe it. I just left you at home."

"Slightly older, but it is me," Toby said, jovially. Terri started to walk away. "Please don't go. We need your help."

"I can't, I..." words failed her. She crossed the road and

hesitated on the other side, Toby's eyes penetrating her back. Slowly she turned and waited, her mind taking in every detail of the strange man in front of her, the strange man that resembled her husband.

A stand-off ensued. Terri not quite willing to give in, and Toby not being able to approach her. Finally, gingerly, she moved towards him.

Her first question seemed rational to her yet she knew the answer, it was staring her in the face. "Who are you?"

"I am Toby. I know none of this will make any sense to you now but it will, one day, you just have to be patient, we were hoping," he indicated to Edward, "that we would find you closer to two-thousand-and-eight." Toby felt the words 'but it's not an exact science' rising up, and knew they would not placate, or steady her. "It is difficult to explain and part of a puzzle that we need you to help us solve."

"Who's he?" She pointed to Edward. Toby's first reaction was to say he was a friend, but knew Terri deserved more, but also he knew, if he wasn't careful, she would bolt.

"Terri, he is Edward. You will find out more about him, I promise, but I need to ask you a favour, and you can't tell Toby about it either." Alarm flashed across her face, "Look, it's nothing sinister. Firstly, I need to give you this." She looked at his hand to see a silver coin, on the back Toby had scratched roughly 'I luv u x'. "Promise me you'll keep it, and whenever you enter this cottage in the future you'll have it with you." She held out her hand and Toby pushed the coin firmly into her palm. A static charge made her retract her hand slightly but then let it be drawn back into Toby's. "It's pure silver and important. Remember always enter here with silver on you." As their hands touched there was a charge of something that ignited a fire in each other's soul. Suddenly Terri wasn't afraid anymore, she felt at ease, whoever this stranger was. Toby continued.

"Secondly, in four year's time I need you to visit a reporter called Matthew Gilbert and ask him for the Pineapple Amethyst Crystal he took from this place."

Terri's bemused look and quick retraction of hand, shook Toby.

"What is this? This some sort of joke." She looked at the coin in her hands. "What's going on? Who are you?"

"It's me, Toby," Toby pleaded, not thinking how it must look. Suddenly Terri looked at her hand remembering the familiar touch of his in hers and not being able to fathom it.

"No, Toby's at home, you're an imposter. I don't know…" Terri stopped mid-flow, enlightenment of a cruel joke being played on her. "I'm going." And with that she about-turned and was gone before Toby could do anything about it. He turned to Edward.

"There's nothing we can do if she won't believe." Edward placed a firm hand on his shoulder. "Come on let's go back."

"Back where?"

"Wherever the cottage wants to take us, we'll try again." The sky had grown dark rapidly causing the street lamps to flicker on. As Edward led Toby back to the cottage Toby saw the glint of something round and silver on the ground. Edward saw it to.

"We can't do anything about it now. She has made her choice."

163

"Where have you been?" Toby enquired as Terri returned home. "Stacey still upset?"

"Huh, oh yes," she answered wondering if indeed she had dreamt everything that had happened.

"Maybe they just weren't right for each other..." Toby went to kiss Terri on the cheek but she pulled away, her mind unsure of what was going on.

"How bloody inconsiderate. Of course she's devastated. What did you think? She would just go 'okay then'", Terri's anger at Toby's off-hand remark was more to do with her stupidity at going to that cottage.

"Woah, sorry, its' just... forget it. Do you want a drink?" he asked, changing the subject "There's a Poirot on TV later if you want to watch it."

"No, no. I think I'm going to bed," Terri said, preoccupied with the cottage and the other Toby.

"Not a bad plan," Toby answered, a smile oozing across his face.

"Look, I'm tired, do you mind?" She kissed his cheek, but the emotion she would normally have felt was gone, she was overcome by an emptiness, a distrust.

"No, I suppose I can entertain myself," he replied, grinning mischievously.

"You've got a one track mind you have." Almost forgetting her confusion for a second.

"What?!" he said, in a subjective gesture.

"Night. I'm sorry"

"Night. For what?" He patted her bum as she walked away from him but she didn't answer him.

Clearly shaken by events, she found sleep was not comforting, In her dreams she saw both Tobys standing side by side, identical in every detail, even wearing the same clothes, but one was an evil version of the other. She found herself torn between the two, being forced to choose. Each coercing her with words of love and promises of a better future. Hands grabbing at her, pulling at her like a tug-of-war match. She couldn't make up her mind. Then, without notice, a decision had been made, she couldn't remember making it. It was the wrong decision, immediately she regretted it, tears streamed down her face as she tried to break free and run to the other Toby. 'NO!' she screamed. She heard the words reverberating round her head. 'Let me go'

"It's alright," Toby was saying. "What's wrong, you're safe with me."

"No, let me go," she screamed louder, thumping Toby's chest.

Suddenly the voice changed and became more real, telling her to 'wake up, wake up'. Wearily she opened her eyes to stare at Toby, the bedside light on.

Terri's eyes darted about the room for confirmation that she was safe again, staring into each dark-shadowed corner cautiously. Toby's reassuring voice came to her.

"Terri. Are you okay?" He placed a hand on her shoulder. She flinched, the visions still fresh in her mind. "What's wrong?" He tried to cuddle her but she stiffened briefly. "Fine." Toby stated, offended, "Be like that."

Immediately she apologised, "I'm sorry, it's just, just... a horrible nightmare."

Toby rolled over onto his back, the duvet exposing his naked torso. Terri sidled over to him and rested her head on his shoulder, draping her arm over him; squeezing him tight, feeling safe and warm in his embrace, he pulled her in tighter and she let herself being consumed by the softness of his skin under her touch.

"You okay?" he asked tenderly.

Terri closed her eyes muttering, 'Mmm', soaking up his essence.

Toby let it go, turning out the light he stroked her shoulder in a reassuring way.

Edward took the silver coin from Toby, the one that had been tuned to 2008 and nutrealised it, making another incantation to break the anchor of time.

"Now what?"

"We need to see where the cottage takes us to so we can start again."

"And what do we do in the meantime?"

"What do you mean?"

"Well, what do you get up to, here, in this cottage, with no interaction with anyone?"

Edward, stood up and looked Toby squarely in the face, a sadness rested there.

"Think about the past, think about my life. Wonder what if? Talk to my parents, or at least their essence. Try to find…"

"How can you talk to your parents?" Toby enquired, wondering if maybe it would be possible to talk to his.

"Its simple magic really and requires an object that they held dear to their hearts, then you can pick up on their essence that was left there when they were alive." Seeing Toby's querying glance, he continued, "We all leave shadows in this world, every object has a frequency and, by tapping into them, you can manipulate the shadows, especially if it is something special."

164

"You want to speak with your parents?" Edward asked, seeing the question burdening Toby thoughts.

"No," he answered abruptly, before adding, "Yes, I think so. I don't know, I have some strong memories of them, and…"

"Then don't, it will not always be as you remember, it is only a shadow of them, they are not real. Think of them as little parcels of themselves, they will look real, they will look as you remember them, they will sound real enough. But they aren't." Edward placed a hand on Toby's shoulder. "Not everyone can handle it."

"But what about yours? You did."

"They helped me, they made sure their essence was left on the pendants. Edward pulled two pendants from an inside pocket of his jacket.

Toby stared at them. He didn't really have anything of his parents, everything had been taken to pay off the bills, the debts.

Pacing the room, sadness consumed him as Edward caressed the pendants carefully. They were both in limbo waiting for time to slip by, his family carrying on without him present. An eternity locked to this cottage. What was he meant to do with that time?

"How do you cope with this?" he finally exploded. "There's nothing to do. I want to see my family, my son, and I am stuck here."

Edward felt the torment in the words that came out. 'I tried to help, I tried to warn you but you didn't listen'. He bit them back. He had sacrificed his existence and now they were both tied to the cottage like immortal souls.

"We could play chess?" Edward threw in, so far out of left field, that Toby laughed.

"Play chess?! Is that it, we wait for time to end playing chess."

"Toby, I have tried everything to leave this place, to go back to where I belong, and although the cottage will take me back to the time where I first came in, it will not let me out, I can't change that." The words rose again inside him and this time he couldn't help but let them out, "I tried to stop you coming here, tried to prevent this from happening, hoping to correct things, but you didn't listen…"

"If you hadn't have been so bloody cryptic, I might have understood. Then I would be with my family now. You started this. You dragged me to this place. I missed eight days because of you. What was I meant to think?" Anger dissipated as they both finally said what had been on their minds.

After a minutes pause Edward was the first to break the ice.

"I'm sorry, it was a crazy idea. A thousand things were going round in my head and the only thing that was clear was that I wanted to save Jake, your son, my best friend. The guilt I felt for letting him down, abandoning him when he needed me."

"He's his own person, you can't control someone else's destiny."

"No, but you can sure as hell help to steer the ship," Edward steamed.

Another silence engulfed the room as the two men sized each other up, realising that they liked the person opposite them. They each had compassion and love that rendered them idiots at times but also great friends and parents respectively.

Toby sighed. "How about that game of chess?"

Edward looked on, a tear was on the brink of falling, he saw Jake in the man that now sat on floor waiting for a game of chess. It was comforting.

"Not here. It's in the lounge." Baffled, Toby followed Edward to the lounge.

Edward reached up into the fireplace and pulled out a package wrapped in a piece of leather. Inside was a faded cardboard board with sixty-four coloured squares and then in two canvas sacks, were two sets of pieces, brown and off-white. Perplexed Toby watched.

"You thought I was going to magic up a set?" Edward smiled.

"Yeah," Toby answered nonchalantly.

"I probably could, but I found this set buried in the garden one day. I hid it here for safe-keeping.

Sitting down they played chess, Toby was a little rusty but it passed the time.

"Toby," a voice called.

Edward and Toby stared incredulously at each other.

"Toby," the voice repeated.

165

Terri appeared at the lounge door.

"Terri," Toby called, jumping up to hug her, but the affection wasn't reciprocated, a strange wary look on her face. "What's the matter?" he asked, before panic settled in. "No, wait, you can't be in here you'll…"

Terri pulled from her pocket a round silver object, which Toby saw plainly as the silver coin he had handed to her.

"But I thought you threw it away."

"No," came the stammered reply.

"But I saw it on the ground and I thought," he stopped. Maybe he hadn't seen what he thought he saw. It could have been a piece of silver foil.

"Hello, Terri." Edward offered his hand, which she gingerly took, edging away from Toby.

"What's wrong Terri?"

"Look, I don't really understand, but you have been missing for seven months and I was searching through my things, ready for the move and I came across this," She held up the coin to make the point. "I'd forgotten." Her words were cautious as she still felt uneasy, the cottage had consumed Toby ever since they had inherited it from Peter.

"How is Jake?" Then thinking about it, added, "He has been born, hasn't he?"

"Of course he's been born? What stupid question is that? What's going on Toby?"

"It's this cottage, Terri." Edward spoke, remembering his vagueness before, he decided it was time to be frank. "If you allow it, it will destroy your lives, especially my friend Jake's"

"Who are you? Who is he Toby? Have you turned gay?"

"No," Toby said, dismissing the idea as preposterous.

"I am your son's best friend from the future. This cottage has a curse. It takes Toby from you and will eventually take Jake from you."

"But he's here. The future? Is this some sort of joke? Am I in a movie or something?"

Toby stepped forward to calm her agitated mind. "No, it's not. How else did you get that coin."

Shaking her head. "I don't know, I don't know anything anymore. I've lost my husband, I have had to sell the house because I can't pay the mortgage, I don't want to touch the inheritance as it's brought nothing but misery. I want my husband back, I want Jake's father back in my life."

"That's all I want." He took her in his arms, this time the hug was reciprocated and for a few moments they were both lost in the love that they felt.

"Come home then," she said into his shoulder, his scent intoxicating her.

"I can't."

Terri fought to break free. "Can't or won't? Do you love me Toby Grant?"

"I have always loved you, I want to be with you forever."

"But you won't come home now," she snapped, anger forcing its way to the fore.

"That's not true. Terri."

Edward butted in. "Terri, I came back here to correct something, but in doing so feel that I only made matters worse. In order to put things right we need something, Matthew Gilbert, a reporter, took an object, a Pineapple Amethyst Crystal from here. We need it to correct the time fracture." Terri was vehemently shaking her head, trying to shake off the words. "It's the truth."

"Terri, listen to him, please. I didn't believe it myself but everything I have seen..." he left the sentence unfinished.

Terri started to leave the room. "If you want to see your son we'll be moving into my Mums. You know where that is don't you?"

"Terri, please find it in your heart to believe us. You always looked out for me after my parents died, treated me as your own. I just want to give something back, a thank you." Edward stepped forward, the fondness that he always had foremost in his thoughts.

"Give me something back." Terri marched toward Edward her face contorted in anguish, Toby had never seen her so upset. "Give me my family back," she said coldly.

There was silence and Terri eyed both men. Then she bolted from the room.

Toby rushed after her. "Don't go, please, it's the only way I can get back to you."

She was through the open front door and steaming down the path, blindly rushing forward, tears running down her cheeks. Outside the gate she turned, to see Toby running after her. Her heart leapt, He did want her. But as he reached the open gate he disappeared.

Terri's jaw dropped open in wonder. She couldn't be sure how long she had been standing there, all anger gone, but Toby reappeared, coming through the front door.

Regaining her composure she threw the silver coin at him.

"No!" Toby cried.

Before he could do anything Terri was gone from view. Toby collapsed on the ground after failing twice to break through the gate that sent him back up to the room where it all started.

166

Terri woke up with a start, her mind racing, new memories flirted with older memories, a tingling inside her head, a restless ache. It was still dark. Switching on the bedside light she got up and looked in the mirror, wondering whether she was imagining things or not.

She tried to put recent events in order, her new haircut, which had grown out slightly but still gave her the confidence boost she needed to cope, the house auction and the failure to secure a buyer, talking to Toby and Edward – no, that's new! Her frenzied mind couldn't work it out, a new memory, or it felt new, something bright and shiny. She remembered throwing it. It was important. It was to do with the cottage. With Edward, Jake's best friend – it was alien to her, but there in her head.

A coin.

That was it, a silver coin. What was so important about it? Then a name came to her, Matthew Gilbert. Why was that familiar? Something she remembered but was just out of reach. She paced her bedroom, her head in turmoil as thoughts cascaded into view.

Again the name came to mind, Matthew Gilbert. Why? And why was he holding a pineapple? It didn't make any sense.

Too restless and awake to sleep, she went to the kitchen, the 1950's style oversized clock on the wall read, 4.22, the minute hand appeared to be zipping round at double speed. Switching the kettle on, she pulled a mug off the mug tree.

Something was trying to clarify itself in her head.

It had started to rain, and Toby hadn't noticed, although he was getting soaked.

"Toby, come inside." Edward attempted to help Toby up.

"Why? Eh? Why? There's nothing for me, you saw her, she doesn't believe me. We failed."

Edward had to concede they had. "Staying out here won't make that change."

Toby jumped up causing Edward to reel backwards. "Neither will going in there." Toby ran for the gate, knowing it was hopeless but deep inside praying that he could break the hold the cottage had. Again he found himself upstairs in the bedroom.

His angry sobs were intermingled with hysterical laughter as he realised that he had done what Edward had suggested, ended up inside, in the dry.

Edward sauntered reluctantly through the door expecting

more verbal berating but was surprised to see Toby on the floor, in fits of laughter, finally dispelling his anger.

"Like father, like son."

Toby wanted to reply but he couldn't as the hysterical laughter caused cramps in his stomach. "Ow, ow it hurts."

"Well, stop laughing then," Edward said, solemnly.

"I can't, ow." Toby rolled around the floor holding his stomach.

Edward's face started to crack and soon he found himself laughing too, tears of joy rolling haphazardly down his cheeks. Abruptly Toby stopped, his face growing serious. Standing up he faced Edward, whose laughter took a minute to die away.

"He hasn't been here yet."

The comment was so out of kilter that Edward was stumped by the statement.

"Who?"

"Matthew Gilbert."

"Toby, I know…" but he wasn't allowed to finish.

"No, no. If Matthew Gilbert hasn't been here yet, then he can't have taken the crystal, then it must still be there, here. We can do whatever it is we need to do." Toby couldn't contain the excitement in his voice.

He ran from the room before Edward could stop him.

167

Edward caught up with Toby in the lounge, he had thrown the loose floorboard excitedly across the room and was scratching at the ground below. Dirt was piling up and falling back into the hole. Toby rushed to scoop it out, placing it on the floor haphazardly. All the time muttering to himself.

"It has to be here, it has to be. He hasn't been yet, he doesn't come for another few months. Ouch. It's here." Furvour in Toby's words almost made him sound insane.

"Toby." Edward called from the doorway, following Toby's train of thought but knowing the reality was something different, "you won't find it."

"I've got it." Toby was struggling to pull an object from the soil, the tight space between floorboards was making it difficult to get a decent hold of it.

"It's not there Toby."

"Got it," Toby cried, pleased. Edward was temporarily phased by this. As his hands appeared from the floorboards he could see all he had was a rock.

More assuredly, Edward added, "It's not there Toby. I know it should be but it won't be."

"But that's impossible. Matthew doesn't take it for another few months. If it is not here then how can he take it."

"An object can only exist once."

"Exactly, if it was placed there in the sixteenth century, then it has to be here now, until Matthew takes it, otherwise how else could he get it?"

Edward looked at Toby who was still searching the hole,

convinced his logic was correct.

"Toby, if I gave you some money," Toby peered back at Edward, eyebrows furrowed, "just listen okay?" Edward said, holding out his hand in platitude. "If I gave you some money, say, a five pound note and you left this property, you couldn't then go back in time and take the same five pound note."

"Where would it be though?"

"You'd have it." Edward stepped forward, his words sounding more forceful.

"Yes, but if I went back again and met you then surely you'd have to have the five pound note. You must have, I can't take something from you if you haven't got it. You have to have it."

"You have to think a little more in depth than that. More fourth-dimensionally. If what you're saying was true then you could make a lot of money, looping round in time taking the same five pound note. It can't be. You can't have more than one of everything existing."

"So how does it work?" he asked, sitting back on his haunches.

"The crystal will have been planted, as it should be, in my parents' time. Then over the next few hundred years it will gradually fade out, its physical matter and essence fading over time, here in this place. It has to, to make sure no one else takes it . However, as we get close to the time that Matthew has it, will manifest itself when he is here."

"But surely," Toby's face expressed his confusion.

"By taking it from here, Matthew has skewed its physical presence, as such, meaning that it is pulled out of kilter the rest of everything around it."

"I don't understand."

"It is not an easy thing to understand and I have tried to simplify it. I have also had the same thought processes as you, thinking I could correct the time rift, but no. How about this then?" Edward knelt down to face Toby. "Imagine Matthew is a magnet that attracts crystals, the crystals timeline is here."

Edward drew a straight line on the ground in the dust. "Now when Matthew takes it, it starts a new timeline/presence here, "Edward drew another line this time parallel to the first but starting where the first finished. "You follow so far?" Toby nodded.

"Now imagine these points are places." He pointed to the end of the first line and the beginning of the second. "Because we have come from a time where it was taken, and we know it was taken, then how does it get from this point to this point?" Again he pointed to the two ends which he had marked 'A' and 'B'. It won't be instantaneous. Over time it fades from here to appear there."

"Yeah, but if we go back to the five pound notes, surely, by going back in time, the one from the future will disappear?"

"Why?" Was Edward's simple question.

"Because…"

"Toby, once something is physical, it is physical. Do your clothes disappear when you travel back. NO."

Edward's words were starting to ring some truth despite the convoluted theory behind them.

"Why would they though?" Toby asked.

"If what you're saying is true then, your clothes haven't been made yet so how could you have bought them?"

168

In a strange sort of sense it was starting to become clear. "So where is the crystal now?"

"Somewhere between being a real object and being here. It will be here when Matthew comes to take it. But we cannot make use of it now to correct the time fracture. If it were possible to go back and take the crystal before Matthew did, we would create a paradox that would probably implode."

Terri sat down at the kitchen table her mind still reeling from the new memories, and they did feel like new memories, a phenomenon she couldn't quite get her head round, little snippets of information that formed a collage with a hidden meaning. She cradled a hot, sweet tea in her hands listening to the house breathing, wishing Toby was here. Somehow she felt closer to him, an aching in her heart to say that he was close by, now, closer than he had felt for months.

Her thoughts started to whisk her away to a future she hoped would come true, her family back together, forever.

The kitchen door opened and Vivien walked through.

"You alright Terri?" She yawned, rubbing her weary eyes.

"What you doing up?" asked Terri, startled from her dream.

"I needed the loo and saw the light on." Vivien stepped over to the table. "Jake's okay isn't he?"

"He's fine." There was a pause between them.

"Do you mind if I…"

"Mum, do you…"

They both spoke at the same time. Vivien waved for her

daughter to continue. "Mum, can you I ask you something strange?"

"I'm not sure I am going to like this. Do I need a strong drink?" Vivien smiled warmly, sitting down.

"No, it's nothing sinister, well, at least I don't think so." Seeing her Mum eye's looking at her mug, "Do you want one, the kettles not long boiled?" Terri went to get up.

"I'll make it. What did you want to ask?" Vivien grabbed a mug from the draining board whilst Terri thought about how to word her question.

"I know this is going to sound strange, but," she paused, turning the question over in her mind, "do you have any new memories?"

"What?" Vivien froze, holding the tea bag above the mug.

"Any new memories? It's really strange but I woke up and have these pictures in my head that I don't recall as real memories." She looked at her Mum whose pensive face indicated her brain working overtime at this early hour. "I know that sounds weird, but they feel fresh."

"You mean like, of your father?"

"No, not necessarily. These ones are of Toby, and, in particular, a name, Matthew Gilbert, and now this is going to sound totally weird I know, a Pineapple."

Vivien couldn't help but smirk as she sipped her drink. "A Pineapple? I think you're working too hard dear. Why don't you go on holiday, you've got that inheritance?"

"NO," was the sharp response from Terri, I'm not touching that money until Toby's back and we can move on from this."

"Sorry, I was only…" She let the sentence die. "No, in answer to your question then, I have no new memories. Although I do sometimes think of your father and remember something that I'd forgotten, before feeling the regret of the accident that took him from us." For a moment sadness flashed in her eyes.

"Does it ever get easier?"

"It gets easier, but, it doesn't get better." She looked at Terri. You will always miss Toby, but the days won't seem so hard." She placed a reassuring hand on Terri's as she sat down at the table. "It's Jake I worry about."

"Me too."

169

Terri got dressed and decided to take advantage of the sunny weather. Jake had proved to be a model baby when it came to sleeping. He slept through the night and very rarely woke up before seven. He was now in his cot, trying to eat his toys.

Standing in front of her chest of drawers, Terri looked at herself in the vanity mirror and, in particular, at her jewellery. She had always worn gold, it suited her colouring. She hadn't given it a thought to change, even after her new sharp hairdo and makeover, but today something was niggling at her, tempting her to look again. The gold heart that Toby had given her on Valentine's Day - the year of their engagement - glinted in the light. She held it, in her mind changing it to silver. Why silver?

'Oh, yes, the dream'. Like a revelation she started to pull her jewellery box apart, taking out all the segments, not realising how much jewellery she had accumulated over the years, she lifted the final piece out, a broach that had belonged to her grandmother, a cheap piece of costume jewellery.

Where was the silver coin she had expected to find?

"So we just have to wait?" Toby concluded.

"Afraid so." Edward stood up again. "Obviously with the help of the time fracture moving us around time. Come on, we'll find out exactly what year we are in." They walked into the garden. The sky was dull and grey. It didn't look like it would rain but there wasn't a sign of a break either.

After a while, a person walked by and they managed to engineer the conversation around to the day's date.

Terri stopped at the cottage, a familiar memory nagging at her. "I don't know what it is about this place, Toby, but I feel I should be here."

"Morning." Terri turned sharply. Standing there was Gareth. Terri recognised his face but was not sure why.

"Morning," she replied cautiously.

"Excuse me for coming across as rude, but I noticed you looking at the cottage," Terri nodded. "I wouldn't go in, there are some strange things going on, I have a whole history that I have put together and believe me, it is weird."

Under normal circumstance's Terri would have walked away from this stranger but she sensed a connection. But what?

"I see," was all Terri could answer. "Have you been in?"

"Oh no, that would be trespassing, but I have seen and heard stories of people who have."

"Really." Terri sounded more interested. It was Gareth's turn to nod. "Would you mind filling me in on them?"

Surprised, Gareth almost tripped over himself leading Terri back to his house, where Elaine made tea, and listened as, once again, Gareth told all he knew about the cottage, thrilled to have an interested ear.

Two hours later Terri left, her mind buzzing with new information. She didn't believe in witchcraft but it backed up some of the new memories, which she had not divulged.

A new resolve gripped her, to visit at least once a day. Hope cascaded through her, hope that she was going to see Toby again, and soon.

Toby kicked at the long grass as Edward was engaged in conversation with yet another passer-by from a different time. They had leapt about in time eighteen times and Toby, despite wanting to get to the bottom of it, was getting bored at the tedium and the lack of precision.

"Toby?"

Edward turned to look at Toby, who stood mesmerized by the figure standing near the garden wall. He then thanked the person he had been speaking to and walked to where Toby was standing.

Toby stood speechless.

170

For a moment Terri was speechless. There was a connection that had been missing before on every encounter previously. This time is just felt right, permanent.

Toby was the first to break the deadlock. He felt it to, sensed that she believed this time. What was different he couldn't tell. "Hi." It sounded lame but he couldn't help it.

"I've got new memories." The words were strange on her lips.

Edward was now standing behind Toby's left shoulder. He

nodded his greeting and Terri reciprocated. Her eyes darted between the two of them as she tried to confirm everything she could remember, to pull the pictures together.

"I don't understand what I remember, Toby," Toby was going to answer her but she continued. "Matthew Gilbert and Pineapple?" Toby and Edward couldn't help but smirk. "What is it?" she asked defensively, concerned that maybe this meeting wasn't real and that she was still stuck in a dream.

"Pineapple Amethyst Crystal," Edward chipped in. "It is what we need to undo what has been done and correct the time fracture." Terri cocked her head slightly still confused by what she knew from experience and what was actually a new memory.

"And Matthew Gilbert?"

"He stole it from this cottage," Toby added. "Why don't you come inside and we can talk more?" She took Toby's offered hand and, as he led her round to the gate, an electric charge surged them both; yet they held tight, afraid to let go. "Take this." He handed her the silver coin she had thrown away. She looked at him, remembering. Turning to Edward, Toby sought his acknowledgement that everything would be okay. Edward nodded his aggreement.

Glaring at Toby, she wanted his reassurance.

"It will be fine as long as you keep that silver coin with you, at all times." He emphasized the last three words.

"Silver," she repeated, as clarity cleared the fog in her head.

"It's what will hold you in time, in this place. That is why some people have never experienced…"

"… losing time," Terri finished.

"But how have you appeared?" The question was directed at Edward, and then at Toby, as more thoughts tumbled through her mind. Whenever Toby had vanished, he showed up weeks, months, a year later. If he could go back, Why didn't he? "How have you appeared today?"

"Edward has a device, he is a wizard." Terri's face showed her disbelief at that statement, believing it might be more mockery. "It's true, he also has a good understanding of science and… look it's hard to explain. I know." Then turning to Edward as they approached the front door. "Can you demonstrate it, so Terri knows. I want to be honest with her."

Edward stopped and sighed. "Did you find Matthew Gilbert, Terri?"

Abruptly Terri faced Edward. "Yes, well not exactly." Curiously both men waited for her to explain. "I didn't really understand the pineapple part, but yes, I did look for a Matthew Gilbert. It's a fairly common name but at least I remembered he was a reporter so I started my search there."

"And?" Toby enquired eagerly.

"If you let me finish, I'll tell you." She paused. "He disappeared."

"When? He can't, he has to take the crystal. If he doesn't then, then…" he looked to Edward to clarify.

"What time do you think this is Toby?" Edward asked.

"I don't know, I didn't hear your conversation with those people.

"This is one week after you got yourself trapped here. The coven has gone…"

Terri agreed. "That's right." Edward and Toby looked at her. "After a bit of digging I found out about the White Hats, but their partners have not seen or heard anything from them since last Friday. Matthew has also gone, vanished."

After a pause to absorb the information, Toby's eyes lit up. "That's alright if we go back again a week or so, we can stop it, you have that device. If we take Terri with us, everything will be good. And I won't get caught in the cottage."

"No Toby, it's too late for that, and, no, I won't let Terri experience the time travel." The statement was cold, showing Edward's determination to not let anymore harm come to anyone.

171

Toby grabbed Edward's arm as he tried to turn away from them.

"What do you mean 'no'?" Toby's words were harsh as he immediately saw red. "You mean it's okay for us to be trapped here, but we can't show Terri what has happened."

Edward gritted his teeth, trying to lessen the annoyance in him. "Toby, how do you think we got here?" Toby started to mouth an answer but stopped as Edward continued heatedly. "I sacrificed my life to enter here, although I didn't know it at the time. I contacted you because I thought we could stop it, yet all I have done is perpetuate it. By using the device and tuning into different times I have inadvertently got stuck here, I can't leave this place, like you. If I run out that gate now, I end up in the lounge, which is where I started.

I do not want that for Terri." The tirade stopped and left Toby feeling empty, taking in Terri's face only compounded the matter.

"So you really are Jake's friend?" Terri said, subdued. Edward confirmed with a mouthed yes. "When did... do you meet him?"

"When we started infant school."

A silence settled between the three as each became consumed by their own thoughts. A first drop of rain was enough to break any tension and send them into the cottage to seek shelter.

"So what happens now?" Terri asked after about an hour of looking around the cottage, really taking in the details.

"I don't know," Edward replied.

"If Terri goes, we will have to find her again in time," Toby said, hating the thought of losing her again.

Edward was about to speak when Terri interrupted,

surprising them both.

"What's to stop me moving in here?"

"What?" Toby said, astounded.

"You said something about the silver coin holding me in time, right?" Toby nodded. "Well, if I always have something silver, I, we could live here, right?" She looked to each for confirmation. "Right?" She repeated as neither answered. The thought like a silver lining.

Logic tumbled through Edward's head like a steamroller. Everything he had witnessed, every experiment he had tried, every result did give the impression that there was no reason why it would not work. Silver was the key, As long as anyone in the house always wore something that was silver, they should always be safe.

"But I can never leave," Toby stated.

But Terri was there with a reply, it was so simple. "But at least Jake would have his father, at home, all the time. Maybe that could change his future?"

Edward flumped onto the floor sending a small plume of dust across the room. Toby looked to him for confirmation.

"It makes sense, I don't know why I didn't see it before."

"You're a man. Only a woman can find a simple solution." Terri smiled, she was joking with them to protect their male pride, but she meant it and for the first time there was a lighter side to all that had happened.

"It's going to need a lot of work," Toby said, hugging his wife, to her surprise, then a thought occurred. "What about when they leave, won't we move forward in time?" Toby looked to Edward again, he was the oracle as far as Toby was concerned.

"What? Toby you feel…" Edward didn't let her finish.

"Not if, maybe, we tune silver coins to the same frequency and never change that, of course they will all move forward at the same rate, therefore anchoring us all together," Edward said, pleased that at least a solution had been found, it was not what he had wanted but if the end result was the same, then so be it.

Terri pulled Toby in tighter. "Oh, you feel so nice."

"I've missed you so much." Toby held her as tight as he could, feeling her buxom figure squashed against his chest, he felt the desire that he always felt when near her.

"Yes, I think I can tell" She looked suggestively into Toby's eyes and he smiled so wide that he thought his face was going stay like it.

Every emotion raced through his body, he was alive again, so in love. He planted a kiss on her lips and, when withdrew and beamed. "I can't wait to see Jake again, it feels like it has been weeks."

"It has," Terri slighted.

An hour later Toby walked Terri to the gate. Life was finally complete again the future was their's, and Jake could be helped. So many plans had been discussed that it was like a whirlwind as he walked around the cottage once more after she had gone, imagining all the ideas they had talked about. It was going to be a great family house, home.

"I want a daughter," Toby said aloud.

"Pardon?" Edward asked, as he walked up behind Toby, who standing in what was to be the main bedroom. "I would like a daughter. If she is anything like her mother…" he didn't finish the sentence, letting the made-up pictures of a baby girl fill his thoughts.

Edward placed a hand on Toby's shoulder and squeezed it, proud that at least some good had finally come out of everything. Yet still saddened that amongst all the good he had tried to do a proper resolution hadn't been forthcoming. He vowed to keep on working at it in the hope that one day he could release both Toby and himself from the prison that was Thyme Cottage.

TOBY:
MICHAEL AND ISOBEL

1

3 years later

"Come on Jake, stop dawdling or you'll be late."

"Don't wanna go." Jake sulked snatching his arm back.

"Jake, I don't have time for you to mess me around, I have got to get to work." Terri felt the stress rising inside her; at times like these she wished Toby could help her, but confined to the cottage was all she could expect. At the time it had seemed a marvelous solution but now she wondered whether a future like this was really possible, it had already proved awkward. They'd been forced to make silver charms to give to anyone who came into the cottage, which, up to now, had been relatively few. However as Jake grew that was changing.

The front gate was locked all the time so no one could walk freely onto the property. The first few months when they were busy renovating the place it had been bliss, Edward had left them to it and gone back into another time, popping by infrequently, he was still searching for a permanent cure, but he tried to stay out of the way to let them get on with their lives. He knew his younger self would meet them soon.

All the workman who appeared on site, had been issued with the little silver charms, much to their bemusement, in the shape of an anchor. It did the trick, with the exception of one young builder, who vanished; Toby and Terri knew why, but had to maintain their silence. In private they hoped he would turn up in time and that they would be there for him.

The workmen did find it odd that Toby never left the premises, instead choosing to work in the garden, planting vegetables and creating a lovely play area for Jake. He even started to speak to Gareth, the one person, whom they could talk to about all that had happened.

Those rosy months and years were fading as the true implications of Toby being tied to the cottage became a reality, he could only help with Jake at home. He couldn't leave; that meant no family holidays, no time away, even for an evening at a friends house. It was the curse of being mortgage and debt free. Deep down she loved Toby with all her heart but at times, like today, when she needed him to do other things it was hard to be a part of this lifestyle.

Toby waved Jake goodbye at the gate, it was his first day of infant school, and he was going to miss it; miss watching his son walk into that huge building for the first time. The pain of the parting was getting harder. He missed that they couldn't even go for a walk in the woods, what sort of a future was this. Thyme Cottage was quickly turning into a prison.

He sat down on the front step and watched the day drift by. The sun was soothing his weary body, but could not ease his unhappy, troubled, mind. The first year had been blissful, the three of them tucked up in their own home, paid for, mortgage free, no financial worries; the joy of making it theirs. They had grasped every opportunity to enjoy the time to its fullness, but as Jake grew it became obvious that he needed more than the world Thyme Cottage could offer, and Terri needed it too. He could see the longing in her eyes to go for a stroll, sometimes just the two of them, elsewhere, away from this place, it was like a fresh loaf of bread spoiling fast.

Toby looked at his watch, only an hour had passed, it had felt like a day, time was moving slowly for him, Terri had started a part time job, to earn some money to pay for a few luxuries and the bills. He could see she enjoyed it, and now a chasm was opening for them, a chasm that soon they wouldn't be able to cross.

"Jake, you are going to school." Terri changed tack, realising that she had been harsh on Jake, when it was really Toby that she was upset with. She knelt down to be Jake's height. "You'll meet lots of new friends. Don't you want to meet new friends?"
"No." Was the simply stated answer as Jake continued to sulk. Terri played slyly, "Okay, we'll go for a walk instead." She jollied.

Instantaneously Jake's face changed and he started to bob along the street, singing to himself oblivious that they were still walking in the same direction.

Five minutes later they were outside the grounds of the Leigh Infant school.